Believe in Us

Believe in Fairy Tales : Book One

by

Suzie Peters

Copyright © Suzie Peters, 2018.

The right of Suzie Peters as the Author of the Work has been asserted by her in accordance with the Copyright, Designs and Patents Act, 1988.

First Published in 2018
by GWL Publishing
an imprint of Great War Literature Publishing LLP

Produced in United Kingdom

Apart from any use permitted under UK copyright law, this publication may only be reproduced, stored or transmitted, in any form, or by any means, with prior permission in writing of the publishers or, in the case of reprographic production, in accordance with the terms of licences issued by the Copyright Licensing Agency.

All characters in this publication, with the exception of any obvious historical characters, are fictitious and any resemblance to real persons, either living or dead, is purely coincidental.

ISBN 978-1-910603-66-6 Paperback Edition

GWL Publishing
Forum House
Sterling Road
Chichester PO19 7DN

www.gwlpublishing.co.uk

Dedication

For S.

Chapter One

Lottie

"You sure this is the right address?" The cab driver pulls to a halt outside the enormous gates.

"I'm positive. If you pull forward a little further, you can swipe my entry card to let us in." I hand it to him and he takes it, inching closer and lowering the window beside him, which lets in a blast of cold December air. "Just run it from top to bottom," I explain and he obeys my instructions, then hands my card back as the little light on the entry system turns from red to green. The gates hesitate for a moment, as though they're just as uncertain as I am about my return to Boston, and then finally make up their mind and start to open inwards.

"Jeez," he murmurs under his breath, raising the window again and starting to move onto my father's property. I call it my father's property, but it isn't really. Not anymore. It's my stepmother's property now and this is the first time I've been back here since my father's funeral, just over four months ago. To be honest, I wasn't entirely sure my entry card would still work, or whether Catrina would have had the access codes changed. Nothing that woman does would surprise me.

"Dear God." The words leave my mouth before I can stop them.

"Well, that's sure lit up," the driver says at the same time, and I stare out the window at the monstrosity of coloured flashing lights that cover the entire front surface of the house. "I guess it's festive," he adds, trying to sound positive.

"That's one word for it." I can think of several others. Cheap. Gaudy. Vulgar. They all spring to mind, and yet they all feel inadequate for the ostentatious show of tasteless flamboyance that lies before me. "What do I owe you?" I ask the driver as he pulls up right outside the front door.

He checks his meter. "Call it forty," he says, rounding down the numbers.

He's obviously noticed that, despite the showy surroundings, I'm not the best-dressed person in town and I guess he's taking pity on me. Or maybe it's just the Christmas spirit kicking in a few days early. I give him fifty and tell him to keep the change. I've worked a few extra shifts myself in the last couple of weeks and can afford to pass a little on. And besides, the Christmas spirit works both ways, doesn't it?

He gets out and opens my door. Luckily, because some of my clothes are still here, I've travelled light and only have my rucksack, which I pull out behind me and sling over my shoulder. "Thanks for the ride," I say to him.

"My pleasure," he replies. We've spent the forty-five minute journey from the airport talking about all kinds of things, but mainly his kids, and although I've only been able to see his eyes in the rear-view mirror, his pride and pleasure in talking about them has been obvious, not to mention refreshing. Working in the retail sector in the lead up to Christmas is pretty much guaranteed to leave you feeling jaded, and I'm sure it's no different for cab drivers, but this guy is more interested in the time he's gonna spend with his kids than anything money can buy.

"Enjoy the holidays," I say to him as he gets back into the cab.

"You too, ma'am."

He gives me a wave and turns the car around, going back down the long driveway and disappearing from sight. I wait until he's gone before turning and looking up at the building which, if previous Christmases are anything to go by, should have a simple tree outside, decorated with white lights. My father – and my mother, when she was alive – never went in for anything ostentatious, and their Christmas decorations reflected their modest tastes. Instead of that though, I'm looking at a flashing, rainbow colored building, with almost none of the actual fabric visible, other than the windows, and the intermittent flashing of the lights is enough to make my eyes ache. So, as much as I'd like to stay out here and prolong the inevitable meeting with my supposed family, I climb the steps to the front door and insert my key.

Inside, the decorations are just as bright, the wide marble-floored hallway having been filled with fairy lights. There's also a life-size Santa Claus model at the far end beside the stairs, which is bad enough, except it's also illuminated and is rocking back and forth ho-ho-ho-ing to itself.

"Oh, good Lord," I murmur to myself.

"Hello?" A familiar voice sounds from the direction of the kitchen, and I move toward it, smiling, and then start running and throw myself into the arms of Mrs Hemsworth, who returns my greeting, hugging me tight. "I thought it might be you," she says, eventually pulling back and looking me up and down. "You've lost weight," she adds and takes my hand, leading me back to the kitchen.

"A little… maybe."

She shakes her head and I sit up on one of the high stools at the wide breakfast bar, dropping my rucksack at my feet. This has always been my favorite room in the house. Dad had it remodeled about three or four years ago, and it's very sleek and chic now, with every modern convenience you can imagine, but that's not why I like it in here so much. I like it because Mrs Hemsworth makes it feel so homely. Every day, when I finished school, I used to come back here and have a glass of milk and a couple of her home made cookies, or a slice of cake, and we'd sit and talk about my day. Then my mom would come home from the foundation she used to run about an hour later and she'd join us and, while I did my homework, they'd cook our evening meal together, like two old friends. Dad always did his best to get home in time to eat with us, even if it meant he had to carry on working afterwards in his study. That was one of the best things about my parents. Despite their wealth and how busy their lives were, they never forgot the value of family time.

"Eating too little, or working too hard?" she asks, opening the oven and pulling out a lasagna.

"A bit of both," I reply. "Is that for me?" I can hear my stomach grumbling already.

"Sure is," she says, smiling. "Your favorite." She cuts into it and the heady aromas of tomato, Italian herbs and cheese assail my nostrils.

"That smells so good," I tell her truthfully as she places the plate in front of me, and fetches a bowl of salad and some cutlery, before taking a seat opposite and looking over at me. She hasn't changed at all, but then I suppose it's only a few months since I last saw her, standing holding my hand at Dad's funeral. At least she's not wearing black now, but she's in her usual smart skirt and blouse, an apron tied around her waist. I've never known how old she is, and never been brave enough to ask, but I imagine she's in her mid to late fifties. She's got brown hair with a fair amount of gray running through it, and pale blue eyes that always seem to know when I need someone to talk to…

"Well, eat up," she says, smiling.

The way the lasagna is calling to me, I don't need telling twice, and I cut through the crispy cheese topping to the rich meaty sauce below.

"Where is everyone?" I ask, taking my first delicious mouthful and closing my eyes in appreciation of one of life's finest things.

"They're all out," she replies. "The twins have gone to a party, and her ladyship went out for dinner." She rolls her eyes. "Again," she adds.

"You'd better not let her hear you calling her that," I warn. "And what do you mean 'again'?"

"I think that's the third time this week she's gone out." She gives me a knowing look.

"You think she's got another man… already?" Although I hate my stepmother with a passion, I can't help the emotion from seeping into my voice. The thought that she can have forgotten my father so quickly is appalling to me.

Mrs Hemsworth shrugs. "I don't know," she says. "Let's face it, she was never around that much, even when your daddy was alive, not once she'd persuaded him into marriage, anyway. But you've seen what she's like with Jack. She was all over the poor boy today…" She lets her voice fade and we both smile now, but then it's hard not to. Jack is the gardener and handyman. He comes in three times a week, usually on Mondays, Wednesdays and Fridays and whenever he's around, Catrina does her best to attract his attention, wearing the skimpiest clothes imaginable, even in the middle of winter, fawning over him like a lovesick teenager, complimenting his impressive physique and generally making a fool of herself. The reason we're smiling is because Mrs Hemsworth and I know something that Catrina doesn't... namely, that it would have to be a very cold day in hell before Jack would ever be interested in 'her ladyship'. That's because he's already in a relationship, with an equally attractive lawyer, by the name of Alex, which is short for Alexander.

"Is he responsible for decorating the house?" I ask.

She nods. "Yes, but she didn't give him a choice, and he didn't like doing it. Your stepmother had all the lights delivered last week and it's taken poor Jack all his time to put the darn things up, which is why she's got him coming in tomorrow as well as Friday, to make sure the garden looks just right for the party on Saturday..." her voice fades again and she looks across at me.

I pause, my lasagna-loaded fork poised mid-air. "Excuse me? Did you say 'party'?"

Mrs Hemsworth nods her head, then rests her elbows on the countertop, letting her chin fall onto her upturned hands. "You know how your father always used to have a Christmas party?" she says thoughtfully.

"Yes."

"Well, Catrina's decided to do the same thing."

"But I don't understand. Why does it matter what the garden looks like? Dad always held his parties at a hotel, not at home." Dad's Christmas parties were legendary, but he never hosted one at our house. This was always a place that was private, for us to be alone, away from it all.

"I know, but she's holding it here," Mrs Hemsworth confirms.

"She is?" I can't disguise my surprise. "And did you say it was going to be on Saturday?" She nods. "This Saturday? But Christmas Day is only next Wednesday. It's too close..."

"Yes."

"But…" I'm stunned into silence. That was something my dad would never have done. His appreciation of family time wasn't limited to us Hudsons. He'd never have held a business function like this on a weekend so close to the holidays, because he knew people had their own family commitments. They had relatives to see, shopping to do, children to be with. The last thing they needed was to have to attend a business party, even if it was being thrown by a man who'd done a lot to help them and their community.

"I know," Mrs Hemsworth replies and I realize that I don't need to explain it to her.

"Why's she doing it?"

"I have no idea." She gets up and goes over to the coffee machine, filling it with ground coffee from the container that sits beside it, and then going to the sink. She turns around to face me again. "But she told me to tell you that she wants to talk to you tomorrow."

"She did?"

"Yes. She said she's got something in mind, and she needs to talk it through with you."

"That sounds ominous," I reply, suddenly feeling nervous. When Catrina says she's got something in mind, it's usually time to be worried, because I know it's going to mean work for me. Even before my father's death, she dropped not very subtle hints – out of his earshot, of course – that, once I came back from university, I needn't think I could live at the house rent free. She told me in no uncertain terms that I'd have to earn my keep if I thought I could continue to live in luxury. That rule doesn't seem to apply her twin daughters, Christa and Chelsea, who swan around, doing whatever takes their fancy. But with that thought in mind, I dread to think what she's planning for me.

Paul

I stare at the invitation in my hand, trying to make a decision.

I've been to this particular Christmas party every year for the last ten years, but this time around, it feels wrong. Charles Hudson only died a few months ago, so for his widow to be throwing the customary Hudson Investments annual Christmas party feels a little inappropriate, to put it mildly. I check the date again. The party's this coming Saturday, which is really close to the holidays, and although I'm supposed to have replied by now, I've been putting off making the decision. I mean, I know I'm supposed to have gone back to them by the end of the day – one way or the other – but being as it's only just after five in the afternoon, it's not the end of the day yet. Not my day, anyway.

I put the invitation down again and check my emails, answering one from my newest potential game designer. He's based in Detroit and, so far, we've only communicated by email and Skype, but I'm supposed to be flying to meet him in the New Year. In his message, he details out a couple of questions about the draft contract I sent through to him earlier in the week, which I refer to the legal department, just as there's a knocking on my door.

"Come in," I call out.

"What's going on?" My friend Fin Price comes into my office, looking around, with a surprised expression on his face.

"Sorry?" I stare over at him, feeling confused.

"I expected to find you running around, in a state of panic, your share price tumbling through the floor, the bottom having fallen out of the market..." He comes over and flops his six foot three frame down into the chair opposite me.

"What the hell are you talking about, Fin?" I sit forward.

He leans over and rests his arms on my desk. "Since when do you ignore my text messages?" he asks. "I assumed there had to be some kind of national emergency going on..."

"You sent me a message?"

"Yeah... about Friday night."

Fin and I have known each other since high school and we usually meet up for a quiet drink after work at least once a week. Mostly it's on a Friday, but sometimes we'll change the evening, if we have to. I guess this is one of those times.

"I've gotta pull a late shift on Friday, which on the upside means we could play golf in the morning, if you want to, but it means I won't be able to come out in the evening, so I was suggesting we could maybe do something tonight... except you didn't answer my text."

I check my phone, which is on silent and look up at him, sheepishly. "Sorry," I murmur.

"So you did get the message then?"

"Yeah. I just didn't realize."

"And you call yourself a chief executive," he mumbles, rolling his eyes. "It's a good thing I have to drive past your office to get home," he adds.

"I've been distracted," I point out. "So shoot me."

"Why would I wanna do that? I'd only feel obliged to fix you up again." He shakes his blond head at me. "So, what's been distracting you?" he asks, leaning back again and crossing one long leg over the other. He's wearing jeans and a button down shirt, although I know he'll have spent his day in scrubs, being as he works as an Emergency Room doctor in the city hospital. "It's not a sexy new secretary," he continues. "I recognized Maureen the moment I walked in."

"Yeah... and she's the only one who'd let you walk in here unannounced," I reply. She's been with me for nearly five years and feels more like a mother than a secretary sometimes. "And besides, you know I never mix business with pleasure... unlike some doctors I could mention."

"It was once," he replies, rolling his eyes. "Just once. And in my defense, she was the sexiest theater nurse I've ever seen." He smiles, clearly remembering something I'd probably rather not know. "But, like you, I prefer to keep my personal life and my professional life separate."

"Except when you find a particularly sexy theater nurse, evidently," I joke.

"Yeah… except then." He folds his arms across his broad chest. "You still haven't told me what was distracting you," he says, looking across at me.

"Oh, it's this," I reply, tossing the invitation across the desk at him.

He leans forward and picks it up. "Hudson Investment Corporation," he murmurs. "Isn't that the guy who first invested in you?"

"Yeah," I confirm. "Charles and I met at a conference when I was just finishing college, we got talking over a beer and Charles said he saw something in me. It just kinda blossomed from there really." I can't help remembering that meeting, in the hotel bar, and how he'd listened to my young and occasionally naive dreams, not in a critical or judgmental way, like some of my lecturers, nor in a jokey, disbelieving way, like many of my peers, but in a supportive and helpful manner. A few weeks later, Charles called me up and arranged to meet me again, and told me he wanted to invest in me, to give me a head start in forming a computer gaming company. I've never looked back.

"So, how much did he invest?" Fin asks, still looking down at the invitation.

"Half a million," I reply.

He lets out a soft whistle.

"On a kid he didn't know?"

I nod my head and Fin locks eyes with me. "You could probably buy Hudson Investment Corporation several times over now, couldn't you?"

"Yeah. If I wanted to."

He smiles. "So, how much are you worth?"

"I don't know really," I reply honestly. "It changes every few minutes. Last time I checked, I think it was about two point eight…"

He looks surprised. "Million?"

"No… billion."

His jaw drops and the surprise becomes shock. "Holy shit, Paul. I had no fucking idea…"

"It's taken more than ten years of hard work to get here, but I'm here." I glance across at him, noticing the invitation he's still clutching. "And no matter how much I'm worth, it still doesn't help me make a decision about the goddamn party, does it?"

"What's stopping you from saying 'yes'?" he asks.

"I've gone to Charles' Christmas parties every year since I first met him," I explain. "It's something he always did, bringing together all the people he'd invested in so he could catch up with us all and see how we were getting along."

"But?"

"But he died in the middle of August, and this feels…"

"Too soon?" he prompts.

"Yeah. But it's more than that. It feels inappropriate, especially as he won't be there, and the whole point of these parties, as far as I was concerned, was to see him." I pause for a moment. "But at the same time, I feel that if I don't go, I'm dishonoring his memory."

He nods his head. "The invitation's from Catrina Hudson," he says, looking down at it. "Is that his widow?"

"Yeah." He must be able to hear the distain in my voice, because he raises his eyebrows and tilts his head to one side. "They were only married for about a year before Charles died," I add, "and this feels like a fairly typical, and cynical ploy of hers."

"You like her then," he says.

"Yeah. I'm a huge fan."

"Hmm. I can tell." He smiles at me. "Well, maybe she just wants to carry on the tradition, or perhaps she's looking for some moral support from the people he helped over the years?" he suggests.

I shake my head. "No, that's not how Catrina operates," I reply. "She couldn't give a damn about tradition, and I've never met anyone who needed moral support less."

He leans forward again, putting the invitation back on my desk and looking hard at me. "Whatever you think of her," he says softly. "Charles obviously loved her, or he'd never have married her, would he? Maybe you should remember that?"

"I'd love to. I really would. But I'm not convinced he did love her. I think he married her because he was lonely."

"Really?" He leans a bit further forward, clearly interested.

"Yeah. Charles was married to his first wife, Olivia, for years. He told me they were childhood sweethearts and she was the love of his life." I pause and think for a moment. "It was odd, you know, he was a fairly hard-nosed businessman, but he was complete mush when it came to Olivia." I always remember feeling kinda jealous of that, knowing I'd probably never have anyone like that in my life. I'm just not that kinda guy. I can't imagine myself being in love, or even coming close to it.

"So what happened?" he asks, interrupting my train of thought.

"She died about three years ago. She ran a foundation which helped disadvantaged children, and was working really hard, so she missed the early signs…" I let my voice drop.

"Cancer?" he asks.

"Yeah. By the time they caught it, it was too late. She died within a couple of months. I was out of the country at the time, doing some work in Europe, but I went and saw him when I got back. He was in pieces, being fawned over by Catrina."

"She was on the scene even then?"

"She was his secretary," I explain. "And she obviously wanted to be more."

"If he and his first wife were so close, how did she manage to convince him?"

"I think she played on his loneliness," I reply. "And of course, there was Lottie…"

"Lottie?"

"Yeah. Charles and Olivia's daughter."

"They had a daughter?"

"Yeah. And Catrina had a couple of kids too… twin girls, if I remember rightly. I think she convinced Charles that she'd take care of Lottie and be a mother to her."

"Well, maybe that wasn't such a bad idea," Fin says.

"Maybe not, in normal circumstances. But I don't think Catrina has a maternal bone in her body. She's the last person you'd want to mother your child. I guess Charles wasn't thinking straight at the time and, after a year or so of her wearing him down, he asked her to marry him. She jumped at the chance and the rest, as they say, is history."

"So, the daughter is now living there with the stepmom and the twins?" he asks.

"No. I think she was going off to college when her mom died. As far as I know she did so, which is probably a good thing. At least she escaped Catrina's poisonous influence."

"Sounds to me like you should avoid this party," he says, tapping the invite with his fingertips.

"Except I kinda feel I owe it to Charles to go… not just to pay my respects, being as I missed his funeral, but also to make sure Catrina's not ruining his company and taking his good name down with her."

"Then go," he says, sitting back again, seemingly a little exasperated with my inability to make a decision.

I reach across and pick up the invitation again.

"It says 'To Paul Lewis and guest'," I remark and look up at him. "What are you doing on Saturday evening?"

"Um…"

He fumbles around mentally for an excuse. "You're free? Great. You can come with me." I check the email and start typing out my reply, giving them Fin's name as my guest.

"You're kidding, right? You must have a list of women who'd willingly accompany you. Let's face it, most of Boston's finest young ladies are positively gagging to be seen with you, and your billions."

"Yeah, but none of them will watch my back like you will."

"Will you need to have your back watched?" he asks.

"I might. It depends on what Catrina's done to Charles' company, and what her real motives are for throwing this party."

He stares at me for a moment. "I guess I'd better find my tux then, hadn't I?"

I smile at him and press 'send'.

Chapter Two

Lottie

"Wakey, wakey," Catrina's shrill voice crashes through my dreams and I sit bolt upright in shock.

"What?" I cry out. "What's happened?"

"Nothing's happened yet," she announces, going over to the large floor-to-ceiling window and pulling back the drapes. "But that's all about to change."

"It is?" I stretch my arms above my head and then pull them down again and rub the sleep from my eyes.

Catrina stares across at me, then walks over and perches on the edge of my bed, right at the end, ensuring she maintains her distance. Even though I'm not properly awake yet, I'm still alert enough to take in the fact that she's wearing an almost transparent pale pink robe, which reveals a lot more than I'm comfortable with seeing. She's obviously been in the shower; her dyed blonde hair is still wrapped up in a toweling turban, although she's found the time to put on her makeup. Lots of it. This must be for Jack's benefit, being as he's coming in today. I'm almost tempted to laugh, but then she'd want to know why, and I'm certainly not about to explain.

"What time is it?" I ask her.

"Just after seven," she replies, inspecting her red-lacquered nails.

"In the morning?"

"Of course in the morning." She gives me a harsh look. "You can't laze around all day, you know?"

"All day? It's seven in the morning…" I flop back down onto the pillows, any thought of a relaxing lie-in forgotten. And I'd been so looking forward to it as well. I have to get up at six every morning so I can squeeze in some study time, grab breakfast and head out for classes. Then I work three evenings a week, plus weekends at the bookstore. A lie-in is unheard of for me – even on my vacation, evidently.

"I want to talk to you about the party," Catrina says.

"What about it?" I can't disguise my disapproval for her scheme, but she fails to notice. That doesn't really surprise me. Catrina rarely pays attention to anything that isn't brightly colored, and flashing, and directly in her line of vision.

"Well," she continues, with enthusiasm, "just about everyone I invited has said they're gonna come, which is great."

"Fantastic." Again, my sarcasm should be obvious, but it sails right over her head.

"I'm employing a local catering company," she goes on. Then, as though we're in some kind of conspiracy together, she leans forward and adds, "Let's face it, this is hardly the kind of event Mrs Hemsworth is used to handling." I want to object to her insult, but what's the point? Catrina's not going to listen to me. "And the caterers are supplying some waiting staff…" She pauses.

"Right?" I don't know where she's going with this, but she's got a slight smile on her face and that's usually a bad sign – for me, anyway.

"The thing is, I'm not sure there are going to be enough of them, so I'm expecting you to help out." The last few words come out of her in a rush, like a speeding train, and hit me with appropriate force.

"Excuse me?" I can't believe she expects me to wait on her guests, in my own home, like I'm hired help… except, unlike the hired help, I won't even be getting paid for the privilege.

She stands up and looks down at me. "There's no need to adopt that tone of voice, young lady," she says, not that I was aware I had. "The company have provided me with a uniform for you." She stops talking, walks over to the door, opens it and goes out, returning a few moments later, carrying a hanger on which there's a white blouse and what appears to be the shortest skirt ever. "Look," she says, triumphantly, holding out her hand, "they've even had a name badge made for you."

She drops the badge into my hand and I turn it over, seeing that it says 'Charlotte'.

"Charlotte, not Lottie?" I query, although why that's a priority, given what she's just demanded of me, I have no idea.

"Lottie sounds cheap and tacky," she replies and I want to laugh out loud that she clearly thinks the monstrous decor and her own personal tastes are stylish and tasteful, but my abridged name, that my father used all the time, is 'tacky'.

"It was good enough for my father," I counter.

She rolls her eyes and hooks the blouse and non-existent skirt on the back of my door.

"I won't do it," I tell her, getting out of bed and folding my arms resolutely.

"You will," she replies.

"You seem to forget, Catrina. This is my home, just as much as it's yours. More so really, being as my parents lived here for years, and I was born here. I—"

"Ancient history," she interrupts, waving my argument away with a flick of her manicured hand. "The house and your father's money are mine now," she chirps.

"That's not true." I march over to her, staring up into her eyes, noting the slight crows feet that are beginning to form at their corners. "He left me his money. You only got the house."

She shakes her head slowly from side to side. "Yes, but your money's held in trust until you graduate, if you remember."

"Yes, Catrina. It's in trust. For me. That doesn't mean you can spend it yourself."

She blinks a little faster and shifts from one foot to the other. "You know perfectly well, I'm entitled to use your inheritance to support your education…"

"Support my education?" I round on her. "You haven't even paid my allowance for the last four months."

"There are expenses to be taken care of, Charlotte." She waves her hand dismissively. "You're too young to understand..." Her voice fades for a moment, then she looks down at her watch. "Dear Lord... I don't have time for this," she says. "Jack's coming today... I need to get ready." Without another word, she wafts from the room, leaving nothing more than the heady scent of her perfume and a sour taste in my mouth.

I could have pointed out to her that, since my dad died, she hasn't contributed a single cent to my education or my living expenses. My dad bought the apartment I live in when I started college, for its convenience to the campus, rather than its style, and I share it with my friend Heather. I always did, because I liked the company, but since Dad died, I'm even more glad I made that decision, because Heather now helps pay the bills. She also got me a job in the bookstore where she works, so I can buy food, and I take public transport everywhere I go, because I can't afford a car. It's all so different to when Dad was alive. I sit down on the edge of the bed and fight back the inevitable tears. I miss my dad so much – but not because he paid for everything. I miss him because, when he was around, I was never scared, or lonely. I never doubted myself, and I never feared for my future.

I wipe away the tears with the backs of my hands and take a deep breath. There's no point in feeling sorry for myself. I've learned very quickly over the last few months that it doesn't get me very far. I glance out the window. It looks like being a sunny day, even if it is cold, so I guess I may as well have a shower, get dressed and go and see Jack.

"I wish you'd eat something a bit more substantial for your breakfast," Mrs Hemsworth says, standing with her back to the countertop and her arms folded across her chest, watching me eat a bowl of granola.

"This is what I usually eat," I tell her. "It's fine."

"But I could make you some pancakes, or bacon and scrambled eggs."

"Yeah, and I could go back to college weighing ten pounds more than when I arrived, with a whole bunch of clothes that don't fit me anymore." I give her a wink and a smile and she just about manages to smile back.

"That'd be a bad thing, would it?" she asks.

"Well, I can't afford to replace the clothes," I point out.

"You could if madam paid you what you're due," she says.

I chuckle. "Don't get me started. I've already had that argument once today… and it got me nowhere."

Mrs Hemsworth's response is curtailed by a knocking on the back door.

"That'll be Jack," she says, a full smile appearing on her lips as she pushes herself away from the countertop and goes over to the back door, pulling it open. "One day, you'll let yourself in," she remarks, standing to one side.

"Maybe," he replies, coming in. Although it's cold and I can feel the chill from the other side of the kitchen, Jack's just wearing blue jeans and a red check shirt that fits him well and shows off his muscular physique.

"Hi," I say and he turns, a broad grin settling on his handsome face.

"Hi you." He's pleased to see me, which is gratifying. "How's things?"

I shrug. "You know… Same old, same old." I get up and go over to him, and he pulls me into a big hug. I haven't seen him since my father's funeral and it feels good to be held by him again.

"You are okay, aren't you?" he asks, leaning back and looking down into my eyes.

"Yeah. I'm fine."

"Then why don't I believe you?"

"Because she's not fine," Mrs Hemsworth puts in.

"I am. Really."

"Why don't you come outside with me and tell me all about it?" Jack suggests.

"There's nothing to tell, but I'll come outside with you anyway. It'll give us a chance to catch up."

"You'll need a jacket," he says. "It's cold out there."

"Is that you, Jack?" We all stop dead at the sound of Catrina's voice.

"I'm gonna grab a jacket and meet you outside," I say, pulling away from Jack and retreating toward the kitchen door, just as Catrina comes through it. She's dressed now. Well, she's got clothes on, anyway. Her mini skirt and low-cut top seem to be trying to meet in the middle, and while I think the overall effect is horrendous, I have to admit, she's got an amazing figure for a woman of her age. Not that I know what her age is, but with two twenty year-old daughters, I'm guessing it's around forty something.

"There you are," she simpers, walking over to him, oblivious to everything and everyone else in the room.

"Mrs Hudson," he replies quietly, his embarrassment obvious.

"How many times, Jack?" she says, placing her hand flat on his chest. "You must call me Catrina."

Jack looks over her shoulder at me, giving me an entreating look, but I smile back and shrug my shoulders, beating a hasty retreat. I love Jack dearly, but he can fight his own battles today. I can't handle another skirmish with Catrina. Two in one day is too much for anyone.

"How did you get out here so quickly?" I ask. I'm surprised to find Jack already tending to the flower beds when I get outside, having run upstairs and grabbed a coat and scarf.

"I got lucky," he says. "The caterer called and Mrs Hudson had to go speak to them." He stands and looks at me. "Thanks for nothing, by the way."

I hold up my hands. "I already had her in my room at seven this morning, telling me I've gotta be a waitress at this dumb party… the last thing—"

"Wait a second," he interrupts. "She said what?"

"That I have to be a waitress at this party she's having on Saturday night."

He shakes his head. "Is that why you're looking so down?" he asks.

"I wasn't aware I was looking down," I reply.

"Well, you don't seem quite your usual self."

"Maybe because it's the first time I've been back here since Dad's funeral?" I explain and he runs his fingers through his thick dark hair.

"Yeah. Of course. Sorry. I should've thought."

"It seems very different around here," I say, wanting to distract him from feeling guilty.

"You mean it seems a whole lot more tasteless," he replies.

"Yeah. That would be it." We both smile at each other and the moment of awkwardness is gone. "How's Alex?" I ask him.

He doesn't reply, but after just a moment's hesitation, takes my arm and leads me over to the outbuilding where the tools and garden equipment are all stored. "I was hoping to talk to you about him," he says quietly, once we're inside. At least it's warmer in here, away from the chilly breeze, and I perch up on the work bench while Jack sits down on a stool, looking up at me.

"Why? What's happened?"

"Nothing's happened. Not yet, anyway."

"This sounds ominous." He tries to smile, but fails dismally. "Tell me what's wrong, Jack."

He sighs. "Alex has gone home to his parents for the holidays," he says.

"Already?" Christmas Day isn't until next Wednesday. I'm surprised he's gone this early. Okay, so I know I've come home early too, but that's only because the flights were cheaper than waiting until nearer Christmas. Alex is a lawyer. I doubt he has to think about such things.

"Yeah," Jack replies. "He hasn't seen them for a while, so he decided to spend a few extra days with them."

I nod my head. "And you're missing him?" I suggest, trying to work out what Jack's problem is.

"Well, yeah. I am, obviously. But that's not what's wrong…"

"Jack!" Catrina's voice interrupts him.

"What now?" he mutters.

She calls again, a little louder this time. "You're gonna have to go out there," I whisper to him. He looks deflated. "Hey, why don't we go out somewhere tonight?"

His face brightens in an instant and he gets to his feet, going over to the door. "That sounds perfect," he replies, his voice barely audible. "I can pick you up at the end of the drive at… seven?" I nod my head. "We'll go into the city. And I don't care what you say," he adds, "it's my treat." I'm about to argue when he opens the door and steps outside, calling, "Yes, Mrs Hudson?" as he closes it behind him.

I wait until their voices have disappeared into the distance before opening the door myself, just a crack, to make sure they're really gone, and then going back across the lawn to the kitchen and letting myself back in.

Jack sits opposite me, as the waiter holds my chair and allows me to get comfortable.

"I'm glad I bothered to put a skirt on," I whisper, looking down at my gray lambswool sweater and black skirt. "I was gonna just wear jeans, but I changed my mind at the last minute."

"I don't think they'd care," he replies and I feel relieved that at least he's not wearing a tie, although looking around, a lot of the men in here are. Even so, Jack looks amazing in his white button down shirt and dark gray jacket, and he's getting a lot of admiring glances from the women around us. A couple of them have looked me up and down, presumably wondering why someone who looks as good as he does would want to be seen opposite someone like me, but then they don't know Jack.

The waiter hands us the menus and says he'll be back to take our drinks order.

"Well," Jack says, putting down the menu, unopened. "I guess as you're over twenty-one now, you can drink whatever you like."

"I guess." In elegant surroundings like this, I don't like to admit that I rarely drink alcohol these days. It's a luxury I can't afford.

"Would you rather have mineral water?" he asks, taking pity on me.

I nod my head and when the waiter returns, Jack orders a large bottle of sparkling water. The waiter nods and goes away again and I settle down to look at the menu. When I look up, I notice that Jack still hasn't even glanced at his.

"Are you not hungry?" I ask him.

He smiles. "Yeah. But I know what I'm gonna have. Alex and I come here quite often."

"And you always eat the same thing?"

"No. But I'm in the mood for the crab ravioli, and the rack of lamb."

I look down at the menu, reading about the dishes he's just mentioned. "They sound good, but I think I'm gonna have the mussels, followed by the salmon."

"You're in a fishy mood?" he jokes.

"Evidently." I close the menu and put it down in front of me. "So, tell me about Alex," I say, just as the waiter comes back with our water. He pours a half glass for each of us and takes our order, then removes the menus and leaves again.

"Cheers," Jack says, raising his glass. I clink mine against his and take a sip of water.

At that moment, the door to the restaurant opens and a beautiful blonde woman comes in, bringing a chilly breeze with her. She's wearing a stunning short, lacy black cocktail dress, with long sleeves and a very low neckline. However, she's not wearing a coat, so she must be freezing cold – mad woman. She's followed by a tall, dark haired man who closes the door quite quickly, thank goodness, and when he turns around, his eyes lock with mine for a moment and I feel as though all the fresh, icy air that just wafted into the room has been sucked out again. He stares at me and I can't look away as his gaze burns through me. His dark hair is short, but thick and I have an instant urge to run my fingers through it, while he kisses me with his generous lips. I want to feel his slight stubble abrade my skin while his hands explore my body...

"Lottie?" I can hear Jack saying my name, but it's as though he's somewhere else, in the distance, far away. On another planet. In a different universe. The only thing I can see is the beautiful man standing at the front of the restaurant, staring at me. "Lottie? What's wrong?" I feel Jack's hand clasp mine and blink myself back to reality just as the man's blonde companion comes over and stands in front of him, getting his attention.

"Sorry?" I blurt out, trying to appear normal.

"What happened then?" Jack asks, obviously concerned.

"Nothing." I take another sip of water. "You were going to tell me about Alex, remember?"

He pauses for a moment, as though he wants to say something, and then takes a breath. "Yeah," he murmurs. Although I'm looking at Jack, I'm aware of the couple being led through the restaurant and seated a couple of tables away.

"You're missing him?" I try to focus on Jack and his problem with Alex. I'm his friend, after all.

"Yeah, but like I said earlier, that's not the problem."

"Then what is?"

He clasps my hand a little tighter and leans forward. "One of the reasons Alex has gone to visit his parents, and that he's spending a whole week there, is that he's going to tell them," he whispers.

"About you, you mean?"

He nods his head. "They've got no idea. They think he's straight."

"Oh God." I'm completely focused on him now. "Is he worried?"

Jack shrugs and picks up his glass. "Man, I wish this was vodka," he mutters and puts it down again. "He doesn't know how they're gonna react," he says, answering my question, before taking a long pause and looking up at the ceiling. "He's never actually told anyone."

"No-one?" I'm surprised.

"No."

"Not even his friends, or the people he works with?"

Jack shakes his head. "No-one."

"Is there a reason for that?" I look at Jack, who seems to want to look at anything and anyone but me.

"Not that he's told me," he murmurs.

I reach out and place my free hand over Jack's. "Hey…" I whisper. "What aren't you telling me?"

He lets his eyes rest on me at last. "I'm scared," he says simply.

"What of?"

"That his parents will freak out, and that he'll decide he doesn't want me as much as he wants their approval."

"That's not gonna happen, Jack, and you know it."

"Do I?" he asks, with a hint of bitterness, and right at that moment, the waiter arrives with our appetizers. We're forced to let go of each other and sit back so he can put our dishes down.

We wait for him to leave but, before we start eating, I lean over toward Jack again. "What did that mean?" I ask him.

"It means, this has happened before," he replies. "Why shouldn't it happen again?" He picks up his fork, helping himself to his ravioli, and I start to eat my mussels, removing them from the shells and soaking up the rich tomato sauce with some of the bread.

"I don't understand," I say, after a few minutes' silence.

He looks up at me and just says, "My ex, Russ."

"What about him?"

He sighs, deeply. "He and I had been dating for about a year when he came out to his parents," he explains. "They gave him a really hard time. His mom kept crying down the phone at him, reminding him that he was her only child and how much she'd always wanted grandchildren – because she'd obviously never heard of surrogacy or adoption – and both she and his dad were constantly pressuring him to be 'normal', as they put it. It was really getting to him, so I tried suggesting that he should see less of them for a while, to let them get used to the idea, but then they made him feel guilty about that as well. Eventually it became too much for him and he broke up with me. It was easier…"

"And you're scared the same thing will happen with Alex?" I ask, taking another mussel.

He nods. "Yeah."

"But you and Alex live together. You've been with him for two years. It's different."

"Is it?"

"Yes," I tell him firmly.

"How?" he asks.

"Because you're in love with Alex."

He stops eating, puts down his fork and looks at me. "How did you know?" he asks.

"It's written all over your face every time you talk about him, that's how." I watch him closely, sensing his insecurity. "Does Alex feel the same?" I ask.

"He says he does," he replies.

"Then why are you so worried?"

He picks up his fork again, but doesn't eat anything. "I just want him to be honest about who he is, that's all. I came out to my parents ten years ago, when I was eighteen. The fact that Alex has waited until he's twenty-seven doesn't make me feel too confident."

"Maybe he was waiting until he had someone worth coming out for?" I suggest and Jack smiles, just slightly.

"Thanks for saying that," he whispers and picks up his drink, taking a long sip of water and glancing around the restaurant. "Hey," he says, putting the glass back down again. "There's a guy over there who's staring at you,"

I feel myself blush. "There is?"

"Yeah. He's kinda hot."

"Behave yourself, Jack. You're in love with Alex, remember?"

"Don't worry. He's not my type. He's straight for one thing."

"How can you tell?" I ask, trying to keep occupied by taking a small bite of bread.

"Well, apart from the fact that he's looking at you like he wants to take you to bed and pleasure you forever, you just kinda get to know after a while."

I choke on my bread and Jack offers me my water, which I take and swallow down a couple of sips.

"You okay?" he asks.

I nod. "Yeah, thanks."

"Was it something I said?" He smirks.

"No," I reply, trying to sound a lot calmer than I feel.

"Yeah… right," he says, shaking his head slowly. He looks back at the man. "He's still looking," he says. "I guess you've gotta feel sorry for his date. Poor woman. She's trying real hard to impress him, and he's only got eyes for you."

"Stop it," I warn him, daring to glance to my left, where the man is sitting facing me, his eyes locked on mine once more. I can't look away and, for a long moment, we simply stare at each other and it's as though nothing else in the room even exists.

"Hey," Jack says and I drag my eyes away from the gorgeous being a few tables away and look at him. "Wanna give him something to think about?"

"Sorry?"

"Give me your hand," he suggests and I wipe off the tomato sauce and mussel residue on my serviette, before offering him my right hand. "Now, look at me like you were just looking at him," he says, smiling. "And try not to laugh."

"Why are we doing this?" I ask, watching as he raises my hand to his lips.

"Because it never hurts a guy like him to let him think he might have some competition... It keeps his natural arrogance in check."

"Even if he doesn't? Have any competition, I mean?"

He shrugs and very gently presses his lips against my fingers, before slowly taking each one and sucking it into his mouth. Finally, when he's done, he lowers my hand, but keeps a hold of it, in the center of the table, his eyes boring into mine.

"From what I could taste, that was a really good tomato sauce," he whispers. "I'll have to order the mussels next time I come in here."

I can't help it, I have to laugh, and Jack soon joins in. I notice he takes the opportunity glance at the man again.

"He's still looking," he says.

"And? Did we put him off?" I ask.

He smirks, shaking his head. "No. If anything I'd say he's even more determined to get you into bed than he was before." He stares into my eyes. "I think he wants to find out what you taste like too... And if I didn't know better, I'd say the feeling's entirely mutual." He starts laughing and I feel myself blush, although I'm not going to deny the truth of what he's saying.

The thought of going to bed with this gorgeous stranger gives me a warm feeling in the pit of my stomach and I steal a look over at him. His eyes are smoldering and dark now, and I know that if he really wanted me to, I'd let him take me to bed. Actually, I think I'd let him take me anywhere.

Paul

So far, my Thursday has been fairly horrendous. My afternoon meeting was cancelled because the guy I was meant to be seeing wasn't well, and while I could have stayed at work, I decided to get my Christmas shopping done instead. I don't know why I thought that was a good idea, or why I hadn't already done it online, but I thought I'd go out and brave the shops… and I regretted it as soon as I'd walked into the first department store. Christmas may be the season of goodwill to all men, but there's something about buying presents that makes people lose all sense of reason, not to mention good manners.

Still, three hours, two coffees and a really bad headache later, and I'm done. I let myself into my apartment feeling kinda worthy, and completely exhausted. Despite that, I'm still too on edge to relax, so I take a shower, pulling on a bathrobe afterwards, and sit on the bed for a while. I know exactly what I need. The question is, who should I call…?

I've got what can best be described as a 'little black book'. Except I guess that's not really the best way to describe it, because it isn't little – it's expansive. It also isn't black, and it isn't a book. It's a contacts list on my phone, stored in a separate encrypted folder, filled with the names of women who I know will be happy to come out with me, have a few drinks, go for dinner, or maybe to the theater, and then go home with me afterwards. We never come back here though, because I feel as though that would be letting them get too close, and I'm not about to do that. So, we go back to their place, or to a hotel, but whatever happens, they don't seem to mind the fact that I will fuck their brains out for a few hours, and then I won't call them again for several weeks, or even months. At least, none of them have ever complained, so I assume they don't mind. Over the years, I've wondered from time to time, what they do in between our 'dates' – whether they have their own 'little black books' of men who they go out with. It doesn't bother me in the least if they do. They have no more commitment to me than I do to them. A few of them have dropped off the list with the passage of time. A couple of them settled down into relationships and one even got married last year. Weirdly, she was still seeing me until a couple of weeks before the ceremony, when she calmly announced her six month long engagement and invited me to the wedding, maybe to show me what I was missing out on, or perhaps to let me know she was happy for our arrangement to continue, despite her change in circumstances. I don't know her reason. I declined the invite, took her home from the restaurant, and went straight back to my place, where I removed her name from the list. I don't do complicated. I'm not looking for anything other than casual, intelligent company and casual, hot sex. The women on my list have been chosen because they excel in both of those qualities.

Tonight I'm in the mood for stimulating conversation over dinner and something really fiery in bed. And that means calling Ashley. She's a beautiful, very sexy blonde, who happens to also have a brain. She teaches history at the University of Massachusetts, but has always told me that she's too busy to settle down, and likes the casual arrangement she has with me. She enjoys what we do together, evidently. I'm fairly sure she has the same casual arrangement with a few other men too, and that's just fine by me.

I dial her number and she picks up after the second ring.

"Paul," she says, her voice soft and husky, and my cock twitches at the thought of all the things I'm gonna do to her later on.

"Ashley," I reply. "Are you free this evening?" I don't bother with niceties or small talk, but she's used to that.

"Yes, I am," she replies and I can hear the smile in her voice. I guess she's as interested in hooking up as I am.

I check my watch. It's six-thirty now. "I can pick you up in an hour," I suggest.

"Dinner?" she asks, but I know the question is only there because she wants to know what to wear.

"Yeah. Dinner… first."

I hear a slight, very sexy chuckle just as I end the call.

It's colder outside than it was earlier and Ashley, despite being intelligent, didn't bring a coat with her, so she's moaning about the icy wind and freezing temperatures as we walk the sort distance from my car to the restaurant. I'm tempted to tell her that if she'd just brought a damn coat, she wouldn't have anything to moan about. But then I also know that she wore that sexy dress, entirely for my benefit, so it seems kinda churlish to complain. I also know from experience that she won't have put on any underwear, which I guess could be why she's feeling especially cold right now. She goes into the restaurant ahead of me and I close the door as quickly as I can, to keep the chill out, and then turn around, my eyes catching those of… Jeez… the most beautiful woman I've ever seen in my life. She's sitting facing me, her long brown hair curled very gently around her perfect, porcelain clear cheeks. Regardless of the fact that Ashley's standing in front of me, just a couple of feet or so away; regardless of everyone else in the restaurant, I've got an urge to walk right over, lift the woman to her feet and kiss those full pink lips until they're swollen and sore, to pull her soft body close to mine…

"Paul?" Ashley's voice cuts into my thoughts. She comes back to me and takes my hand, leading me further into the restaurant. With my other hand, I pull down my jacket, to hide my erection. The girl has looked away now, presumably distracted by her partner, more's the pity. As we're guided through the restaurant, I get a slightly better view of the guy she's sitting with and my heart sinks. He's good looking. Really good looking, and what makes it even worse is that they're holding hands and leaning in to each other, talking. They look kinda intimate and I feel more disappointed than I ever have before. It's weird. I never had myself down as a sore loser, until now. If a woman isn't interested in me, then so be it. I move on. But the idea of this particular woman being with the guy she's sitting opposite, or with anyone else for that matter, cuts through me like a knife.

The waiter stops by a table just a couple away from the girl and her partner and holds out the chair for Ashley, while I sit, giving thanks that I can see the girl clearly from here – although why I'm grateful to be watching her being fawned over by another guy, I've got no idea.

"Hello?" Ashley says, with a hint of sarcasm.

I focus on her. "Hi," I reply.

"It's good to see you again," she continues as we take our menus from the waiter. "It's been ages."

"What do you want to drink?" I ask her. I don't want to get into reminiscences.

"Red, I think," she replies. "You choose."

I glance down at the wine list. "A bottle of the La Tâche Grand Cru, please," I say, looking up at the waiter. He nods and moves away.

I glance over at the girl. She's wearing a simple gray sweater and some kind of delicate silver-looking necklace, which I can't see properly from here, and she and the guy are drinking mineral water, which either means they're both driving, they don't drink, or they can't afford the wine here. However, she's also eating mussels, picking them from the shells with great dexterity, as though she's been doing that since she was a child. As if it wasn't enough that she's sexy as hell, and beautiful beyond words, she's also got me intrigued. It's like she belongs here, and yet she doesn't. Which is kinda like me, I guess. Okay, so I paid more than most people earn in a year for the suit I'm wearing, and the other dozen or so like it that are hanging in my penthouse dressing room, and I just ordered a bottle of wine that costs thirty-five hundred dollars, but I wasn't raised to these standards. I grew up in a small house on the outskirts of Boston, eating my mom's home cooked food, and didn't see the inside of a restaurant until I met Charles Hudson… all those years ago. Not for the first time, I reflect that, if it wasn't for him, I'd probably be flipping burgers, or washing cars. God, I wish I'd had a chance to really thank him.

"How's business?" Ashley asks, cutting into my thoughts once more. I'm beginning to regret asking her to come out with me now and wish I'd come here by myself. At least I wouldn't have to pretend to make conversation and could just watch the girl... and dream.

"Fine," I reply.

"You're busy?" she perseveres.

"Yeah. Fairly."

The waiter comes back with the wine and I take the opportunity of sampling it to cut the conversation. It's a nice burgundy, light and filled with the flavors of summer fruit, and I give the waiter my approval. He pours an inch or so into Ashley's glass, does the same with mine and leaves the bottle on the table.

"Are you ready to order?" he asks.

I nod and ask for the sirloin steak, cooked rare. Ashley orders the grilled tenderloin of beef. We both skip the appetizers, which is standard practice for us, and for most of the women I see, because we usually want to move on to the main event – namely getting to bed as fast as possible. Tonight, however, I'd just kinda like to take my time, savor the view, sample whatever delights the restaurant has to offer and drink in the beautiful creature who I know I'm never gonna be able to forget.

I look over again and notice the guy glancing in my direction. He leans forward and speaks to her. I wonder if he's telling her that I haven't been able to take my eyes off of her since I walked in here. I also wonder if he's kinda mad about that. He doesn't look it. He looks amused, but that just makes me feel worse. He's obviously real sure of himself. He knows she's his and there's nothing I can do about it. Having just taken a bite of her bread, she suddenly starts to choke and I'm almost on my feet, about to rush over and help, when the guy hands her a glass of water and she takes a couple of sips, calming down again. This is ridiculous. I need to stop it. Just as I'm thinking I should remember the manners my mom raised me with and focus on Ashley, the girl looks over at me. There's a shyness about her, a delicate reticence that makes me wanna hold her and protect her, and keep her safe beside me – which is really strange, being as I've never wanted to do that with any woman before, except maybe my little sister. Sometimes. When she's not being annoying. But that's different. Really different to this overwhelming tidal wave of feeling for a girl I've never even met. I will her to smile, but she doesn't. She looks way again and then offers the guy her hand across the table. He takes it and raises it to his lips, kissing her fingers before taking them into his mouth and sucking them, one at a time. I've gotta give the guy credit. It's a really sexy move and it's obviously got her attention. Her eyes are fixed on him, like there's no-one else in the room, and the moment he lets go of her hand, he says something and they both laugh. I can hear the tinkling sound of her giggle from here, and get a warm feeling deep in my stomach, which is coupled with an overwhelming heaviness in my chest. As far as I'm aware, the former sensation is lust. I wanna be naked with her. I want to touch, kiss and lick every inch of her perfect skin. I want to lay her down and bury myself deep inside her. The very last thing I want to do is to fuck her brains out. I want to make love to her, real slow, real gentle… for maybe the next fifty years or so. I take a drink of wine and try to process that thought, while also working out that the heavy feeling in my chest is jealousy. I've never experienced it before, but I know what it is, because I'm so jealous of that guy, I can taste it. He gets to kiss her, to hold her and, maybe – if he's a really lucky son-of-a-bitch – he gets to see her naked, to make love to her, to make her come. I groan out loud.

"Paul?" Ashley says, her voice filled with concern. "Is something wrong?"

Yeah, everything. "No," I reply and take another long drink of wine.

When we leave the restaurant, the couple are still sitting at their table, drinking coffee and talking. I notice their heads are close together, and that they're still holding hands, and that heavy feeling is back in my chest again. I've just about managed to make conversation with Ashley through the evening and, from the look on her face, I can tell she's impatient to get back to her place. Ordinarily, I would be too, but I've kinda gone off the whole idea now. As I help her into my car, I wonder whether I could make some kind of excuse. Perhaps I could plead a headache? I wander around to the driver's side and open the door. God, I'm pathetic. I can't have the girl, no matter how much I want her, so I just need to get a grip and get on with my life and, right now, that means taking Ashley home and fucking her until she's begging me to stop. Even if I don't really want to.

It's only a short car ride and, throughout the whole of it, Ashley rests her hand on my thigh. Normally, that and the knowledge that she's not wearing any panties, coupled with the anticipation of what's to follow, would have my cock pressing hard against my zipper, but tonight, nothing's happening and I wonder if, for the first time in my life, I'm gonna fail to perform. That would be humiliating. What excuse could I give? I could plead exhaustion. I could plead insanity, I suppose. I certainly feel like I've been 'touched'. Could I fall back on the headache? Why on earth do I keep thinking about headaches?

I pull up outside Ashley's town house and switch off the engine. She looks across at me and for a minute I think she's gonna give me a way out. She opens her mouth and I half expect her to suggest we call it a night. She must have noticed that I'm not in the best of moods, surely? I've hardly said more than a few words all evening. Instead, she moves her hand a little higher so it's resting on my cock. "I can't wait to taste you," she murmurs. My cock twitches, thank God. At least there's some life left in it.

"Guess we'd better get inside then," I say, faking my enthusiasm as best I can. Her eyes widen and she licks her lips, while I get out of the car and go around to help her.

She lets us in and I've barely closed the door before she spins around and pushes me back against the wall, her hands pulling on my tie, releasing it and throwing it to the floor. She drags my jacket from my shoulders and then quickly undoes the buttons of my shirt, before dropping both items at my feet. Then, keeping eye contact, she kneels in front of me and undoes the buckle of my belt, and the button behind it, then lowers the zipper of my pants, letting them fall to the floor and pulling down my trunks. I step out of them and she pushes all my clothes to one side, before letting her hands rest on my thighs, her eyes fixed on mine. I'm semi-hard, which is something, and she puts her hand around the base of my cock and then sucks me deep into her mouth. Within a few strokes, she's got me hard and I gather up her hair, keeping hold of it and start to move back and forth, which makes her groan. I sense her moving, parting her legs and become aware that she's rubbing herself with her free hand. She loves this. It's one of her greatest pleasures, to bring herself off while I fuck her mouth – usually the harder the better. Normally, I might come in her mouth, then in the time it takes us to undress and for me to make her come a second time, with either my fingers, or my tongue, I'll be hard again and ready to fuck her for hours. But I'm not in the mood tonight; not in the slightest. So, I maintain a steady rhythm, waiting for her to come, which she does after a few minutes. She sucks me harder as she rides out her pleasure, then finally releases me and leans back, looking up at me.

"That was amazing," she whispers, smiling softly. "Shall we go upstairs?"

I contemplate what could happen over the next couple of hours, but no matter how hard I try and maintain my enthusiasm, my cock starts to wilt.

"I'm sorry," I murmur. "I thought I could do this, but I'm afraid… I've got a really bad headache." I can't believe I just said that.

"Oh… really? I'm sorry. Why didn't you say?" She gets to her feet and straightens her dress. I'm still naked and I feel like such a loser.

"It only came on earlier, while we were in the restaurant," I add, compounding the lie.

"I thought you'd been quiet this evening," she replies. "We can just go to sleep, if you want. I've got some painkillers upstairs."

She knows perfectly well that I won't spend the night with her. I never do – not with any of the women on my list. Maybe she thinks my 'headache' is a good reason for me to break that rule. I bend down and pick up my shirt, shrugging it on.

"I won't, thanks," I tell her quickly, doing up the buttons and grabbing my trunks. "I've got an early meeting tomorrow. I need to get a good night's sleep." That's a complete lie. I've booked the morning off to play golf with Fin, and our friend Brad.

She smiles, moves closer and rests her hand on my chest. "And you don't think you'll sleep if you stay here?"

I smile back, trying to make it look genuine. "I think it'll be easier at home," I say, quite truthfully.

She nods and bends down, passing me my pants. "Perhaps we can do this again next week?" she suggests.

"I'll have to let you know." I fasten my zipper and pick up my jacket and tie from the floor. "I'm really sorry."

"Hey... it can't be helped," she says, full of understanding, which just makes me feel so much worse about lying to her. I go over to the door and she follows. "I hope you sleep well," she adds, resting her hand on my shoulder.

"I'll do my best." Somehow I doubt I'm gonna sleep at all. Between my guilty conscience and thoughts of the girl in the restaurant, I anticipate a very restless night.

"And call me?" There's a hint of pleading in her voice as I open the door and let myself out.

I don't reply, because I don't want to lie anymore. Part of me knows I'm unlikely to call Ashley ever again. I'm unlikely to call any of the women on my list ever again. The only woman I want to call is the girl in the restaurant, and I don't even know her name, let alone her number, or where she lives. And there's the fact that she's already got a guy in her life, who she seemed to be very intimate with. *Dammit.*

The thing is though, even if I can't have her, I don't think I want anyone else.

Chapter Three

Lottie

Dear God. This feels like déjà vu. Was it really only yesterday morning that Catrina woke me at the crack of dawn? And the same thing's happening today? Except today it's not Catrina, it's the twins, who for some reason are wailing at each other right outside my bedroom door. Being twins, they want to wear the same outfit to their mother's party, but in different colors, which seems incredibly childish to me. From what I can gather, the problem appears to be that they can't agree on the outfit. They're only a year younger than me, but sometimes it feels more like five; they're so immature. They're both at Boston University, studying Sculpture, with varying degrees of success, from what I have been able to see. Chelsea is definitely the better artist of the two. She has more imagination than her sister, but her style isn't something most people would warm to.

I know my father always thought it would be good for them to study at a college that wasn't so close to home, so they could get the experience of living away from their mom for a while, but she overruled him, so while I'm away at Virginia Tech, studying Architecture, they live here, in my father's house, spending my father's money... well, my money now. I swallow down my thoughts and try not to feel bitter, throwing back the covers and climbing out of bed.

I can't help but notice the maid's outfit hanging on the back of the door, which reminds me – as if the twins yelling outside my door wasn't enough – that tomorrow night is the party. I suppose at least I don't have to worry about what I'm going to wear, although I still can't believe Catrina planned this. But then nothing she does should really surprise me.

I wander over to the window and look out at the extensive grounds, thinking back to my meal last night with Jack. He's good company, and fun to be with, and I hope he's calmed down and stopped worrying so much about Alex. I'm sure it'll be fine. Most people are fairly enlightened these days, and Alex's parents will probably just want him to be happy, and he's more than happy with Jack. I've been out with them as a couple on quite a few occasions, and they're just right for each other. In fact, they're perfect for each other. Anyone can see that.

Thinking about Jack and our meal leads my mind onto the gorgeous stranger who sat and stared at me – all night long, if Jack's account is anything to go by. I feel enormously flattered, if what Jack said was true. The thought that the man even glanced twice at me is gratifying, but knowing Jack, he was probably exaggerating. He was the most handsome man I've ever seen in my life, and despite that lovely warm glow I got when Jack suggested the stranger might like to take me to bed, the cold light of day comes with the stark reminder that he was with someone else. He was with a very beautiful blonde. *And* he was out of my league. I feel like I've been given a taste of paradise, I've been shown something wonderful – the perfect man, who wants me and makes me feel wanted – but I can't have him. He's not for me.

Feeling a little despondent, I turn back into the room and go and sit down on my bed. The argument seems to have died down now. Or at least it's moved to somewhere else in the house. The prospect of tomorrow night's party is hanging over me like a deathly shadow though, and I can't get motivated to do anything.

My dad used to throw these parties every year, usually in the first or second week of December, and always at a hotel in the city, so I've never been involved in one before, let alone attended one. As such, I have no idea what to expect, other than that the house will be filled with my father's business acquaintances. He always used to invite the people he'd helped out over the years and I imagine Catrina has done the same. In her case, I'm unsure of her motives, but in my dad's case, it was so that he could catch up with them, see how they were getting along and make sure they were okay. He had a habit of choosing his investments wisely, basing his choice on the person as much as their business. I remember, on one of the few occasions when he actually talked to me about his work, that he told me that it's people who make a business tick – and that if the man or woman at the top isn't ticking, then the whole business fails.

I lie back on the bed, staring up at the ceiling and remember how good my dad was at keeping his work life and home life separate. He always made me feel important and loved, and devoted as much time as he could to us as a family, to the point where I was probably in my early teens before I even knew what my dad did for a living. He rarely spoke about his investments or the people involved, although there was one exception to that. And it was a notable one. It was a guy Dad met about ten years ago, I suppose, by the name of Paul Lewis, and I don't know quite why, but he got under my dad's skin. Paul Lewis, it seems, had been a twenty-two year old graduate from a fairly poor background, but he'd had a good upbringing, despite the lack of money. His parents were both decent and hardworking; they just weren't very well off. Paul Lewis had some really sound business ideas and a brilliant mind when it came to electronics and computers, and he wanted to go into the field of gaming. So, Dad invested some money – although I have no idea how much, because he never used to say – in the man's company, which he called Big Bear. I always remember that part, because as a kid, I used to think it was a great name. I've got no idea why he chose it, but to me, it always sounded like a big cuddly teddy bear, not one of the ferocious man-eating types. Maybe that was just the child in me. Anyway, within twelve months, Big Bear had become the world leader in computer gaming, and my father's financial investment had been repaid. Even so, Dad continued to pay close attention to what Paul Lewis did, following his meteoric rise to his present status as a multi-billionaire. Unlike with most of his investments, where my dad's continued interest was purely a business matter, he and Paul Lewis ended up becoming more like friends. Not the kind of friend Dad brought to the house and introduced to me and my mom, but the kind of friend he'd go out to lunch with and keep a watchful eye over. I know Dad always said that Paul was a genuinely honest man, and that he was really proud of the things he'd achieved and the way he went about doing his business. I just hope Dad got the chance to tell him that.

I turn over and curl myself up into a ball, smiling to myself and wondering about the fact that I know so much about a man who I've never even met; a man I could easily walk past in the street and not even recognize.

By mid-morning, I've managed to drag myself out of bed, showered and dressed, and after a quick snack with Mrs Hemsworth, I catch the bus into the city, where I do some Christmas shopping. It's a challenge, but I resist the temptation to buy truly grotesque things for my stepmom and the twins, and just get them sweaters, which I know they'll exchange anyway. I get Mrs Hemsworth some perfume, but Jack and Alex's presents are already set. I've got them a mug each, with a photograph of the other person printed on the side. I managed to take the pictures when we last all met up earlier in the summer, before my dad died, and went on a picnic together. Given my conversation with Jack at the restaurant last night, I hope those presents don't backfire on me.

When I get back home, there's no sign of Catrina, although I can hear loud music coming from upstairs, so I assume at least one of the twins must be in. What am I thinking? It'll be both of them. They never do anything individually. Rather than risk running into them, I make my way through to the kitchen.

"That smells like ribs," I say, announcing myself.

Mrs Hemsworth looks over from the kitchen sink. "That's because it is." She turns and wipes her hands on a towel, before crossing her arms and studying at me carefully. *What did I do?* "What's this I hear about you and attractive men in restaurants?" she asks.

I'm going to kill Jack. Painfully. "Whatever Jack's told you, it's not true."

"Oh. So there wasn't really a very handsome man who couldn't take his eyes off of you all night?"

"Well, there might have been." I can feel myself blushing.

"And why are you so embarrassed?" she asks. "You're a beautiful young woman. Any man would be proud to be seen with you. I know Jack was." How does she know that? Did he say something?

"Jack's gay, Mrs Hemsworth," I say, justifying myself.

"So? Doesn't mean he can't appreciate a beautiful woman." She shakes her head. "And don't change the subject."

"I wasn't. But there's nothing to tell." I let out a sigh. "There was a man in the restaurant. He spent the evening watching me. He was… he was very attractive. And he was with someone else." I can't disguise the tone of disappointment in my voice.

"And?"

"And what?"

"And you'd have preferred it if he hadn't been with someone else?"

I shrug. "Maybe. But it doesn't matter what I'd have preferred. The fact is, he *was* with someone else. It's past. I'm never going to see him again. And you and Jack both need to stop making mischief." And all I need to do is forget him. If only it were that easy…

She smiles. "Why on earth would we wanna do that?" She rolls her eyes skywards. "There's precious little else to smile about around here…"

She comes over and gives me a hug and I let myself nestle into her, knowing she'll never hurt me and feeling truly safe for the first time in a long while.

Paul

"Wanna tell us what's wrong?" Fin asks, taking a sip of beer and looking across the table at me.

"What makes you think anything's wrong?" I reply evasively.

He glances at Brad and they exchange a look. It's a look that says they know I'm bluffing. Brad leans closer. "Because you just played the worst round of golf – ever."

"I wasn't that bad." I try to justify myself.

"Yeah, you were. So… what's wrong?"

"I met a girl," I explain, and then realize that's bullshit. "Well, I guess that's not strictly true."

"Make sense, will you?" Brad says, looking at his watch. "I've gotta be at work in less than an hour."

Brad's a cop. He looks the part too. He's kinda scary when he has to be, and right now he's got his scowling eyes turned on me. At six foot four, we may be the same height, but I'm not about to argue, or even vaguely disagree with him. I'm no slouch, but this man's made of solid muscle.

"I went to a restaurant last night and saw the most beautiful girl I've ever seen in my life."

"Did you speak to her?" Fin asks.

"No."

"So you didn't actually meet her, did you?" Brad points out.

"No. I just spent the whole evening staring at her."

"I've been known to arrest guys for doing things like that, you know?" Brad says, smiling now.

"Wait a second," Fin interrupts, putting his hands on the table. "Are you telling us you sat by yourself in a restaurant, just staring at a girl across a crowded room?"

"No. I'm telling you I went out for dinner with Ashley, and spent the whole night staring at a girl, who was there with her boyfriend."

"Jesus." Fin's staring at me now. "You were with Ashley?"

"Yeah. And before you say anything, I didn't feel great about it."

"What happened?" Brad asks.

"I just told you."

"No, I mean after dinner?" He's got a smirk on his face now.

"I went home with Ashley."

They're both staring at me. "So you weren't *that* bothered about the girl then…"

"Yeah, I was. When I got back to Ashley's place, I bailed on her." I don't tell them about what happened in her hallway. That feels kinda personal. "I told her I had a headache and left."

"You?" Brad's incredulous. My reputation with women precedes me.

"Yeah. Me."

"And then what?" Fin asks.

"I went home and spent the whole night thinking about the girl."

"The whole night?" Brad's still having trouble coming to terms with this.

I nod my head.

"Well," Fin says, clearly trying to be more understanding than Brad, who hasn't stopped staring at me yet, "nothing's ever gonna come of it, so you need to forget about her. And the best way to do that is to get laid. Just look up someone else, take her out, go home with her and fuck her senseless… like you usually do."

For the first time, I realize how cold, calculating and – frankly – God-awful that sounds.

"I don't want to," I admit. "Actually, I'm thinking about destroying my metaphorical little black book."

"Whoa. Hang on." Fin holds up his hands, a mild panic showing on his face. "Don't do that. I mean, it'd be such a waste. You can just pass their names to us, can't you?"

Brad slowly and deliberately averts his gaze from me, and turns to Fin. "You are kidding, right?"

Fin smirks. "Not entirely."

"Well, you can take his hand-me-downs, if you like, but I'd rather find my girlfriends for myself."

"That's going real well for you at the moment, isn't it?" Fin jokes. We all know Brad's been going through a dry patch, mainly because he's been involved in a tough case at work and hasn't had time for much else. He gives Fin a look which tells us that, if we weren't in a public place, with lots of witnesses, he'd probably shoot him. "Let's face it," Fin continues, "unless one of us is lucky enough to meet a virgin, which at our age is unlikely, pretty much every woman we meet is gonna be someone else's hand-me-down." He's grinning and, from the glint in his eye, I know he's joking, although I'm not sure Brad's realized yet.

"I wouldn't let too many women hear you say that," Brad warns and I know I was right.

"You don't think they'd like it?" Fin replies, feigning innocence.

"Try it with the next woman you meet," Brad suggests. "See what happens." He leans forward. "But I'm not picking up the pieces."

They both turn and seem to suddenly realize I'm still with them. "Sorry, man," Fin says more seriously.

I hold up a hand. "It's okay."

"Well, it clearly isn't," Brad points out and I take a deep breath. "But you've gotta be realistic," he adds. "I know it's hard. She was obviously with someone, and that means you need to put it behind you and move on."

He's right. I know he is. I just wish it was as easy as that.

The problem is, she's all I can think about. Morning. Noon. Night. She's in my head the whole time. She's even in my dreams, or she would be if I could sleep.

I go back to the office and manage to focus enough to answer my emails and sit through a marketing meeting. At least it's Friday and I can make an excuse and leave early.

I need to work this out, before it starts to affect my business.

When I get home, I feel even more restless than usual and, while my solution to that would normally be to call one of the women on my list, that's the very last thing I wanna do.

Instead, I shower and change, and go back down to the underground garage, getting into my car. I drive to the restaurant I went to last night like I'm on auto-pilot. I recognize the waiter who served me and Ashley and, when I tell him I want a table for one, he finds me a space near the back, which is good, because all I wanna do is watch.

I know she won't come in tonight, but this is all I've got.

I order the steak again and, as the waiter brings it over, I ask him about the couple who were here last night, pointing out the table they were sitting at.

"I know you're probably not allowed to tell me," I say to him, "but I wondered if you might know their names?"

"Their names?" He looks down at me.

"Yeah. Did they make a reservation? Or do you keep the credit card records?" He's either gonna call the cops, or take pity on me. I hope it's the latter.

He stares at me for a moment, like I've lost my mind. "She was beautiful, wasn't she?" he says, smiling, and wanders off. I'm not sure what that means and stare down at the amazing looking food in front of me, my appetite now non-existent. Eventually, I pick up my fork and spear a tomato, just as the guy comes back to the table.

"Sorry," he whispers.

"What for?" I look up at him.

"They didn't make a reservation… and the guy paid. His name's Jack McKenzie, if that helps."

"It doesn't, but thanks anyway."

At least he tried. He gives me another smile, even more sympathetic this time, and goes away again.

I give up any pretence at eating after just a few mouthfuls and ask for the check. Brad's right. I need to put it behind me. I need to accept that she's with someone else – although I don't really wanna think about that. And I need to accept that I'm never gonna see her again.

I manage to get my bow tie right on the third attempt. I'm not normally quite so useless, but I'm even less interested in this damn party than I was when I accepted the invite.

Right now, I'd rather just sit at home, watch a trashy movie, order in some take-out and drink a bottle of wine. All to myself. That way I might get some sleep. I certainly didn't get much last night. Again.

I shake my head. I need to stop this.

The entry buzzer sounds and I go out into the hallway and lift the receiver, seeing Fin's face on the screen at the same time.

"Come on up," I tell him and replace the receiver again, going back to my bedroom to put on my cufflinks.

"Where are you?" he calls out.

"Bedroom."

"I take it we're planning on arriving fashionably late?" he says, coming into the room and taking in the fact that I'm still wandering around without any pants on.

"We'll be leaving fashionably early too," I tell him. "I'm really not in the mood for this."

"Can't we just bail and go to the movies, or something?" he asks.

"Dressed like this?" I shake my head. "Besides, like I said to you the other day, feel like I owe it to Charles."

He opens his mouth, but closes it again straight away, and sits down on the edge of my bed, while I finish getting dressed.

We decide to take my car, mainly because Fin likes it and I don't mind driving. Once we've left the parking garage and are heading north, he turns to me and I feel his eyes on me, even though I'm concentrating on the road.

"What?" I say to him.

"How are you?" he asks.

"Not great," I reply, honestly.

"I think that much is obvious."

"I—I went back to the restaurant," I confess, feeling embarrassed and not really sure why I'm telling him.

"You did?"

"Yeah."

"Why?" he asks.

"I wanted to see if she'd be there again… And before you say anything, I know it wasn't very likely."

"I assume she wasn't?"

I shake my head. "No." I bite my lip. "I even asked the waiter if he could tell me who she was."

"How on earth did you think he'd be able to do that?"

"I thought they might have made a reservation, or he might be able to check the credit card records."

"And? Did he throw you out?"

"No. He seemed to understand." I remember the look he gave me, which appeared to show his sympathy. I also recall the shock on his face when I handed him a thousand dollar tip, even though I'd barely touched my food. "He told me they hadn't made a reservation, and that the guy paid for their meal. His name's Jack McKenzie, which tells me damn all."

"Well…" he muses, and then falls silent.

"Well, what?"

"I was just gonna say that maybe you could get Brad to check the guy out."

"Would that be before or after he arrests me for stalking the woman?" I let out a sigh. "I can't," I say slowly. "And don't think I'm not tempted. I am. But it's like Brad said. She's with someone. A lucky son-of-a-bitch called Jack McKenzie, evidently. I guess I'm just gonna have to get over it… and accept that, as far as I was concerned, she was just a mirage. She'll never be real for me."

He hesitates for a second. "You're not looking to just fuck her out of your system, are you?" he asks quietly.

"No." For the first time in my life, I want so much more than that.

We both fall silent for a moment, then I hear Fin take a deep breath and wonder what he's going to say next. "Just so you know," he says softly, "I don't think you owe Charles Hudson anything." He pauses. "I didn't know the man, but I think if he were here, he'd agree with me. He invested in you; you paid back his investment. His friendship with you continued because he liked you. Period. There was no debt involved, Paul. Friends don't owe each other anything. Ever." He takes another breath. "I'm here," he murmurs. "If you wanna talk." I've known Fin for so long I've forgotten what my life was like before him, but that's the first time he's ever said anything like that to me. It's the first time I've needed him to.

Chapter Four

Lottie

I stand in front of the full-length mirror in my bedroom and stare at my reflection. When the outfit was hanging on the back of my door, I thought it would look okay, but it looks absolutely dreadful. The skirt is skin tight and so short, it's ludicrous. I've put on black tights, just to make sure everything's covered, but I still feel exposed. As for the blouse, I'd say it's intended for someone who's a size zero. I'm a size six and the buttons are bulging. Not that there are that many buttons in the first place, because it has a plunging neckline. I'm just wondering if I've got any pins in my room that I can use to fasten it closed a little better, when Catrina barges in.

"You could knock," I tell her, taking in her ultra short bright red cocktail dress. She's put her hair up into a loose up-do and left a few tendrils hanging down beside her face. I'm sure if she didn't try so hard, she could be really pretty. The problem is, she's forgotten how not to try hard.

"It is *my* house," she says, with emphasis on the 'my'.

I want to point out that it's probably my money that's paying for tonight's little gathering, but I can't be bothered to get into that argument again.

"What do you want?" I ask her.

"I just came to make sure you're ready," she says. "The caterer is downstairs waiting for you."

What she means is that she came to make sure I was obeying her orders and hadn't decided to do something truly outrageous, like have a thought of my own.

I turn to face her and her mouth drops open.

"What *have* you done?" she says.

"Nothing," I reply.

"Well…" she splutters. "You can't go downstairs like that." She's studying the short skirt and over-tight blouse.

"Okay. Well, why don't we forget the idea of me being a waitress and I'll put on a cocktail dress instead and—"

She steps forward, holding up her hand to interrupt me. "No," she says quickly coming to stand right in front of me and looking me up and down. "This is very odd. I know I picked out the right size for you." She shakes her head. "I guess you must've gained some weight since I last saw you, Charlotte." She smirks.

"I haven't done anything of the kind." I defend myself, but she just tuts and keeps shaking her head. And that's when I realize that she did this on purpose to make me feel bad about myself. Judging from the look on her face when she first saw me though, I'd say her plan has backfired. Whereas she'd hoped to humiliate me by having me wear something that was obviously a size too small, she's actually put me into a uniform that makes me look like a hooker. And I seriously doubt that was the effect she was hoping to achieve.

"Well, it hardly matters now, does it?" She folds her arms across her chest. "You must have a white blouse and some black pants you can wear?" she suggests.

"Yes, I do." *Somewhere*. That look wouldn't really be my style… well, not since I left for college, and worked out that I actually had a style, but I know I've got them.

"Then at least put them on. Obviously you won't look like the other wait staff, but that doesn't matter, does it?"

I don't reply. It may not matter to her, but if I have to do this, the very least I'd hoped for was to be able to blend in, rather than looking like the odd one out.

She goes over to my closet and opens the door.

"I can find my own clothes, thank you," I say, marching over and nudging her out of the way.

"Just see that you get changed, and be downstairs in five minutes," she says. "You don't need to bother with makeup. It's not like anyone's going to be looking at *you*."

With that, she flounces out of the room, but the way she delivered her parting shot makes me wonder whether that's the real reason for this party. I take off all my clothes, including the tights, which I don't really need under my black pants, and get dressed again. My own white blouse is plain and sensible, and while I do up the buttons, I contemplate the fact that Catrina might just have arranged this evening's festivities with the sole intention of humiliating me while finding suitable partners – or even husbands – for her daughters. The thought makes me shudder and I go over to my dresser and put on a little lipstick and mascara. Catrina will never notice I'm wearing it, simply because she's of the opinion that makeup doesn't count if it hasn't been applied with a trowel.

I dig out my high-heeled black pumps and put them on, wondering how I'm gonna be able to stand in them for the whole evening, and then pin my name tag to my blouse before I shut off the light and go downstairs and straight through to the kitchen. I can hear Catrina shouting instructions at someone in the living room, but I'm not gonna get involved. It's her party, after all.

The kitchen is in chaos, compared to normal and I'm tempted to turn straight back around and go upstairs again.

"Miss Charlotte?" I hear my name being called and look up to see a man approach. He's probably only an inch taller than me – so roughly five foot seven – and he's wearing chef's whites, which seem to swamp him slightly.

"Call me Lottie," I tell him, holding out my hand.

"Ahh…" He smiles. "I'm Claude Mignon," he says. "I understand you are going to be helping us out tonight?"

He has the most glorious French accent, although how genuine it is, I'm not sure.

"I'm not entirely certain I'd use the word 'helping'," I reply. "I've never done anything like this before, so I think I could be more of a hindrance."

He looks me up and down. "Never," he says. "Someone as beautiful as you could never be a hindrance. You'll just make the food look even better." I can't help smiling and he smiles back sympathetically. "Now," he says, clasping my hand and linking it through his arm. "Let's see if we can make some order out of this madness, shall we?"

He gives me a wink and leads me further into the kitchen, and I notice Mrs Hemsworth is over the far side, by the sink, talking to another man, who's dressed similarly to Mr Mignon. They're talking avidly, while working at something, although I can't see what.

We stop by the central island, where an array of trays has been laid out.

"Your job," he explains, "will be to hand out the canapés, along with two of the other waiters. The remainder of my staff will deal with the drinks, so you don't need to worry about that." I nod my head. "Once your tray is empty," he continues, "you come back out here and get a fresh one, and so on until the end of the evening. It's really very simple."

The words 'dumb waiter' spring to mind, but I don't say anything out loud.

"We need to be ready in fifteen minutes," he says, raising his voice so everyone can hear. Then he claps his hands. "Waiters… stand over there." He points to one corner of the kitchen. "I'll call you when we're ready."

The kitchen staff start moving around more quickly, dashing from stove to refrigerator and back. One of the waiters, a man more senior than the rest, judging from his uniform, which consists of a jacket and tie, rather than just the white shirt and black pants or skirt, starts pouring champagne into tall flutes. I'm now relieved that I've been given the task of handing out food. I'm pretty sure I'd manage to drop the drinks, or spill them down someone's expensive dress – assuming Catrina's invited any women, that is.

"Right!" Mr Mignon claps his hands again. "Time's up."

He looks over at us and everyone else starts to move forward, so I copy them as they all pick up trays of intricately decorated and largely unidentifiable hors d'oeuvres.

"Try and keep the tray flat," the girl next to me says, smiling, and I realize I'm tipping mine forward.

"Thanks," I say, correcting my mistake and noticing that her name tag says 'Melanie'. "You've probably guessed that I've never done this before."

"We've all gotta start out somewhere," she replies.

I want to tell her that I'm not starting out; that my stepmom has set this up to keep me out of the way, and put me in my place. But I don't, because that's personal, and my father always taught me to keep quiet about family matters. Instead I just nod and smile and try to look like I belong here.

Melanie suggests I position myself by the fireplace in the living room, and points me in the right direction. She obviously doesn't know that this is my house, but I accept her friendly advice. She says that she and the other girl, whose name I haven't managed to pick up yet, will be closer to the door and will, therefore, attract more of the guests. I'm not sure this is a good thing, as I think I'll be bored rigid. But I realise she's just trying to be kind, knowing I'm new to this.

I take my place, as instructed, and then quickly decide to move a little further away from the fireplace. Catrina has put so many candles and decorations on the mantelpiece, I'm scared the whole thing's gonna go up in flames, and take me with it. I've no sooner got myself settled, than the first of the guests walks through the door.

Paul

When we arrive, the gates are open and there's a man mountain standing beside them, who holds up his hand to stop us.

"Invitation, please?" he says. I reach into my inside pocket and pull it out, handing it over to the tame gorilla. He glances down and then waves us forward, adding, "Just park where you can."

He's not kidding. There are vehicles abandoned all over the place and, while I'm not exactly precious about my own car, I'm not overly keen on the idea of just parking it anywhere.

"There's a spot, over there," Fin says, pointing to a space on the edge of the driveway that looks fairly safe. "We should be able to get out again quite easily too," he adds.

"Good thinking." I maneuver my car into the space and we get out, looking up at the house, which has been adorned with a multitude of colored lights, all of which seem to be flashing – just not in time with each other. "Jeez," I remark, running my fingers through my hair. "Charles would have hated this."

"He would?" Fin looks surprised.

"You're not gonna tell me you like it?" I look at him, not disguising my own shock.

"Not the decorations, no, but the house underneath looks okay."

"Yeah. It does. It's the kind of house I've always wanted to have… when I grow up, that is."

He looks across at me. "You're thirty-three," he says. "How much longer are you planning on waiting?"

"To grow up?" I clarify and he nods. "I wasn't planning on doing it any time soon. It's overrated, if you ask me."

We make our way to the front door, which is open, despite the freezing temperature out here. I'm hoping this means we can make a subtle entrance and just merge in with the other guests, but my hopes are quickly dashed when Catrina Hudson comes rushing forward.

"Paul Lewis," she says, as though she thinks I might have forgotten my own name. She's almost wearing an unbelievably short and very tight red dress, and I'd wager my car that she's not wearing anything else, except a very full pout. There's certainly no underwear beneath her dress – that much is obvious.

"Catrina," I reply, keeping my voice low.

"And who's your handsome friend?" she asks.

"This is Doctor Fin Price," I tell her, giving him his full title, because I know it impresses women like her. She offers her hand, as though she expects him to kiss it, but being Fin he shakes instead and she looks a little crushed.

I glance over her shoulder and pretend to notice someone I know. "There's Mike," I say. "We'll catch up with you later, Catrina?"

She grabs my arm, stopping me. "Just before you go, I'd like you to meet my daughters, Chelsea and Christa." She turns me slightly and I notice two girls taking a step towards us. They're identical, which isn't surprising, being as they're twins. They're both blonde, pretty, slim and, to my surprise, they're wearing identical outfits, namely short cocktail dresses, one in blue and one in dark green. That kind of dressing up in the same clothes is something I would have expected of twins who were, maybe five years old, not two women who are probably around twenty.

"Which is which?" Fin whispers in my ear.

I shrug and move forward to shake their hands.

"Say hello," Catrina prompts and they do, giving me the benefit of ultra white smiles.

"Get me a drink, or get me out of here," Fin mutters.

"I really must go and see Mike," I say to Catrina.

"We'll see you later, Paul," she replies, standing between her two daughters and fluttering her eyelashes.

I don't reply and quickly move further into the enormous hall, knowing that Fin will follow.

"I wonder who her surgeon is," he remarks once we're out of earshot.

"Her surgeon?"

"She's had work done," he clarifies, smiling. "You didn't think those breasts were real, did you?"

I chuckle. "No. I'm not sure about her nose either. It looks different to when I first met her."

Fin shrugs. "Well, I guess she's a rich widow now," he murmurs.

"Yeah." I can't help wondering what Charles would have made of her use of his money though.

"So, where's your friend Mike?" Fin asks, looking around.

"I don't know anyone called Mike," I reply. "It just seemed like a good name to use. There's bound to be someone here called 'Mike', don't you think?"

He laughs. "Nice idea. That woman is hard work. And as for her daughters…" He rolls his eyes.

"Well, hopefully we can avoid them for the rest of the evening."

He nods and we move into the living room and both stop dead. "Welcome to Santa's Grotto," he murmurs and I can't help but laugh. He's not wrong. The hall was highly embellished with Christmas decorations, but this is ludicrous. I don't think there's a single surface in here that hasn't been decked with something festive and tasteless.

I glance around and notice Drew Anderson standing in a corner of the room, looking bored. "There's someone I actually do know," I tell Fin. "Let's go talk to him."

Fin follows my gaze and then says, "I'll see you over there. I'm just gonna grab us some drinks first."

"Okay." I leave him and cross the room to where Drew's standing. His face lights up when he sees me and he holds out his hand so we can shake.

"Hi, Paul," he says warmly. "I haven't seen you since last year's party."

"No. I… I couldn't get to the funeral. Were you there?"

"Yeah. It was awful."

I nod my head. "How's work?" I ask, desperate to change the subject. Drew's company makes an environmentally friendly building insulation which he patented several years ago – with Charles' help, of course.

"Work's great," he replies. "We're expanding into a new factory next month."

"Fantastic." I know Charles would be thrilled.

"What do you think of all this?" he asks, looking around the room.

"I think Charles would have hated it," I reply.

He nods in agreement, just as Fin comes over and hands me a flute of champagne. I make the introductions and we talk about business for a few minutes.

"Will you guys excuse me for a second?" Fin says, all of a sudden. Drew and I both nod and he disappears to the other end of the room. A few moments later, I notice Drew smiling.

"What's wrong?" I ask.

"Your friend," he replies, nodding in the direction Fin just went. I turn and see that he's talking to a very pretty brunette. She's leaning up against the wall and he's standing in front of her, his hand resting beside her head. I'll give him one thing; he doesn't hang around.

I turn back to Drew. "He's got a thing for brunettes," I explain.

"Well, it doesn't look like she's complaining," he says, smirking.

"No, it doesn't."

"Dear Lord," Drew says and I turn again, to see Catrina and her twin daughters coming into the room. "What did Charles see in her?" he asks.

"I've got no idea, but I'm gonna find somewhere to hide," I tell him as Catrina spots me and starts across the room.

"Coward," Drew retorts.

"Every damn time," I reply and, giving him a pat on the arm, I head towards one of the waitresses, hoping to dump my champagne glass and maybe get something a little softer to drink. The girl is standing fairly close to the fireplace, but she's got her back to me, so I skirt around some of the other guests and come up alongside her, just as she turns and bumps her tray into me.

"I'm so sorry," she says, almost dropping it.

I bend and grab hold of the tray, stopping it from falling. "Don't worry," I reply, and look up, my breath catching in my throat.

Without taking my eyes from hers, I stand up straight.

"You," I say.

"You," she repeats at exactly the same time, and we both smile.

I can see her swallowing hard and only then become aware that we're both still holding the tray.

"Are you okay with this?" I ask her, and she nods, although she's still staring. "I know you. I mean, I saw you," I tell her, finally releasing the tray, "at the restaurant, the other night."

"Yes," she replies. Her voice is soft, really gentle and delicate. It suits her. "I remember."

"You do?"

She nods, lowering her eyes, like she's embarrassed, or shy. She's beautiful.

"There you are," I feel a hand on my arm and turn to see Catrina standing beside me. She's glaring at the waitress. "Is there something wrong here?" she asks.

"No," I reply quickly.

She smiles. "Good. My daughters would love to have a longer conversation with you. They're both studying sculpture at Boston University."

"Right?" I'm not sure how that's supposed to interest me.

"Well, don't you ever use models in your work? I'm sure they'd be great at making them for you."

"We don't use anything like that," I reply honestly and I hear the waitress chuckle.

"Even so," Catrina persists, pulling on my arm, "I'd love for you to speak with them... maybe give them some pointers."

What in? How not to dress like you're still at elementary school? I turn to the waitress. "I'll be back," I tell her and glance down, noticing that her name badge says 'Charlotte'. "Don't go away."

"I'm not allowed to," she says, her voice kinda sad now.

"Come on," Catrina says, a little impatiently.

I let her drag me away, rather than creating a scene, or risking getting Charlotte into trouble for not doing her job. I'll talk to the twins if I have to... I'll do anything, providing I can get back to Charlotte again. I can't believe she's here. She's even more perfect close to, and her smile is something else. And as for her voice…

"Chelsea, Christa… Mr Lewis has kindly offered to give you some tips about your work," Catrina says, pulling me to a stop in front of her daughters, who are standing together on the other side of the room, not far from where Fin is still talking to the pretty brunette. Catrina loiters there for a few moments, while an awkward silence descends, and then she moves away, leaving the three of us looking at each other.

"What do you want to know?" I ask them and they shrug their shoulders in perfect synchrony, which almost makes me laugh out loud. I get the feeling their mother set this up and they've got no interest in hearing my opinion on anything.

"Paul?" I turn to see Fin moving closer.

"Yeah?"

"Can I borrow you?" He gives me an almost imperceptible wink.

"Sure." I turn back to the twins. "I'm really sorry. I'm sure this can keep for another time." They both nod their heads and I take a few steps away, moving closer to Fin. "Thanks, man," I tell him.

"I thought you looked like you needed some help," he says.

"You weren't wrong."

He turns to the woman in front of him, who's still leaning against the wall. "Katie," he says, "this is Paul Lewis. Don't be too impressed by the good looks and the fact that he's a multi-billionaire. He's really shallow."

I laugh and hold out my hand. "Nice to meet you," I say to her as we shake.

She nods and looks back at Fin, and I get the feeling I'm no longer required. Even so, I feel like I need to tell him my news.

"You won't believe what's happened," I say, with burning enthusiasm.

"What? You've found a square inch of this house that doesn't look like a Christmas fairy got high and let loose with the decorations?" he jokes and Katie chuckles.

"No. That's never gonna happen. And anyway, it's so much better than that… The girl's here." I tell him.

He turns and looks at me. "The girl?" he says. "The girl from the restaurant, you mean?"

I nod my head. "Yeah. She's working here as one of the waitresses."

He looks around the room. "Which one?" he asks.

"She's over by the fireplace, brown hair… really beautiful."

He moves to his left and stands on his tiptoes, then looks back at me, his face suddenly serious. "She's very young," he says. "She can't be much more than twenty."

I take another look at her myself, moving so I can get a better view. He's right. She is really young. I hadn't noticed before.

"What of it?" I say to him.

He looks at Katie for a moment, then pulls me away from her, lowering his voice. "We both know what you're like," he says. "But you need to be careful with her."

"I will," I reply. "She's different to the others."

"Yeah. *And* she's really young," he repeats, giving me a knowing look.

"And she was in the restaurant with her boyfriend," I point out. "So I doubt she's a complete innocent."

"Aren't you forgetting about him? The boyfriend, I mean?" Fin says.

"No. I've thought of little else since I saw them together. But I might not get to see her again."

"So what are you gonna do?" he asks.

"I'm gonna ask her if I can see her after she finishes work here."

"And if she says 'no'?"

"Then she says 'no'. But if I don't ask, I'll always wonder."

He looks at me for a long moment, then nods his head and steps back to Katie again.

"Are you gonna be needing me to take you home?" I ask him.

"Feeling that sure of yourself, are you?" he replies, a smile forming on his lips.

"No, but I just don't wanna leave you in the lurch, that's all."

"I can give you a ride home," Katie says, looking at Fin.

"You don't mind?" He moves a little closer to her and she smiles.

"I don't mind at all."

Fin turns back to me. "Looks like I'm all set," he says, grinning.

I roll my eyes. "Okay. I'll catch up with you tomorrow sometime."

He nods his head and turns away from me, focusing on Katie again.

I look back at Charlotte and take in the black pants and white blouse that she's wearing, neither of which seem to be her style at all. I guess it's the uniform that goes with the job though. Even so, she looks really nervous and uncomfortable, and I need to do something about that. Now.

Chapter Five

Lottie

He's here. How can he be here? It's not possible. Is it? I suppose it must be, because even from the other side of the room, I can feel his eyes on me. He keeps looking at me, even while he's talking to the man he's standing beside.

Of course, I had to almost make a complete fool of myself by nearly dropping an entire tray of canapés over him. Luckily he's got better reflexes than me and managed to catch them, despite the fact that he was holding a half empty glass of champagne at the same time, and then he looked at me, like I actually meant something. I know I don't, but he made me feel like I did.

Naturally, Catrina had to ruin the moment by interrupting. I honestly thought she was going to show me up in front of him, but she didn't. Instead she just dragged him away to talk to the terrible twins. But even that made me want to laugh. It was the expression on his face, really. He looked like he was being taken to his own execution.

"Hi." I flip around at the sound of his voice, and nearly spill all the canapés again as they scoot across the tray. He's right behind me, his breath soft and gentle on my neck. "You really shouldn't be trusted with that, should you?" he says, catching hold of the tray again.

"Probably not, no." I look up into his eyes, which are deep blue, like pools of water you just wanna dive into. Please.

"What time do you finish here?" he asks, as bold as brass, a perfect smile on his lips.

"Um... I don't know. Late I guess. Whenever the party ends."

His face falls. "Well, that'll never do," he replies. "Where's your boss."

I hesitate, unsure how to tell him that the man I'm working for this evening isn't my boss. "H—He's in the kitchen," I stutter.

He nods his head. "Okay. Take me to the kitchen."

"Now?" I can't disguise my surprise.

"Yeah. Right now." His voice is deep and distracting.

"O—Okay." I've got no idea why I'm stuttering so much, but I look up at him again and then start to walk through the crowd of people, out into the hallway and back to the kitchen, aware that he's following close behind.

Once we've passed through the kitchen door, the man puts down his glass on the countertop and comes and stands beside me. "Which one is your boss?" he asks, looking at the half dozen people who are still working away out here.

"That guy over there," I nod in Claude's direction and the man nods his head.

"Come with me," he says and puts his hand in the small of my back, guiding me to where Claude is working on some more canapés on the far side of the room. The feeling of the man's touch makes me tingle and I grip the tray a little tighter, worried that I'm going to drop it.

"Excuse me?" he says and Claude turns around, looking up at him.

"Sir?" he replies, wiping his hands on a towel.

"I understand you're this young lady's boss," he says, his voice much firmer now.

Claude looks at me. "Well, I suppose so, yes," he replies.

"Good. Then I want you to let her go for the evening," the man continues. "As of now."

"Excuse me?" Claude looks surprised, although I'm sure I'm the one who's most shocked in the room. Out of the corner of my eye, I notice Mrs Hemsworth. She's sitting on one of the stools, clearly taking a break, and she steps down and starts to come a little closer.

"I want..."

"I heard what you said," Claude interrupts. "I'm just not sure I understand." He gives me a look. "Miss Charlotte has to stay here until the end of the evening... on Mrs Hudson's orders."

"I don't care about Mrs Hudson's orders," the man replies. "You and I can both see Charlotte doesn't belong here." I notice Claude's lips twist up into a slight smile.

"You're quite right," he says, after a moment's hesitation. "She doesn't." He looks at me. "You can go," he adds, his eyes twinkling.

Without waiting for me to say anything, the man takes the tray of canapés from me and places them on the countertop. "Thanks," he says to Claude. "And can you do me a favor and not tell Mrs Hudson about this?" He reaches into his inside pocket and retrieves his wallet, pulling out a handful of hundred dollar bills and dumping them beside the tray. "You can use that to tip the rest of the waiting staff for having to cover for Charlotte," he says, and then he turns to me. "Do you have a coat?" he asks.

"Um... no." *Not down here, I don't. It's in my bedroom... upstairs.*

He nods his head and removes his jacket, placing it around my shoulders.

"C'mon," he says and takes my hand, pulling me out the back door. I just manage a glance at Mrs Hemsworth, who's moved closer to Claude. They're both grinning at me.

The man closes the door, undoing his bow tie and top button, leaving the tie hanging around his neck. He looks very sexy like that, and he smiles down at me, then starts toward the front of the house.

"Wait!" I cry out and stop in my tracks.

He stops with me. "What's wrong?" he asks, looking down at me. There are so many lights out here, it's almost as though we're still inside and I can see the concern in his eyes.

"Who do you think you are?" I reply, finally voicing my feelings. "I don't know you, and I'm not gonna just leave with you. You can't buy me, and you can't ride roughshod over me." I want to remind him that he's got a girlfriend already, but I think I've said enough for now.

"I'm not riding roughshod over anyone," he says, staring into my eyes. "And I'm certainly not trying to buy you. I just wanna take you home."

"Whose home?"

"Yours, if that's what you want," he replies. "We can go to mine, if you prefer, but I'll take you wherever you wanna go." He glances back at the house behind me. "Either way, you didn't belong in there." I almost laugh at the irony. It's my home. It's the place I grew up, but I've never belonged here less than I do now. "Where do you wanna go?" he asks.

"I—I can't go back to my place," I reply. "Not yet."

He nods his head, although he's frowning now and looks a little confused. "Mine then?" he suggests.

I hesitate. I know I should tell him to go, to leave me alone, to stop messing with my head. He's obviously in a relationship with someone and, while he may think it's okay to cheat, I don't. But he's right about one thing. I really don't belong here. Standing in my own living room, surrounded by strangers just made me realize that. And that thought makes me so depressed I want to cry. And I don't want to cry in front of Catrina. At least if I let him take me away, I can cry somewhere else.

"Yes," I murmur.

His frown fades and turns into a broad smile. "C'mon," he says, taking my hand and leading me around the side of the house and up the driveway. There are cars everywhere, and I know I couldn't even afford a downpayment on any of them.

"This is me," he says, stopping half way down the drive and pulling me up beside a beautiful red Ferrari.

"You're kidding." I turn to him, smiling.

"No." He opens the door, moving closer to me. "There are three things I never joke about," he says, his voice a low hum.

"Three?" I ask.

"Yeah," he says. "My car… my work… and…"

"And?" I ask, as he lowers me into the passenger seat, leaning in so his lips are almost touching mine.

"You'll find out the third one," he replies, grinning.

"I will?" My voice is barely a whisper.

"Yeah. You will."

He stands and closes the door, going around to the driver's side. I feel like every nerve in my body is alight with anticipation… or is that fear? I'm not sure. Either way, it's too late to turn back now. And even if it wasn't, I don't want to.

Paul

I can't help it if her reaction to my car makes me smile. All she's done since we started the drive back to my apartment, is stare around the interior.

"What is it?" she asks.

"Excuse me?" I'm not sure what she means.

"The car? What is it?"

"It's a Ferrari."

I hear her sigh. "I know that," she replies. "I meant what model."

I smile. "It's an F12 Berlinetta." At that precise moment, I change lanes and floor the gas. Charlotte squeals with delight and then giggles, throwing her head back. Her reaction is cute… and really sexy, and I know I'm showing off, but I don't care. She's here with me. She's in my car, and I'm taking her to my apartment, where she'll hopefully spend the night with me. It's not something I've done before, but I want to be with her and a hotel would have been all wrong. For both of us.

I'm still not entirely sure why she's agreed to come home with me. For a minute, I thought she was gonna change her mind about leaving with me at all, but then she got a really sad look in her eyes, and agreed to come back to my place. I'm guessing that's because of her boyfriend… which I suppose means she's willing to think about cheating. That surprises me, because she doesn't seem the type. But then I shudder as I wonder if she's just like the other women on my 'list'? Does she also have 'arrangements' with men… was he just another on *her* 'list'? Will I be too? God, that's a depressing thought.

"So, what do you do?" I ask her, because I want to stop the way my thoughts are going. "Apart from helping out at parties, that is?"

"I go to college," she replies.

"Where?" I enquire.

"Virginia Tech."

"So you're just back here for the holidays to visit your family?" I ask, still trying to work out what's going on with her personal life, even though I'd rather forget about the guy she was with at the restaurant. I'm also trying to figure out why she just said she couldn't go home 'yet', which seemed weird to me.

"Yeah," she replies, but doesn't elaborate.

We get back to my apartment in no time and I park in the underground garage, getting out of the car and going around to help Charlotte.

I hold her hand as we go over to the elevator and I input the code for the penthouse before the elevator doors open and we step inside. She looks around and then leans against the wall, while the doors swish closed, and I turn around and feel sorely tempted to take the three steps required to stand right in front of her, rip her clothes from her, and take her really hard. The thing is, even though I don't know what's going on with her boyfriend, or in her head, I want our first time to be special, and a quickie in the elevator isn't special. So, I resist the temptation and go over to stand beside her. She rests her head on my shoulder and I gently rest my head on hers. I haven't done this before, but it feels good to stand like that. It's kinda comforting.

The elevator pings and we both jump as the doors open, and I wonder for a moment if she was feeling as relaxed as I was just then.

"I guess this must be you," she says quietly. I can hear her nerves in her voice although I'm not sure what that's about. She must know she's safe with me, surely? She's gotta know I'm not gonna do anything she doesn't want me to. But then the sobering thought comes to me that, if she's thinking about cheating on her boyfriend, it may not be sitting too well with her. God, I wish I could just forget about the guy.

"You've guessed right," I reply, remembering my manners at last, and allowing her to step out first. The elevator opens right into my apartment, straight into a lobby, with marble floors and a long table along one wall. She looks around, then turns to me. "This way," I say, taking her arm and leading her into the massive living space. Two walls are made entirely of glass, and the other two of exposed brick. There's a huge L-shaped pale gray couch in the center of the room, and across the other side is the kitchen, which is very modern and sleek. Beyond that, is the dining area which features a large rectangular table and eight chairs. Needless to say, living by myself, I rarely use it.

"Wow," she says softly, looking around, as I take my jacket from her shoulders and drop it over the back of the couch, pulling off my tie and placing it on top.

"Would you like a glass of wine?" I ask. She's on edge and it feels like a good idea to help her relax.

"Yes, thanks," she replies.

"Take a seat," I offer, going over to the kitchen and getting a couple of long-stemmed wine glasses from the cabinet, before pouring out some chilled white Burgundy. As I'm putting the wine back in the refrigerator, I glance up and notice her pulling her phone from the back pocket of her pants and checking the screen, just as she sits. I wonder if she's had a message from her boyfriend. I wonder where he is and what he's doing; whether he's at home waiting for her, or whether they've got an 'open' relationship and he's with someone else. I also wonder whether she's having second thoughts about being here with me. I shake my head. I've gotta stop thinking about that and focus on her instead. When she's done, she puts her phone down on the table and looks up at me as I bring the wine back over and put it down in front of her.

"Thanks," she says as I sit beside her, giving her a little space.

I'm struck by the irony of how differently I'm behaving to normal. With my usual 'dates', I wouldn't stand on ceremony and we'd normally have ripped each other's clothes off by now. With Charlotte – as I said to Fin – it's different. I'm not entirely sure about the how and the why of that, I just know that it is.

She leans forward, picks up her glass and takes a long sip of wine, before she turns to me, looking me right in the eye.

"Can I ask you something?" she says.

"Of course." I pick up my own glass and take a drink.

"Where's your girlfriend?"

I almost spit my wine across the room, and just about manage not to choke. "My what?" I turn in my seat to look at her properly. She's staring at me, biting her bottom lip.

"Your girlfriend," she repeats.

"I don't have a girlfriend." I've never referred to any woman by that name and it feels like an odd word to have on my lips.

She looks at me like she doesn't believe a word I'm saying. "But I saw you," she says simply. "You were with a beautiful woman."

I put my glass down and move closer to her. "*You're* a beautiful woman," I say softly.

"So who was she?" she asks, refusing to be deflected by my compliment.

I sigh. "She was just someone I know." For the first time ever, I feel embarrassed about my lifestyle. Even so, I want her to know I'm single. "I'm not with anyone," I explain. "But if we're discussing our private lives, can I ask about your boyfriend?"

Her eyes widen. "My boyfriend?"

"Yeah. The guy you were with at the restaurant. You looked kinda… intimate."

She smiles. "Oh… you mean Jack." Her smile widens. "He's not my boyfriend." I give her a moment, hoping she'll elaborate, but she doesn't. I wish I knew if that means the guy was just a friend, or whether she really is like me.

"So you're not with anyone either?" I ask, just to be sure.

She shakes her head.

I move a little closer, wanting to kiss her, but she pulls back and then stands. "May I use your bathroom?" she asks.

"Um… sure." I turn. "It's down that corridor there." I point to the hallway in the corner behind us, which leads to the guest bedroom and main bathroom.

She nods her head and scampers away.

I sit back, leaning into the couch and looking up at the ceiling, still feeling a little confused, despite our brief confessional. I still don't understand why she said we couldn't go back to her place 'yet', even though I feel kinda relieved that she doesn't have a boyfriend. I just wish I knew what he is to her and why he kissed her fingers so intimately, if they're just friends. I shake my head. Who am I to judge? I've got a 'little black book' full of women. The thought of that 'little black book' hits me like a freight train and I sit forward suddenly. I know it's a radical life change, but I can't be with Charlotte knowing that list is in existence. I just can't. I get up and grab my phone from my jacket pocket, inputting the passcode for the list and, without even thinking about it, delete the whole file. Those numbers don't exist anywhere else, so in that one simple step, I've made the first real personal commitment of my life. What I've committed to, however, I've got no idea.

I hear the bathroom door open and close, and drop my phone back on the couch, returning to my seat and picking up my wine again, taking another sip.

"You okay?" I ask Charlotte as she comes back into the room and walks over.

She nods her head. "Yes, thank you," she replies and comes and sits down again, a little closer to me this time, which feels good.

I put my wine glass back and turn to her.

"Would it be okay if I kissed you?" I've never asked a woman that before, but I hold my breath, waiting for her answer.

She turns to me and simply nods her head, just once. Something flares in my chest, and I reach out, clasping her face between my hands and leaning in close, covering her mouth with mine. She's soft to touch, and I run my tongue very gently along her lips. She lets out a gasp and I take advantage, exploring her mouth. She moans into me, moving closer so her breasts are heaving against my chest, and I move one hand down and run it up her leg to the top of her thigh. She deepens the kiss, her moans becoming louder, and I know I've got to have her. Now. I pull back.

"You can say 'no', if you want to, but would you like to go to bed with me?" Again, I've never asked that question before either, and the wait this time is much longer. She looks at me, her eyes studying mine, like she's searching for the answer somewhere inside me.

"Yes," she replies eventually, her voice barely audible.

That flare in my chest bursts into flame, and I get to my feet and hold out my hand, which she takes in hers, and I pull her to her feet.

Without saying a word, I lead her to the corridor on the other side of the room and down to my bedroom, opening the door and letting her pass through ahead of me. The lamps beside the bed switch on automatically, because it's dark outside and they're light and motion sensitive, and when I close the door and turn around, Charlotte's facing me.

I stand in front of her and lean down, kissing her again. She opens up to me straight away and I feel her hands come up behind my head, her fingers twisting in my hair as she pulls me closer. She wants this as much as I do. That much is obvious, and I walk her backwards until she hits the bed, which is in the middle of the room.

"You're wearing too much," I whisper, breaking the kiss.

She doesn't reply, but looks down, breathing rapidly and watching, as I slowly start to undress her. One of the buttons catches on something, and she stops me, placing her hands over mine, then yanks her blouse over her head, and drops it. I bend, planting gentle kisses on the tops of her breasts while I reach around and undo the clasp of her bra. It falls to the floor and I lean back, taking in her beauty. She's stunning, and I palm her perfect breasts, which fit my hands like they were made for each other, feeling her nipples pebble against my skin as she rocks her head back and lets out a long slow sigh. I bend and take one nipple into my mouth, sucking deeply, then running my tongue over the taut surface. She moans and shudders into the contact, and I feel down between us for the zipper of her pants, lowering it. I pull back and kneel down in front of her, pulling down her pants, all the way to the floor, and then, with my eyes fixed on hers, I place my thumbs in the top of her panties, and lower them down to her ankles. She steps out of her clothes and I push them to one side, then lean back on my heels and admire her. She's perfection. Her full breasts lead down to a slim waist, which flares to very slightly rounded hips and further down to long shapely legs, at the top of which is a neat triangle of brown hair.

I stand and lift her in my arms, then lower her onto the downy comforter. She looks up at me, her face a mixture of wonder and fear. I need to get her to relax… and I know the perfect way to do that.

I kneel up on the bed and, placing my hands on her knees, I part her legs, pulling them as wide apart as I can. She's exposed to me, her lips swollen and glistening with anticipation.

Still, neither of us has spoken, but I don't think we need to. It feels like there's a kind of bond between us which makes words superfluous. I lower myself down and, using my hands to part her, I gently run my tongue over her swollen clit. She bucks into me, crying out in pleasure. I didn't expect quite that reaction and give her a moment to calm down again before I repeat the action. This time, she groans deeply and starts to move her hips, grinding into me as I flick my tongue over her. She's close already and, within moments, she lets out a loud cry and clamps her legs around me, writhing and groaning out her orgasm.

Only when I know she's completely calm do I stop and kneel up again. Her eyes are closed, but she opens them slowly, gazing up at me, with a look I'm not sure I recognize. I lean over, my hands either side of her head and kiss her lips, letting her taste herself. To start with, she's a little tentative, but then her tongue's in my mouth and she's licking her juices from me, like she can't get enough. I break the kiss eventually and stand, and Charlotte watches while I undo the buttons of my shirt, shrugging it off. Then I unfasten my pants and let them fall to the floor, kicking off my shoes and removing my socks, before finally pulling down my trunks. She sucks in a breath and bites her bottom lip, but I notice her legs part fractionally wider, like an involuntary action, which makes me smile. I wasn't wrong. She wants this.

Without taking my eyes from hers, I kneel back onto the bed, palming my cock in my right hand and leaning over her, before rubbing the tip very slowly up and down her wet folds. She moans and raises her legs higher, parting them wider still as I find her entrance and very slowly push inside. Our eyes are still locked and I bring my right arm up now, both my hands either side of her head, my cock edging slightly further inside. All of a sudden, I still. There's something stopping me, and my brain takes a second or two to process that thought. She can't be… can she?

"You're a virgin?" I whisper.

She nods her head and for a moment, I struggle to take that on board. She's staring up at me, wide-eyed and expectant and I know I have to do something; say something.

"You're sure you wanna do this?" I ask, because I have to be certain. "With me?"

She nods again.

"Say it."

"I want to do this with you," she murmurs and swallows hard.

This changes everything. Well, it does for me, anyway. I lower myself down onto my elbows, supporting my weight still, while I kiss her very gently, and at the same time, I push a little further inside her. She flinches and cries into my mouth and I swallow down her pain, feeling it right to my core. I still again, waiting, then pull back, looking down at her.

"Okay?" I ask and she nods her head again, smiling.

I raise myself up once more and very slowly edge inside her, giving her every inch until she's got my entire length. Once we're joined, I pause, savoring the moment. She feels incredible, her wet walls clasped tightly around my cock. It's no good though, I have to move. I pull out slowly and then push all the way back in again. She gasps this time, throwing her head back, feeling pleasure, not pain, and I build a rhythm, giving her my whole length with every stroke; giving her all of me. She brings her legs up higher still, clamping them around my waist, so I can go deeper and I increase the pace, taking her just a little harder. Before long, her breathing changes and I feel a tightening deep inside her, and I know she's close. I am too. I give her two more strokes and she comes apart, screaming and thrashing on the bed as I thrust hard one last time and explode deep inside her.

I feel like I've died and gone to heaven. I've watched women come before – I've made women come before – hundreds of times. But it's never felt like that. The connection with her was something else. Something more than physical. I know it was. I felt it. I just hope she felt the same, because I don't want this to stop. Ever. My cock's still rock hard and I want her again already, and I know, without a doubt, that I'm never gonna stop wanting her. I let out a long sigh and fall onto my elbows once more, just as Charlotte moves beneath me… and at that moment, I realize what a complete jerk I've been.

"Oh God. I'm so sorry," I say, pulling out of her. How could I have been so stupid? "Charlotte… That was a mistake. I'd never normally… I mean… Please forgive me. I'm so sorry. I should never have done that." I'm incoherent with panic and she looks up at me, her eyes filled with tears. I guess she's just worked it out as well. Christ, what have I done to her?

"It's fine," she says, her voice choking, and she sits up, moving across the bed.

"Where are you going?" I ask, reaching out and grabbing her arm.

"I need the bathroom," she replies, looking away. I can tell she's trying real hard not to cry.

What can I say? I can hardly stop her from going to the bathroom, even though I really need to talk to her, so I just whisper, "Okay," and she gets up and scampers away into my private bathroom, closing the door behind her.

I lie back on the bed, breathing deeply, trying to regain control. I'll let her finish up, and then we'll talk – properly. I'll even be rational – or I'll try to be, anyway. I won't panic. I should have been more responsible though. I've spent the last fifteen years being responsible, and have never had unprotected sex before. And I chose my first time to be *her* first time? I'm a fucking idiot. Well, when she comes back, I can at least reassure her that I'm clean – because I am. I get tested every year when I have my medical. But I guess that might not be the thing she's most worried about. Somehow I doubt she's on birth control… and if she's not, then I can also reassure her that we'll deal with any consequences of that. Together. Because we will.

The bathroom door opens and she reappears, one hand across her pussy, the other arm clasped across her breasts, trying to shield herself from my view, even though I've already seen her naked; even though I've already been inside her. She's obviously feeling really shy.

"Charlotte?" I say, keeping my voice soft, trying to put her at ease.

She looks over at me, staring at my face, then she lets her eyes wander down my body to my still-hard cock. She looks away quickly, like she's embarrassed, and walks across, picking up her clothes, holding them in front of her, and covering herself.

"What are you doing?" I ask, sitting up.

She doesn't reply. She just looks me in the eyes and, without a word, she runs.

Chapter Six

Lottie

I run, clasping my clothes against my chest, my shoes dangling from my hand, and I don't look back. I make it through his apartment and press the button for the elevator, on tenterhooks, and the doors open immediately, thank God. I dart inside and press the button for the lobby, hoping I'll be able to get out of the building without some kind of passcode. The doors start to close, and right at that moment, I hear my name being called.

"Charlotte? Where are you?"

I don't reply, but I see him, stark naked, still perfect and still aroused, evidently, striding into view. Our eyes meet just as the doors shut tight. He looks shocked, confused, maybe even a little hurt. I've got no idea how I look. A mess, obviously. I feel embarrassed, shamed, belittled.

In my panic, I drop my clothes, but decide the floor is probably the best place for them at the moment, and reach down, picking up my bra, putting it on as fast as I can, followed by my blouse. I grab my panties and my pants and pull them on, and finally slip my shoes back on. I know I probably still look disheveled, but at least I'm decent. I laugh and then struggle not to cry. 'Decent'? After what I've just done? I shake my head and take a deep breath. I can't think about that now. I'll think about that later.

The elevator doors open and, without even thinking, I run straight for the entrance, taking care not to slip on the shiny marble floor. The last thing I need is to fall and break something in his apartment building.

Outside, it's freezing cold, but I don't care. I run to the edge of the sidewalk and raise my arm, hailing a cab. Please, please let there be one…

A few cars pass me by, a couple of the occupants staring at me – I guess because I'm not wearing a coat, despite the temperature out here. Finally, a cab pulls over and I jump in the back.

"Just go," I tell the driver.

"Where to, lady?" he asks.

"Anywhere. Just go."

He shakes his head and the car moves forward. I glance out the window, just as the main apartment building doors open and the man appears, wearing sweat pants and a t-shirt. Our eyes meet again. He calls out something, although I can't hear what, and he starts to run toward the cab, but we move off into the traffic, and he stops, raising his hands in exasperation, I think, and that's the last I see of him.

Tears are welling in my eyes and I blink them back.

"I can drive around all night, if you want, but I'm guessing you wanna go somewhere?" The driver's voice makes me jump and I take a deep breath before giving him my home address and leaning back in the cab, staring at the ceiling just above me.

What's the matter with me? I just let a complete stranger take my virginity. I don't even know his name, and I let him do *that* with me? I must be insane. And to make it worse, he said it was a mistake. Actually, he said a lot more than that. He said he shouldn't have done it. He asked for my forgiveness. Dear God, I must have been really bad at it if he felt the need to say all that *and* to apologize. His regret was palpable. I don't think I've ever felt so humiliated in my life. Not even Catrina, at her worst, could make me feel this bad, and that's saying something.

I shiver. This has to be the most embarrassing experience ever and I wish I could turn the clock back and undo it. Except I don't… because until he felt the need to apologize for making such a heinous mistake as having sex with me, it felt so good. It really did. It was a truly amazing feeling, because while he was making love to me, I honestly felt completely connected to him, like it wasn't just our bodies that were joined, but our minds and maybe even our hearts as well. It was so much better than I ever imagined it could be. And he regretted it.

"Looks like there's a party going on," the driver says, pulling up outside the gate, and I remember I don't have my purse, or any means of paying him.

"Can you just wait here?" I ask him. "I'll need to run inside and get some cash."

He looks at me in the rear-view mirror. "I'm not going anywhere." His voice betrays his suspicion.

"I promise I'll be right back," I say and, as he parks up alongside the kerb, I dart out of the car. There's a security guard on the gate and he holds his hand up as I make my way in. I want to tell him I live there, but I know he'll insist on calling Catrina to make sure, and she's the last person I wanna see right now.

"I'm with the catering company," I tell him, showing him my name badge. "I just need to get some cash to pay the driver."

He looks down at my badge and gives me a nod of his head, standing to one side and letting me pass. I run up the driveway and around the back of the house, letting myself in through the kitchen door. Everything is very much as it was when I left, but I keep my head down and ignore everyone, rushing through into the hallway and straight up the stairs. I'm just a couple of minutes finding my purse and retrieving all the cash I've got, which is just under fifty dollars. I hope it's enough, because I have no idea what I'm gonna do if it isn't.

Back outside, the security guard ignores me this time and I go over to the cab where the driver's tapping on the steering wheel, waiting for me.

"What do I owe you?" I ask, leaning into the car.

"Forty two bucks," he says, checking his meter.

I give him everything I've got. "That should cover it," I tell him and he starts counting through the money.

"You've given me four dollars too much," he says, going to hand it back.

"Keep it," I tell him. He gives me a slight smile and pulls away, leaving me standing in the middle of the road.

I turn and walk past the security guard, making my way more slowly up the driveway this time, no longer really aware of the cold, or the cars still parked all over the front of the driveway, or the flashing Christmas lights. All I can think of is that I've ruined my life. I'm a slut. And my heart aches.

I go back into the kitchen again, closing the door softly behind me.

"What happened?" Mrs Hemsworth asks, coming straight over to me. "You came flying through here just now… You had me worried."

I look at her and try really hard not to cry. "I had to pay cab fare," I explain.

Claude comes over and stands the other side of me. "Is everything okay?" he asks, his kindness taking me by surprise.

"Yes. It's fine," I lie. I attempt a smile and almost get there. "I may as well get back to work."

"You don't have to," he says.

"I don't mind."

There's a tray of canapés on the countertop and I pick them up and wander out into the hallway, taking my place in the living room again. I glance around and notice that there's no sign of the man's friend – thank goodness.

"Where have you been?" Catrina's standing right behind me, her voice whispering in my ear.

"I didn't feel very well, so I stepped out for a moment."

"A moment?" she says, coming around and standing in front of me. "You've been gone for ages."

I don't reply and eventually she gets the message and moves away.

It's already after ten-thirty and, within an hour or so, the guests have started to disperse. Melanie comes over and tells me I can go back to the kitchen, and I smile my genuine gratitude. I can't wait to put tonight behind me.

The kitchen is much quieter now. There are couple of guys over by the sink, and someone's stacking the dishwasher. Claude and Mrs

Hemsworth are sitting together at the island unit, cups of tea set in front of them. I place my tray down on the countertop and turn back to the door, hoping to make a quick getaway.

"Not so fast," Mrs Hemsworth says. "What happened?"

She pats her hand on the stool next to her, indicating I should sit down. I love Mrs Hemsworth. I really do. But I don't want to talk right now. "Nothing happened," I say quietly.

She gives me a glare. "Is this something to do with that young man?" Claude asks, obviously not picking up on my rebuff, but then he doesn't know me, so why would he?

"No," I reply, maybe a little too quickly. I notice Mrs Hemsworth's eyebrows rise slightly. "I'm gonna go to bed," I say quietly. "I'm really tired."

I don't give either of them a chance to say anything else. I turn and go back out into the hallway. Catrina's just seeing off the last of the guests and I take the opportunity of sneaking up the stairs and into my room.

I close the door and lean back against it, wondering how the evening can have gone so horribly wrong. I catch sight of myself in the full length mirror on the other side of the room and wonder why I don't look any different. I should do, shouldn't I? I'm not a virgin anymore. Surely that makes me a woman. And yet, I still feel like a little girl, who really needs a hug, a shoulder to cry on and someone to tell her it's all gonna be okay.

My image becomes a blur as the tears start to fall and I stumble into the room, undoing the buttons on my blouse as I go. I undress quickly, leaving a trail of clothing behind me, until I'm naked, trying hard not to remember how good his tongue felt when he licked me, how sexy and exciting it was to taste myself on his lips, or how incredible it was to feel him inside me. I've always known I'm a complete innocent when it comes to sex, but I didn't realize how little I knew until tonight. I've got no idea what he did to me. All I know is it felt wondrous. And that he regretted it. He apologized. He said it was a mistake. A mistake? Dear God... I sob and fall onto the bed, my hand automatically reaching for my necklace, for the comfort of my dad's gift to me, for the connection to him. I clutch at my throat, but there's nothing there.

Sitting bolt upright, I kneel, hunting around on the the bed… nothing. I get up again and search the floor, and go through my clothes. It's gone. My necklace is gone. It's too much. I collapse to my knees, tears streaming down my face, as the sense of loss overwhelms me. While I'm weeping, I tell myself I'm crying about the necklace, about the loss of that link to my dad, but I know deep down I'm not. I'm sobbing over the loss of my virginity, and the fact that I'll never again see the man who took it. That's what hurts so much.

Paul

I wander slowly back inside the apartment building and, like I'm on autopilot, input the code for the penthouse. The elevator doors open and I get in, waiting for them to close.

What the fuck just happened? Why did she run? I'm so confused, my head hurts. I know she saw me coming after her. Our eyes connected when she was in the elevator, standing with her clothes clasped against her, an expression of fear on her face, coupled with something that looked like embarrassment. But then the doors closed and she was gone and I was the one enveloped by fear. Fear that, for some reason, she was running away from me; fear that I might never see her again. I ran straight back into my bedroom, grabbed some sweats and a t-shirt from my dressing room and went back to the elevator again, pulling them on while I pressed the button and waited for it to come back up.

That was the longest few minutes of my life – as was the ride down. And when I got there, she was already in a cab. She saw me though. I know she did. Why didn't she stop? Whatever was wrong, she could've told me. We could've talked about it. I would've listened. I run my fingers through my hair just as the elevator doors open and I exit into my own lobby, only now realizing that I've got nothing on my feet – and they're freezing. I step onto the deep pile carpet in my living room, savoring its softness, and go over to the couch.

Our wine glasses are still on the table, almost untouched, and I bend to pick mine up, when I notice Charlotte's phone. For the first time since she got out of bed, I feel that flare come back into my chest again. I've got a way of contacting her. I press the button at the bottom of her phone, to be met with a keypad. It needs a six-digit number for me to get into it. This is just marvelous. My one hope of getting hold of her, is resting in my hand, and there's nothing I can do with it. I wonder, for a moment, if she might come back to collect it, but I highly doubt that. The way she ran out of here, I don't think she'll be coming back anytime soon.

I put her phone down on the table and wander into the bedroom, trying to avoid looking at the bed, although my eyes are drawn to the tiny blood stain in the middle of the white sheets, and I feel a sharp pain which starts deep inside me, somewhere near where that flaring hope had been a few minutes ago. I go and sit down on the couch over by the window, holding my head in my hands. She was a virgin. That was the last thing I expected. Because she was with that guy the other night, I assumed she'd be experienced, but then she did tell me he wasn't her boyfriend… so, I guess… I shake my head. Just because that guy wasn't her boyfriend, I had no way of knowing she'd be a virgin… did I? If I had known, I'd have taken more care, given her more time, but she did say she wanted to make love with me. I know she did. I got her to say it out loud, just to be sure. I know she wanted me as much as I wanted her. Her body and her eyes told me that. Although, wanting someone so much you can't breathe properly, is no excuse for forgetting the condom… Because there's no excuse for being an inconsiderate, careless, fucking idiot.

I raise my head and something on the carpet catches my eye, glinting in the glow of the bedside lamps. I get up again and go over to the bed, bending and picking it up. It's a silver chain, with the letter 'C' attached. I remember seeing a chain around her neck in the restaurant, so I guess this must be it, although I didn't notice her wearing it tonight. I saw she was wearing a couple of woven leather bracelets, but this seems like a very different item. It's more delicate and refined. I run it through my fingers and notice that the clasp is missing from one end of the chain. I guess it must have fallen off, maybe when her button got caught and she pulled off her blouse. Her need, her desperation was just as great as mine. I know it was.

I place the necklace on my nightstand and sit on the edge of the bed, deciding that I'll get it repaired, and if I ever manage to I find her, I'll return it to her.

I wake early, feeling absolutely dreadful.

I couldn't face going to sleep in my own bed. It smells of her already. So, I slept on the couch in the living room – having first finished the rest of the bottle of Burgundy.

It's Sunday. I've got nothing planned for the day and the thought of sitting around here, trying to work out what happened last night fills me with gloom. I've never really been a sitting around kind of guy anyway. I'm more of a getting on and doing kind of guy. And today, that means getting up, showering, getting dressed and going back to see Catrina Hudson. I worked out last night, just as I was finishing the wine, that my best hope for finding Charlotte is to discover where Catrina hired her waiting staff for the party. Once I know that, I can contact them and see if they'll give me the girl's full name, so I can track her down. I'm not giving up that easily – even if it does mean seeing Catrina again.

I pull up outside the gates of the Hudson house. They're shut today and I press the entry button and wait.

"Hello?" a woman's voice says.

"Hi. I'm here to see Catrina Hudson," I reply.

"Can I ask your name?" the voice says.

"Paul Lewis. I was at the party last night."

"Okay. Come on in." There's a moment's pause and then the gates start to open. As soon as they're wide enough, I drive through and continue toward the house, parking up outside.

I have to say, the place looks better in daylight. It's easier to see that, without the addition of the Christmas lights, it's a really nice colonial style property. I glance around while I'm getting out of the car, and notice a guy working in the garden. He's quite a distance away, but there's something about him that's vaguely familiar. I can't place him though, and close the car door, going over to the house.

I climb the five steps to the front door, and am about to ring the bell, when it opens and I'm faced with Catrina herself, wearing a poor excuse for a negligee. It's almost transparent and I avert my eyes, looking at the space between us.

"Paul," she gushes, holding her arms out. I hope she doesn't expect to hug me, because that's not happening. I hold back until she puts her arms down again, then offer my hand for a formal handshake. She accepts, giving me a demure look at the same time. It doesn't suit her style. "This is a lovely surprise," she says, stepping to one side to let me in.

I enter, and wait for her to close the door. "I've got a question I need to ask," I say, cutting to the chase.

"Oh?" She indicates the living room and I follow her, my eye settling on the spot by the fireplace where Charlotte was standing last night. "How can I help?" she prompts, sitting on the couch, and crossing her long legs.

I focus on her face, which is overly made up, especially considering the time of day, and come straight out with my story. "I noticed a waitress here last night," I tell her. "She was wearing a distinctive necklace and, when I was leaving after the party, I found it outside." It's a complete fabrication, but hopefully she won't question it. "I was too tired to come back in last night, so I thought I'd drive over and see you today."

She smiles up at me, and very slowly gets to her feet again. "I understand," she says softly.

"You do?"

"Yes. You're making this up, aren't you?" My mouth dries as I wonder if she's worked out what really happened, then she continues, "You were just looking for an excuse to come over here again, weren't you?" She adopts the demure look again and I struggle to control my temper. Does she actually think I'm interested in her?

"No, Catrina. I can assure you it's nothing like that."

"Come now, Paul. I know your secret." *No you don't.* She smiles. "It's one of my girls, isn't it? I knew you wouldn't be able to resist. So, which one is it?" she asks.

Well, at least she doesn't think it's her, but the idea of being with either of her daughters is almost as bad. They're too vacuous for words. "Neither," I reply.

She slaps my arm, playfully. "You don't need to be shy with me," she says. "Do you have this necklace with you?" she asks, like she doesn't believe in its existence.

I reach into my pocket, where it's nestling beside Charlotte's phone, and pull it out.

I notice her eyes widen and she takes a step closer.

"I don't think that belonged to any of the waiting staff," she says, her voice suddenly harsher.

"How can you possibly know that?" I reply.

She raises her eyes to mine and see the anger behind them, just fleetingly. "Because… because it belongs to one of my daughters," she says, and although she's making an effort to sound calm, I can hear the barely suppressed rage in her voice. What on earth is that about?

"It does?" I've got no idea what's going on here, or why she's lying to me, but I'm willing to play her game long enough to find out.

"Yes." She puts her hands on her hips. "I noticed one of the waitresses disappeared for a while last night. I bet she went upstairs and stole it…" Her voice fades.

Seriously? I'm even more intrigued now. "Call your daughters down," I suggest. "Let's ask them about it."

She bites her bottom lip and goes to speak, then changes her mind and wanders out into the hallway, calling her daughters' names up the stairs, before coming back into me.

"That's the problem with having staff come into the house," she says, continuing the charade. "You can't always trust them."

I don't reply and, within a moment or two, Christa and Chelsea appear in the doorway, both still wearing very short pajamas.

"Girls… you could have gotten dressed," their mother scolds, although she's smiling as she walks over to them and is clearly secretly pleased at the amount of flesh they're showing. She whispers something briefly, then turns, links arms with them and pulls them over in my direction.

"I have a necklace here, which your mother seems to think belongs to one of you." I hold out my closed hand, then unfurl it to reveal the silver chain and its attachment.

"It's mine," Christa says, looking up at me and fluttering her eyelashes.

"Oh you found it," Chelsea chimes in at the same time, and Catrina rolls her eyes.

"Girls…" she says through gritted teeth.

"It can't belong to both of you," I reply, closing my hand around the necklace. "So which of you is it?"

"Me!" they both say in unison.

I shake my head and stare at Catrina. Whatever her plan was, it's backfired, mainly because her daughters aren't bright enough to have picked up on it. "I'm done here," I tell her. "Give me the name of your caterer." Charlotte said the guy I spoke to was her boss, so that seems like a good place to start.

Anger flashes through Catrina's eyes, but I match it with my own and she takes a step back. "Claude Mignon," she says. "His company is called Mignons Morceaux."

I nod my head and leave, without another word.

Outside, I notice the gardener has gone, but I don't care about him anymore. I've got a lead. I've got a chance.

Back home, I check out the catering company on the Internet. Their opening hours are Monday to Friday only, so I can't call them until tomorrow. I feel a little deflated. I'd hoped to be able to track her down today. I can't face just sitting here thinking about her all day, so I pick up my phone and call Fin. I need to talk.

Chapter Seven

Lottie

I wake late, having slept – or rather, not slept – very restlessly. I spent most of the night dreaming about what the man did to me, worrying about what he must think of me, wondering if he's already in the arms of another woman – like the blonde he was with at the restaurant – desperate to find someone who can actually give him what he wants… being as I so obviously couldn't. I shudder at the memory of his words and try to stem back the tears, squaring my shoulders, taking a deep breath and heading for the shower instead.

I'm still dressing and trying not to think too much, when Catrina barges into my room.

"Please… will you knock," I say to her, not bothering to disguise my anger.

"No," she replies, standing with her hands on her hips. In the distance, I can hear the twins bickering about something, but I ignore them and pull on my jeans.

"What do you want?" I ask Catrina.

"I just wondered if you had anything you want to tell me?" she says.

"No," I reply, shaking my head at the same time.

"I see you aren't wearing your necklace," she comments as I put my arms into a thick sweater before pulling it over my head.

I stare across at her. "No… I lost it."

"Where?" she asks, her eyes narrowing.

"At the party," I reply, saying the first thing that comes into my head. "I guess someone must have picked it up."

I've got no idea how she knows it's even missing, but I'm certainly not going to tell her I lost it at the apartment of a total stranger, just before losing my virginity to him as well.

"Well, I doubt you'll see it again," she says, still watching me closely.

I shrug, but don't reply. She's almost certainly right. There's no way the man is going to return my necklace to me. I have no doubt he's glad to see the back of me.

She glances over my shoulder to the window, and the garden beyond. I follow the line of her gaze and notice Jack, tending to the flower bed.

"I'd better get dressed," Catrina says and quickly leaves the room, slamming the door behind her.

I don't know why she's bothering. She'll wear something that's almost as revealing as her negligee, but whatever she puts on, Jack won't care. I look back out the window and see him heading for the outbuilding where the garden equipment is stored. If I'm quick, I can beat Catrina down there, and talk to Jack. I need to talk to someone…

"How's things?" I ask as I open the door.

"Don't *do* that," Jack replies, turning to me. "I thought you were her."

I smile. "Scared?"

"Terrified." He smiles back.

"So… how's things?" I need to talk, but the least I can do is to find out how he is first. "I can't believe she got you to come in on a Sunday."

"She said she needed me here this morning to clear up after the party."

"Even though there's nothing to clear up outside?" He rolls his eyes in agreement. "Does this mean you get tomorrow off?" I ask.

"No." He smiles at me. "But she's paying me a bonus for today, so I can't complain."

"And how are things with Alex?" I change the subject, fed up already with talking about Catrina.

"A little better, I think," he says, leaning back on the workbench. I sit on the stool and face him.

"You've gotta give me more than that," I tell him.

"Well, Alex has told his parents," he begins.

"And?"

"And they weren't exactly delirious, but they were okay. They've invited me to visit with them for New Years." He looks a little doubtful.

"And that's a problem?"

"Not for me, but I've gotta break the news to Catrina that I'm gonna miss a couple of days of work."

"Go for it," I tell him.

"The thing is, I can't tell her I'm going to visit Alex's parents, so what am I gonna say to her?"

"Just say you're gonna stay with your own parents for a few days. Maybe do it in the kitchen, though, with Mrs Hemsworth there, so Catrina can't ask for any kind of payback…"

He pulls a face and shudders in an overdramatic way. "Don't," he says. "Just the thought makes me wanna vomit." He falls silent for a moment. "Although…" He seems thoughtful. "I wonder if she's got a new man in her life."

"You do?"

"Yeah."

"What makes you say that?" I ask, intrigued.

"A guy came to the house really early this morning, and Catrina let him in the front door herself."

"That doesn't tell us anything. Can you describe him?"

He thinks for a minute. "Tall, dark, built like a god." He shrugs. "He was a long way away. He had a lovely car though."

"Oh?"

"Yeah. A bright red Ferrari F12 Berlinetta."

I feel light headed and grab the shelf beside me for support.

"Hey," Jack says, pushing himself off the workbench and coming over to stand in front of me. "What's wrong?"

"This guy…" I say. "Did he look anything like the man we saw in the restaurant the other night?"

He stares at me. "I guess. Yeah. Like I say, he was a way off, but he did look kinda like him. Why?"

I close my eyes. "What was he doing here?" I whisper to myself.

"Who?" Jacks says and I realize I just spoke out loud.

"The man," I say, opening my eyes and looking at him.

He folds his arms across his chest. "You're gonna have to tell me what the hell you're talking about," he says, "because right now, you're not making any sense at all."

I stare at him for a moment longer, then suck in a deep breath. "He... he was at the party last night," I say quietly. "And I was waitressing for Catrina."

"I know you were," he says.

"And we met..." He nods, still clearly not understanding. "We recognized each other from the restaurant," I continue and I see the penny drop in his eyes.

"Something happened, didn't it?" he asks, his voice filled with concern.

"He... he took me back to his place. In his bright red Ferrari F12 Berlinetta." Jack smiles.

"Did you have a good time?" he asks.

I shake my head, then stop and nod, then shrug. "It all went so wrong," I tell him and the tears start again.

"Oh, Lottie," he says and puts an arm around me. "Tell me."

"I—It was really nice," I say through my tears. "He was really nice. He asked about you – about whether you were my boyfriend."

"Did you tell him about me?" he asks.

"Well, not really. I just said we were friends."

"You should've told him," he replies.

"It's not for me to tell people about your life." He shakes his head.

"What about the woman he was with?" he asks.

"He said she was just someone he knows. He made a point of telling me he wasn't with anyone."

"So, what happened?"

"H—He took me to his bedroom, and... we had sex." I blurt out the words.

"You did want to, didn't you? He didn't force you?" Jack stands back, looking worried.

"No. I wanted to." More than anything.

"But?" he says. "There's a but somewhere in here. I can sense it."

"It's just that, afterwards, he said it was a mistake and he shouldn't have done it, and he apologized…" I sob out a long wail and feel Jack pull me into a hug.

"What did you do?" he asks me, when I've managed to calm down a little.

"I grabbed my clothes and ran out of there. Then I got a cab and came straight back here."

"You ran out?" he says, evidently incredulous.

"Yeah." I lean back and look up at him.

"Why?"

How can he not understand this? "Because I felt humiliated. He apologized for having sex with me, Jack."

"Do you think you might have misunderstood what he was saying?" he asks. "Because as far as I'm aware, most guys don't usually apologize for having sex with women, they just don't call them again. And let's face it, there are all kinds of reasons why he could have been saying sorry, aren't there?"

"Yeah… like discovering I'm really crap at sex," I say without thinking.

"I doubt that very much," Jack replies, giving me a kind smile.

"I'd never done it before," I murmur.

"You were a virgin?" He's even more surprised now.

"Yeah." I lower my head. "And he *apologized*." I start crying again. Jack puts his finger underneath my chin and raises my face to his.

"You liked him, didn't you?"

I pause, then nod my head. "Yes. I liked him."

"A lot?" he queries.

I nod again. "I wanted there to be something… more between us," I say, struggling to find the words. "And while we were… well, together, I thought he did too. But I obviously got that wrong. I was a mistake to him."

"You don't know that."

"It's what he said," I reply, raising my voice a little. "Anyway, what does it matter? I'm never gonna see him again, am I? He regrets what we did, and I'm not exactly going to go looking for him." I huff out a sigh. "I don't even know his name, Jack," I wail. "God, I feel like such a slut."

He pulls me into a hug. "You're not a slut," he says firmly. "You just needed someone to make you feel special for a little while."

"Yeah. But maybe I should've asked his name before I went to bed with him? That makes me a slut, doesn't it? To throw myself at a man like that?"

He smiles again. "No. It just makes you like the rest of us." He pulls back and cups my face in his hands, looking into my eyes. "We all wanna be loved."

I stare at him. "I wonder why he came back here?"

His smile widens and he murmurs, "Maybe because he wants to be loved too?"

Paul

"What kind of fucking time do you call this?" Fin doesn't sound very pleased, to put it mildly.

I check my watch. "It's nearly eleven. Why?"

"God... is it?"

"Did I wake you?"

"Yeah."

"Sorry," I reply with as much feeling as I can muster.

"No, you're not." I hear him yawn.

"What time did you get to bed last night?" I ask him.

"I got to *bed* at about ten-thirty," he replies. "I got to sleep at about three am." I can hear the smile in his voice and a female cough in the background.

"She's still there?"

"Yeah."

"Sorry. I'll call back later."

"Hey," he says, stopping me from hanging up. "What's wrong?"

"It'll keep."

"No it won't. Hang on…" He must have covered the mouthpiece, because all I can hear now is muffled voices. I wait for a minute and then he comes back on the line. "Katie's gone for a shower," he says.

"And you'd rather be in there with her?"

"Yeah, but I'm gonna make coffee instead."

"You can do that and talk on the phone at the same time?"

"Yeah. It's called multi-tasking. You should try it some time."

I ignore his jibe. "So… is Katie a keeper?" I ask.

There's a short silence and then he replies, "No. She's transferring to Seattle in the New Year."

"And you can't do long-distance?"

"It was nice," he says quietly, "but not *that* nice." He doesn't sound even vaguely disappointed, so I don't worry about commiserating. "Gonna tell me what's wrong?" he asks. "I'm guessing it's something to do with the girl from the restaurant… the waitress."

"Charlotte." I offer her name.

"Okay. Charlotte. What happened?"

I take a breath and lie down on the couch, staring at the ceiling. "I brought her back to my place," I tell him.

"You did?" He knows this is unusual – unheard of – for me.

"Yeah. It felt like the right thing to do."

"Okay… And?"

I'm not sure how to put this, but then I remember something he said on Friday, after we'd played golf together. "And… you remember how you said that at our age, we'd be unlikely to meet a virgin?"

"Yeah," he says slowly.

"Well, you can take that back."

"Jeez. I knew she was young, but…"

"Yeah."

"Paul, what did you do?" There's more than a hint of suspicion in his voice.

"I didn't do anything she didn't want me to." I've gone over last night so many times in my head, I know I've got that right. "I made sure of it."

"Okay." I hear the sound of his coffee machine bleeping. "Can I assume she's not a virgin anymore?"

"You can."

"Right. But I'm guessing it didn't go well, or you wouldn't be calling me. You'd still be in bed with her."

"Well, that would be kinda hard, being as she ran out me."

"She ran out? Paul, what the fuck did you do to her?"

I sit up. "I didn't do anything. Honest. I already told you, she's different. She's…" I want to say that I'm pretty sure she's the one, but I hold back. I need to talk that through with Charlotte before I admit it to anyone else.

"Alright. Calm down and tell me what happened."

I take a long breath. "I made love to her," I say simply. "And before you ask, I was gentle. I've never been that fucking gentle in my life." I wonder for a moment if I should be telling him this, but I need someone to help me make sense of it all, and I don't have anyone else.

"Right. And then?"

"And then, afterwards, I realized I'd forgotten the condom…"

"You did what? Jesus. How the hell could you do something like that?"

"Because I wasn't thinking straight." If I remember rightly I was just starting to contemplate what forever might feel like with her. "So shoot me."

"I won't need to. Her dad'll probably do that for me, when he catches up with you… you fucking idiot."

"I feel bad enough already, Fin," I say quietly and I hear him suck in a breath.

"Okay. I'm sorry. I'm not helping much, am I?" I don't want to confirm that he isn't, but he isn't. I couldn't feel any worse about what I've done if I tried. "So what did you do next?" he asks after a moment's pause.

"I apologized, obviously."

"And then what happened?"

"That was when she ran out on me."

The line goes silent. "You need to find her," he says quietly.

"I know," I tell him, with renewed determination. "And when I do, I'm gonna get her to talk to me. I'm gonna find out why she ran, and I'm gonna make damn sure she doesn't run again."

"You're really serious about her, aren't you?" he says, although he doesn't sound as surprised as I might have expected in the circumstances.

"Yeah. I am."

"Then I suggest you tell her that."

"I intend to," I reply. "Maybe not the minute I find her, but when I think she's ready to hear it."

"And if there are consequences to your forgetfulness? If she's pregnant?"

"I'll be there for her, Fin. I'm not gonna be a fucking idiot anymore."

I spend the afternoon finding a jewelry store willing to repair Charlotte's necklace on the spot. It's a simple enough job but, because it's a Sunday, and a lot of them don't have repair facilities on site, it proves harder than I thought. I eventually find a little place where the guy says he can do it while I wait and, when he's out the back fixing a new clasp, I find myself looking around his shop, wondering what kind of things she'd like. Obviously, I know she owns the necklace, but then I also remember she was wearing leather bracelets around her wrist and the two styles seem really different. I want to find out why that is. I want to get to know her. Right after I've apologized again – for everything I so obviously got wrong in the first place.

I'd thought about calling Claude Mignon, but by Monday morning, I've decided to go to his offices instead. So, I call Maureen on her cell as early as I dare and tell her I'll be in late, although I don't know when. I also don't tell her where I'm going, or why, but she agrees to handle anything that comes up, and only call me if she absolutely has to.

Claude Mignon's offices are fairly opulent, attached to the front of a warehouse-looking building, and made of smoked glass and chrome. I guess there must be money in catering. I go in through the main entrance and walk up to the reception desk.

"I'd like to see Claude Mignon, please," I say to the young woman behind the desk.

She looks up and her eyes widen. She even licks her lips. That happens sometimes, and occasionally – if I'm interested – I'll play along, but today I'm not in the mood. I doubt I'll ever be in the mood again. I just tap my fingers on her desk impatiently. "Do you have an appointment?" she asks, like she doesn't already know that I don't.

"No," I reply.

"I'm afraid he only sees people by appointment," she starts to explain, but I cut her short, holding up my hand.

I take one of my business cards from my inside pocket. "Tell him Paul Lewis is here. Ask if he'll make an exception."

She glances down at the card and then back at me again. "Paul Lewis?"

"Yes."

My face may not be overly familiar, but if she's even vaguely aware of the business columns, she'll know my name, and judging from her change in attitude, I think she does.

"Take a seat," she offers, nodding toward a white leather couch on the other side of the reception area. I nod my head and walk over, sitting down and selecting a magazine, which I pretend to look at while she picks up the phone and says something quietly. She replaces the receiver, but nothing happens, and I'm just thinking of going back over and finding out what's going on, when a side door opens and Claude Mignon himself steps out.

"You?" he says, looking at me. "The man from the party." A broad smile forms on his lips. "I had no idea…"

I get up and take his offered hand, giving him a firm shake, which he returns. "Come into my office," he says and leads me back through the door, down a corridor and into an office at the end. It's a large space, the walls of which are filled with photographs of food, very beautifully and artistically shot. His desk is made of glass and is set at one end of the room, and he goes over and sits behind it, offering me a seat in front of him.

"Would you care for a coffee?" he says, his French accent still fairly pronounced. I noticed it at the party, so I guess it's not as faked as I thought it might be. Let's face it, he hardly needs to pretend when it's just the two of us.

"No, thanks."

"Then how may I help you?"

I'm not sure how to put this. I can hardly tell him the same things I told Fin, but equally, the story I gave Catrina is no good either, being as this guy saw me leave with Charlotte on Saturday evening. I decide to come clean – well, kind of.

"I'm sure you remember me leaving the party with one of your waitresses," I say, maintaining eye contact with him.

"Yes," he says, nodding his head and smiling, just slightly.

"Well, she left a couple of things at my apartment, and I was wondering if you could give me her address, so I can return them to her?"

He leans forward, resting his elbows on his desk. "Or… you could just give me these items, and I could return them to her myself?" he suggests.

"I could," I say. "But then I wouldn't get to see her again."

His smile widens. "And you'd like to?"

"Yes."

He nods his head. "Can I ask how you found out my name?"

"Sure. I went to see Catrina Hudson yesterday morning. She told me. Eventually."

He smiles. "Well, that makes more sense of her telephone message."

"She's left you a message?" I can't hide my surprise.

"Yes. Early this morning. I've been busy and was just going to call her back when my receptionist said you were outside. I decided Mrs Hudson could wait…" His voice fades for a moment. "You really don't know who the girl is, do you?" He tilts his head to one side, the smile returning to his lips.

"I know her name's Charlotte," I point out.

"Yes. Because that was the name on her badge," he says, and I sit forward.

"You mean that's not her real name?"

"It is, but it's not the name she chooses to go by." He must notice my confusion. "You don't need me at all, you know," he says cryptically. "You already have her address."

"I do?"

"Yes. You were there on Saturday night." I guess my puzzlement must be really obvious now, because his eyes soften and he leans even further forward. "Charlotte is the daughter of the house – well, she's one of them, anyway. Her stepmother, who I have to say is probably one of the most evil women I've ever come across, is Catrina Hudson."

"Seriously?" I can't hide my surprise.

"Yes." He nods his head for emphasis. "Only Mrs Hudson didn't want Charlotte to attend the party as a guest, so she called me and asked if she could be used as a waitress instead."

"Excuse me, but how do you know she didn't want her at the party?" I ask. "Did she tell you that?" I find it hard to believe Catrina would open up like that, but you never know, I guess.

He frowns, like he's remembering something. "No," he says. "I was at the house one afternoon, making the arrangements with Mrs Hudson. Her daughters came in, saying that, if Charlotte was allowed to be there, none of the men would even look at either of them." He shrugs his shoulders in a very Gallic way, holding out his hands at the same time. "I've got to admit, they did have a point, because even in her uniform, Charlotte outshone every other woman there. Anyway, Catrina called me a few days later with her plan for Charlotte." He smiles again. "She's a lovely girl," he says. "And she didn't complain about being forced to work for the evening… not once."

"And you didn't say anything to Catrina?" I ask.

"She was paying me," he reasons. "I did give Charlotte an easy ride," he adds. "And I made sure the other staff looked out for her."

I nod my head. I guess there wasn't a lot else he could do.

"I was thrilled when you brought her out to the kitchen and took her away."

"Did she come back later?" I ask. I need to know she got home safely.

"Yes," he replies. "She was… upset.'

Shit. "Just so you know," I tell him, getting to my feet, "I didn't do anything to hurt her. Not intentionally anyway. I really hope it's gonna turn out to be a misunderstanding."

He stands and smiles at me. "I hope so too," he says.

Once we've said our goodbyes and he's shown me out of the office, I settle into my car and think over what Claude Mignon has just told me. This means that, when I was at the Hudson house yesterday morning, asking Catrina for the name of her caterer, Charlotte was probably upstairs in her room, maybe sleeping… maybe still crying. Hopefully thinking about me. The irony of that situation isn't lost on me. It also means that I'm gonna have to go back there again, even if the thought of seeing Catrina again is kinda daunting. Still, I didn't get where I am today by being scared – I gave that up years ago – and not even a man-eating cougar is gonna stop me. Not now.

I feel like I still have so many questions, but at least I have one answer. I know why she said we couldn't go back to her place – yet. We were already there. I shake my head and let it fall back onto the head rest behind me. I'll call round to her house after lunch. I'm not waiting any longer than that, but I've got several messages on my phone from Maureen, so I've gotta get into the office and deal with a few things first, and I need to take some time, think through what I'm gonna say, and make sure I get this right. I want to find out why Charlotte ran, and I want to persuade her to let me spend some more time with her, so we can get to know each other and I can persuade her I'm a good guy – well, I am when I'm with her – and that I'm not gonna hurt her, if she'll just trust me to take care of her. I also realize that I should probably stop calling her 'Charlotte', even in my own head, because I know who she is now. I know exactly who she is. She's Charles's daughter. She's Lottie.

Chapter Eight

Lottie

It was only last night, when I went to check my messages, to see if Heather had gotten in touch about the new work schedules for next year, that I realized I don't have my phone. I went through my purse and scoured my bedroom and then remembered the last time I used it was at the man's apartment. I left it on his coffee table and forgot to pick it up when I ran out of there.

So, this morning, I'm faced with the prospect of buying a new phone and having to let everyone know my new number. In the meantime, I've managed to contact Heather on Facebook, using my desktop computer, which is still here. She came back quite quickly and told me our boss at the bookstore has flu, which probably just means that he has a bad cold, but either way he won't be looking at the new schedules for a while. It doesn't really matter, but we both need to make sure he's not going to cut our hours. We need all the work we can get. Well, we need all the money we can get, anyway.

"What are you going to do today?" Mrs Hemsworth asks, when I get down to the kitchen. Jack's sitting with her at the island unit, having a coffee break, which I guess must mean Catrina's out, being as he generally avoids hanging around inside the house when she's home.

"I'm gonna have to go into town," I tell them, helping myself to coffee and joining them.

"Why?" Jack asks. "Christmas shopping?"

"No. I've done that. I—I lost my phone. I'm gonna have to get a new one." I let out a sigh. "It won't be a very nice one, because I can't afford it." My dad bought my last one, but the best I'll be able to afford is something very basic.

Mrs Hemsworth gives me a sympathetic glance and reaches over, squeezing my hand.

"You lost it?" Jack says. "But I sent you a message on Saturday night. You had it then."

I glare at him. "Yes."

"You didn't leave it at that guy's apartment, did you?" he asks.

"Yes, I did." There's no point in lying.

Mrs Hemsworth sits up, paying attention. "I assume we're talking about the guy who took you out of here on Saturday night, like a knight in shining armor?"

"In a tux," Jack corrects, grinning.

"And who you evidently abandoned to come back here and hand out fancy canapés?" Mrs Hemsworth adds.

"Yes. We are talking about him," I say.

"You never did tell me what happened with him," she replies, taking a sip of coffee.

"You mean you don't know?" Jack says and I give him one of my hardest glares. He smiles at me. "Lottie got cold feet," he adds simply, not elaborating.

"And you ran out on him?" Mrs Hemsworth's surprise is obvious. "A gorgeous hunk of man like that?"

"We're all entitled to get cold feet every so often," Jack says, sensing my discomfort and defending me.

Mrs Hemsworth shakes her head, like she doesn't quite believe anyone would turn down the chance to be with a man like that. "You know his address, don't you?" she asks. "I mean, you went back to his place, didn't you?" I nod my head, not altogether sure where she's going with this. "Then why don't you go around and see him? You can get your phone back." She smiles, obviously thinking she's found the perfect solution to my problem.

"I—I'm not sure I can," I stutter.

"Why not?"

"Because... because I ran out on him."

"I know, but I'm sure he'll let you have your phone back."

He probably would. But I imagine he'd also want an explanation for my sudden disappearance. I'm too embarrassed to even start to explain it to him. It was bad enough telling Jack. The thought of facing the man again makes me shake with fear. It was humiliating having to look at him after coming out of his bathroom, so the thought of doing so again, in the cold light of day... I feel myself shudder.

"Maybe you should just get a new one," Jack says, helping me out. Mrs Hemsworth looks at him, like he's mad.

"Exactly," I reply, finding my voice again at last. "I can hardly go marching into his penthouse apartment. There's all kinds of security to get through... I really don't wanna have to explain to complete strangers that I left my phone there on Saturday night."

Mrs Hemsworth nods her head. "No... I see what you mean."

I don't add that one of the 'complete strangers' I'm talking about is the man himself.

I spend the morning wrapping Christmas presents and listening to music. It transpires Catrina and the twins have gone out, and won't be back until this evening. They're all evidently 'exhausted' from the weekend's festivities and Catrina's booked them into the spa for the day. I have to say, it's really nice having the house to myself, with just Mrs Hemsworth and Jack for company. I'd like to say it reminds me of when my dad was alive, but it doesn't, because he's not here.

The three of us take advantage of Catrina being out, and have a late lunch together. Mrs Hemsworth has made some goats cheese tarts, which we have with potato salad and iced tea. Being as it's the last time I'm going to see Jack before the holidays, we all exchange gifts, and afterwards, Jack goes back outside and I help Mrs Hemsworth clear away. Luckily, she's avoided talking about the man, or my phone since this morning, which is a blessed relief.

"You're going into town this afternoon, is that right?" she asks.

"Yeah. I was gonna see if I could get a ride with Jack when he goes home." He normally leaves sometime around four, which will give me time to deal with my phone before the store closes.

She nods her head as I pass her the glasses to put into the dishwasher, just as the doorbell rings.

We look at each other. "Who can that be?" she asks. "And how did they get in through the gate?" She looks out through the window. "Oh… Jack's doing some work up by the entrance. I guess he let them in, whoever they are." She turns to me. "Do you mind getting the door?" she asks. "Just while I finish this?"

"Of course not."

I go out into the hallway feeling perfectly safe in the knowledge that Jack won't have let in anyone untoward. Pulling open the door, though, my heart stops beating and my mouth drops open.

The man looks nearly as shocked as I feel and stares at me for a few seconds before reaching into his jacket pocket.

"I—I've got your phone," he says, sounding a little nervous, and handing it to me.

"Thank you," I reply. I don't ask how he found me, and it doesn't really matter. What matters is getting away from him, before he starts asking awkward questions, so I go to shut the door, right at the same moment as I notice Jack. He's walking up the driveway. He gives me a nod and a 'thumbs-up' sign and I know he'll have let the man in. I don't know what his game is, but my immediate thought is to march down the driveway and give him a piece of my mind.

The man turns, obviously having noticed my distraction. Then he looks back at me again.

"Is that your boyfriend?" he asks, his voice sounding more normal now. "From the restaurant last week? Is that why you ran out on me on Saturday night? Because you really do have a boyfriend after all, and you felt bad about what we did… about sleeping with me?" He fires his questions at me, one after the other, a confused expression on his face.

"No," I reply, wishing I'd been able to close the door now, although a part of me wants to justify myself. I mean, does he actually think I could date one man and lose my virginity to another? "I didn't lie to you on Saturday night. Jack is our gardener."

He gives me a weird look that I don't understand. "So what?" he says. "You think a gardener can't be your boyfriend?"

I shake my head and take a step toward him. "No. That's not what I meant. What I meant was that I don't have a boyfriend at all, and the night you saw me and Jack in the restaurant, we were having an evening out… as friends, just like I told you." I can feel myself blushing. "I'm really grateful to you for returning my phone," I say, feeling embarrassed now that he's in front of me, his eyes boring into mine, and I'm transported back to Saturday night, remembering how it felt to be underneath him, his hard, naked body on top of mine… "But I have to go."

I push the door closed, but he raises his hand and stops me. "Wait," he says. "Just wait a minute."

"Why?" I ask, maybe a little harshly.

"Because I feel like I'm getting this all wrong, and I really don't want to." I stare at him, feeling even more confused now. What does he mean by that? He takes a deep breath. "The phone isn't the only thing I've got to return to you," he adds and while he's speaking, he reaches into his other pocket and pulls out a box. He opens it before turning it around and handing it to me. "I found this on my bedroom floor," he says, not even remotely embarrassed to be telling me that, doubtless knowing that we'll both be thinking about what we were doing in his bedroom. I know I am, anyway. "The clasp was broken, so I took it and got it fixed. I hope that's okay?"

My eyes are now filled with tears and, although I take the box from him, the contents are a blur. Still, I know what's inside it. "Thank you," I whisper. I'm so confused now. He's obviously gone out of his way to find out who I am and where I live. He's also fixed my necklace for me… and yet going to bed with me was a mistake. He said so himself. In that case, why didn't he just throw my necklace away, dump my phone and forget all about me?

"I know who you are," he says softly, still staring at me. "I know you're Charles' daughter, and that your name's Lottie – or at least, that's what your father used to call you."

"You knew my father?" I ask, saying the only thing that comes into my head.

"Yeah, of course." He smiles, just slightly.

I nod. "I suppose that's why you were at the party. It makes sense…"

He holds out his hand and I take it. It swamps mine and he shakes very gently. "I suppose I should introduce myself," he says, and I feel myself blush, thinking about what we've already done together, without bothering about introductions. "I'm Paul Lewis," he says.

Now I know my mouth has dropped open. "You are?" He's the man my dad invested in? The one who became a friend; the one he always told me he was most proud of; the one he trusted more than anyone else.

"Yeah… what of it?" He looks confused again.

"My dad always used to talk about you when I was little," I explain, still clutching his hand, and looking into his deep blue eyes. He laughs, and all my nerves tingle.

"That's a good way to make a guy feel old," he says eventually.

"Sorry," I murmur.

"Hey. Don't be sorry," he says. "C—Can I come in?" he asks, stammering slightly.

"Sure, if you want to." I stand to one side, letting him pass, unable to believe I forgot my manners that badly. "I'm really sorry."

He turns to face me as I shut the door. "I just said… I don't want you to be sorry," he murmurs, taking a step closer and looking down into my eyes. "But I'd really like you to tell me why you ran out on me on Saturday night."

I can feel the blush spreading up my face. The last thing I want to do is to have to explain how it felt when he apologized for making the mistake of taking me to bed. That would be beyond humiliating. "I—I shouldn't have done… what we did," I murmur.

He moves closer still, so he's almost touching me and I lower my gaze to his tie, which is pale gray in colour, but then he places his forefinger underneath my chin and slowly raises my face to his.

"Why not?" he asks, his voice soft and gentle, his eyes burning into mine now. "Didn't you enjoy it?"

"Yes," I reply immediately, without thinking.

He smiles. "Well then…"

I don't know what to say next, and it feels awkward standing in the hallway with him this close, my head filled with images of the two of us together, my ears filled with his apologies. "Would you like a coffee?" I offer.

He moves away, just a fraction, seemingly surprised by my question. "Um… sure," he replies.

I know I should take him to the living room, but that feels a bit too formal. And besides, I don't want any more strained silences. Hopefully, with Mrs Hemsworth there, we can avoid that.

"This way," I say quietly, and lead him down to the kitchen.

Paul

I follow her down the hallway, by-passing the living room. For a moment, I wonder where she's taking me. Perhaps it's somewhere more private? Maybe she wants to talk some more… or, better still, to re-live Saturday night? *No, don't be an idiot.* It can't be that. She seems really embarrassed about the fact that we made love. Actually, if I'm being honest, she seems to regret it, and as I watch her hips swaying in front of me, I feel utterly despondent about that. She ran because she feels we shouldn't have done it? And yet, she definitely said she wanted to at the time. I know she did. That has to mean she liked the idea, but not the execution… but she just told me she enjoyed it. Was she just being polite, or have I missed something? Man, I'm confused.

Focusing on where we're going, I realize all of a sudden, that she's taking me to the kitchen, just as she pushes the door open and stands to one side to let me pass. I didn't expect that, but a part of me feels kinda reassured that she's treating me so informally. A lot of people think they have to stand on ceremony with me, and I'm really much happier just kicking back in the kitchen or the den, with a coffee or a beer.

"Hello?" I look up at the sound of a female voice and see a middle-aged woman standing over by the sink. She's got slightly graying hair and a fuller figure, with a flowery apron tied around her waist. I vaguely recall seeing her on Saturday night when Charlotte… sorry, Lottie, brought me out here. But I assumed she was part of the catering crew. I guess not.

"This is our cook-housekeeper, Mrs Hemsworth," Lottie says, making the introductions. "Mrs Hemsworth, this is Paul Lewis."

Mrs Hemsworth wipes her hands on a towel and comes over, offering me hers. I take it and shake.

"Nice to meet you," she says, smiling, then she looks at Lottie.

"We came out here for coffee," Lottie explains.

Mrs Hemsworth raises her eyebrows but says nothing and I get the feeling that this isn't Lottie's usual course of action with guests.

"Let me get that for you," Mrs Hemsworth offers. "And I baked some brownies this morning. Sit yourselves down."

I'm not a great chocolate fan, but it would be rude to say 'no', so I take a seat at the island unit. Lottie sits beside me, pulling nervously on the cuffs of her thick sweater and I can't help notice the leather bracelets she's wearing again. I want to reach over and take her hands in mine. I want to tell her everything's gonna be okay; that whatever it is that's troubling her, we can work it out. If she's worried she might be pregnant, then she needs to know, I'm not going anywhere. If she's unsure about what we did together for some reason, then we can talk it through. If she needs reassurance from me that I'm not gonna disappear on her, I can give her that. But I'd rather do it without Mrs Hemsworth in the room.

"Mr Lewis…" Lottie glances up at me, although she's clearly talking to Mrs Hemsworth.

"Call me Paul," I interrupt, smiling at her. *I've been inside you, Lottie. I took your virginity, at least use my first name.*

"Okay, Paul… He called round to return my phone," she continues, explaining my presence. "And my necklace." *I called round because I wanted to see you. Returning your phone and necklace were just good excuses.*

"That was kind of him," Mrs Hemsworth replies, bringing over two cups of coffee and putting a plate of brownies in front of us. "It saves you going out and buying a new one, anyway."

"You were going to buy a new necklace?" I ask.

"No." Lottie smiles. "I was going to buy a new phone."

"Oh. I see. Why? You could've just come and got it back from me."

"Except I didn't even know your name…" Her voice fades and she looks down at the countertop, and I understand what she might have meant about regretting what we did together. She let me make love to her and take her virginity, without even knowing my name. I guess that probably didn't make her feel too great about herself. But if she'd just waited around for a few minutes more, we could have dealt with it. I know it's not the usual way of doing things, but I could've introduced myself. I think we could've even laughed about it. I could've explained that my desperation to be inside her made me forget everything else, including using a condom and telling her my name, because I'd kinda forgotten it myself at the time. All she had to do was wait. She must see that, surely?

"You know where I live," I reason.

She blushes. "I know, but it… it didn't feel right."

It didn't feel right for her to come back and get her phone? Jesus. What did she think I was gonna do?

Mrs Hemsworth has gone back over to the sink and is humming to herself and I wonder whether Lottie brought me back here so she'd have someone with her; so she wouldn't have to sit with me by herself. Is she scared of me? God, I hope not. Or is it that she just wants to avoid talking about Saturday night? I want her to feel comfortable with me, in any situation, so neither of those thoughts is sitting very well with me.

"What are you doing for the holidays?" I ask, just to make conversation.

She glances up at me. "Staying here, trying my best to ignore Catrina and the twins," she replies. There's a note of sadness in her voice, which I like even less than my thoughts about her motives for bringing me into the kitchen.

"Is that easy?" I ask, trying to make light of the situation.

She smiles. "Not really, no."

We both take a sip of our coffee and she pulls forward the plate of brownies. "Help yourself," she says and I take one, to be polite. After one bite, though, I think I may have been converted to chocolate.

"That's amazing." I wait until I've finished chewing to praise Mrs Hemsworth's cooking.

"They are good, aren't they?" she replies, taking one for herself, breaking off a piece and putting it into her mouth. Watching her chew makes me want to kiss her. Hard.

"With someone around who cooks like that for you, I'm surprised you look as good as you do," I tell her, lowering my voice just slightly.

She blushes and I know she's remembering that I've seen her naked, and maybe I'm not playing fair, but I want her to know that I've got no regrets about Saturday. None whatsoever. Hell, I don't even regret forgetting the condom. Not anymore. Whatever the consequences.

"I—I don't live here most of the time," she murmurs.

"Oh yeah… You're at Virginia Tech," I say, recalling what she told me in the car on Saturday night. "What do you study?"

"Architecture," she replies, speaking a little louder and turning to look at me.

"Do you enjoy it?" I ask.

She nods her head with enthusiasm. "Yes. I do."

"And that's the field you wanna go into?" I enquire. "When you leave college, I mean."

"Yes. It's not easy to get into…" She falls silent.

"What's wrong?"

"Oh… nothing."

I turn to face her. "It's clearly something. Tell me." *Talk to me; tell me what you're thinking. I'm no expert on relationships, but as far as I'm aware, communication is a vital part of making them work. And now I've found you, I wanna make this work.*

She looks up at me. "It's just that my father was going to help me out. I know I should've wanted to get by on my own, but it's a really hard field to get a head start in, and he knew a few people and was going to just give them my name and see if they could put in a good word for me.

I fully expected to start at the bottom and work my way up, but just the introduction would have been useful. Now… well, I'm gonna have to do it by myself." I can see the self doubt and lack of confidence written all over her face.

"I'll help you," I tell her, without hesitating for a moment.

She leans back and stares at me. "You don't have to. And besides, you're in computer gaming, aren't you?"

I smile. "Yeah. But thanks to your dad, I know all kinds of people." I realize I don't even know how old she is, or when she'll be graduating. "When are you gonna be leaving college?" I ask.

"Next summer," she replies.

"So, I guess that makes you about twenty-one?" I ask and she nods. "Only twelve years younger than me then," I add without thinking, and I let out a sigh. She frowns, clearly confused. "I was talking to a guy at the party on Saturday," I say quickly, so she can't ask why working out her age, when compared to mine, should bother me so much. In most ways, it doesn't, but I guess it does help with making sense of her fears and her discomfort over Saturday night. I should have been more of a grown-up, for once in my life. I should've taken more time… more care of her.

"Oh?" She interrupts my train of thought.

"Yeah." I focus on our conversation once more. "His name's Drew Anderson. Your dad started him off in business about seven or eight years ago. I guess he's in his late twenties now. Anyway, his company makes a new kind of insulation material, and I know he works with all kinds of construction companies. If you want me to, I could speak to him and see if he can make some introductions for you."

Her eyes widen. "You'd do that?"

I'd do so much more than that to make things right with you. "Of course," I say out loud. "I'll speak with him in the New Year and put the two of you in touch with each other."

"Thank you," she says and I notice tears brimming in her eyes. I'm not sure why she'd be crying over anything I've just said, but I don't like the idea.

"You don't have to thank me," I whisper, leaning into her just slightly. I finish off my coffee and notice on the kitchen clock that it's gone three-thirty. "I should probably get out of here." I've been with her for over an hour, and the last thing I need is to bump into Catrina – or her daughters.

"So soon?" Her words, and the hint of disappointment behind them bring back that flare in my chest. "Thank you," she adds quietly.

"What for?"

"For offering to help me find some work after graduation… and for bringing back my phone and my necklace."

I get to my feet and move my stool to one side so I can stand right next to her. "I didn't come here just to return the phone, or the necklace," I tell her, twisting her around on her stool so she's facing me.

"You didn't?" She looks up at me with wide eyes.

"No. I wanted to see you again."

"Oh." She seems shocked.

"Can I take you to dinner this evening?" I add quickly, in case she thinks I'm only interested in taking her to bed.

"Dinner?" she says, hesitating. She glances over toward the sink and I follow her line of sight and see Mrs Hemsworth giving her a reassuring smile before she turns and continues with her chores. I wonder why Lottie needed the housekeeper's approval. That seems kinda odd to me.

"What do you say?" I ask.

"Thank you. I'd love to come," she replies, giving me a very sweet smile.

I'm not sure whether to jump for joy, or collapse in relief. I don't do either – because they'd both be embarrassing. Instead, I take her hand in mine. "I'll come by and pick you up at seven?"

She nods. "I'll be ready."

I'm back at work, although I doubt I'll be able to concentrate on anything, but I figure I should at least show willing. Maureen has a couple of messages for me, and I pick them up and go into my office, closing the door behind me and fixing myself a coffee.

I put my feet up on my desk and lean back into my chair. I'm still feeling mystified by a lot of what's going on with Lottie, but right now, I'm just thankful that she's giving me another chance; that her evident regrets over what happened last time we were together aren't so bad that she doesn't ever want to see me again.

My phone beeps, bringing me back to reality and I sit forward, picking it up and checking the screen. It's a message, from Fin.

— *Just thought I'd check in and see how things are going? Fin*

I type out a quick reply:

— *Better than they were. I've found her. She's Charles' daughter and I'm taking her to dinner tonight. P*

He comes back right away.

— *Charles' daughter? What a small world. Remember what we talked about. Go easy on the girl (emphasis on the word 'girl'). F*

— *Give me some credit. P*

I feel a little offended, although I know he's just thinking about Lottie.

— *I do. Let me know how it goes. F*

I'm about to put my phone down again when I realize I should probably book a table for tonight. I want take Lottie to my favorite restaurant, which is a great seafood place in the center of the city. I smile to myself as I dial their number, remembering how at ease she looked shelling mussels in the restaurant last week. I guess she likes seafood, in which case, she's gonna love this place. Knowing that she's Charles' daughter makes sense of why she looked so at home in those surroundings. Unlike me, she was brought up among the finer things in life. I start to chuckle at the irony of that, just as the call connects and I force myself to concentrate.

Once the table's booked, I wonder if I should maybe order some flowers. That's not something I've ever done before, but I seem to be doing a lot of things for the first time with Lottie: taking her back to my place, thinking about having her spend the night, wanting to date properly, being considerate, asking for kisses, forgetting the condom…

falling in love. I can't be completely sure about that last one, being as it's never happened to me before, and unlike all those other 'first time' things, it's harder to work out – even with the benefit of hindsight – but when I was driving back from her place earlier, I was thinking about the fact that I missed her already. I'd only been away from her for maybe five minutes, and I wanted to turn around and go back. I got to thinking about how, even when I'm not with her, she's the only thing can think about, that seeing her seems to make me breathless, being with her makes me smile, just looking at her makes me happy, and the thought of not doing any of that makes me desolate. I figured out she was different the moment I met her; on the way back here, I think I figured out why. I'm in love with her. Well, like I say, I think I am, and that being the case, I may as well add buying flowers to the list of firsts. I go onto the Internet and find a local florist, going through their list of arrangements. I know red roses are traditionally romantic, but the white ones look good to me, and they feel kinda appropriate for Lottie, for some reason. I'm about to call them up when I think again. Is it too much? She seemed really unsure about me earlier and, while she said 'yes' to dinner, I don't wanna push her too far too fast. I don't want her to get the idea that I'm all gestures and no substance. I get the feeling I've only just got my foot in the door. If she thinks I've got some kind of ulterior motive, she might just slam that door in my face.

Chapter Nine

Lottie

"What was that all about?" Mrs Hemsworth asks, as I come back into the kitchen. She looks up at me and stops clearing away the cups, her hands resting on her hips expectantly. I just took Paul to the door and he confirmed our arrangements for dinner. He didn't even try to kiss me and, I've got to be honest, having seen him again, I felt a little disappointed by that. He really is gorgeous.

"Sorry?" I glance over at her and then pretend to pick at a loose thread on my sweater.

"Why did you need my approval to go out for dinner with that young man?" she asks.

"I didn't."

"Oh… so that's why you looked over at me, all doubtful and unsure of yourself, was it?" I never could get anything past Mrs Hemsworth.

"You know what happened on Saturday night," I say by way of explanation, even though she doesn't know the whole story. She doesn't even know the half of it. "I'm not sure what he wants from me."

"Well," she says, coming closer and putting a hand on my shoulder, looking me in the eyes. "There's only one way to find that out… Dip your toes in the water and see what happens."

"And if there are sharks in there?"

She shakes her head. "I don't think there will be," she replies. "He seemed like a really nice man. He brought your phone back, and got your necklace fixed too."

"I know."

"Well… why not give the guy a chance?"

"I am. I'm having dinner with him."

She puts her arm around me. "What I meant was, don't be so unsure of yourself. Live a little. Let yourself be happy. You never know, you might like it." She gives me a squeeze, then lets me go. "Now," she says, with purpose. "I think you'll find you've got a date in a couple of hours. And, unless I'm very much mistaken, that means you should be upstairs getting ready."

"So soon?" It's not even four yet. That means I've got three hours at least.

"Of course," she replies, giving me a nudge. "This is part of the fun. Go. Enjoy…" She nods toward the door and I take the cue and go out and up the stairs to my room.

I'm not entirely sure how I'm going to fill three hours with getting ready, but I start by putting on some music and taking off my clothes, looking at myself in the full-length mirror, in the hope that I'll get some inspiration from the bare canvas, as it were. After a few minutes' reflection, I suppose a bath would be a good place to start, so I go into my bathroom and turn on the faucet, adding some scented oils. I check the cabinet above the sink and find a new razor, putting it on the side of the bath, as a thought occurs to me. Heather shaves herself 'down there'. I know this because she decided to use a sales bonus she got paid a few months ago, to get a wax, rather than shaving. She hated it. She said it was the most painful thing she'd ever experienced and she'd rather die than go through that again. She told me she'd stick to shaving from then on. It's not something I've ever considered before, but I wonder if I could try it too. Do men prefer women to be shaved 'down there'? I wonder, sitting down on the closed toilet seat while I wait for the bath to fill. Is that one of the reasons Paul said he regretted what we'd done? God, I wish I understood what's going on. I wish I knew what he expected of me.

An hour later, I'm wrapped in a towel and I wander back into my bedroom, feeling clean, and buffed. I decided to throw caution to the wind and shave… everywhere, and I have to admit, it feels really smooth and comfortable.

I settle down on the bed and paint my toenails with pale pink nail polish, using the same shade on my fingers, lying back for a while and letting it dry. I've never really given myself a pampering session like this and, I'm surprised by how much I'm enjoying it. Once I'm sure my nails are dry, I sit at my dresser and do my makeup. I don't usually wear much anyway, and I don't want to tonight either. I wouldn't feel like myself if I was made up like Catrina or the twins. Even so, I want to make an effort and, while I wear pretty much the same things as usual, I take a little longer putting them on. I'm mid-way through when I hear my stepmom and her daughters return from the spa. They're really noisy, even though they're downstairs, so I turn the music up a little and concentrate on my mascara, safe in the knowledge that they won't disturb me. I don't mean a damn thing to them.

Once I'm happy with the effect, I dry my hair, leaving it long, but curling it a little more than I normally do. By the time I've finished, it's nearly six-fifteen, and I realize I haven't even decided what to wear yet. I've got no idea where we're going, but somehow I doubt a skirt and sweater are going to cut it. Luckily, most of my clothes are still here; I have little call for cocktail dresses at college, so at least I've got a choice – a grand choice of three. I pull them all out and put them on the bed, side by side. I dismiss the black one straight away. I know it looks okay on me, but it also reminds me of the dress Paul's date was wearing the other night, so I push it to one side. That leaves a navy blue one, which is embellished with sequins in a leaf pattern, and comes down to my mid thigh. Or there's the deep red one, which is a little longer, and is made of lace. It's got spaghetti straps and a flesh-colored lining, which comes down to a few inches below my panty-line, so it's perfectly decent. The blue one, with its sequins seems to scream 'party' to me. The deep red one is a little more understated and perhaps more suitable for a restaurant, especially if I put it with my black cashmere wrap. I nod my head. Decision made.

Mrs Hemsworth must have let Paul in through the main gate, because I hear the doorbell ring at seven on the dot and race down the stairs to get there before anyone else.

Pulling the door open, he stands before me, looking glorious in a dark gray suit, with matching tie. He looks me up and down for a few moments without saying a word.

"Is this okay?" I ask, feeling nervous all of a sudden.

"Yeah. It's perfect," he replies, smiling at last. "It's absolutely perfect. And you look very beautiful."

I can feel myself blushing. "Thank you," I whisper.

"What's going on?" Catrina's voice makes me jump and I spin around. She's standing by the entrance to the living room, with Chelsea beside her. I don't know where Christa is – and, frankly, I don't care.

"I'm going out for dinner," I say.

"You are?"

"Yes."

"With Mr Lewis?" She walks forward very slowly, eyeing me critically.

"With Paul, yes." Her eyes flicker with anger.

"And if we don't leave now, we're gonna be late," he says, taking my hand and pulling me out the door.

"Bye!" I call over my shoulder, giving them a vague wave.

Paul leads me to his car and helps me into the passenger seat, giving me time to swivel around and get comfortable before he closes the door and goes around the other side. Once he's seated, he switches on the engine and revs it a few times, then drives off.

I can't help giggling.

"I hate showing off like that," he says, turning and smiling at me. "But sometimes you just kinda have to."

I'm still chuckling as he pulls out of the driveway and onto the street.

"It wasn't that funny," he says.

"It's not that," I reply. "It was the look on Catrina's face."

He laughs himself now. "It was a picture," he replies, then pauses. "I take it from the fact that she got you to pose as a member of staff on

Saturday evening, that you don't have a great relationship with your stepmom?"

I stop laughing. "That would be the understatement of the century." I sigh deeply. "I really wanted to get along with her when she and Dad got together, but she just made it impossible."

"You must have known her when she was his secretary, surely?"

"I did, but that was business and Dad was good and keeping his personal life and his work life separate. I only met her on the odd occasion, and she was always really nice to me – probably because my dad was there and she was on her best behavior."

I turn and look at him, and notice he's nodding his head. "She changed when your mom died, didn't she?" he asks.

"Oh God, yeah." I pause for a moment, remembering how bad it was back then. "Dad went into shock," I tell him.

"I remember," he says.

"I tried to be there, but Catrina always seemed to get to him first. I didn't want to have to compete for his attention – or his affection." I've never really said that to anyone, but sitting in the dark, in Paul's car, it's easy to be myself for once.

"He didn't see it like that, Lottie. I promise you. He loved you."

"I know he did," I tell him. "I just wish she could've left us alone to grieve together, instead of always getting in the way, telling me to leave my dad alone, and then shutting herself away with him. I felt so… excluded." He forms his lips into a thin line, like he's angry or something. "Did I say something wrong?" I ask.

"No." He turns to me, just briefly before focusing back on the road. "No, not at all. I just felt kinda mad for a minute that you were treated like that. You were what? Eighteen or nineteen at the time?"

"I was eighteen when mom died. It was only a few weeks before I was due to go to college. I think Catrina was glad to see the back of me, really. It meant she could make her moves on Dad without any interference from me."

He nods his head slowly. "I was blown away when they got married," he says.

"So was I. I knew she was plotting something, but I didn't see it coming – probably because I wasn't here so much."

"She didn't seem like his type, not to me anyway," he adds.

"She isn't, but she likes money and she's manipulative. And I'm being a bitch, aren't I?"

He smiles. "No. From what I've seen, you're just being accurate." He glances over at me again, just briefly. "How bad is it?" he asks.

"When Dad was alive it wasn't too bad," I tell him truthfully. "But then he died and… well, it was awful…"

"I wanted to be here," he says, and I can hear the sorrow in his voice. "I was on the west coast at the time and couldn't get back – not even for the funeral."

"Well, Catrina arranged it in double-quick time for some reason. I think she just wanted the whole thing over and done with, so she could get on with her life. So, I'm not surprised you couldn't get back."

"I really regretted that," he says, then stops, seeming to think for a moment. "I still do," he adds.

I stare at him. He obviously cared about my father and I decide to tell him what it really feels like. "Even that soon after his death," I say quietly, "I already felt out of place in my own home." I let out a half laugh. "That's why I felt the full irony when you told me on Saturday that I didn't belong at the party. I didn't. Not in any sense of the word."

We pull up at traffic lights and he turns to look at me. "I'm sorry," he says softly. "If I'd known who you really were, I'd never have said something so insensitive."

"It wasn't your fault."

He looks out through the windshield again, checking the lights. They're still red. "Can't you tell Catrina to leave?" he asks as they change and he pulls away again.

"I wish. God, my life would be so much simpler if I could do that…"

"What does that mean?" He glances over again, looking confused.

"It means it's her house now."

"What?" He raises his voice a little, obviously shocked.

"Dad left the house to Catrina," I explain.

"He did?"

"Yes. And she loves reminding me of that at every chance. She loves letting me know that I'm only there because she's allowing it, not because I have a right to be. I'm pretty sure she only lets me stay because then she can control my money."

"I'm sorry?" he says. "She can do what?"

"Control my money. Dad may have left the house to her, but I got all the money."

"Thank God for that," he says, seemingly relieved. "I was starting to think Charles had taken leave of his senses."

"No," I reply, smiling. "He changed his will after he married her, leaving his property to her, but he stated that the remainder of his estate – namely all his money – was to be held in trust until I graduated, or turned twenty-five."

Paul falls silent. "How do you feel about that?" he asks.

"Ordinarily, I'd feel just fine," I say. "I don't blame him for making me wait. Dad had seen a few people screw up their lives by getting money too early on. He made a point of never investing in anyone until they'd at least proved themselves able to see something through – even if it was just studying for a degree."

He pulls into a parking space at the side of the road and turns to me. "You said 'ordinarily'," he says, shifting in his seat to face me. "What did you mean by that?"

"Only that I wish Dad hadn't made the mistake of making Catrina the trustee. That's what I meant about her controlling my money."

"What's she done with it?" He leans closer, his eyes fixed on mine.

"I can't prove anything, but I'm fairly sure she's been using the money to finance her lifestyle. Either way, she hasn't been paying my allowance. That stopped as soon as Dad died…"

"Seriously?" he interrupts.

I nod my head.

"Have you spoken to anyone about this?" he asks.

"Like who?"

"Like a lawyer. You need to get your allowance paid, and you need to ensure the capital sum isn't being wasted by your stepmom. It's your money, Lottie."

I laugh. "I can't afford a lawyer, Paul. Dad may have bought my apartment for me, but I share it with a friend, and she helps with the bills. I'm working evenings and weekends just to buy food and pay for bus fare and books, although my job's in a bookstore, which means I get discount…" I let my voice fade.

He huffs out a long sigh. "Let me help you."

"I can't." I feel tears welling in my eyes. That happens when people are nice to me. I didn't expect so much kindness from him; it's taken me by surprise. "And anyway, I don't really care about the money. I'd rather have my dad back…"

He reaches out and takes my hand in his. "I know you would, but I don't think he'd like the way you're being treated – do you?"

I stare at him for a moment and find that I can't disagree with him.

Paul

"You don't have to make a decision now," I say, sensing her discomfort. "Think about it. Just remember, I've got a really friendly lawyer, and I can help you deal with this, if you want me to."

She nods her head, although she doesn't say a word. Judging from the tears that are still brimming in her eyes, I'm not sure she's capable of speech.

"Shall we go in?" I suggest, because I think she needs a change of subject – and scene.

"Yes," she whispers. "Thank you."

I get out of the car and walk around to help her out, trying hard to keep my anger in check. I'm so livid with Catrina, I feel like driving back there and demanding she gives Lottie what she owes her, but I doubt that will help. Not with someone like Catrina.

We go inside the restaurant and the head waiter, a guy called Henri, comes straight over.

"Mr Lewis," he says, smiling broadly. "It's been a while." He looks at Lottie, seemingly surprised, but then I can understand that. I don't think I've ever brought a woman here before. I've brought Fin and Brad, my sister and her husband, and my parents, but never any of the women I've been with.

"This is Lottie Hudson," I tell him.

"It's a pleasure, miss," he says, giving her a slight bow.

Even in the dim candlelight, I can see Lottie blush and I take her hand in mine, giving it a light squeeze.

Henri turns and starts walking through the restaurant, which is about half full. "I've given you your usual table, Mr Lewis," he says over his shoulder.

"Perfect," I reply and Lottie looks up at me, raising her eyebrows.

Henri leads us through to the back corner of the restaurant. I like it down here. It's secluded and, even when this place gets busy, it's still quiet enough to hold a conversation. He holds out his hand to take Lottie's wrap, which she gives to him, and I swear my heart just stopped beating. I'd realized she was wearing a really sexy lace dress the moment I saw her on the doorstep at her house… well, at Catrina's house. I hadn't realized she looked this good in it. Henri moves to one side and holds Lottie's chair while she sits, although I'm tempted to ask him to wait, just so I can look at her for a little longer.

I sit opposite her and find that I can't stop staring. She's just perfect.

"Would you like something to drink?" Henri offers.

"Two glasses of Pol Roger," I say and he nods, turning away.

"Champagne?" Lottie queries. "Are we celebrating?"

I smile. "Well, I am."

"What are you celebrating?" She leans forward, like she's expecting me to announce it's my birthday, or something.

I inch nearer to her too, so we're as close as we can get without one of us standing up. "Finding you," I tell her, keeping my voice low.

She blushes and lets her eyes drop to my tie. She did that earlier this afternoon, when I called at the house. She's very easily embarrassed and, for a moment, I wonder how she'd react if I told her I'm in love with her. Seeing her again has made me realize it's true, but somehow

I doubt it would go down too well. For some reason, she's still got doubts about me.

"Do you want to look at the menu?" I suggest.

She raises her eyes to mine and smiles at me gratefully. "Yes," she says and sits back again, opening the large white menu.

She studies for a few moments, then looks up at me. "I'm spoilt for choice," she murmurs.

"Just have whatever you most feel like," I tell her. "I'll bring you back again so you can try something different."

She bites her bottom lip and looks back down again.

"What's the octopus like?" she asks, raising her eyes to mine again.

"Octopus," I reply and she giggles.

"Thanks. That was helpful."

"Well, personally I think the best thing about that dish is probably the capers, but that's because I'm not the world's greatest fan of octopus."

She studies me for a moment, then shakes her head. "And the lobster?"

"Can't go wrong with lobster," I reply.

"So you like lobster?" she asks.

"I love lobster. I'm going to have that to start."

"I think I might join you," she says. "And I think I'll have the monkfish for my main course."

I nod my head. "A woman of taste."

"What are you going to have?" she asks, closing her menu.

"The salmon, I think."

At that moment, Henri comes over with our champagne.

"We're ready to order," I tell him, once he's deposited the glasses. Normally, he'd send one of the waiters over, but he stands, looking down at us expectantly. We are being honored tonight…

I give him our order, and add a bottle of Montrachet Grand Cru, and he leaves us alone again, with a smile to me and a bow to Lottie.

"He's very sweet," she says.

"I think he's very sweet on you," I tell her and she blushes again. "He never normally gives me this kind of service."

"Well, I'm sure that's because you're a good customer, who's just ordered a really expensive bottle of wine. It's not because of me," she says, firmly.

"Yeah. It is."

I raise my champagne flute and she copies my action. "Cheers," I say and we clink glasses. "Here's to finding each other." She doesn't comment, but gives me a very slight smile and takes a sip of her drink.

"That's lovely," she says, putting it back down on the table.

I'm tempted to tell her that it's nowhere near as lovely as she is, but I don't want to embarrass her again. I want to talk to her; find out about her.

"You like seafood?" I ask, because it's a reasonable place to start.

"I like a lot of things. Mrs Hemsworth's ribs take some beating," she replies, smiling more broadly. "You may think that my upbringing makes me used to places like this, but there was nothing Dad liked more than sitting in the kitchen, elbow deep in a bowl of ribs. And I am my father's daughter."

I'd kinda worked that out for myself and I wonder if that's one of the many reasons I'm so attracted to Lottie; simply because she's the daughter of the man I've always respected more than any other – with the exception of my own father.

"I need to get friendly with Mrs Hemsworth," I say, taking a long sip of champagne. "She sounds like my kinda cook."

"She's amazing. She makes great lasagna too."

"I'm liking her more and more," I joke.

"And she keeps me sane."

"That's it. I'm adopting her." I pause for a moment. "Or is there a Mr Hemsworth who's gonna object to that?"

"No," Lottie replies. "She was married, very briefly a long time ago. It didn't end well. I think he ran off with another woman, but don't quote me on that. It's not something she talks about."

"He gave up lasagna and ribs… for a woman? What an idiot," I joke and Lottie laughs. "I like that sound," I say, seriously.

"What sound?"

"You… laughing. It suits you." I reach across the table and take her hand in mine. "I doubt you've had much to laugh about in the last few months, have you?"

She shakes her head. "No, not much."

"Let let me help you laugh again."

She smiles, and raises her glass. "To laughter," she says and I clink my glass against hers in a worthy toast.

She puts her drink back down and stares at me for a moment. "Can I ask you a question?" she says, tilting her head to one side.

"Sure." I've got no idea what's coming, but I guess if we're gonna make this work, I've gotta be willing to open up to her, not just expect her to tell me all about herself. It's a two-way street…

"Why did you call your company Big Bear?" she says, after just a slight hesitation. I wasn't expecting that, and I chuckle. She looks down at the table and adds, "I think I told you already that my dad used to speak about you a lot. He said your company was called Big Bear, but he never explained why."

"Probably because I never told him," I tell her, smiling across the table as she finally looks up at me. "I've never told anyone."

"Oh… I'm sorry. I didn't realize it was a secret. You don't have to tell me."

"Hey." I reach across the table for her hand and clasp it tight. "I wanna tell you." Her lips twitch upward and she leans forward in anticipation. She's probably gonna think I'm a complete sap, but what the hell. I want her to know all about me. Childhood secrets and all. "When I was a kid," I explain, keeping hold of her hand, "I used to be scared of the dark. I'm not just talking about feeling a little bit afraid, I'm talking about complete night terrors. I used to scream the building down." She smiles and nods her head, like she understands. "Anyway, for my fifth birthday, my dad got me an enormous pale brown teddy bear, probably around four feet high. And he sat in the corner of my room. My mom told me he was there to protect me from the dark and, as far as I was concerned, he kept me safe. I stopped being afraid."

"And he was called 'Big Bear'?" she guesses.

"Yeah. Not the most original name, but that wasn't really the point. Then, I met your dad, just after I'd finished at M.I.T. We talked, and after a while, he made the offer to invest in me. And for the first time in years, the fear came back. I guess there was still a part of me that remembered what it felt like to be a frightened kid. I was about to take a huge risk with my whole life, and someone else's money, and I remember going home that night and thinking that I wished I could take Big Bear on that journey with me. I know that sounds pathetic for a twenty-two year old guy, but that was how it felt. So, I decided to use the name instead. In a strange way, once I'd made that decision, I knew nothing could go wrong." I've really let my guard down now. I've shown her a side of myself that I've never shown to another living soul. "And if you ever repeat that story…"

She draws a cross over her heart with her right forefinger, interrupting me with her action. "Cross my heart," she says. "Your secret's safe with me. Although I can't believe you've managed not to tell anyone before now."

"You'd be amazed at the stories I've come up with over the years to avoid revealing the truth," I reply.

"You're good at telling stories?" Her eyes narrow just slightly and I know she's asking if I'm good at lying.

"Only to people who don't matter," I reply and her mouth drops open. That floored her.

"I—I…" she starts to say, just as Henri arrives with our appetizers.

I wait for him to go, and then lean over to her. "You matter," I whisper, taking the plunge. She blushes, but smiles, and based on the sensation flooding my chest, I'd say my heart just burst with love for her.

Dinner was magnificent, as usual, but the conversation and company were better. We spent the evening talking about everything from food, to movies and music, her course at college and my work. We've laughed a lot too, and I can honestly say I've never had so much fun just talking. Actually, I've never had so much fun. Period. And once I've paid and tipped Henri very generously, he hands me Lottie's black shawl, which I wrap around her shoulders, letting my hands linger on her just a little longer than is strictly necessary. It feels good to touch her again, but I want more than that. I want a lot more.

I help Lottie into the car, knowing that our perfect evening has to end very soon, even though I don't want it to, and we drive home in silence. Me, because I'm feeling kinda low, in the certainty that, although we've had a great night, Lottie's still not ready to take things further yet. She's still got doubts about me I think, which means I've gotta work to gain her trust. Lottie, on the other hand, is quiet because she's tired – evidenced by the fact that she can barely keep her eyes open.

She has a card to let us in through the gates and hands it to me when we reach the house. I pass it back to her and start up the driveway.

Parking up right by the front steps, I switch off the engine and turn to face her.

"I don't want to leave you," I say and she looks up at me, wide-eyed. "Apart from anything else, I don't like the idea of you being here alone with Catrina and the twins."

She smiles. "It's fine. I'm pretty used them now." I'm not sure I believe her, but I can't argue. "And anyway," she adds, before I can say anything, "I've got Mrs Hemsworth."

"Yeah. And the gardener." I don't really know where that came from, but it's out there now.

"Yes, but he's only here three days a week." I guess she didn't notice my little fit of jealousy then. I don't even know why I feel like that. She's told me twice now that the guy is just a friend. My problem is that I keep remembering the way he kissed her fingers in the restaurant last week. There was something really intimate about that…

I decide I have to be honest with her. Earning her trust and her love means I've gotta give her my honesty. That's the very least I owe her. "The thought of leaving you with Catrina isn't the only reason I don't want to go," She tilts her head to one side. I guess she doesn't understand. "I want you," I say simply. It's hard to miss her gasp, even though it's quiet. "I want you with me. I want to spend some more time with you. I want to get to know you better. And I want to take you to bed again." I spell it out because I need to make sure she understands what I'm saying.

"You do?"

She's surprised? "Yeah. Being with you was amazing. It was incredible. And I want more."

She bites her bottom lip again, like she's not sure about something. I hope the 'something' isn't me.

"Hey," I say, reaching over and cupping her face with my hand, making sure she can't look away. "I get that you're new to all this, and if you need to slow it down, that's fine."

"But you just said…" She looks really puzzled now.

"Yeah. But just because I want you doesn't mean I can't wait. We can date for a while, if that's what you want. I'll wait for as long as you need me to."

She pulls back just slightly, although I manage to keep hold of her. "And while you're waiting?" Her voice has a definite tone of suspicion but I don't really understand what she's talking about.

"What do you mean?" I ask.

"I saw you with that blonde," she says. "You said she was just someone you know, which suggests there might be other people you know… and you're obviously a fairly regular visitor to that restaurant we went to tonight, presumably with other women. So, while you're waiting for me, will you be seeing your blonde friend – or someone like her?"

Well I'll be… She's interested. At least, she's jealous, and that means she's interested, and that has me so relieved and so filled up with stupid male pride, I can't help smiling.

"I've never taken another woman to that restaurant," I explain, keeping my voice really quiet and soft. "I reserve that place for the important people in my life, which means my parents, my sister, my friends… and you. And, while I'm waiting for you, I won't be seeing anyone – unless you count my family, because I'm going up to see them for the holidays. I'm leaving really early tomorrow."

"Sorry," she whispers. "I didn't mean to be so…" she's struggling for the word, and I could easily fill it in for her by saying 'jealous', but I don't want to make her feel any worse than she already does.

"Don't be sorry," I reply instead. "I don't want that." I move closer to her. "I just want you."

She looks into my eyes and I sense a change, like the fear, or uncertainty, or whatever it was, has suddenly evaporated. "You're going away?" she says.

"Yeah. Just for the holidays." She nods her head, looking a little sad, which is kinda gratifying. "Have you got your phone?" I ask her.

She reaches into her purse and hands it to me. "What do you want it for?" she asks.

I hand it back again. "Can you unlock it?" I ask her. She puts in the six digits and gives it to me. I go to her contacts list and add myself. "I've just put my number on there," I say, handing it back to her.

She looks down at the screen. "Don't you want mine?" she asks, raising her eyes to mine again.

"No."

Her eyes widen. "Why not?"

"Because if I have your number, I know I'll end up pulling over and sending you a message, or calling you before I get home. Hell, I might not even get to the end of the driveway," I tell her and she laughs, just lightly. "I don't wanna hassle you. But this way, if you wanna talk to me, you can, and I really hope you will. I'll answer your texts, or I'll pick up, anytime you call me. I've never let a woman call the shots like this before, Lottie, but I'm going to with you, because I want you to know that everything we do from now on is on your terms. You decide what happens, and you decide when." I lean in, really close to her, and caress her cheek with my fingertips. "I hope you get in touch real soon though," I whisper, "because I'm gonna miss you."

Chapter Ten

Lottie

As I close the door, I hear his car pull away. I don't dwell though. I don't even stop to think about what a wonderful evening I've had. I race up the stairs and go straight to my room, desperate to avoid any kind of confrontation with Catrina. It's only when I've closed my bedroom door and am leaning back against it that I realize the house is silent. I guess that means she's probably out herself. In a way I'm relieved, being as she'd almost certainly barge in here and demand to know why I thought I had a right to go out to dinner with 'Mr Lewis', but on reflection that just means postponing the inevitable until tomorrow.

I move away from the door, flicking on the lights, and go over and sit on the edge of my bed, my feelings in a turmoil. I've had a really lovely evening. We talked about so many different things, and I feel like I know him so much better than I did. At the same time though, I still feel confused. He told me he wants me. He made it very clear. He wants to go to bed with me again. And yet, I still can't forget the fact that he regretted it the first time. He apologized for heaven's sake. But now it seems he wants to do it again? Is that normal behavior? I've got absolutely no idea. I have no understanding of how these things are supposed to work. The only thing I do know is that when I'm with him, he makes me feel really good. He also makes me feel really good about myself. I flop back down on the bed and stare at the ceiling. Is this what love feels like, I wonder. Part of me really hopes so, because it's the only thing that explains the lack of logic going on here. It accounts for my humiliating level of jealousy, my overwhelming need to be with him all the time, my fear that he might not want me, and my euphoria when he said he did. It has to be love, doesn't it?

I let out a long, slow sigh and turn onto my side, wishing I knew more – not just about relationships in general, but about what's going on between Paul and me. Are we even in a relationship? He hasn't made that very clear. Wanting to take me to bed doesn't mean he wants anything long-term, does it? And he made a point of not giving me his phone number, although I suppose his reason for that was sound. Maybe he sensed my insecurity and wanted to give me the reassurance that I'm in control; that he's not going to push me into things I'm not ready for… If only I knew what I *was* ready for.

I wish I could see him again, and could ask him what it all means. But I can't. He's going away tomorrow for the holidays. He didn't even tell me when he was coming back. Tomorrow's Christmas Eve, so I guess he'll be gone for at least two days, maybe three. If we were in a relationship, he'd tell me things like that, wouldn't he? Or should I have asked? Does the fact that I didn't ask mean he'll think I'm not interested? And if he thinks I'm not interested, will he be tempted by other women? I sit up straight. He wouldn't… He told me he'd wait for me. He definitely said he wouldn't be seeing anyone except his family. And if there's one thing I do know, it's that I should at least try and trust him. I have to try.

I get undressed and go through to the bathroom, thinking back over the evening again, and all the wonderful things he said, the way he looked at me, the feeling of his fingers when he touched my cheek. I feel myself blush as the thought crosses my mind that I wish he'd done more than that, but I can't help myself. I want him too.

I put on some short pajamas and climb into bed, still feeling a little sad that I won't get to see him again until after the holidays. And that, if he stays with his family for too long, we won't get to see each other even then, because I'm due to go back to Virginia on the 28th. Maybe I should have told him that. But then he didn't ask about my plans either. Does that mean he's not interested in anything long-term? Is this just a 'fling' for him? Oh God. I feel like I'm going around in circles, getting nowhere.

I get up again and go over to my purse, which I left lying on the dresser. I pull out my phone and, while I'm walking back to the bed, I call up his details, going to my message app. I'm not going to tell him my plans, because then he might feel obligated to shorten his time with his family, and I don't want that. This is a time for families, and he's entitled to see them. But at least I can let him know I'm thinking about him.

I'm not sure what to type though, and I think back to what he said to me just before I got out of his car… 'I hope you get in touch real soon, because I'm gonna miss you.'

I suppose the response to that is simple really and I wouldn't be lying. I take a deep breath and start typing:

— *I'm gonna miss you too. Lottie.*

And then I press send, before I can get cold feet, or change my mind.

I climb back into bed, switching off the lights, so that if Catrina comes home, she'll think I'm asleep and hopefully leave me in peace, but I keep my phone clutched in my hand, so I'll know if Paul texts back.

I turn onto my side and look out the window. It's a clear night, the inky black sky filled with stars and I wish he were here with me, holding me in his strong arms and we were staring at the sky together. My phone beeps and I jump out of my skin. That was quick. I glance at the screen and read his message, my heart in my mouth.

— *Hello, beautiful. Didn't expect to hear from you so quickly. Well, that's nice to know. But now you've contacted me, I'll feel free to bombard you with messages, so you won't have time to miss me. Now, it's late. Go to bed, and dream of me. Paul x*

I can't stop myself from smiling at the fact that he's added a kiss to his message. Although I mustn't read too much into that. After all, Jack always adds kisses to his texts, and we're just friends. My smile doesn't fade though, as I tap out a reply.

— *I'm already in bed. Not sure I said this earlier, but thank you for a lovely evening. Sleep well. Lottie x*

I decide to add the kiss, just because he did, and press send.

His reply is almost immediate.

— *__Wish I was with you ;) The evening was my pleasure entirely. We'll do it again, real soon. Sweet dreams. Paul xx__*

He's put two kisses this time, but I decide to call it a night. Apart from the fact that we could go on like this forever, I'm getting tired. I turn over onto my back, letting my phone drop onto the bed beside me and, within moments, I'm fast asleep.

I wake up to a bright blue sky, the comforter wrapped around me, like a cocoon and that warm, satisfied feeling you get, knowing you've slept well and don't have anything to rush up for. I stretch my arms above my head then bring them down by my sides and my right hand lands on my phone. I can't help myself. I have to check to see if there's a message from him. I know there probably won't be, as he was leaving so early this morning, but even so…

The smile that forms on my lips is entirely involuntary, as I read his words.

— *__Good morning, beautiful. Hope you slept well. I did. I dreamt of you. Have a good day. Maybe talk later? Paul xx__*

He called me 'beautiful'. Again. And he dreamt about me? My smile widens and I feel my stomach flip over with excitement – at least I think that's what it is. It feels good, anyway.

I need the bathroom, but I delay long enough to type out a reply.

— *__I slept wonderfully well, thank you. Hope you have a safe journey. We can definitely talk later. Let me know when you get to your parents'. Where do they live, by the way? Lottie xx__*

I realize he didn't tell me that. Or that I forgot to ask.

I put down my phone on the mattress and leap out of bed, running for the bathroom. On my return, the screen is alight with a message.

— *__Good. I'm already half way there. Just stopped for coffee. I'll text you when I arrive. They live in Cape Elizabeth, Maine. Sorry, should have told you that. Call me if you need anything. Paul xx__*

I'm not sure what he thinks I'm going to need, but I'm grateful that he's thoughtful enough to make the offer.

— ***Thanks. Enjoy the coffee and drive safe. Lottie xx***

I wait for a few minutes, but he doesn't come back again and I work out that he's probably started driving again. It may be only just after nine, but I imagine he's keen to see his family and spend as much of the holidays as he can with them. Looking at the time, I suppose I should get up and face the day, so I go back into the bathroom and turn on the shower.

I had hoped that by coming down fairly late, I would have been able to avoid Catrina, but unfortunately, when I get into the kitchen, she's sitting at the island unit, cradling an empty coffee cup. If I didn't know better, I'd say she was waiting for me.

"Good morning," she says, eyeing me up and down.

"Hello, Catrina." I'm finding it harder and harder to be civil to her, but I know I have to try, if I want to keep a roof over my head when I'm not at college, and maintain the tie to my parents that this house still gives me, despite her presence.

"Did you have a nice evening last night?" she asks, getting straight to the point.

Mrs Hemsworth is over by the sink and she turns to look at me, frowning. We both know Catrina's enquiry isn't genuine.

"I had a very nice time, thank you," I reply, being as evasive as I can.

"Where did you go?" She persists with her questions.

"Oh, just a small restaurant in the city." I don't mention how expensive or exclusive it was. "I can't remember the name," I add, before she asks.

She turns in her seat and looks at me properly. "And why did he invite you to dinner?" Mrs Hemsworth puts her hands on her hips and opens her mouth to speak, but I give her the tiniest shake of my head. I don't need a scene. I really don't.

"He didn't," I reply. "I asked him. I wanted to thank him for returning my phone and necklace. He very kindly offered to pick me up, that's all." It's all a complete lie, but it's better than telling her the truth and facing yet more questions.

She smiles and nods her head very slowly. "Well, that makes more sense," she says with some satisfaction, and I wonder how long she's spent pondering over the logic of Paul Lewis taking me for dinner. She gets to her feet and stands, looking down at me. "I mean, why would a man like Paul Lewis want to be seen with someone like you, unless he absolutely had to?" She smirks. "I wondered, when I saw you'd come back so early yesterday evening." It wasn't that early; it was after eleven. "I mean…" she continues, "let's face it, if he was really interested in you, I'm sure he'd have found *something* to do with you after dinner." She gives me a knowing look but I try my best to keep my expression blank. "Don't read too much into him accepting your offer, dear," she adds, obviously thinking that her insults haven't hit home enough yet. "I'm sure he just said yes out of politeness, probably for the sake of the relationship he used to have with your father… so whatever you do, don't go getting your hopes up. Men like Paul Lewis simply wouldn't be seen dead with the likes of you."

With that, she flicks her hair and flounces out of the room.

Mrs Hemsworth makes a move toward me, but I hold up my hand to stop her.

"Don't," I say through my, as yet, unshed tears. "Just don't. Please."

She stops and looks at me, like she wants to hug me, or shout at me. I'm not sure which. I don't hang around to find out either. I head straight back upstairs to my room, where I throw myself on my bed and cry my eyes out.

Paul

I pull up outside my parents' house in Maine and switch off the engine. It's only a two hour drive up here, but I feel quite tired, despite the fact that I stopped for coffee. I shouldn't feel so exhausted really. Okay, so I had a fairly late night, but I slept quite well, helped by the fact that Lottie sent me a message within a few seconds of me getting back to my apartment. Such was her distrust last night, I fully expected to have to wait days, if not weeks to hear from her. I'd have given her that time, to make sure she felt certain about me, but it seems she didn't need it, and that thought had me smiling to myself, even as I fell asleep. I suppose I did have to get up earlier than usual though. I needed to make a stop at a store in the city before setting off. There was something important I had to pick up.

I glance over at my parents' fairly expansive house and am just about to grab my phone from my jacket, which I threw onto the passenger seat after my short coffee stop, when the front door opens, and my two nephews appear, and hurtle straight towards the car. Noah is three and Logan is five, and they're great kids. Great, but noisy, and boisterous. And destructive. And before they can do any lasting damage to my car, I jump out and grab them both, tucking one under each arm, and spinning them around. They squeal loudly.

"You found them then," my sister Morgan's voice hails from the front door and I look up to see her standing with her arms folded, studying me with a fond expression on her face. She's three years younger than me, slim and beautiful. We share the same coloring, in terms of our hair and eyes, but our temperaments are very different. Unlike me, she settled down and got married young – at just twenty-two. She's happy though and motherhood suits her. "They only ate breakfast about an hour ago," she adds. "They're likely to be sick if you do that much longer."

I heed her warning and stop the spinning, to loud cries of dismay, carrying them both to the entrance of the house and letting her take Noah from me, while I set Logan down on the floor. I lean over and give her a quick kiss on the cheek, just as her husband Austin appears behind her. He's the same age as me, and is an engineer by trade. He's probably around six feet tall, well-built and loves my sister to death. He's got a great sense of humor too, but he needs that with their two kids.

"I heard mad screeching," he says. "I might have guessed it was you."

"Not me," I reply, shaking his hand. "Your kids."

"Encouraged by you."

I smile at him. "They don't take a great deal of encouragement."

"You're right there," he says, looking at them with the kind of affection only a parent can feel.

"Do you want to come in?" Megan says. "Mom's just making coffee."

"I'll just grab my jacket," I reply, going back to the car. "I'll bring my bag in later." I give her a wink, which she understands means I've got presents for the boys, presents which they obviously can't see, as they expect Santa to bring them.

"Fine," she says, nodding.

I get my jacket from the car, and join them, going into the house, where I'm greeted by the smell of strong coffee and fresh baking. I'm home.

"Mom?" I call out, going into the enormous kitchen, which features a large farmhouse table, as well as two sizeable couches. Basically, you could live just in this room, and be very comfortable, even if there wasn't another separate living space on the other side of the house, alongside my parents' bedroom.

"Paul?" She comes over and envelopes me in a hug. I haven't been up here since the summer and I've missed her. Judging from the way her arms come around me, I'd say the feeling's mutual.

"Everything okay?" I ask, pulling back and looking down at her. She seems worried, her hair appears to have grayed more since the last time I was here, and she's obviously tired. "What's wrong?" I ask her. "Is it Dad?"

She nods her head. "It's nothing to worry about," she says quickly, resting her hand on my chest.

"Then why are you worried?"

"I'm not. I'm tired."

I pull her over to the table and sit her down. "You're tired *and* worried. Tell me what's wrong," I say, as Morgan takes over making the coffee and brings it across, sitting down with us, while Austin takes the boys through to the other side of the house.

"You've only just walked through the door," Mom says, patting my hand.

"So what? Tell me."

She takes a deep breath. "Well... I—I noticed that your father seemed a little slower than usual," she says quietly, blinking a lot, I guess to hold back tears. "And he was having trouble swallowing too. I was worried he might have had another stroke... just a little one, you know?" I nod my head, giving her hand a squeeze. "So, I took him to the doctor last week."

"And was it a stroke?" I prompt.

Morgan nudges me, telling me I think to let Mom tell the story in her own way, in her own time.

"And they did some tests. It wasn't a stroke," she replies.

"Well, that's good, isn't it?"

"Wait," Morgan says and I try to reign in my impatience.

"They called us back in two days ago," Mom continues, "and told us he's got Parkinson's Disease."

Although she's facing the table, and I'm sitting sideways to her, I notice a tear falling onto her cheek, and I pull her into my arms. "Oh, Mom."

She sobs gently, turning into me as I stroke her hair. "They gave Mom a whole handful of leaflets," Morgan says, getting up and going back into the kitchen area, returning with several brochures and sheets of paper. "But I think she's finding it a lot to take on board."

Mom pulls away again and looks up at me. "There are all kinds of exercises and diet plans, and different therapies to consider..." She falls silent, and I rest my hand on the side of her face.

"We'll look at it together," I tell her. "We'll sit down while I'm here and work it out, and if you need someone to come in and help, I'll arrange it."

She smiles and leans into me. "Thank you, Paul," she murmurs.

"You didn't need to worry," I say. "You know I'll do anything for you."

I glance up at Morgan and she's smiling at me. "You've done so much already," Mom says. "I don't like asking for any more."

"You and dad gave up so much for me, to get me through college," I tell her and tears fill her eyes again. "I can never hope to repay that, no matter what I do for you."

She nestles into my arms and rests her head on my shoulder. It's a strange role reversal, but it feels good to know I can help her. She and Dad don't deserve this. They've already been through so much. Still, I'll do whatever I can to make this as easy as possible, and I know Morgan will too.

Once Mom's calmed down and we've drunk our coffee, I make an excuse and head to the bathroom, taking my phone with me. I've been here for nearly an hour already and haven't let Lottie know yet. Still, I'm sure she'll understand.

— ***Hi. Sorry for delay. Wanted to let you know I've arrived safe and sound. Paul xx***

I want to suggest we have a phone call later, but I can work up to that. I don't want her to think I'm pressuring her. I did touch on the idea last night, so maybe she'll suggest it. I hope. Her reply comes through almost straight away.

— ***Good. Lottie xx***

'Good'. Is that it? She was quite loquacious yesterday and this morning, and now I'm getting one word answers? Is she mad because I didn't contact her straight away? I've got no idea, but I'm gonna find out.

— ***What's wrong? P xx***
— ***Nothing. Lottie x***

Only one kiss this time. And 'nothing'? Bullshit.

I can't leave it like that, but I think she's just gonna keep fobbing me off with monosyllabic replies, and even if she is mad at me, at least if I call her, we can talk about it. So I call her.

"Hello?" She answers after the second ring.

I don't bother with niceties. "Are you mad with me?" I need to know.

"No." She seems surprised. "Why would I be?"

"Because I didn't text you straight away. I've been here for over an hour, and…"

"Paul," she interrupts, "I didn't expect you to contact me the moment you arrived. You're visiting with your family. I understand that you need to spend time with them."

Her voice is gentle and filled with kindness, and I can just imagine the expression on her face, the softness in her eyes. God, I really do love her… so much.

"Then what's wrong?" I ask her.

She sighs loud enough for me to hear, and I feel the deep sadness behind it. "It's nothing…" I'm about to call bullshit on that, when she continues, "I was just on the receiving end of Catrina, at her worst, that's all."

"Tell me what happened," I say, leaning back on the edge of the vanity unit.

"Oh, she just wanted to know about last night," she replies.

"And what did you tell her?"

"Well, I told her that I'd asked you out to dinner, to thank you for returning my phone and necklace…" her voice fades to silence.

"Why did you do that?" I can't quite believe what I'm hearing.

"Because I didn't want her to start questioning your judgement."

"Excuse me?"

She lets out a half laugh. "It didn't work," she says, like she didn't hear me. "All she did was to tell me that she wasn't surprised I'd had to ask you out, because a man like you wouldn't be seen dead with someone like me." She pauses, just for a moment. "I think those were her words, anyway." I hear her voice crack and then a small sob.

I'm so fucking angry, I want to hurl my phone across the room, or punch the wall, or just break something. Badly.

Instead, I keep my voice as calm and quiet as I can and say, "I want you, Lottie. Nothing she says or does is gonna change that. I wasn't lying last night when I told you I wanna be with you." She sobs again, a little louder this time. "Don't you remember what your dad used to say about me?' I ask her. She falls silent. "You said he used to tell you about me, so if nothing else, he must've told you I was honest, didn't he?"

"Yes," she whispers through her tears.

"Well, that hasn't changed, baby." It's the first time I've called her anything so romantic. I just hope she knows I mean it. "I'm still honest. I went out of my way to find you after you ran out on me, because I think you're the most beautiful, kind, interesting, generous woman I've ever met, and I want you in my life, as well as my bed. God, I wish we weren't having this conversation over the phone. I wish you were standing in front of me, so you could see in my eyes how much you mean to me." I wonder if I've said too much and the silence on the end of the line is deafening. Scarily deafening. Then I hear another sob. "I'm sorry," I murmur. "I'm sorry if that just made you feel pressured. That wasn't my intention and I know you need to take things slow…"

"That's not what's wrong," she murmurs.

"Then what is? Tell me."

"No-one has said anything that nice to me since my dad died. It— It's just a bit overwhelming, that's all."

I smile into my phone. "In a good way?" I ask.

"Yes. In a good way."

We both take a deep breath at exactly the same time. "Is Catrina like that a lot?" I ask. I'd like to keep paying her compliments and letting her know what she means to me, but I'm slightly worried I'll end up blurting out 'I love you' over the phone, and I don't want to do that.

"Yes. All the time. But it's okay. I can handle it."

I smile to myself again. "Oh, really? Is that why you were so offhand with me in your texts just now?"

"Sorry," she says softly.

"I don't want you to be sorry," I tell her. "I want you to be happy."

"Well, that's kinda difficult these days," she says.

The desperate sadness in her voice overwhelms me completely and I know I have to be with her. Now. Not in a few days' time. Right now.

"Do you want to come up here?" I ask her.

"Sorry?" She speaks a little more clearly.

"I asked if you wanted to come up here, to my parents' house." I know my mom and dad have just had some bad news about my father's health and this new diagnosis is going to take some getting used to for both of them, and we need to work that out as a family, but I also know that if I went to my mom and told her that the woman I love is in trouble, she'd tell me to move heaven and earth to make it right. I'm not gonna tell my mom that – well, not the part about being in love, anyway, because I haven't told Lottie yet. But I know she'd want me to do whatever's necessary to make sure Lottie's okay.

"I don't have a car," Lottie says, breaking into my thought process.

"Ignore that. Just answer the question. Would you like to come up here and spend the holidays with me?" I can hear the hesitation on the end of the line and wonder if she's still having those trust issues. "My parents have a big house," I point out. "You'd have your own room, and I wouldn't pressure you into anything. As far as you and I are concerned, nothing would be any different. You'd still be calling the shots. You'd just be calling them from here. And my sister and her family are here too, so it wouldn't just be us and my parents." I pause. "I guess I should warn you that my sister's kids are kinda noisy."

She laughs. "I'd love to come," she says. "If only I could."

"Can you be ready in an hour?" I reply.

"Um... yes."

"Okay. Pack some warm clothes and leave everything else to me."

Having made the arrangements I need to, I know I have to clear this with my mom. Obviously it's a little late for her to say 'no', but somehow I don't think she will. I come out of the bathroom and go through to the kitchen, where I find Mom and Morgan starting to get the lunch ready. I'd probably rather have this conversation with my mom on our own, but I don't have much choice.

"Can I speak to you," I say, going over to the kitchen island and leaning against it. Mom and Morgan are on the other side, chopping up vegetables for a salad.

"Of course," Mom says, looking up at me. She puts down her knife. "What's wrong?" she asks. Morgan stops what she's doing too and stares at me. I'm not sure what expression's written on my face, but from the way they're both looking at me, I guess it must be one they haven't seen before. My next question is, where do I start?

"I've met a girl," I say.

"Oh yes?" My mom smiles. I have to say, it's worth the humiliation of saying that in front of Morgan, just to see my mom look so happy.

"Yeah. She's... well, she's having some trouble at home, and I wondered if she could come up here for the holidays."

"What kind of trouble?" Morgan asks.

"She's not married, if that's what you're thinking." I turn to her. "It's her stepmom, if you must know."

"How old is this girl?" my mom asks.

"She's twenty-one."

My mom nods her head, while Morgan raises her eyebrows. I glare at her, defying her to make a comment, considering she was twenty-one when she met Austin. Okay, so he wasn't twelve years older than her, but…

"I know the timing sucks," I continue, "and I wouldn't ask…"

"She's unhappy?" Mom asks.

"Yeah. Very."

"Then of course she should come."

I knew it. I knew she wouldn't let me down.

"I'm so glad you said that," I reply. "Because I've already sent a car for her."

Mom lets out a laugh. "So you asking was a formality then?" she says.

"No. If you'd said 'no', I'd have taken her to the hotel down the coast."

"And you'd have gone with her?" Morgan asks.

"Yeah. I know Christmas is a family time for us, and we've got things to do, and I'd have honored all of our arrangements, but I could hardly invite her up here to get her away from her stepmom and then dump her in a strange hotel by herself for the holidays." Mom nods her head. "Besides, I knew Mom wouldn't want me to abandon my girlfriend." That's a word they've never heard me say before – well, not in association with myself anyway – but it sounds right. It sounds fucking perfect, actually, even though Morgan's eyes just lit up like fireworks.

"Your girlfriend?" she says, coming around to my side of the island and nudging into me.

"Yeah." I look down at her. "You wanna make something of that?"

"Lots," she replies. "Oh, boy… I'm gonna have so much fun with this." She rubs her hands together with glee.

"Morgan," Mom says, with a warning note in her voice. "Behave yourself."

"Of course," she replies.

I lean into her. "You're not meant to have your fingers crossed when you say that," I tell her, and she looks up at me.

"Spoilsport."

"You bet."

Chapter Eleven

Lottie

I've packed a bag with warm clothing, just as Paul suggested, and have been sitting on the edge of my bed for the last fifteen minutes, waiting. Quite what I'm waiting for, I've got no idea. I know he's not going to come and pick me up, because he's over two hours away, and he told me to be ready in less than half that time.

I hear the buzzer ring for the main gate and jump to my feet, going over to the window to peek outside. After a minute or so, I see a limousine coming down the drive. Is this for me? Is this what he told me to wait for? He's gone to the trouble of ordering a limousine, just for me? I'm in shock, and stand, staring, waiting to see what's going to happen next.

"Lottie?" I hear my name being called from downstairs.

"Yes?" I go over to the door and open it.

"There's a chauffeur-driven car here for you," Mrs Hemsworth calls.

"Okay. I'll be right down."

I guess this is about me then. I grab my bag and my coat and purse, and head down the stairs.

"What's going on?" Catrina appears from the living room.

"I—I'm going away," I stutter, looking from her to Mrs Hemsworth, who's standing by the open front door. Outside, I can see a middle-aged man, wearing a pale gray suit, waiting beside the sleek black limousine.

"You are?" Catrina steps forward.

"Yes. For the holidays. I've left your presents under the tree." The monstrous purple plastic tree in the living room, that is.

"Oh." Catrina smiles, obviously pleased that I won't be here to spoil the festivities for her and her daughters. "Where are you going?"

"Away," I reply evasively. "With Paul Lewis." Her smile drops and her mouth falls open, but I don't wait around to hear what she's got to say.

"Miss Hudson," the chauffeur says, opening the rear door for me as though he hasn't just witnessed everything that's been said in the hallway, which I'm sure he has. "Let me take your bag."

"Thank you," I reply, handing it over and climbing into the back of the car. I sit down on the plush seat and glance around. It's very opulent and comfortable in here, with soft leather seats and what appears to be a mini-bar in front of me.

"Just make yourself right at home back there," the chauffeur calls out as he gets into the driver's seat. "Help yourself to anything you want."

"Thank you," I repeat.

"That's my pleasure," he says. "If you need anything, just press the button to your left." I check and find the button, as a smoked glass panel comes up between us and I'm cocooned by myself in the lap of luxury.

I let out a slight giggle, unable to believe this is really happening, although I know someone who'll enjoy it even more than I am, and I pull my phone from my purse to type out a message.

— *Hey, Jack. Just thought I'd let you know that I'm going away for the holidays. I'm currently in the back of a very luxurious limo, courtesy of Mr Paul Lewis... aka my knight in a tux. See you when I get back. Love, Lottie xxx*

Sure enough, his reply comes through almost immediately.

— *A luxurious limo? And you didn't invite me? I'm offended. Make sure to enjoy yourself, hun, and tell me all about it when you get back. And I mean ALL about it. Love you, J xxx*

I smile, not even vaguely surprised by his effusive response and start typing.

— I'll try to enjoy myself. And if I don't see you before the New Year, have a great time with Alex's family. Hope it goes okay. Love you too. L xxx

I put my phone down, not expecting a reply, but it beeps again straight away and I check the screen.

— Don't be afraid of being loved. J xxx

I shake my head, then let it rock back onto the seat behind me. This morning, I felt so despondent, after Catrina's vile words, but now... well, now I feel like I'm on cloud nine. And, glancing around me, cloud nine seems to be very comfortable indeed.

My phone beeps again. *Honestly Jack... give me a break.*

I sit forward and look at the screen, and I have to smile. The message isn't from Jack, it's from Paul.

— Gary just called to say you're on your way. The next two hours can't go quickly enough. See you soon. Paul xx

I type out a response straight away.

— Yes, I'm on my way, but who's Gary? Lottie xx

— He's my driver. The guy who just picked you up. Paul xx

I'm surprised. No, actually I'm shocked.

— Your driver? I assumed you'd hired this car. Lottie xx

— No, it's mine. I can't always drive my own car, so I have Gary to take me places when I need him. I kept you up quite late last night. Lie down and sleep, if you want. The seats are really comfortable. Paul xx

How does he know that, I wonder. I shift in my seat, sitting forward. What's he done back here to find that out? And who's he done it with? I hesitate, putting my phone down for a minute, then picking it up again and turning it over. I want to ignore my thought process, but I can't help it and now the image of him writhing around back here with some gorgeous woman is set in my head, I can't get rid of it. I move right into the corner of the seat, somehow hoping that'll make me feel better. It doesn't.

My phone beeps.

— Are you okay? P xx

Should I tell him what's wrong, or just try and forget about it? As if that's going to happen any time soon.

— ***No. L xx***

At least I was honest, even if I was abrupt.

The phone rings in my hand. It's Paul. But then that's not a surprise, really.

"Hello?"

"What's wrong?" he asks.

I want to say 'nothing', but that would be a really big lie. "How do you know the seats are comfortable in here?" I ask, my voice really quiet and nervous.

"Because I've slept back there myself a few times," he says, without even a second's hesitation. "Sometimes I've been jet-lagged, and other times I've just been plain drunk, but whenever it's happened, I've managed to get off to sleep within moments of lying down." He pauses. "Can I assume you thought I knew about the comfort of my own car seats because I'd been using them for something other than sitting and sleeping?"

"Yes," I whisper. "I'm sorry."

"Hey," he says softly. "Don't be sorry. It's okay."

"No it isn't. I need to try and trust you."

"Well, maybe over the next few days, we can spend some time together and I can show you that you can – trust me, that is. And it won't be hard. You won't have to try, I promise." He sighs. "You've had a shitty morning, Lottie. You're probably not feeling yourself. Just get up here, and we'll talk. Okay?"

"Okay." He's being very understanding. And very kind. "Thank you," I murmur.

"You don't have to thank me."

"Yes, I do."

"Okay… well, get up here and do it in person then," he says and I can hear the smile on his face.

It's nearly three by the time we arrive, having made two stops – one for me to use the bathroom, and the other for lunch. I sent Paul messages, so he knew what we were doing and didn't get worried about the fact that the journey was taking longer than he probably expected.

When Gary finally parks the car up, I glance out the window at the beautiful, modern, ocean-front property and feel my breath catch in my throat. My dad had always told me that Paul came from fairly humble beginnings, but this house is the opposite of humble, and for a moment, I wonder if we're in the wrong place. Then the wide front door opens, and Paul appears, wearing jeans and a white button down shirt, his hands tucked in his pockets, looking every inch the relaxed billionaire. I loved how he looked in a suit, and in a tux he was amazing, but I think this is my favorite look so far. He's so relaxed.

He comes over and opens the door before Gary can even get out of the car.

"Hi," he says, leaning down and looking straight at me. "Come here." He holds out his hand and I take it, grabbing my purse and coat, and letting him pull me from the car and into his arms. "That's better," he says, smiling down at me. I want to nestle into him and tell him to never let me go, but right at that moment, I hear a soft female cough from behind Paul. He turns, keeping his arm around me and bringing me with him, to face an older couple, probably in their late fifties, or early sixties. "Lottie," he says, taking a step toward them. "Let me introduce my parents." I fumble with my purse and coat and manage to hold out my hand to his mom, who takes it and gives me a gentle shake.

"It's lovely to meet you," she says, with a very kind voice. "And please, call me Linda."

"Thank you," I reply. "And I'm very grateful to you for letting me come visit."

"It's our pleasure," she says. Then she turns to the man beside her, whose arm is linked through hers. "This is my husband," she says. "He won't shake hands." I notice that his right arm hangs limply by his side and just nod my head.

"I'm Michael," he says, his speech a little slurred.

"It's a pleasure to meet you, sir," I reply.

"Michael," he repeats, giving me a slightly lopsided smile.

While we've been talking, Gary's taken my bag from the car and deposited it in the house.

"That's everything, Mr Lewis," he says, standing just off to one side.

"Thanks, Gary," Paul replies. "I'll see you after the holidays."

Gary nods his head, then smiles at me and goes back to the car, before getting in and starting the engine.

"Where's he going?" I ask Paul, looking up at him.

"Back to the city," he replies.

"Already?"

"Yeah. He's got a wife and a couple of teenage kids he wants to spend the holidays with."

"And you made him drive me up here? On Christmas Eve?"

"I made it worth his while," he says. "Although I didn't need to. He'd have done it anyway."

"And then he'll drive back after the holidays to collect me again?"

"No," he says, pulling me closer. "I'll drive you home. I guarantee it'll be a lot more fun." He squeezes me tight, giving me a twenty-four carat grin. "Shall we go in?"

I look up at him and nod, and his mom turns his dad around, keeping a firm grip on him. We follow them into the house and, as we do, I notice that his dad shuffles his feet along the floor, not picking them up properly, and leaning on Paul's mom for support the whole time. Michael obviously isn't well and realizing that makes me fearful I might be intruding.

We go into a large, wide hallway. The staircase is right ahead of us, and there are two open doorways, one to the right and one to the left.

"This way," Paul says, leading me to the right, and into the biggest living space I've ever seen. It's dominated by the kitchen, which is in the center of the room, with a long dining table at this end, and beyond I can see two huge couches, set either side of a coffee table. There's a wood burning stove against one wall, and opposite, at the other end of the lounge area, is an enormous, ten foot tall Christmas tree, decked with baubles and coloured lights. The smells of fresh baking, cinnamon and pine fill the room and I have to smile. This is basically everything you could want in a big family home at Christmas, which makes me a little reminiscent of the holidays I used to share with my parents.

I don't have time to contemplate that though, because from behind us, comes a whirlwind of noise as two young boys run through the room and crash onto the couches, yelping and screaming.

"My nephews," Paul says, nodding toward them.

"My sons." I spin at the sound of the female voice from behind me, and come face to face with a very beautiful woman. She's about the same height as me, so roughly five foot six, with brown hair and the same deep blue eyes as Paul. "Hello," she says, smiling and holding out her hand, which I take. "I'm Paul's sister, Morgan."

"Hi. I'm Lottie."

Paul takes a step closer, suddenly going all protective on me, and I wonder if I should expect some kind of hostility from his sister. I hope not. That's the last thing I need.

"So what exactly do you see in him?" she asks, grinning.

I laugh, just lightly. "I'm still trying to work that out," I tell her, and Paul looks down at me, shaking his head and chuckling at the same time. It seems as though I'm on fairly safe ground here. The only bickering will be of the sibling variety – and I guess that, while that's a novelty for me, it could be quite good fun. It'll be interesting to see that side of Paul, anyway.

For the first time, I notice the man standing behind Morgan. He's shorter than Paul, although he looks about the same age, and he's very handsome.

"This is my husband," Morgan says, turning to him and resting against his chest.

"Austin," the man says, supplying his name. "And the noisy troublemakers over there are Noah and Logan." They're very cute kids. Boisterous, but cute.

"I'll show you to your room," Paul says, taking my hand in his and pulling me back toward the hallway.

"Dinner's in three hours," Morgan says, with a wink. "Will that be long enough for you?" She's got her eyes fixed on Paul, and a wide grin on her face. Hopefully no-one's noticed me blushing at her implication.

"Morgan," Linda says, her voice maybe a little stern. "I warned you to behave."

"I am behaving," Morgan says, trying to sound innocent.

"Could've fooled me," Paul replies. "And, for your information, no… three hours isn't long enough."

And with that, he drags me out of the room, grabs my bag from the hallway and leads me up the stairs. At the top, we turn left and then go along a corridor to a door on the right. "This is you," he says, opening it wide and letting me pass through before him. "I hope it's okay."

I'm met by a breathtaking panoramic view of the ocean on two sides. The rest of the room is painted white, with a large picture of a seaside view above the huge bed.

"The bathroom's through there," Paul says, following me into the room and pointing to a door in the corner.

"This is incredible," I breathe and turn to face him.

"I'm sorry about Morgan," he adds, and puts my bag down on the bed, looking over at me. "She can't help herself."

"That's okay. I—I can't thank you enough for this."

He comes over and stands in front of me, his hands in his pockets. "Don't thank me," he whispers. "I just didn't want you to be unhappy, and I could tell you were unhappy with Catrina. Here… well, here I hope you'll be happier, anyway."

"I'm sure I will."

"Just so you know," he adds, "my room's right across the hall. And that doesn't mean anything has to happen. I'm just letting you know."

"Thanks. And also just so I know, where are your sister and her family sleeping? I don't want to run into your nephews in the early hours of the morning."

He smiles. "I don't wanna run into them anytime of day," he quips and I giggle. "But don't worry. You're quite safe. They're on the other side of the house, with Morgan and Austin." He leans down. "Why do you think I stay on this side? It's quieter."

I laugh. "They're cute," I say.

"Yeah. And annoying. And best kept at arm's length."

"If we're on this side of the house and your sister's family are on the other side, where do your parents sleep?"

"Downstairs," he says. "They've got a suite, with a sitting room on the opposite side to the kitchen."

"Oh… I see." And I wonder if that's because his dad has mobility problems.

He smiles down at me. "And I'm sorry about my little joke," he says softly.

"What little joke?"

"About three hours not being enough time with you."

"That was a joke?"

His eyes widen slightly "Well, yes and no." He moves closer still, so we're almost touching. "It was a joke in terms of putting Morgan in her place, but it was the absolute truth in terms of the fact that three hours wouldn't be enough." He pauses. "What I'm trying to say though, is that I don't want you feel pressured. It really was just a line, to shut her up, that's all."

I nod my head, not sure whether I feel gratified, or disappointed.

Paul

I'm close enough to kiss her, but I don't. There's something in her eyes that I think looks like disappointment, but I can't be sure, so I take a step back.

"I'll give you some time to freshen up," I offer, "and I'll see you downstairs."

"Oh, okay." Again there's that hint of regret in her voice, but I don't want to read too much into her reactions. "I won't be long."

"Good," I say, giving her the reassurance I think she might need.

I want to touch her so badly, but I know I've gotta behave myself. I got her up here to make her happy and keep her safe, not to gratify my own desire for her. The last thing I need right now is to scare her off.

I leave the room, before I end up doing something one of us might regret, and go back downstairs and into the kitchen.

Austin's taken the kids off somewhere and Dad's sitting on the couch, looking at the newspaper. He likes sitting by the fire in here, because he feels the cold more than he used to. Mom and Morgan are sat at the table, cradling cups of coffee, although they both look up when I come back into the room.

"Is Lottie alright?" Mom asks.

"Yeah, she's just freshening up." I help myself to coffee, thinking that I'll go sit with Dad for a while. Mainly because it gets me away from Morgan's prying eyes.

"So, tell us all about her," my little sister says, before I have the chance to move away.

I glare at her. "I already did, earlier."

"You told us she's your girlfriend, and she's having trouble with her stepmom. That's it."

"And?" I lean against the countertop and she and Mom turn around to face me.

"And there's more to it than that," Morgan persists.

"So?"

She rolls her eyes. "Now I know I'm right. Not only did you go all doe-eyed over her the moment she arrived, but now you've gone coy on us. You're hiding something."

"Leave him alone," Dad calls from the couch, slurring his words just a little.

"See, Dad's on my side."

"He would be," Morgan replies. "You guys always stick together."

I ignore her and turn to my mom. "You're sure you're okay with Lottie staying here?" I say, nodding toward my dad.

"Yes," she replies and gets up, coming over to me. "It'll do us good not to dwell on our own problems for a while."

Apart from a short errand I had to run in the nearby town, we spent the few hours while we were waiting for Lottie to arrive, sitting around the kitchen table, going through the information the doctor had given Mom. It seems that, to start with, there shouldn't be too many changes required to Dad's lifestyle. Although Dad has a few symptoms already, he might stay as he is for some time yet, without any noticeable deterioration. So, the only thing we made a very quick decision about was that, because he shuffles around a bit more than he used to, we'd remove the rugs from the ground floor, leaving just flat wooden surfaces, so he can't trip over so easily. Austin and I took them all up, and stored them in the garage for now. Mom didn't want to make any further decisions or alterations at the moment. I think she wants to see how things go for a while, which seems fair enough to me. There's no point in worrying about something that hasn't happened yet.

"You know you don't have to dwell on your problems, don't you?" I tell her, keeping my voice quiet.

"Yes," she replies.

"And you'll call me, if you need anything?"

I must've said that ten times already today, but it doesn't hurt to say it again.

She nods her head and rests her hand on my arm. "Thank you," she whispers.

"Stop trying to change the subject, Paul Lewis," Morgan says, coming to join us. "There's more to your girlfriend than meets the eye. Who is she?"

"If you must know, she's Charles Hudson's daughter."

My mom pales a little. "Really?" she says. "Lottie's Charles' daughter?"

I nod. My parents met Charles a few times years ago, when he first helped me get started. One of the things I liked most about him was that he didn't make them feel like failures because they couldn't afford to give me the start he could. He praised the way they'd raised me. He told them that, without that beginning, I'd never have been the man I was, the man who attracted his attention and made him want to invest in me in the first place.

"I didn't realize you knew her," my mom says, after a few moments' silence. "I thought your connection with Charles was purely business."

"It was. I knew Lottie existed, but I'd never met her before."

"Before when?" Morgan asks.

"Before last Saturday."

"You only met her last Saturday?" Morgan's surprised and, judging from the expression on my mom's face, I think she is too.

"Yeah."

"And you've fallen for her… already?" Morgan crows.

I'm not about to confirm, or deny that, especially not when I haven't told Lottie yet.

"Leave him alone," my mom says.

"And pass this up?" Morgan replies, grinning. "Not a chance. Not when there's a woman upstairs, who's finally gotten on the inside of my big brother."

"And I'd kinda like her to stay there," I admit, if only to shut her up. "So behave yourself."

"Hello?"

I spin around at the sound of Lottie's voice and hope to God she didn't hear what I just said.

"Hi," I say, going over to her and taking her hand.

"Would you like a coffee?" Mom offers and Lottie nods her head.

"Let's sit, shall we?" Morgan suggests, pointing to the table.

I wonder what she's scheming, but steer Lottie to the table, where Mom joins us, bringing the coffee with her.

"So," Morgan asks, almost as soon as we've sat down. "Paul tells us you only met last Saturday?"

"Yes," Lottie replies, blushing.

"How did that happen?" Morgan says, giving Lottie a smile.

"We met at a party, if you must know." I get my answer in before Lottie can.

"Oh?"

"Yeah. A Christmas party." I'm not giving her any more than that.

"And you're from the Boston area?" Morgan says, clearly fishing. She knows as well as my mom that Charles lived to the north of the city.

"I am, yes. Although I'm at college at the moment."

"Whereabouts?" Mom asks, before Morgan can say anything else.

"At Virginia Tech. I'm studying architecture." Lottie takes a sip of coffee and, when she's put the cup down again, I reach over and take her hand.

"Paul... son?" My dad's voice carries from the other side of the room.

"Yes?" I let go of Lottie. "Excuse me," I say to her, and then I get up, going straight over to him.

"C—Can you put some more logs onto the fire?" he asks me, nodding toward the wood burning stove.

"Sure." I go to the log basket beside the fire, to find it's empty. "I'll need to go and fetch some more," I tell him. "I won't be long." He looks up at me and nods, attempting a smile. "I'm just gonna fetch some logs," I call out to Lottie and my mom. "Back in a minute."

"Take your time," Morgan replies. "We'll be just fine." She grins over at me, her eyes sparkling with mischief, as I grab the basket and head out the back. I need to hurry up. If I'm too long, she'll have talked Lottie out of seeing me ever again.

Chapter Twelve

Lottie

As soon as Paul leaves the room, I feel nervous. I know he won't be gone for long and I know I'm perfectly safe with his family, but I still feel unsure of myself, especially as his sister is so full of questions. I decide to pre-empt her.

"You have a lovely house," I say quickly, addressing myself to Paul's Mom.

"Thank you." She smiles, looking around. "Paul bought it for us a few years ago."

"He did?"

"Yes." She nods and pours more coffee into my cup. "Michael had a stroke, you see," she explains. "About four years ago, and he found our old home too difficult." She sits back. "We were still in our small town house in Boston at the time, where Paul and Morgan grew up," she continues. "It was a nice enough place, but it had a lot of stairs."

"Oh. That must've been hard for your husband."

"Yes, it was. So, Paul stepped in and bought us this place. It was a godsend, being as Michael wasn't well enough to work any more, and I had to give up my job to care for him."

"I can imagine," I say quietly. I had no idea he'd done that.

"And it's so lovely up here," she says wistfully. "Michael was doing a lot better, being so close to the ocean."

"Was?" I pick up on the past tense.

"Um… yes." She hesitates, like she wishes she hadn't said that, and Morgan leans forward, taking her mom's hand.

"What Mom's referring to is that Dad's just been diagnosed with Parkinson's disease."

"Just?" I query.

"Yes. We only found out a couple of days ago," Linda replies. "It came as a bit of a shock."

"Then I should go," I say, getting to my feet. "I shouldn't be here. You need some family time."

Linda reaches out and takes my hand in hers. "No, dear," she says softly. "Paul wants you here. He wants to help you too. And you should let him. He's good at it." She looks into my eyes. "And anyway, I've spent the last few days worrying about Michael, and the whole morning talking about him with Paul. It'll be nice to have someone else to focus on for a change."

I'm more than taken aback by her generosity, and I let her pull me back into my seat. "Thank you," I murmur.

"If you only met my brother on Saturday, I guess you probably don't know how generous he can be," Morgan says. She's not fooling around this time, or making fun of Paul. She's being serious.

"No. I don't," I reply. I don't tell them that I don't know him at all, but then I think they've probably worked that out for themselves.

"Well, after Dad had his stroke and it became clear that Mom and Dad needed somewhere else to live, he went house hunting with Mom…"

"And I'd have settled for somewhere a lot smaller," Linda puts in.

"Only Paul wanted us to be able to have family times together, so when he and Mom saw this place, he bought it, there and then. We get together every Thanksgiving, and at Christmas, and for at least a week in the summer."

"We have odd weekends too, throughout the year, but they're not set in stone. We just arrange them whenever it fits in with everyone's schedule," Linda adds, smiling. "And Paul pays for everything, including our food and bills, and the upkeep of the house," she says. "I don't have to worry about a thing. I have someone who comes and cleans three times a week, and then there's Harold, who does the garden for us…"

I had no idea. Well, obviously I didn't, because I don't really know him. Oddly though, I'm not that surprised. He's been so kind to me in the last couple of days, and I'm a comparative stranger. It makes perfect sense that he'd be that generous to his family.

"That's not all he's done," Morgan says, interrupting my train of thought. "Austin and I have always been very fortunate," she continues. "He's well paid, and we've never really needed Paul's help, although I know he'd be there for us if we ever did. But, he's set up a trust fund for the boys – for when they graduate college." I'm struck for a moment by how similar that sounds to my dad's way of doing things. "He's put aside a very generous amount of money," Morgan says, "so they can either buy a property, or set up a company. He won't just let them blow it on having a good time; they've got to use it wisely. As far as he's concerned, it's for them to have a head start – the same head start your father gave to him, when he needed it."

"My father?"

"Yes," Linda says. "He told us that you're Charles Hudson's daughter."

I nod, blushing again. "It seems odd that I know so much about Paul from my father, but I never met him until a few days ago," I confess.

"He lived up to your father's generosity," Morgan says and I feel myself swell with pride for the things my dad achieved. "Austin and I have a nice home and two cars, and we'll be able to put the boys through college by ourselves, but what Paul's given them… well, that's the kind of thing we could never hope to have done. I didn't ask him to do it either," she adds. "He just came to see me one day when Logan was about one, or maybe just a little older, and told me he'd done it. He said he'll do the same thing for any other kids we might have in the future… Although that won't be happening. The two I've got are more than enough." She laughs, just as Paul reappears, carrying the log basket in one hand, with one of the boys tucked under his other arm, squealing with delight.

"Look what I found," he says, followed by Austin, who's got the other boy on his shoulders. I'm still not sure which child is which yet, but they both make enough noise.

Paul dumps his human cargo on the couch opposite his dad, then goes over to the fire, loading it up with fresh logs.

"I'm gonna put a movie on for these two," Austin announces, switching on the TV and getting the boys to sit together on the couch.

"Whatever my sister's been telling you, it's all lies," Paul says, coming over and standing beside me.

I look up at him. "Oh… so you didn't really buy your parents this house then? And you didn't set up trust funds for your nephews for when they graduate college?"

He frowns, just slightly. "Well, yeah." He turns and looks at Morgan. "Only she's not meant to tell anyone about that."

"Why not?" I ask him. "It's very kind and generous."

He crouches down beside me. "I don't do any of it to be kind, or generous," he says softly. "I do it because they're my family, and I love them." His eyes bore into mine. "Even if Morgan can be the most annoying little sister in the entire world."

Morgan laughs. "It's my job to be annoying," she says. "But you're not getting away with it that lightly. You might be as generous as you are to us because we're family, but how do you explain all the other things you do?"

Paul's eyes close and his chin drops to his chest.

"What's this?" I ask, turning to Morgan.

"I think he's put roughly fifty or so kids through college now." I can feel my mouth opening in surprise. "He stayed in touch with his old high school in the city, and he gets them to tell him about the kids who have potential, but don't have the financial backing to get through college. And then he sponsors them – anonymously."

"You do?" I turn and look at him. He shrugs almost like he's embarrassed.

"And it's not just helping kids get an education," Linda adds.

"Jeez, Mom," Paul says, clearly wishing they'd both stop now.

"What? Why shouldn't I tell Lottie what you do?" She turns to me. "There was a nurse," she explains. "She looked after Michael when he had his stroke. She used to sit and read to him when I couldn't be there, even after her shift had finished. She was a lovely girl. One of those nurses who works for the love of the job, not for the salary. Anyway, Paul found out her husband had left her with a couple of teenage kids, and she was struggling to make her mortgage payments, so he paid it off, and settled all her outstanding bills."

"And set up college funds for her kids," Morgan adds.

"Okay, that's enough," Paul says, getting to his feet and holding up his hands in surrender.

"We're just telling it how it is," Morgan replies, looking up at him.

"Yeah, maybe you are, but what you don't understand – and what you're not explaining – is that whatever I do for other people, is just my way of repaying the debt." He looks at me, his eyes locked with mine. "I was given such a head start by Charles, and I can't repay that. Especially now. So, if I can make life better for other people, then I intend to."

"You did repay my dad," I say simply.

He crouches down again. "I repaid his financial investment," he says softly. "I can never repay everything else I owe him. I'd talked to so many people about my ideas and they'd all treated me like I was insane, or told me to go away and come up with prototypes, which I couldn't afford to do. Your dad had faith in me. Not my ideas. Not my products. Me. *That's* what I owe him for, Lottie."

I shake my head. "No you don't. Why do you think he always talked about you?" I turn to face him. "He never talked to me about any of his other investments, Paul. Just you. He knew you were special." I swallow down the lump in my throat. "My dad made a point of keeping in touch, of knowing everything about the people he'd invested in, so you can be pretty sure he knew about your... your random acts of kindness. I think that's why he was always so proud of you. You became exactly what he knew you would... exactly what he always wanted you to be. You owe him nothing, Paul."

Paul

I want to tell her that's not true. I want to tell her that I owe Charles everything – because he's given me her. But that's a conversation we need to have when we're alone.

Instead, I stare at her for a long moment and hope she'll see in my eyes how much I love her. She blinks a few times, struggling with her own emotions, which doesn't surprise me in the least given that we're talking about her father and I know that's still kinda raw for her.

"I've made lasagna," Mom says out of the blue, breaking into the highly charged atmosphere – thank goodness – and Lottie turns to face her.

"You have?"

"Yes. I asked Paul this morning what I should make, and he said you liked it."

She looks back at me. "Yes, I do."

"Good." Mom gets up and goes into the kitchen. "It just needs to bake in the oven, and dinner will be ready."

I take Lottie's hand, pull out a chair, and sit beside her, staring into her eyes. I don't care if Morgan finds this amusing, or spends the rest of the holidays making fun of me, I don't ever want this moment to end.

Mom has to help Dad with eating, which we're all used to, and the boys are as boisterous and noisy as ever, but Lottie seems to take the whole thing in her stride. I keep her close to me the whole time and, as soon as we're finished, I tell everyone that we're going out to look at the ocean. I fully expect Morgan to make a comment, but she doesn't, so I get up, pulling Lottie with me, grab our coats from the hooks in the hall, and take her out the front and around the side of the house, onto the deck, pulling her close in my arms.

"I'm real sorry about my family," I say, looking down into her eyes in the moonlight.

"You don't have to be. I think they're lovely."

"Loud, but lovely."

"It's how families should be," she replies. "And speaking of which, I feel bad about being here."

I lean back. "Why?" I ask her, feeling scared about what she's gonna say.

"Your mom and Morgan told me about your dad's diagnosis. You should be having this time together as a family…"

"Bullshit," I interrupt. "You honestly think I was gonna leave you to Catrina's mercies? And anyway, Mom agreed to you coming the moment I told her you were having problems."

"You told her?" Her eyes widen and she tenses.

"I told her you were having trouble with your stepmom. I didn't give her any details."

She relaxes again.

"You're sure it's okay?" she asks. "Me being here, I mean?"

"I'm absolutely positive."

"What's the outlook for your dad?" Her voice is tentative and I hold her closer.

"It's kinda hard to say," I reply honestly. "From what I've learned today, talking it through with Mom and Morgan, and reading the information Mom was given by the doctors, the disease itself won't kill him, but it'll eventually make life much harder for him, and for my mom."

"Do you think she'll manage?" Lottie asks. I can see a touching concern in her eyes. If I didn't already love with with my whole heart, I know that after seeing that look in her eyes, I would now.

"She won't have to," I explain. "When Dad had his stroke, I offered Mom the chance to have a live-in nurse. She said no at the time, but we left the option open for the future, and I had a separate apartment built above the garage, in case Dad deteriorated. Mom decided she'd rather have someone take care of the house, while she looked after my dad. But the offer still stands, and she knows that. I've made it very clear to her today, I'll do whatever she wants… whatever she needs."

She leans into me, which feels incredible, and I tighten my hold on her still further. "Can I ask you something?" she says, looking up at me.

"Sure."

"You remember you said you had a lawyer who'd help me get my allowance paid, and get the capital sum protected?"

I nod. "Yeah. Why?"

She pauses, just for a moment. "I've decided I want to do something."

I smile. "Okay."

"It's not that I want the money," she adds quickly. "Well, not the capital sum, anyway. The allowance will be quite useful, in terms of not having to work myself to death when I should be concentrating on my finals."

"Yeah… like I'm gonna let that happen."

She narrows her eyes, but doesn't speak for a moment. "I—I just realized that Catrina is blowing the money on stupid things, like manicures and cosmetic surgery. And I could actually do some good with it. I could carry on what my dad started, in some small way. If you'd help me?"

I can't do a damn thing about the broad grin that's spreading across my lips. "I'd love to. I'll make an appointment with my lawyer when we get back to the city."

"And you'll help me? I mean, you'll advise me on what to do with the money?"

"Of course I'll help you. Your father wanted you to have that money, because he knew you'd do the right thing with it. And this is the right thing."

"And that's the same reason he invested in you. Because he knew you'd always do the right thing too. I meant everything I said earlier."

"I know. So did I. And helping you get your money is about the best way I can think of repaying your father."

"I already told you, Paul. You don't owe him anything."

I take a step closer to her, so our bodies are touching. "Yeah I do," I whisper. "I owe him everything I have."

She starts to shake her head and goes to speak. I quickly bring my hand around and place it over her lips.

"Let me finish," I murmur. "I owe Charles all that I have for the very simple reason that he's your dad. And that means he, together with your mom, gave the world the wondrous gift that is you." I pause to take a breath, because I need to get this right. "I know you need to take things slow with me, and I get that you need to learn to trust me, but I can't wait another moment to tell you that I'm in love with you, Lottie, and I don't wanna even imagine my life without you in it."

She sucks in a sharp breath and I wonder if I've gone to far, maybe spoken too soon.

"It's okay if you don't feel the same," I say quickly.

"And if I do? Is that okay too?" she whispers.

I feel like my heart just burst in my chest and I'm so full of love and joy and happiness that, for a moment, I can't speak. "D—Did you just say you feel the same?" I ask her.

She nods her head very slowly, her eyes fixed on mine. "Yes, I do."

I put my arms tight around her and lift her, swinging her around. "I love you so much," I whisper in her ear.

"I love you too," she replies, then squeals and throws her head back.

I put her down eventually, and we stand for a moment, in each other's arms, looking out across the ocean.

"It's beautiful here," she says quietly.

"Yeah. Nowhere near as beautiful as you though."

She looks up at me, smiling.

"Thank you for helping me," she whispers, resting her head on my chest.

"It's my pleasure. I'll always help you." I smile to myself. That's not a hollow promise now. She loves me. Dear God… she loves me. And that means I'll always be there to help her, and that's a pretty amazing feeling.

I've got no idea how long we stand outside, holding each other and looking at the ocean, but eventually Lottie starts shivering and I realize it's turned colder. Personally, I can't feel a single thing, except love.

"Let's go back inside," I say to her. "It's freezing out here."

"Yeah. I think my nose is about to fall off," she jokes.

"Well, we can't have that," I reply and pull her down, so her face is buried in my chest. "Better?"

There's a muffled reply that I can't make out, and she pulls back.

"Yes," she says. "You're lovely and warm."

"Even so, I'd better take you in, before you start to lose body parts to frostbite."

She giggles – which has to be the most perfect sound on earth – and I lead her back into the house, taking off her coat in the hallway.

"Do you wanna sit up and watch a movie, or go to bed?" I ask her. I'm kinda hoping she opts for the movie, because at least I'll get to spend some more time with her.

"Bed, I think," she says. "It's been a long day."

I suppose it has, and I do my best to hide my disappointment. The boys have gone up to bed already, thank goodness, and Mom and Dad have gone over to their side of the house. Morgan and Austin are cuddled up on the couch when we go in.

"We're heading up to bed," I tell them.

Morgan gives me a cheeky smile, even though she knows perfectly well we're sleeping in separate bedrooms.

"Sleep well," she says, grinning.

"Thanks. You too," Lottie replies, clearly missing Morgan's implication.

"See you in the morning," Austin adds, with a wave of his hand.

I pull Lottie from the room before Morgan can say anything else, and lead her up the stairs and around to our wing of the house, taking my time in going down the corridor, just to savor every last second of the day with her.

Outside her door, I pull her close.

"Can I kiss you?" I ask her.

She looks up at me and nods her head, just once, and I lean down and very gently press my lips against hers. She lets out a soft moan, bringing her arms around the back of my neck and opening her mouth to mine. Our tongues dance as our breathing hots up and I feel her press her breasts into my chest. My cock is rock hard and, without thinking, I grind my hips into her, letting her feel my arousal. She stills and I wonder if I've overstepped the mark, but then she groans and matches my movement with her own. She may have had some regrets about our first time – for a reason I'm still trying to work out – but she's told me she loves me and she's responding to my kisses, so I guess maybe that means she's willing to try again. At least I hope so. I pull back, breaking the kiss.

"You can say no," I breathe. "You can always say no… but do you wanna go to bed with me?"

She stares into my eyes, like she's looking for something and it's only now that I realize that I used exactly those words the last time – our first time. And while I don't regret a single second of what we did together, I know that me using the same words is only gonna have reminded her of her lingering doubts about me. I wait, unable to speak, or even breathe and eventually, after a heart stopping pause, she whispers, "Yes," and I hear the crack of emotion in that single word.

I try to ignore my overwhelming relief, or at least not to let it show, and lean down, lifting her into my arms, and carrying her across the hall and into my own bedroom. I kick the door closed behind me and set her down on the floor.

I'm just about to pull her sweater over her head, when she puts her hands on mine, stopping me. She wants to stop? Now? Even though she only said 'yes' a few seconds ago? Well, I guess if that's what she wants…

"You're sure you want me?" she asks, with undisguised doubt in her voice. How can she think I wouldn't?

"Fuck yeah," I murmur. Even I can hear the hoarse emotion in my voice.

"No doubts?"

"No. Not one."

I've got no idea where that moment of uncertainty came from – presumably from the things Catrina said to her earlier – but I'm gonna do everything I can to make sure she knows how much I want her.

"I'll prove it," I whisper, leaning down and capturing her lips with mine. She moans loudly, running her hands down my back. God, that feels good. I break the kiss and pull her sweater over her head, then undo her bra and drop it to the floor, before bending and capturing one of her perfect nipples between my teeth, biting real gently on her soft flesh. She groans and holds the back of my head in place.

"Yes…" she hisses. "That's…"

"That's what?" I release her nipple and look up at her. "Tell me how it feels."

"Amazing," she whispers.

"Well, I'm sure we can do better than that," I reply and I kneel before her, undoing her jeans, and pulling them down, with her panties. My heart stops beating as I gaze upon her. "You shaved?" I look up at her, unable to disguise my surprise.

"Y—Yes." She puts her forefinger in her mouth, biting the tip of it, evidently unsure about my reaction. Fuck, that's hot.

"Why?" I ask – just because I want to know.

"I—I wanted to know how it would feel," she replies.

"And?" I glance back at her perfectly shaved pussy, her lips swollen with desire.

"And it feels good," she replies.

"It looks incredible."

"You like it?" she asks and I look back up at her again. She's smiling.

"I love it. I loved it before, but this is… this is something else." I move closer, settling between her legs. "Move your feet apart," I tell her and she does. Then I reach up and, using my fingers to part her glistening folds, I run my tongue across her clit.

"Oh… Oh yes," she murmurs, clutching the back of my head. I don't need any encouragement, and I start to flick my tongue across her, circling her tight bud. I bring my hand up between her legs and insert my middle finger into her entrance, feeling her soaking walls clamp around me. "Please…" she whispers, as her breathing changes and she pulls my head even closer onto her. I lick and suck her clit until she stiffens, lets out a soft whimpering moan and comes apart. I place my arm around her, holding her up while she rocks her hips into me, riding out her orgasm.

Eventually, she calms and, once I'm sure she can stand unaided, I get to my feet.

"Taste," I say, leaning down and kissing her lips. There's no holding her back this time, as she licks her juices from me, kissing me deeply. "I need to be inside you," I murmur, breaking the kiss.

She nods and I walk her backward to the bed, keeping our eyes locked. I let her fall back onto the soft mattress and quickly undo my shirt, letting it fall to the floor, then kick off my shoes and unfasten my jeans, pulling them down, with my trunks. I discard my socks and lean over to the nightstand and grab a box of condoms. I'm not making that mistake twice. I owe her that much.

She watches avidly while I pull out a foil packet, open it and roll the condom over my length, then I kneel up on the bed, letting my hands rest either side of her head, just like last time. *Just like last time.* The thought of her running out on me crosses my mind, but I banish the memory. She loves me. It won't happen again. It can't.

She parts her legs wide and I push inside her welcome entrance, and she gasps, grabbing my arms, staring at me.

"Lottie?" I say, stilling inside her. "Are you okay?"

"Yes," she nods. "It just stretches me a bit."

"Is it too much?"

"No." She gives me a sweet smile and I start to move, building a steady, gentle rhythm, which she quickly matches, bringing her hips up to meet mine with every stroke. I keep my eyes fixed on hers as I give her my whole length, letting her feel every inch each time I enter her. She parts her legs even wider, clearly wanting me to go deeper, and who am I to disappoint? I force my cock hard inside her and grunt out my pleasure as I take her.

"It's happening again…" she says, and tips over the edge. Feeling her muscles clamp around my cock is too much and, with two final strokes, I let go deep inside her.

I give her a few moments to calm, before I pull out of her and remove the condom. I'm still hard and she looks down at me.

"Is it meant to still be like that?" she asks.

"Not necessarily, but I want more."

"You do?"

"If you do… yes."

She bites her bottom lip and smiles up at me.

"Can I take that as a 'yes'?" I ask, reaching forward and pinching her nipples between my thumbs and forefingers.

"Oh… ahh. Yes," she whimpers, throwing her head back.

I grin and lean over to the nightstand, grabbing another condom from the box.

"You wanna do it this time?" I ask her, kneeling back on my ankles.

"What? Put that on?"

I nod my head.

"I don't know how," she replies.

"Then I'll show you." She sits in front of me and I hand her the foil packet. "You need to open that," I tell her.

"I think I worked that out." She rips through the foil and pulls out the condom, holding it out in front of her. Then she stops abruptly, staring up at me, her eyes fixed on mine, although they're suddenly filled with uncertainty.

"How… I mean why do you have condoms here?" she asks. "This is your parents' house."

"I know. And, believe me, I don't routinely keep condoms here. I went out this morning into the town and bought them."

She tilts her head to one side. "So you knew we'd end up doing this?"

I shake my head. "No. No of course not." I take the condom from her and throw it to one side, pulling her closer to me. "I hoped, Lottie, that's all." I stare down at her. "I wanted to be prepared, just in case." I half expect her to mention my lack of preparedness when we first made love, but she doesn't. Instead, she gazes into my eyes.

"And you've never slept with anyone else here?"

"God no." I smile at her. "Do you honestly think Morgan would have reacted the way she did to me inviting you here, if I did it all the time?"

"No, I suppose not." A slow smile settles on her face.

"So, shall we try that again?" I ask her, feeling reassured that her moment of doubt about me seems to have passed.

"But you threw the condom away," she replies, sitting back and looking over the edge of the bed.

"Then get another one."

She giggles and pulls another condom out of the box, ripping through the foil packet and looking at me expectantly. "What now?" She's breathing hard and her eyes are shining with anticipation.

"Now you need to pinch the end…"

"Of you?" she asks, her surprise obvious.

"No. Of the condom. Please don't pinch me… not if you can help it."

She nods her head, smiling. "I'll do my best." She leans down, pinching the tip of the condom between her thumb and forefinger. "Like that?" she asks, looking up at me.

"Perfect. Now put it over my cock, while you're still pinching the end – of the condom," I clarify and she grins at me, doing as I've instructed. "And now roll it down."

She fumbles a few times, trying to get the condom over the end of my swollen dick, but eventually she gets there, and manages to roll it down as far as it'll go. I'm holding my breath and let it out slowly as she finishes. Just her touch is enough to make me wanna come again, and I'm trying real hard not to.

"It won't go any further," she says, looking at her handiwork. "Are you okay?" she asks.

"Um… yeah."

"Did I hurt you?" She sounds genuinely concerned.

"No."

"Then why were you holding your breath?"

"Because it was real hard not to come," I explain. She looks confused. "Feeling your hands on me was very arousing," I explain.

"Oh." She bites her bottom lip.

"That's a good thing," I clarify, because she still seems unsure, and she rewards me with a beautiful smile. "And now, I wanna be inside you again." She goes to lie down, but I pull her back up. "Not that way," I tell her.

"Oh? Which way then?"

I look down at my cock thinking the answer to that ought to be obvious, until I remember she's never done anything like this before and she's gonna need instructions. "Kneel up," I tell her, and she does. "Now put your knees either side of my legs." I watch while she obeys. "And move forward, toward me." She sucks in a breath and bites her bottom lip as she obviously works out what's gonna happen next. "Now," I say, placing my hands on her waist and lifting her, "lower yourself down onto me." She starts to move downward. "Just take it slow," I add quickly. "The stretch might be more noticeable this way." She nods, looking me in the eye as she lowers her body down, taking my length deep inside her, inch by inch until I'm buried to the hilt inside her perfect body. Her eyes are on fire now and I know she needs to come again – soon. "Now move," I whisper, leaning down and kissing her neck. She slowly raises herself up and then back down again, taking it easy to start with, and then increasing the speed and force until she's slamming herself down on my cock and groaning out her pleasure, her head rocked back, her nipples hard, like pebbles. She's close, but being ridden like this, so am I.

"Come for me, baby," I murmur and she rocks forward, her eyes locking with mine as she explodes around my aching cock. That's all it takes for me to come apart and I pull her down onto me, giving her everything I've got.

I take a moment to catch my breath, holding her tight, and then lift her off of me, lying her down gently on the bed.

"Back in a second," I tell her, kissing her briefly on the lips.

She smiles into the kiss, and moans softly, then stretches and curls up. God, she's cute.

I jump out of bed and go over to the bathroom. By the time I return, she's asleep. She's on top of the comforter, so I grab the blanket from the end of the bed, lie down beside her and cover us over. She seems to sense me and moves closer, and I put my arms around her, pulling her in tight.

"Thank you," she murmurs.

"Don't ever thank me for making love to you," I whisper back. "I love you."

She nestles closer and I just about manage to hear her say, "I love you too," before her breathing alters and she's fast asleep again.

I lie still, savoring the feeling of her warm body along the length of my own, her soft skin next to mine, her breath whispering across my chest, as my eyes close.

Waking up on Christmas morning, with Lottie in my arms feels like the most perfect place to be and I take the chance to watch her sleeping, the early morning sun dappling across her closed eyes. Like so many things with Lottie, this is new to me. I've never spent the night with a woman, so waking up beside one hasn't been an option. But I've gotta say, I like waking up beside her and I really wanna do it every day. I'm aware of not rushing things with her, though, so I guess I'll keep that thought to myself. At least for now, anyway.

She looks angelic, her hair spread out on the white pillow and her skin downy soft, and I can't resist planting a light kiss on her slightly pouting lips and, as mine rest gently on hers, she wakes.

"Hello," she says, seemingly surprised.

"Happy Christmas," I reply, smiling.

"Oh, yes. Happy Christmas."

"Wanna make my day?" I ask her.

"How?" She looks inquisitive.

"Shower with me?"

There's a moment's pause, before she nods her head. "If you want me to," she whispers.

"Oh... I want you to."

I get out of bed and her eyes drop to my erection, then widen, and creep up again to my face. "You're sure you want to shower?" she asks.

I chuckle. "Yeah."

"You don't want to... um..." She glances down at my hard cock once more and blushes.

"Yeah I do. That's why we're gonna shower." I love her innocence. It's who she is.

Her brow furrows and she tilts her head to one side, but I don't want to explain. I want to show her how much fun a shower can be. So, I reach over and pull her across the bed.

"Come with me," I say, grabbing a condom from the drawer before lifting her to her feet and taking her hand.

She follows me into the adjoining bathroom and we both go straight into the walk-in shower, where I turn on the water, letting it fall onto my back until the temperature is just right. Then I pull Lottie beneath the jets and kiss her deeply, placing my hands on her perfect ass and pulling her onto me. She moans and grinds into me. Maybe she doesn't need too much showing after all.

Downstairs, after the best shower I've ever had, and once we've all had a delicious breakfast of bacon, pancakes and maple syrup, we decide it's time to put the boys out of their misery and keep them quiet for at least a few minutes, by allowing them to open their presents. They've had a few already, upstairs with their parents, but the bulk of their things are under the tree, which is in the living area – as usual. Mom got Harold to bring it in at the weekend, but I know she'll have decorated it herself. It's something she always did, even when we were kids and she was working a couple of jobs to make ends meet.

We sit around on the couches, and Morgan helps the boys to sort out the gifts. While Logan and Noah are busy ripping the paper from various boxes and toys, she pulls out a small square present, and I feel myself tense, wondering if I should have done this in a more private setting. I bought it, expecting to give it to Lottie when I got back to the city, and only snuck it under the tree this morning, when no-one was looking. Morgan checks the label and crawls over.

"This one's for you, Lottie," she says, smiling.

"It is?"

Lottie looks at me, and takes the gift from Morgan, who's grinning now. I will her to move away and supervise her kids, but she stays exactly where she is, her eyes gleaming.

Lottie turns over the card and takes a moment to read the words. I know what they say, because I wrote them:

'*Dear Lottie,*
Happy Christmas.
I hope you love this as much as I love you.
Paul xx'

She pauses, then turns to me, and I see there are tears glistening in her eyes.

"I didn't get you anything," she whispers.

"You didn't have to," I tell her. "Why don't you open it?"

She nods and I'm aware of Morgan moving away, showing a little sensitivity for once in her life, even though I know she's still watching, and I'm fairly sure the rest of my family is as well.

Lottie carefully opens the parcel, revealing a red box, with the word 'Cartier' on top.

"Paul," she murmurs, shaking her head.

"Open it." I want to know I did okay.

She flips open the box. Inside is a thin, black leather cord, joined together with three small rings; in different shades of gold, one white, one yellow and one pink. She's staring at it, and then turns to me again.

"I noticed you wore leather bracelets," I say, hoping I've done the right thing. It's not feminine, or delicate, like her necklace, but I hope it's 'her'. "And I saw this one and liked it." I pause and she doesn't reply. "Obviously, if you don't…"

"I love it," she replies, interrupting me, and I heave an inward sigh of relief. "It's perfect."

"I know it's nothing like your necklace," I point out.

"Well, my dad gave me that years ago," she says, "for my fifteenth birthday. My style has changed over the years, but I still wear it, because he gave it to me."

"Oh, I understand now," I say, leaning into her a little.

"I feel bad for not getting you anything," she murmurs. "Not that I could hope to compete with Cartier, anyway." She smiles up at me.

"Well, you've already given me the only thing I want." I wink at her and lean in closer, so my lips are right next to her ear when I whisper the word, "You."

Chapter Thirteen

Lottie

Christmas Day has, so far, been spectacular.

I've never woken up in bed with anyone before – well, obviously I haven't because I've never slept with anyone before. The sleeping part was fine. The waking up part was surprising, because I'd slept so well, I'd actually forgotten Paul was there. So when I opened my eyes to find him looking down at me, I found it hard to disguise my shock. He didn't seem to notice though, which is probably because he's done this before, many times I imagine. I did my best to banish that thought and focused on us, on now, on being together. Paul wanted me to shower with him, which surprised me too, because he was very aroused and I assumed he'd want to make love again. It turned out he did. In the shower. With me held in his arms. There was something very intimate about that.

Making love is intimate anyway – well, it is with Paul. He looks into my eyes the whole time, and makes me feel like I'm the center of his world. Last night and this morning have been so different to the first time and I wonder if maybe that's because he loves me now. I have to admit, him saying that came as quite shock. I'd thought it was just me who'd gotten in deep, so to hear him confess his feelings was unexpected. I suppose being in love with someone does make a difference, doesn't it? In any case, that feeling when he entered me, and when he was buried deep inside me was so intense, so magical, it was almost enough to make me forget my doubts, and his apologies. Almost.

After the mammoth present opening, at which he gave me the most beautiful bracelet, Linda and Morgan got on with cooking the lunch. I offered to help, but they had everything covered, so I sat with Paul and his nephews, helping them with the iPads Paul had bought them for Christmas. We loaded up several apps for them to play with. Paul tried to keep it educational; I tried to keep it fun.

Lunch was amazing and I'm realizing very quickly that Paul's mom is a brilliant cook. After we'd finished, we went for a walk on the beach, leaving Linda and Michael to rest quietly at home for an hour or two, and then came back and played some games. For once, the boys were actually tired, so we settled down and watched a movie together, while Linda made some sandwiches and popcorn, and then it was time for bed. It really was the perfect family Christmas, and just what I needed.

I'm standing outside Paul's bedroom door, with him, his arms close around me.

"Do you want to spend the night with me again?" he asks and I can hear the doubt in his voice. "You don't have to, if you don't want to."

"I want to," I say, without a moment's hesitation, because I do.

He smiles and opens the door, leading me inside and closing it again. "I'm so relieved you said that," he says. "Obviously, if you hadn't wanted to, I'd have respected that, but I don't think I'd have slept very well. And I know I'd have missed you."

"I'd have missed you too." It's the truth. I may have only spent one night with him, but I've already gotten used to the feeling of his arms around me.

He leans down and kisses me, just softly, but I want more. I want him, and I deepen the kiss, pulling him closer and running my tongue along his lips. He opens his mouth and I taste him. He's delicious. His hands are at the hem of my sweater, then I feel skin on skin as he touches me and I suck in a breath.

"You need to be naked," he whispers, breaking the kiss.

"So do you." I look up at him. His eyes are burning into mine and he yanks my sweater over my head, undoing my bra and releasing my breasts. I reach out and start unfastening the buttons of his shirt, but they're small and fiddly, and I'm impatient to see his perfect, muscular chest, to touch his soft skin, so I rip hard and tear his shirt open. He chuckles and walks me back to the bed, letting me fall down onto it, then leaning over and undoing my jeans, and I raise my hips off the bed so he can pull them and my panties down.

"That's better," he says, looking down at me.

I raise my head off the mattress and notice the bulge in the front of his jeans. He's already aroused and I want him. Now. Luckily he's obviously thinking the same thing and he quickly takes off his jeans and underwear and stands before me.

"You're beautiful," I say, without thinking.

He smiles, then leans over and grabs a condom from the drawer, pulling it onto himself like I did last night. Then he kneels on the bed, crawling up over me. "I think you'll find that's you," he replies and I feel his erection prodding into me. I instinctively part my legs, pulling them up so I'm exposed to him and he glances down. "You look perfect," he says, the head of his arousal finding my entrance, like we're meant to be joined. His eyes lock with mine as he pushes inside me and I let out a low moan, tensing slightly at the way he stretches me. He fills me very slowly, edging inside until he can go no further.

"I love you," I whisper, staring up at him.

"I love you." He starts to move, pulling almost all the way out of me, before plunging deep inside again. The feeling is incredible. It sets off sparks of pleasure inside me and I clutch his biceps to try and maintain some control, some grounding, as he builds a slightly faster rhythm, pounding into me.

"Can I have more?" I ask, needing to feel him as deep as he can go.

He stills, then looks at me. "Sure," he says, then without disconnecting us, he kneels back and grabs my legs, pulling them up onto his shoulders. "Let me know if it's too much," he says, and he leans over me again, bending me back on myself, so my knees are by my ears. He pauses, and then pushes himself deep inside me, so deep it almost hurts – except it doesn't because the pleasure is overwhelming and I start to pant straight away, unable to control the feelings any longer. He strokes in and out of me as I'm overcome once again and give myself up to him, to the joy he gives me, as stars fill my eyes and ecstasy consumes my body. I'm aware of his erection getting even bigger, stretching me still further, then his loud groan as he explodes deep inside me.

I must have fallen asleep in Paul's arms again, although I have no recollection of anything after he lowered my legs to the mattress. This morning, he made love to me in the shower again. I love being in bed with him, but there's something really intense and romantic about being held up in his arms while he penetrates me. It feels like I'm putting all my faith entirely in him, not to drop me, not to hurt me – and for me, that's a big step, especially after our first time.

We stay with his family for lunch, after which we pack up our things and say our goodbyes. I make a point of thanking his mom for letting me stay. I know it's not been an easy time for her, but she's made me so welcome. Paul gives his mom a really long hug and spends some time talking quietly to her. I guess that's got something to do with his dad's illness, so I hang back and don't intrude. Once we're ready to go though, he helps me into his car and we drive off.

"Thank you," I say to Paul as he pulls out onto the highway.

"What for?" He glances over at me.

"Inviting me. Making me so welcome into your family. Letting me sleep with you."

He slows the car slightly and looks at me for just a little longer. "Firstly, I've already explained that I invited you because I couldn't bear the idea of you being unhappy with Catrina, so you don't need to thank me for that. Secondly, you're always welcome in my family. I love you. As far as I'm concerned, that makes you family. And thirdly, I didn't 'let' you sleep with me. I asked you to sleep with me, because I wanted to share my bed and my body with you." He pauses, like he's going to say something else, and then speeds up again.

"Are you mad at me?" I ask, feeling slightly scared. His speech, followed by his silence have gotten me a little worried.

"No, of course I'm not." His voice softens. "I just don't always understand you, that's all."

"Why not? What's so hard to understand?"

"Well, I don't see why you need to thank me."

"Because I'm grateful?" I point out the obvious.

"But you've got nothing to be grateful for. Like I said, I love you. Whatever I do for you and with you, I do, because I love you."

It's hard to tell him that I'm not used to being loved. I've grown out of the habit since my dad died – and I'm not sure that's the same kind of love, anyway.

I turn and look out the window.

"Don't go silent on me," he says.

"I'm not."

"Yeah, you are."

"Okay, I am."

"Tell me what you're thinking," he persists.

"I'm thinking that it's a shame our time away has to end. I don't relish the prospect of returning to reality." That's not really what's wrong, but like I say, some things are too hard to tell.

"Yeah," he replies, smiling. "Reality is vastly overrated." He checks his mirrors and changes lanes. "Speaking of reality," he continues, "I'll get in touch with my lawyer when we get back, and I'll let you know when he's free to see you."

"Do you think he'll be able to fit me in sometime in the next couple of days?" I ask.

"You're that keen?"

"Well, no, but I'm going back to Virginia the day after tomorrow. I'm booked on the eleven o'clock flight on Saturday morning."

He pales and turns to glance at me again. His eyes are filled with sadness. "You're leaving? So soon?" he whispers.

"Yes."

"But why? I mean, surely your lectures don't start for another couple of weeks, do they?"

"No, they don't. But I've got a job, remember? I got some time off to come visit my so-called family for the holidays, but I'm due back at work on Sunday."

His shoulders drop. "I see," he murmurs. "Well, I'll speak to Anthony as soon as I can, and see what he can do. If he can't squeeze you in, will you be able to come back at some time?"

"I'm not sure. I work three evenings a week and all weekend, so I can pay the bills and eat."

"Let me help you," he says.

"No, Paul." I look down at the beautiful bracelet around my wrist. "You've already done too much."

"I don't like the idea of you working so many hours. I can…"

"Paul, you're helping me already, by arranging for the lawyer. Please, let me do this my way?" I can feel tears welling in my eyes and he reaches over and clasps my leg.

"Okay," he says softly. "Just promise me, if you need anything, you'll call me."

"I promise."

He smiles very slightly. "And you really have to go home on Saturday?" he asks.

"Yes. I'm sorry."

"Don't be sorry," he whispers, and then he focuses on the road.

I feel every ounce of his disappointment. In reality, there's nothing I'd like more than to stay here – preferably with him. I'd like to spend more time with him, get to know him better, get to understand what's happening between us and what love is all about. As it is, I'm terrified that, when I'm a few hundred miles away, he'll remember that I'm a mistake and I'll be all too easily forgotten. And all too easily replaced.

I hand him the entry card to get into the house and he swipes it, returning it to me before driving inside.

"You're sure you're gonna be okay?" he asks.

"I'll be fine," I tell him. "At least I've got Mrs Hemsworth. And Jack's coming in tomorrow."

"Yeah, right." There's something odd in his voice, but when I turn to look at him, his face is blank, maybe a little pale.

"Is everything okay?" I ask him.

"Sure."

He parks up outside the house and turns off the engine, then leans over toward me.

"Thank you for making it such a special Christmas," he says, looking into my eyes. He's back to his usual self again. Thank God.

"No… thank you."

He moves closer and brushes his lips against mine, his tongue flicking against my lips. I open to him and we kiss intensely, both becoming breathless in an instant.

"I—I think I'd better go," he says, pulling back and smiling down at me. "Otherwise, I'm gonna really give Catrina something to think about."

I can't help chuckling. "She'll be bad enough as it is," I say, without thinking.

He puts his hand on my leg. "If she gets too much, call me," he says, more purposefully. "We'll work something out."

"Don't worry," I say, trying to sound reassuring. "I'll be fine. I've got…"

"Yeah, I know. You've got Mrs Hemsworth and Jack," he says, with a trace of bitterness.

"No. I was gonna say I've got my memories of the most perfect few days with you."

He smiles and leans his forehead against mine. "Sorry," his whispers. "I just wanna be the one protecting you, that's all, baby. I really don't like the idea of leaving you here."

I don't like that idea either. I'd much rather be with him, preferably lying in his arms, where I can feel safe.

"I know you're busy, but you will call me, won't you?" I suddenly feel really unsure about everything, like a shadow's descended over us. The shadow of reality, of his world and mine, and their differences.

"Of course I'll call you," he says, pulling me close to him.

When I get inside, Catrina's waiting, leaning on the wall by the entrance to the living room.

"You're back then," she says, her sarcasm more than obvious.

"So it would seem."

I head for the stairs, but she steps forward, getting in my way.

"So, where have you been?" she asks.

"I told you where I was going," I reply, looking her in the eye. "I spent the holidays with Paul Lewis." I don't mention his family.

"I hope you're behaving yourself," she warns.

I turn to face her. "Whatever I do, or don't do, is no concern of yours, Catrina. And now I'd like to go to my room…" I go to move around her, but she sidesteps me, glaring into my eyes.

"You'd do well to remember this is my house," she hisses.

"As if I could ever forget… given the amount of my money you've spent decorating it."

She opens her mouth for an instant, then stops herself and turns away, flicking her hair into my face as she storms off.

I sag with relief and run up the stairs, bolting to my room and closing the door behind me. God, I wish Paul was here.

I fling myself down on my bed, turn over and stare at the ceiling, wondering why I bothered to come back. I suppose because I don't have any alternatives. Paul might have said he didn't want to leave me here, but he wasn't offering to take me anywhere else either. He didn't suggest going to his place, did he? So this is about the best I've got, at least until Saturday, when I can go back to Virginia. As much as I love Paul – and I really do – the thought of my little apartment near the campus seems wonderfully normal and very uncomplicated.

I curl myself up in a ball, wishing I could work out what's going on, what Paul wants from me, whether this is something long-term, or whether he says he's in love with every woman he takes to bed, when my phone rings. I check the screen, find it's Paul, and answer straight away.

"Hello?"

"Hi," he says, and his voice is like a soothing balm. "You okay?"

"Well, I've been better."

"Yeah. Me too," he replies, sounding desolate.

I sit up. "Why? What's wrong?"

"I'm missing you," he says, with disarming honesty. "I'd say we could meet up tonight, but I've already made plans and I can't really cancel. That's why I didn't invite you back here. It didn't seem fair to do that, and then leave you sitting in my apartment all by yourself."

Well, I suppose that makes sense, except… "You've made plans?" I say, unable to keep the doubt out of my voice. Or is that jealousy?

"Yeah. I'm just going out for a drink. I'd cancel, but it's been arranged for ages…" His voice fades and I struggle to find a reply. "Are you okay?" he asks.

"Yes, I'm fine." I wish I could stop the voice that's ringing around my head, wondering who he's going to be meeting. I shake my head. I need to stop this.

"I spoke to Anthony while I was driving home," he says.

"Oh? Did you?" I welcome the change of subject.

"Yeah. He's not actually working until the New Year."

The disappointment is almost overwhelming. Heaven knows when I'll be able to get back here again. "Oh well," I reply. "Thanks for trying."

"Man, you give up easy," he says. "I'm a very good client of his, and he's agreed to see you at his home tomorrow afternoon."

"He has?" I feel like the weight of the world has been lifted from my shoulders, even though I'm fully aware that I might meet this man and be told there's nothing he can do. "That's very kind of him." A thought occurs to me. "How much is this costing you?" I ask him.

"He owes me a favor," Paul replies evasively. "Your appointment's at four-thirty."

"Okay. Give me the address."

"I'll come by and pick you up at four."

"But surely, you need to work, don't you?"

"Yeah. See you at four," he replies, laughing, and hangs up the call.

I lie back down on the bed again, just as my phone beeps in my hand and I check the screen. It's a message. From Paul.

— *Forgot to say. I love you. xx*

A smile spreads across my lips as I type out my reply:

— *I love you too. L xx*

Paul

I meet Fin and Brad in our usual downtown bar just after eight. I know they've both had to switch shifts for us to keep this meeting, which is why I didn't dare bail on them to spend the evening with Lottie, as much as I wanted to, especially knowing she's going back to college so soon. But then, I've always hated people who dump their friends when they get into a relationship. That said, I don't want two separate lives. Once things get more settled, I want to include Lottie with my friends, and my friends with Lottie, especially as she went really quiet on me after I said I was coming out tonight. I'm not sure what that was about. It's another one of the many things about her that I don't really understand, but which I'm prepared to spend time figuring out.

"Hey, man," Brad says, slapping me on the back. "Did you have a good time with your family?"

"I had a fantastic time with my family." I can't help smiling at them, and they both sit across from me, staring, a little confused.

"Okay," Fin says, sounding doubtful. "That look in your eyes has gotta mean something. So, tell us what happened?"

"Everything happened," I reply, grinning and taking a long sip of my beer.

"Define 'everything'." Brad leans forward.

"Well, I invited Lottie…" I let my voice fade, and watch while they work out what I'm saying.

"This is the girl you met at the party?" Brad asks. "The one you first saw at the restaurant?"

I nod my head, realizing I haven't seen him since we played golf, but that Fin must have filled him in on what's happened since – or at least some of it, being as Brad didn't mention Lottie running out on me after our first time together.

"And, based on that brief acquaintance, and the amazing success of your relationship to date, you invited her to spend Christmas with your folks?" Fin says.

I nod my head. "Yeah."

They both stare at me for a little longer. "Are you serious?" Brad asks.

"Absolutely. And we had a fantastic time, thanks."

"You're not… you're not… in love, are you?" Fin asks, falteringly.

"Yeah. I am."

Brad lets his head drop into his hands, while Fin just continues to stare at me. "And Lottie?" he asks eventually.

"She feels the same," I tell him, and his expression clears a little.

"Thank fuck for that," he murmurs.

"I wasn't sure she did," I explain, "but when I told her how I felt about her, she said she felt the same."

"You said it first?" Brad asks, looking up again.

"Yeah."

"Who the fuck are you, and what have you done with Paul Lewis?" he says.

"I'm right here," I reply. "I'm still the same guy."

"No, you're not." Brad's clearly in shock. "The Paul Lewis I know would've run a mile before declaring his love for a woman. He'd probably have run straight into the arms of the next woman, just to avoid that kind of commitment."

"Yeah. Because he hadn't met the woman he wanted to commit to," I explain. "Wait till you meet her. She's incredible."

Fin sits forward. "I have met her," he says. "And I know how beautiful she is."

"No. You've *seen* her. There's a difference. And it's not just about her being beautiful. It's about so much more than that. I don't really understand her most of the time, but when I'm with her, I just feel different. I feel so much… better."

They both groan and lean into each other. "We really have lost you, haven't we?" Fin says.

"No. I'm still gonna come out with you guys. We'll still do things like this."

"Yeah, until she ties you down to date nights, and weekends away. And suddenly you won't have time for us anymore…"

Brad nods his head, smiling sagely. "Yeah. And before you know it, she'll be talking about weddings and kids, and then it'll be all diapers and breast feeding, and no more sex, and then within the blink of an eye, you'll be obsessed with schools and college funds." He shudders theatrically.

"You're getting way ahead of yourselves, guys."

Fin gives me a knowing look. "You sure about that, are you?"

"Well… not yet, no." I know right away that he's referring to the possibility that Lottie could be pregnant, but Brad looks confused. He glances from me to Fin, and back again.

"Did I miss something?" he asks.

"No," Fin replies. "But our lovestruck friend here did."

I scowl at him and turn to Brad. "The first time Lottie and I were together, I forgot the condom," I whisper.

"You what?" He's even more shocked than Fin was.

I hold up my hands. "Okay," I say, calmly. "I know I'm an idiot."

"What did she say?" he asks.

"She didn't say anything," I reply. "She ran out on me."

He seems to ignore that little bombshell, focusing on the other little problem instead. "And you still don't know? If everything's okay, I mean?"

"No."

"But you've talked about it, right? The consequences, I mean?" Fin asks.

"Well, no we haven't actually."

"Paul," he says testily. "That's a conversation you really need to have. You told me you'd be there for her. But if she's unaware of that, she's probably worried sick."

"She's…" I pause, thinking about how relaxed she was over the holidays, how she didn't seem to think about it, not even we were talking about condoms, and the memory might have realistically come back to haunt her.

"She's what?" he asks, pushing me.

"It's weird," I say, thinking out loud. "She hasn't mentioned it."

Brad leans closer. "Not once?"

"No. When I first found her again, I asked her why she ran out on me, and she didn't say anything about the condom, or about the fact that she might be pregnant – not even to say that it might have been unlikely, that the timing might have been out, or something. There was nothing like that. She just said she felt like we shouldn't have done what we did… like she regretted it."

"Regretted what though? You forgetting the condom, or the whole thing?"

"It felt like she meant the whole thing," I reply remembering the look on her face.

"Well, that's not good," Brad says, stating the obvious.

"Yeah. I know, but then I realized later on that was probably because she didn't know my name at the time."

"You took her to bed without even telling her your name?" Fin says. "I thought I told you to be careful with her."

"I was careful with her."

"Hmm… Sounds like it," Brad puts in, shaking his head.

They both look at me, long and hard. "And despite all of that, despite being unsure about what you'd done, despite you rushing her into bed, despite you forgetting the condom, she still says she loves you?" Fin says.

"Yeah," I reply, somewhat wistfully. Hearing it put like that is sobering. "Although I didn't rush her into bed." I didn't, did I? Did I? "I asked her if she wanted it. She said yes."

"Yeah, and you didn't hang around long enough to tell her your name," Brad interjects.

I fall silent. Their words are like a kick to the gut. I resolve that, after we've been to see Anthony tomorrow, I'm gonna take her out to dinner, and we're going to talk everything through. I need to get this straight. And I need to apologize. Again. And I have to hope to God that when she works out the consequences of my actions – which, for some reason, I don't think she has – she can find a way to forgive me. I thought I was being considerate, making sure she wanted what I was offering, but now I've heard it put into words, I realize that I didn't do enough. I worked out a while ago that I was too focused on getting her naked that first time. I was so intent on getting her into my bed and getting inside of her, I forgot about her. And, more importantly, I forgot to protect her.

Chapter Fourteen

Lottie

I've spent a sleepless, fitful night, missing Paul and wondering what he spent yesterday evening doing. No matter how hard I try, I can't get the image of him with that blonde woman out of my head, only now – because I'm a little more experienced than I was when I first saw them – my imagination is capable of going a little further than them having dinner in a candlelit restaurant. Now I can see them writhing in ecstasy on a silk-lined bed, while he pleasures her. I can hear her calling his name as he penetrates her. I can feel his body shuddering into hers as he takes her and makes her his. Even in my waking moments, my mind is filled with those images. So much so, that I didn't even try to get to sleep.

When I got up, I had a message waiting on my phone from Paul. It just said 'I love you'. It was sweet and, even though I was feeling very frayed around the edges, it helped. Well, it helped me get through the day, anyway.

I decided to spend the day in my room, reading. I desperately wanted to avoid Catrina and the twins, and while I know I could've gone outside and spent a few hours with Jack, I wasn't even sure I wanted to see him. I just needed some time to myself, rather than facing questions and scrutiny, no matter how well intentioned. I don't know that it helped though, because all I've done is wonder about what Paul's doing – or more precisely, who he's doing it with. *What's wrong with me?*

Mrs Hemsworth lets Paul in through the gate at just before four and I go outside to meet him, rather than having him come face-to-face with Catrina. Now he knows how badly she treats me, I'm not sure how he's going to react to seeing her.

Jack's working on the flower beds over to my right and I catch his eye and give him a wave, as Paul's car appears on the driveway. I feel bad about not spending any time with him today, but he gives me a smile and then puts his spade down, making a 'phone' signal with his hand, to let me know he'll call me later. I nod my head and blow him a kiss, which he returns, just as Paul pulls up in front of me.

He climbs out of the car and comes over, looking serious.

"Is everything alright?" I ask him.

"Yeah, I think so," he replies. He glances over his shoulder to where Jack's now gone back to work, and then looks back at me, his eyes a little darker than usual. Surely he's not jealous of Jack, is he? That's ridiculous.

I lean up and kiss him, just gently. To start with, he doesn't really respond, but then suddenly, he brings his arms around me, pulling me close, his tongue darting into my mouth, and I'm leaning into him, my breathing ragged and heavy.

"I know I shouldn't, but I wanna take you," he whispers as he breaks the kiss. "Right here. Right now." I stare into his eyes, wishing he would, wishing he could banish the images from my mind, give me the reassurance I need that he really does love me. Me and no-one else. "But if I do that," he adds, "we'll be late for Anthony."

He takes my hand and leads me to his car, helping me into the seat and closing the door. As he walks around the front of the car, I notice him staring at Jack again. Maybe he does have a problem with us, even though I've explained to him – twice – that Jack's just a friend. I hope he's not gonna be one of those men who doesn't like me having friends of my own, because that would be very hypocritical of him, considering I don't know where he spent yesterday evening.

He sits beside me and I wonder about raising the topic, but he turns and looks at me, then leans over and kisses me deeply. "I've missed you," he says softly. "After we've been to see Anthony, will you come out for dinner with me?"

"If you want me to," I reply, still feeling uncertain.

"Yeah. I want you to. We—We need to talk."

I swallow down the lump that's just formed in my throat. "We do?"

"Yeah."

He sounds unsure of himself. "Should I be worried?"

He caresses my cheek with his fingertips. "No," he says. "You've got nothing to worry about at all. I promise."

"Then why don't I believe you?" I ask him. "Please tell me what's wrong?"

"I'm sorry. I shouldn't have said anything yet. Can we talk about this later?" he says. "We've gotta be at Anthony's in twenty minutes."

He puts the car in gear and sets off down the driveway.

"We can't talk while you drive?" I ask, feeling fearful.

"No. Well, I can't. Not about this."

"Paul... I'm scared," I whisper.

He looks over at me. "I promise, you have nothing to be scared about." His voice carries such sincerity, I feel like I have to believe him. All I want now is to get this meeting over and done with, so we can go out and he can tell me what's wrong.

Anthony's house is modern and stylish, probably a fifteen minute drive from the city, set on a small plot of land behind a high wall.

He greets us at the door, a man of medium build, with salt-and-pepper hair, black rimmed glasses and steely gray eyes, and shows us to a home office, which is just off the main hallway.

"Thanks for doing this," Paul says, taking a seat beside me.

"It's a pleasure," Anthony says, sitting opposite us and looking at me. "So, you're Charles Hudson's daughter?" he says.

I nod my head. "Yes," I reply.

"I was sorry to hear about his death."

"Thank you." I didn't even know he'd met my dad, but it seems like he must've done.

He leans forward slightly. "Paul has given me a rough outline of the issues you're having with your stepmother and I've taken the liberty of obtaining a copy of your father's will."

"You have?" I'm surprised by his efficiency.

"Yes. I can see straight away that your father left you the bulk of his capital, to be held in trust until you either graduated from college, or achieved the age of twenty-five. And that you're entitled to an allowance of three thousand dollars a month until then." I nod my head in agreement. "I also note that the trustee is Mrs Catrina Hudson – your stepmother?" He looks up at me and I nod again, before he glances back at the notes in front of him. "But I understand from Paul that your allowance stopped when your father died, in August, and that it hasn't been paid since. Is that correct?"

"That's right."

"Have you spoken to your stepmother about this?" he asks.

"Several times," I reply. "All she tells me is that I should think myself lucky that she's continuing to let me live in 'her' house, and that my education is really expensive."

He stares at me for second. "I'm not sure what she means by that last statement," he says. "She doesn't pay for your education."

"I know."

He looks down at the document in front of him again. "As for her comment that the house is hers, I'm afraid that is true. And unfortunately, your father made no stipulation in his will that you should be granted a right to live there after his death."

"Wait a second," Paul says, leaning forward. "Are you saying Catrina can kick Lottie out any time she likes, and there's not a thing Lottie can do about it?"

"What I'm actually telling you is that she can – if she feels so inclined – prevent Miss Hudson from gaining entry to the property at all. She can't stop her from taking items which Miss Hudson can prove are rightfully and legally hers. But, if she wished, she could prevent her from setting foot on the property itself."

I've always been aware of this. Well, let's face it, Catrina never let me forget that my former home is now hers, to do with as she pleases.

Hearing it put into blank, legal words is still kinda hard to take though.

"I'm afraid that's not the worst of it," Anthony continues and I sit forward, paying attention. *There's more?* "I understand you live in an apartment in Virginia when you're attending college. Is that right?

"Yes." I nod my head slowly.

"And your father bought that property several years ago, before you started your degree?"

"Yes."

He glances down at the document he's holding, takes a moment to read something and then looks back up at me again. There's a look in his eyes I don't understand. "Unfortunately," he says quietly, "due to the wording of your father's will, your stepmother is entitled to claim ownership of that apartment as well. You see, the way the will is phrased is unusually loose and it just states that she inherits all property to which he had ownership at the time of his death."

I can't believe this. "You mean she can evict me from my own apartment?"

"Yes. From what you've said, I'm not sure she's aware of that, but yes she can."

I feel Paul move closer and put his arm around me. Tears are falling onto my cheeks before I'm even fully aware of them. How could my father have been so blind? Surely he must have realized the power he was handing Catrina over me. Did he really love me that little? "And there's nothing I can do?" I manage to ask.

"No, I'm afraid not," he replies, then holds his hands up as though he's trying to stem my inevitable questions. "But let's not worry about things that haven't happened yet. At the moment, our main concern is to get your allowance reinstated, while we also take steps to ensure your capital sum is being properly administered."

"And you don't think me doing that is likely to push her into forcing me out of the apartment, and the house?" I ask him.

"Well, that's a risk, I suppose," he says, mulling it over. "But then she could do that anyway, even if we don't take any action against her."

He's got a point.

"What do you wanna do?" Paul says, turning to me.

"Well, I'm not going to sit back and just let her spend my dad's money..."

"You want me to write to her?" Anthony asks.

I nod my head. "Yes... please."

He stacks up the papers in front of him, putting them into a file. "I understand you're returning to college tomorrow," he says. "In which case, you'd better give me your contact details in Virginia, and I'll correspond with you there."

I give him my cell number and dictate my address, which he types into his computer.

"Thank you," I say, getting to my feet. I reach across the table and shake his hand. "I appreciate you giving up your time like this."

"It's no trouble," he replies, giving me a sympathetic look, which almost makes me start crying again.

Paul and I drive silently into the city, I think still taking on board what Anthony said. Catrina has always threatened that she could throw me out, and reminded me that the house is hers, but I had no idea how far her power went... until now. I don't think she did either though, because if she'd known she had the right to evict me from the apartment, I'm sure she'd have threatened that too.

Paul parks the car outside the same restaurant we went to the other night and I look over at him. I'm not sure I'm in the mood for fine dining on this scale, not after the meeting we've just had, and knowing that he wants to talk to me about something that's making him unsure of himself and has me scared. I'd rather be somewhere private if we're gonna talk like that. "I'm not properly dressed for this," I tell him, thinking up the only excuse I can.

"You're fine," he replies.

Maybe it's best to just tell him the truth; namely that I'd rather go back to his place, where we can talk in private. "I—" My phone rings, interrupting me and I pull it from my purse, checking the screen. It's Jack, and for a moment, I recall Paul's reaction to him at the house and wonder if I should leave it, but then I think about it. Why should I? Jack's my friend.

"Excuse me," I say to Paul. "I need to take this."

He nods his head and looks out the window.

"Hi," I say into the phone.

"Hi yourself."

"Are you okay?"

"Well, I've been better," he replies. "Are you free to talk?"

"Not really. Can I call you later? Or tomorrow?"

"Are you with your knight in shining armor?" he asks.

"Yes. Very funny, Jack." He laughs.

"Then call me tomorrow," he replies. "And tell me all about it."

"You're sure you're okay?"

"I'm fine." I'm not convinced, but I've got problems of my own, and anyway, I can hardly discuss Jack's issues in front of Paul. "Speak soon," he adds.

"Take care."

We say our goodbyes and I put my phone back in my purse, looking up at Paul to find him staring at me.

"What's wrong?" I ask him. "And don't say 'nothing'."

"I wasn't going to," he replies. "I was going to ask if you've got anything you want to tell me."

"No. You're the one who said you wanted to talk."

"That was before you took a phone call."

Did he really just say that? "So? Am I not allowed to take calls when I'm with you?"

He sighs and shakes his head very slowly. "Of course you are."

"Then what's your problem, Paul? What do you want from me?" I twist in my seat to face him.

"I want to know what the gardener means to you," he says, very calmly.

"I've told you already. He's a friend."

"With benefits?" he asks.

"I don't even know what that means, although I can hazard a guess." I feel my blood boiling, but there's nothing I can do to stop it. "How dare you judge me, or criticize me? For the umpteenth time, when you saw me at the restaurant with Jack, I was out with him as a friend. That's all. But can I remind you, that on that same night, you were out with a blonde woman, who I have no doubt you took back to your place and entertained..." His eyes widen just slightly and I know I've hit the mark. "Oh my God... You did, didn't you?" He reaches out for my hands but I pull away from him, cowering into the seat. "You went to bed with her?"

"No."

"Don't lie to me," I scream.

"I'm not lying. I didn't take her to my place and I didn't go to bed with her. I swear on my mother's life."

I can't disbelieve that, but even so. "Okay, but what about all the other times? All the other women?"

"What other women?"

"Well, I'm sure you've got a list, somewhere..."

He sucks in a breath. "No. Not anymore."

"Excuse me?"

"Nothing..." His voice falls silent.

"No." I move closer to him, trying to read his face. "You said 'not anymore'. That must mean there was originally a list."

"There was," he admits.

"You had a list of women?" My voice has dropped to a whisper – mainly because I can't believe what I'm hearing.

"Yes," he replies, looking out the front windshield.

"So where is it now?" I ask.

He turns to look at me again. "It was on my phone. I deleted it. It doesn't exist anymore."

"When did you delete it?" I feel really cold all of a sudden.

"Right before we first made love, at my apartment."

"Why?"

"I don't know, Lottie," he says with a hint of sarcasm. "I suppose because I thought you and I might have something."

I freeze and my heart stops beating. "You *thought* we might... You mean, you don't now?"

"I don't know. I don't know what's going on anymore."

I swallow down my tears. "Why?"

"Because I don't understand you," he says, raising his voice a little.

"Right back at you."

"What does that mean?" He stares at me, looking almost angry.

"It means I don't know what you want from me. I've got no idea what you're doing when you're not with me. You went out last night, but how do I know where you were, or what you were doing?"

"Because you said you loved me… and that means you're supposed to trust me," he says. "Except you obviously don't."

"I don't even know you, not really. And before you say anything, that's as much my fault as yours. I have no right to judge anyone, do I? Dear God… I had sex with you without even knowing your name."

A shadow crosses his eyes, but it's gone before I have the chance to think about it. "Yeah," he says, "and then ran out on me, without even saying a word, evidently regretting what we'd done together. How do you think that made me feel?"

"About as good as I felt when you apologized, I should imagine. About as good as when you said you'd made a mistake, and regretted it too."

"I never said I regretted it," he says, trying to justify himself.

"Yes you did."

"When?"

"Right after I came back from the bathroom. You said we should never have done it, and you apologized."

"I apologized for forgetting to use a condom, Lottie," he says, slowly and deliberately. "I was letting you know that I regretted doing that; that I made a mistake by forgetting to use protection. That's all. I wasn't apologizing for anything else."

I feel foolish for misunderstanding him; for not realizing. Jack told me Paul could have been apologizing for something else, that I was probably misinterpreting his words, but I wouldn't listen. I was so wrapped up in feeling bad about myself, I refused to admit there could be any other explanation. But how was I supposed to know? I'm not exactly experienced, am I? Not like all the other women he sleeps with… "That's not how it sounded to me," I reply.

"Well, if you'd hung around long enough, you'd have found that out, wouldn't you?" He's still mad. I can hear it in his voice.

"It was my first time, Paul. Why would I want to hang around when the man who'd just taken my virginity told me he regretted it?"

He flinches at my words. "I didn't say that," he says, raising his voice. "I've just explained. I never said I regretted what we did. You made me feel like you wished we hadn't made love; I never regretted a moment of it. But, don't you see? If you'd waited around, instead of running out on me, we could have talked it though, like adults..." He stops speaking suddenly. "I'm sorry. That was uncalled for."

And then it hits me. Despite everything we've done, I'm a child to him... well, maybe not a child, but I'm not a woman either. I'm not worldly-wise, or experienced. I'm still at college. I've got no idea how things like this are supposed to work. I let out a long, slow sigh. "No..." I murmur softly. "Don't apologize. You're only saying what we're both thinking."

He twists in his seat, moving closer. "What's that?"

"That I'm too young for you. Too immature."

"Lottie?" He almost sounds afraid now and I look up at him, to find his eyes glistening a little.

"Well, I am, Paul. Let's face it, you're used to being with sophisticated women, who can take the rough with the smooth, who understand your world, your ways... your needs; who don't mind what you get up to in your spare time, who are a lot less questioning, less... demanding, I suppose."

"I don't have 'ways'," he says, his voice a soft whisper. "And the only thing I need is you. I don't mind you asking questions. I get that you're new to all this and I think it's kinda cute that I get to teach you the things you're not familiar with. You're not demanding, Lottie. Not at all."

"Well, it seems I'm too demanding for you."

"You're not. I promise..." His voice fades.

It doesn't matter what he says now. I can't escape the fact that I can never be the kind of person he's used to. "I'm sorry. I can't do this." I can hear the cracks in my own voice.

He turns to me, his face white. "Don't you love me? Was that a lie?"

The first of many tears falls onto my cheeks. "No. No, it wasn't. I do love you. I honestly do. But I can't be the kind of woman I think you need. Or the kind of woman you want."

"Yes, you can. You are. It was just a misunderstanding. I should have made myself clearer when I apologized."

"It's not just about that, Paul. It's about my jealousy, my insecurity… my need to be with you a lot more than you're able."

"Hey, I need to be with you too. All the time. I can't, because I have commitments, but that doesn't mean the need isn't there. I promise, you have nothing to be jealous of," he says. "I spent last night with Fin and Brad. They're old friends of mine from…"

"I don't want you to have to justify yourself to me all the time," I interrupt. "I want to be better than that." The tears start falling again.

"Don't cry." He reaches out for me, but I pull away.

"I'm sorry." I open the car door and almost fall out onto the sidewalk.

"Lottie?" he calls after me.

"Just go."

Paul gets out of the car, looking at me over the top of it. "No. I'm not leaving you here."

"And I'm not getting back into your car." I fold my arms across my chest. I know I'm being childish now, but I'm scared. I'm really scared. I'm scared of how I'm feeling; scared of the turmoil of emotions swirling around me; scared of losing him, even though I know I'm pushing him away.

He holds up his hands. "Okay. If you won't go anywhere with me. Call a cab to take you home, and I'll wait with you until it arrives."

"Home?" I say to him, trying hard not to laugh, because I know I'll cry even harder. "I don't have a home. My father gave both my homes to my stepmother, remember?"

He closes his eyes. "Is that what this is about? You're feeling unsafe and insecure because of the fact that Catrina can put you on the streets at a moment's notice? You have to know, I'd never let that happen to you."

"Because you'll ride in like a knight in shining armor and throw money at the situation?"

"No, because I love you and I'll always take care of you," he reasons.

"Why can't you just accept it, Paul? There's nothing you – or anyone – can do to stop her," I yell at him. "My dad saw to that."

"Please, Lottie?" He goes to step around the car.

"Let's face it," I say abruptly, holding up my hands. "It's over. I've said too many horrible things to you now. I know you won't be able to forget what I've said tonight, or forgive me for it. So, let's just pretend we never happened…"

"You think you could do that?" he asks, raising his voice again. "Because I damn well can't."

"Yeah, you can. Just start another list."

He glares at me, and I know that hurt him. I can see the pain etched on his face and I want to take back the words, but then he gets back into his car, and with a screech of tires, he pulls away from the sidewalk.

It's already dark and I'm standing in front of the restaurant, staring into the space where Paul's car was, regretting every single word I just said to him. I've never felt so alone in my life as I do now and I'd give anything – everything – for him to come back and hold me, and tell me he can make it alright. Except he won't, because the one true thing I said to him in all those harsh, uncalled for words, was that he won't be able to forgive me. He won't. Ever. Why would he? I was hateful.

I start to cry a little harder. I don't have enough money for taxi fare, and if I use my bank card to pay for a cab, then I won't have enough in my account to pay the rent at the end of the month. This is the kind of real life existence Paul Lewis isn't used to, the living from hand-to-mouth that the rest of us have to deal with on a daily basis.

I wonder for a moment about calling him and asking him to come back and get me. I'm fairly sure he would, but what we'd say to each other, I don't know. And I don't have the right to ask. Not any more.

I pull out my phone and do the only other thing I can. I call Jack.

Jack's Dodge pulls up by the side of the road about ten minutes later. I'm cold and I'm tired, and I've never been so grateful to see him in my life.

"What the hell happened to you?" he asks, jumping out of the vehicle and coming over to me.

"It's a long story."

"Well, you can tell me on the ride home," he replies and puts his arm around me.

Then, from somewhere up the road, I hear a screech of tires, which makes me jump and I turn to see a bright red Ferrari roaring away into the distance.

Paul

My hands grip the steering wheel and I floor the gas, glancing back in the rear-view mirror and seeing him putting his arms around Lottie, helping her towards his dark blue Dodge. What the fuck? I look back at the road and realize the lights ahead of me are red and I'm way too close to them. I slam the breaks on, skidding and stopping just in time. I take a few deep breaths. Christ, I need to calm down. I close my eyes and take a few deep breaths, then I look back in my mirror and see the Dodge pulling out into the traffic, going in the opposite direction.

"She's safe," I murmur out loud, letting out a sigh of relief, because that was the whole reason I pulled over in the first place.

I was mad at Lottie for suggesting I start another list – like I'm ever gonna do that. I love her, why the hell would I wanna be with anyone else? I didn't say that though. I didn't say anything, because I was mad at her, and because she just broke up with me for reasons I don't understand. And I didn't really feel like putting my heart out there. Again.

There was no way I was gonna leave her standing on the sidewalk though, so I pulled up across the street and watched her. She stood for a while, looking distraught, wandering up and down, like she was lost. I thought about running over the road and putting her over my shoulder, and just carrying her back to my car, so she'd be safe, so we could talk, but I didn't think she'd appreciate that. And then she made a call. I assumed she'd taken my advice and called a cab, so I waited for one to arrive... and then *he* turned up. I shake my head as the lights change to green and I pull away, a lot more slowly, a lot more in control. I've gotta stop thinking about him like that. She said she wanted to stop feeling jealous of me; that she wanted to be better than that. I guess I want the same thing. If I hadn't jumped down her throat about him the moment she came off the phone, none of this would've happened. It's all my fault, because I didn't trust her. I didn't believe her. Well, I did, but I just keep seeing him kissing her fingers and wondering what kind of 'friend' does that. Still, whatever he did, she told me he's her friend, and I should have trusted her. And because I didn't, we're over.

I keep remembering the sight of her, crying in front of me and I want to hold her, to make it better. I guess he's doing that now. He's the one hugging her, stroking her hair and drying her tears, and in a way, I'm pleased. I never thought I'd say that, but I'm glad she's got someone to hold her. I'm glad someone's there for her – even if it isn't me.

I get back to my apartment and get out of the elevator, going over to the couch and throwing my keys onto the table. Then I flop down into a seat and lie my head back, looking up at the ceiling, remembering how she felt in my arms, how her body felt underneath mine, how good it felt to be inside her. Everything blurs and I blink quickly trying to clear my vision. It doesn't work, and a tear falls onto my cheek. I haven't cried since I was about ten years old, but the thought of never seeing her again is too much.

I pull my phone from my jacket pocket and, through the blur, manage to look up Fin's number.

He picks up after the second ring.

"Tell me you're not working," I say by way of greeting.

"No. I've just finished. What's wrong?"

"Everything." I swallow hard. "Can... Can you come over?" I feel pathetic, but I really don't wanna be by myself.

"Sure. I'll be there in ten minutes." He doesn't ask why. He just hangs up, probably guessing that I can't talk.

I get up and go through to my bedroom and into the bathroom, running some water and splashing it onto my face. I look up at myself in the mirror. I look pale, drawn, tired. Put simply, I look wrecked. And I bury my face in a towel for a few minutes, hiding, pretending my world didn't just end on the sidewalk outside my favorite restaurant. Except it did. The irrefutable evidence is staring me in the face when I look up again.

I can't bear to see my own reflection any longer and return to my bedroom, quickly changing out of my suit and into jeans and a t-shirt, just as Fin arrives and I buzz him in.

"What happened?" he asks, as he exits the elevator. He looks at me, but doesn't comment, although I can tell from the expression on his face that I don't look good – even if I hadn't seen the evidence for myself.

"Lottie… she broke up with me," I say simply.

"Fuck," he murmurs under his breath, and we go over to the couch and sit down together. "Have you eaten?" he asks.

I shake my head.

"Okay." He pulls out his phone and presses a few buttons, then holds it to his ear and places an order at our usual Chinese take-out. When he's finished, he drops his phone down beside him on the couch, then gets up and goes into the kitchen, grabbing a couple of beers from the refrigerator and bringing them back, placing one in front of me. "Drink that," he says.

I open the bottle and take a long swig. "Is it meant to help?" I ask.

"No, but it can't hurt." He takes a gulp of his own beer, puts the bottle back on the table and turns to face me. "Do you wanna get drunk, or do you wanna tell me what happened?"

"Can we do both?"

"Sure." He takes a breath, understanding I think that he's gonna have to start this conversation. "I thought you guys were doing okay. I thought you'd done the whole 'I love you' thing over Christmas."

"We were. We did."

"So what went wrong?"

"Everything… I think."

"You think?"

"Yeah," I reply. "It got complicated."

He shrugs. "I'm not going anywhere."

"While we were up in Maine, she asked me to help her get her inheritance back."

"Her inheritance?" he queries.

"Yeah. Charles put all his money in trust until Lottie graduated, or reached the age of twenty-five."

"Okay. So what's the problem?"

"Catrina stopped paying her allowance, and started spending the capital sum."

"Nice."

"Yeah. So Lottie asked if I'd help her out. I took her to see my lawyer this afternoon, and he explained that, while Lottie has a great case for getting her allowance back, and having the management of the trust fund investigated, under the terms of the will, Catrina has the right to throw her out of the house, and her apartment in Virginia, and there's not a damn thing Lottie can do about it."

"Wow. That's harsh."

"Yeah. Although to be honest, I was so focused on the conversation I wanted to have with her – about the way I'd behaved when we first got together, and her reaction, and wanting to make sure she really had been okay with what we did, and maybe finally getting around to talking about whether she might be pregnant – it didn't fully hit home with me about what Charles had done, and how she might feel about that, until we were arguing outside the restaurant."

"You were arguing?"

"Yeah."

"About the way you'd treated her?" he asks.

"No. We didn't even get to that. I was about to take her to dinner, and she got a phone call from her friend, Jack."

"Jack?"

"Yeah. He's the guy I saw her with that first time, when I was with Ashley."

"I get the feeling there's something you're not telling me. You thought she was with him at the time, didn't you?"

"Yeah."

"So is she? With him, I mean? Is that what this is all about?" His voice hardens.

"No. She says they're just friends, but what I didn't tell you then was that he—he did this thing to her..." My voice fades to silence.

"What thing?" Fin asks.

"He kissed her fingers and then sucked them." He nods his head, but doesn't say anything. "It was really intimate," I continue. "That's the reason I thought they were together."

"I can understand that. It doesn't sound like the kind of thing a friend does."

"Exactly." I feel kinda relieved he said that. Maybe it's not me. Maybe I'm not being completely irrational.

"So, he called her this evening?" he prompts.

"Yeah, and she took the call. It was clear who she was talking to, and she said she'd call him back later, which made me think she wanted to talk to him when I wasn't around." I look over at him. "I've never been so jealous in my life as I was right then, but I was just overwhelmed with it... and with anger."

"Toward her?" he asks.

"Toward both of them."

He nods his head. "So what happened?"

"I asked her if she had anything she wanted to tell me."

"And?"

"She said she didn't. So I asked her outright what he meant to her, and she kinda lost it. She told me he's a friend, and reminded me that I'd been with a woman too that night, and then accused me of being a hypocrite."

"Because of Ashley?"

"Yeah... and all the other women."

"How does she know about the other women?"

"Well, she didn't, until she made the sarcastic suggestion that I probably had a list of them."

"Oh God…"

"I told her that I don't… not anymore."

His eyes close. "Fucking hell, Paul."

"I know. I wasn't thinking straight. I was mad with her at the time. It just came out."

"So what happened then?"

"I explained that I'd destroyed the list, before she and I went to bed the first time."

"You did?" He's surprised and it shows.

"Yeah. It didn't feel right for that to be out there. I thought she was different. I thought we had a chance at something different. That's what I told her."

"And what did she say?"

"She asked if I was talking in the past tense, about having something special with her."

"Right…"

"And I told her I didn't know. I said I didn't understand her — because I don't, not always — but she threw that back in my face."

"She did?" He looks confused now.

"Yeah. She pretty much accused me of cheating on her."

"When? When you were with Ashley? Because that's not fair; that was before you guys even got together."

"No, this had nothing to do with Ashley. She was talking about last night, when I was out with you and Brad."

"Excuse me?" He sits forward and picks up his beer, letting the bottle hang between his fingers. "She does get that, just because you're seeing her, doesn't mean you're not allowed to see your friends, doesn't she?"

"She thought I was lying. She assumed I was with another woman."

"What did you say?"

"I told her it'd be real nice if her love came with a little bit of trust." He winces, but doesn't say a word, and takes a sip of his beer. "She said it was her fault as much as mine, but that we don't really know each other. She said she felt bad about having sex with me, when she didn't even know my name."

"I'm not gonna say 'I told you so' but…"

"Yeah, I know. And I get that. Let's face it, that's exactly what I was planning on talking to her about before we starting arguing. But it's like I said to her… if she'd hung around, instead of running out on me, we could have talked it through. As it was, she made me feel like she regretted it."

He tilts his head from side to side. "I can see that."

"But then she said she felt I regretted it too."

"Why would she say that?" he asks.

"Because I told her I'd made a mistake, and apologized for it."

"When?"

"When we'd finished… after she came back from the bathroom." I let out a sigh. "And before you say anything, I was apologizing for not using a condom. I was telling her I'd made a mistake by forgetting it. The problem was, she ran out before I got the chance to explain that."

"It does all sound like a huge misunderstanding," he points out.

"Yeah. I told her that. I said it was something we could have worked out, if she'd hung around… like an adult." I lower my voice as I say the last three words.

"Oh shit," he murmurs. "You actually said that?"

"Yeah. I apologized straight after though. I felt bad about it." I take another swig of my beer. "The thing was, she agreed with me. She told me she feels she's too young for me."

He shakes his head slowly. "That doesn't sound good."

"No. It was about then that I realized we weren't just having an argument, that it wasn't just a misunderstanding, and she was breaking up with me." I lie back on the couch and close my eyes. "She told me she loves me. She even said that one of her problems is that she wants to be with me more than I want to be with her, which is bullshit, because I wanna be with her all the time – and I told her that. But she still didn't wanna try and work it out. She told me to go." I hear my own voice crack and swallow hard, trying to keep it together.

"You left her there?"

I shake my head. "She got out of the car and refused to get back in, so I told her to call a cab to take her home, and that I'd wait with her until it came." I look over at him again. "That's when she really lost it. She yelled at me that she doesn't have a home, because her father gave it to her stepmother. I—I told her I'd never let anything bad happen to her, and she... she got even more defensive, saying how I'd rush in and throw money at the problem, like a knight in shining armor, or something. I tried to tell her that wasn't what I meant, but she just said it's over and she wanted to pretend we never happened..." I stop talking, because I have to.

"Can you do that?" Fin asks, his voice very gentle.

"No. I told her I couldn't."

"And?" He looks at me expectantly, knowing there's more.

"She told me to start another list."

"Fuck... That had to hurt."

"Yeah."

"What did you say?" he asks.

"I didn't say a fucking thing. I didn't trust myself to. So, I got in my car and drove off."

"So you did leave her there?"

"No, I couldn't do that. I parked up on the other side of the road. I thought I'd wait and see what she did."

"And? What did she do?"

"Well... she wandered up and down for a few minutes. She was obviously crying and she looked really distressed. I was gonna go back to her, but then she made a call, and I assumed she was gonna get a cab home. I waited. And then *he* turned up."

"He?" Fin stares at me, then realization dawns in his eyes. "Oh. The 'friend'."

"Yeah. Jack."

"She called him?"

"Yeah." I hold up my hand before he can say anything. "And I'm okay with it. She told me she loves me and I have to give her my trust, the same as I was asking her to give me. If she says they're friends, then I believe her."

He raises his eyebrows, but doesn't say a word.

"Okay, I know the finger kissing thing is weird," I admit, "and maybe that means he wants more from her, but I do believe that for her, it's just friendship."

He nods his head just as my door buzzer rings.

"I'll get it," Fin says, and goes over to the intercom, letting in the guy with the take-out delivery. He pays him and brings the bags back over to the kitchen. "You need to eat," he says, looking over at me.

"I need Lottie," I reply.

"Come here and get some food, and then we'll talk some more," he says.

I get to my feet, knowing it's useless to argue with him. "At least use plates?" I ask, going over to him.

"I know better than to do anything else when I'm here," he says, getting some dishes from the cabinet above his head.

We help ourselves to take-out and grab another couple of beers, going back into the living room. Once we're both comfortable and he's taken a mouthful of Kung Pao Shrimp, he turns to look at me. "First I'm gonna be your friend," he says. I stare at him for a moment.

"And second?" I ask, not sure what to expect.

"Second, I'm gonna be a doctor."

I swallow down the special fried rice I've just put in my mouth. "A doctor?"

"Yeah. It's what I do, remember?"

"I know. But why do I need a doctor?"

"You don't." He takes another forkful from his plate and says, "Speaking as your friend, I think you need to hang onto the fact that she said she loves you."

"Why?"

"Because, if my medical opinion is correct, what's coming next could be kinda hard to handle. And she's gonna need you."

"Even if she doesn't want me?" I ask.

"Except she does." He takes a sip of beer. "She told you she does. She told you she wants you more than you want her, remember?"

"Yeah, right before she dumped me."

He sighs. "I'm trying to be your friend here. Hold onto the good things she said and try real hard to ignore the negatives. I think she needs you *and* wants you. She's just in a really bad place at the moment"

"Is this you being a doctor now?"

"Yeah. The last part is. Obviously I'm not a psychologist and I've never met her or examined her, but from everything you've told me, I think she's struggling over the death of her father, and her feelings of being abandoned by him."

"By Charles?"

"Yeah. From her point of view, it's only a few months since he died and she just found out that he left her family home – the place she always felt safe and loved – and her apartment, which is the place where she now lives, to a woman who hates her. She probably feels like she doesn't belong anywhere. For all she knows, she could be homeless tomorrow."

"I'd never let that happen to her."

"I know. Hell, she probably even knows that too. But can't you see? It's not about you, Paul. From her perspective, her dad didn't care about her enough to keep her safe. She's just lost him, and on top of that, she's just found out that he put her stepmom first. He may not have meant it that way, but that's how it probably feels to Lottie right now. She's still grieving for a man she no longer feels sure about. I imagine she's in all kinds of turmoil."

"In which case, why end it with me? I can keep her safe."

"Because she's not necessarily being logical. She only just found out about her dad's will and all its implications. She needs to work things out for herself…"

"Yeah," I murmur, thinking through what just happened. "And the first thing I did was to accuse her of lying to me about her friend."

"Your timing may not have been the best, but don't beat yourself up too much. You were hurting too."

"Not in the same way. I was feeling jealous. She's falling apart… There's a difference."

"Yeah, there is." He nods his head, then pauses for a moment before continuing, "And you've gotta bear in mind that she might also be pregnant – with your child. Pregnancy does weird things. If she is pregnant, her hormones will be all over the place, so you can't necessarily expect rational behavior. Even if she didn't have all this other shit going on in her life."

I close my eyes. Why didn't I think about that? "We didn't even get around to talking about the possibility of her being pregnant," I murmur. "Even after I explained that I was only apologizing for not using a condom, she didn't seem to register the consequences of my fuck-up. She was so focused on the misunderstanding of what we'd said to each other, she didn't seem to realize she might be pregnant."

Fin stares at me. "She's fragile," he says. "She's not thinking straight at the moment. It's not a medical term, but she's emotionally lost right now. She needs your help."

"And how the fuck am I supposed to help her when she just broke up with me?"

"You love her, don't you?" he says calmly.

"Yeah, of course I do."

"Then don't give up on her."

"I'm not going to." I can't. I love her too much to give up on her.

Chapter Fifteen

Lottie

Jack looks over his shoulder. "That car," he says, turning back to me. "The red Ferrari... Is that him?"

I nod my head and then collapse into him.

"What's going on?" he asks, putting his arms around me and pulling me toward his car.

"I didn't know he was still here," I reply. "I thought he'd gone."

"Why would he go?"

"Because I broke up with him."

Jack helps me up into his Dodge. "You did?"

"Yes."

"Give me your phone," he says, holding his hand out. "Let me call him. You guys need to talk."

I shake my head. "No. I need to go... home." I can't help the smile that forms on my lips as I say that last word. What home? It's like I said to Paul, I don't have a home anymore.

"You're clearly upset at breaking up with him, and he obviously waited around. You need to speak about this, not just walk away," Jack persists.

"No. It's over. And anyway, he'll be madder than hell at seeing you here."

"Why? What did I do?"

"You didn't do anything. He... he got the wrong idea about you at the restaurant."

"Because of that dumb thing I did with your fingers?" he asks. Oh. I'd forgotten about that. Is that why Paul's found it so hard to believe in Jack as a friend, I wonder. I suppose it was quite an intimate thing for him to have done to me. And now I come to think about it, his reaction isn't that surprising. After all, I've been raging with jealousy over seeing him sitting opposite another woman, and he's had to picture Jack kissing and sucking on my fingers. Even so, it was just a bit of harmless fun. At the time, we had no idea Paul and I would ever even see each other again.

"I don't know," I reply. "He just asked me – for the third time – whether you're more than a friend."

"The third time?"

"Yeah. I've explained it to him before, and it seems he didn't believe me. Again."

He leans into the car. "Give me your phone," he says. "I'll talk to him. I can tell him I was fooling around when I kissed your fingers. I'll tell him I'm gay…"

"No. Now, shut the door and take me home. Please. I'm freezing."

He stares at me for a moment, then does as I ask, coming and sitting in the driver's seat beside me. He pulls away into the traffic, heading out of the city.

"Gonna tell me why you just broke up with a man you're so clearly in love with?" he asks. "Because I really don't believe it's just because you're friends with me."

"It wasn't. That was just the catalyst for the argument." I turn to look at him. "I've had such a shitty afternoon."

He puts his hand on my knee and gives me a light squeeze. "Tell me about it."

I suck in a breath and lean back in the seat, staring out the front window at the oncoming headlamps. "Paul took me to see his lawyer," I explain.

"He did?"

"Yeah. I asked him to help get my allowance reinstated, and to stop Catrina blowing my inheritance."

"Good for you, girl," he says, grinning.

"You'd have thought so, wouldn't you?"

"What went wrong? Can't the guy help?" he asks.

"He can help. But he'd gotten hold a copy of my dad's will, and found a clause that says Catrina has the right to evict me from the house and my apartment whenever she wants, and there's not a damn thing I can do about it." I start to cry again and reach into my purse for another Kleenex.

"Oh, Lottie," Jack says. "That's awful."

"I know. I feel so alone," I wail.

"Hey. You're not alone. You've got me and Alex, and Mrs Hemsworth. And I'm pretty sure you've still got Paul Lewis, if you want him."

I shake my head. "We're completely wrong for each other," I tell him.

"Is that why you broke up with him?"

"Yeah. He doesn't really want me," I murmur, even though I vaguely remember him saying he does. "He wants someone older, more sophisticated. Someone who doesn't get jealous every time he's out of her sight."

Jack chuckles. "I'm sure you're not that bad," he says softly. "And don't you think that's for him to decide? If he's happy with you, despite your numerous faults, then who are you to make him miserable?"

"But I never knew what I was to him." I sniff into my Kleenex. "He never called me his girlfriend… and then there were all his other women."

"What other women?" Jack says, with a sharpness in his voice. "Was he cheating on you?"

"No, but he had a list," I explain.

"How do you know this?"

"Because I accused him of having one, as a kind of joke, and he confirmed it."

"He's got a list of other women?" I can hear the shock behind his words and his hands grip the steering wheel a little tighter.

"No. Not anymore."

"Lottie, I'm really confused. Can you explain this properly?"

"He used to have a list of women, on his phone. He destroyed it."

"When?" Jack asks. "When did he destroy it?"

"Before he and I slept together the first time."

He smiles. "Then I don't see what your problem is. If he had a list of women who he used to see before he met you, then it's nothing to do with you. You can't judge him based on who he was before you knew him. But he erased the list before he took you to bed, Lottie. That shows he was committed to you, and to the chance of a future with you, not the list, not the other women." He reaches over for my knee again. "And as for not calling you his girlfriend, you hadn't been together for very long, so maybe he just didn't get the chance. Besides, who cares about labels anyway?"

"I do," I grumble through my tears.

He smirks at my childishness, then shakes his head and sighs patiently. "Okay. Well, I guess we all like to know where we stand. But is that the most important thing here? I mean, isn't it more important that you love each other?"

I pause for a moment before nodding my head. "I was always so jealous of him though," I point out. "And I despised myself for it. Surely, if it was right – if it was meant to be – I'd have trusted him."

"Everyone gets jealous sometimes, honey," he says. "Maybe you need to sit down somewhere quiet and talk this over with Paul?"

"What would be the point in that?"

"Lottie, if you're gonna have any chance of a future…"

"A future?" I interrupt him. "We don't have a future. After everything I just said to him, he'll never want me back. I think that much is obvious from the way he just drove off."

"I think the only thing that's obvious from the way he just drove off is that he's as jealous of you as you are of him," Jack replies.

"Either way, you weren't there. You didn't hear the things I said to him…"

"And it was all one way, was it?"

"Well, no…"

"Exactly. That's what happens when people fight. They say things they regret. Then they apologize, they make up and they work it out. It's called being an adult, Lottie." I burst into noisy tears, covering my face with my hands and sobbing loudly. "What?" he asks, and I feel the car stop. He leans over and pulls me into his arms. "What did I say."

"The same thing as him," I cry. "He said I ran out on him, rather than staying and talking it through, like adults."

"What? When you and he first got together?" he queries.

"Yes." I nod my head.

"But that was because he said he regretted what he'd done. I think most people would be upset about that."

I pull back and look up at him. "Yes. Except he wasn't apologizing for what he'd done… well, not in the way I thought, anyway. That's why he said I should have waited, because then he'd have been able to explain. He wasn't saying he regretted what we'd done. He was apologizing for not using a condom…"

"Excuse me? He was what?"

I stare at him. "He was apologizing for…"

"I heard what you said, Lottie," he interrupts. "I just can't believe you said it." He pauses for a moment. "He forgot to use a condom?"

"Yes."

"And you're only mentioning this now? Nearly a week after the event?"

"Well… yes. Does that matter?"

He sighs deeply and lets his head rock forward into his hand. "Yeah. It does." He looks up at me again. "I'm gonna give this guy the benefit of the doubt and assume he's clean, but what about you?"

"Excuse me? It was my first time, Jack…"

"I know that," he says quickly. "I'm not suggesting you wouldn't have been clean. I'm just saying that you might be pregnant."

I can feel the blood drain from my face. "Oh God…"

"Has that only just dawned on you?" he asks.

I nod my head. "Yes. I—I was so upset because he was apologizing, and then so happy that he was in love with me, it didn't even occur to me…"

"I wish you'd told me earlier, like the next day, when you were telling me everything else," he says.

"Why? What difference does that make? The damage was already done by then." I stare down at my shaking hands, unable to believe that my life has changed so much in the last couple of hours, that I'm facing the possibilities of homelessness and motherhood at the same time.

"There is such a thing as emergency contraception, Lottie."

I look up at him, seeing a ray of hope. "Is it too late for that?" I ask, although I don't know how I think my gay friend is going to know the answer to that.

"Yeah. My sister used it once. I'm not sure why she felt the need to tell me about it, but she did. Anyway, I think you've gotta take it within the first couple of days. So it's too late now…" He takes my hands in his and turns me to face him. "Look, you don't know for sure that you are pregnant. Chances are that you're not."

"My period's due next Friday," I say quietly. "So I guess I won't have long to wait." I shrug my shoulders and lean into him. "As if the prospect of being homeless wasn't bad enough…" I whisper.

He pulls back and takes a firm grip of my shoulders, twisting me to face him. "You'll never be homeless," he says. "If that old witch kicks you out, you'll always have a home with me and Alex."

"Except you live here, and I'm at college in Virginia," I point out.

"Well, I'm sure we'll be able to work something out. And if you are pregnant, Alex and I will make the best uncles you can imagine."

I look up at him and try really hard to smile. I can't though. All I can do is cry.

Paul

I woke up this morning and, for a moment, I forgot about yesterday and thought Lottie and I were still together. I turned over, for some reason expecting to find her next to me, and found the bed empty. I've got no idea why I thought I might see her beside me, considering that she's never slept here with me, but the disappointment on finding she wasn't there was overwhelming and I buried my face in the pillows for a good half hour, unable to face the reality of a day without seeing her.

Fin stayed until gone midnight. We didn't get drunk in the end. He let me have three beers and then switched us to coffee, using the excuse that he was on an early shift this morning. I felt guilty for keeping him here so late, but he assured me he's used to going without sleep. He's a good friend. I know if the roles were reversed, I'd do the same for him, although I'm not sure he'll ever fall in love. He's not like I used to be, with a list of women he can call on, but he does like to play the field and I can't see him giving that up.

Thinking about my list just reminds me of my argument with Lottie and I roll over onto my back. It all went so badly yesterday. Everything I wanted to say came out wrong, and everything she said was so final. I know Fin said she needs me, but her words to the contrary keep rolling around my head.

I can't bear the memory and I get up and go through the bathroom, walking straight into the shower and turning on the water, trying real hard not to think about taking Lottie in the shower at my parents' house – twice. I loved the way she looked into my eyes when I penetrated her, like she was placing all her faith in me, which I guess she was, because in that position, she kinda had to trust me not to drop her. I really felt that belief in her, when I held her in my arms, joining our bodies. She was giving herself to me completely at that moment, and I knew it. Everything blurs again, just like last night, and I know it's not just because I've got my face under the shower.

I step out of the water and hear my phone ringing. For some reason, hope flares in my chest that maybe Lottie's calling. Maybe she's saying she's changed her mind, she wants to talk before she flies back to Virginia later this morning.

I race through to my bedroom, dripping water all over the wooden floor, thinking to myself that I'll agree to anything. I'll go wherever she wants, I'll do whatever she wants, if she'll just give us another chance.

"Lottie?" I say, without checking the screen.

"No. It's me." My mom's voice brings me down to earth with a crash.

"Oh. Hi, Mom."

"What's wrong?" she asks. I guess I can't hide my feelings from her, any more than I can from Fin.

I wander back onto the bathroom and grab a towel, putting the phone onto speaker and resting it on the shelf while I dry off.

"It's obviously something to do with Lottie," she continues when I don't immediately answer her.

"Yeah." I suppose I'm gonna have to tell her. "We broke up."

"You only just got together." She states the obvious. "What happened?"

I tell her the same things I told Fin, leaving out some parts. I don't tell her I forgot to use a condom, or that I used to have a list of women and that Lottie called me out on it. I do tell her that Lottie had a really bad day yesterday, that I wasn't there for her like I should've been, and that she ended it with me.

"Why?" she asks. "And don't tell me it's because you weren't there for her," she adds. "That's a reason to have a fight with someone. It's not a reason to break up with them."

"She feels she's too young for me. Well, that's what she said, anyway."

"And you don't believe her?"

"No. I think she's feeling insecure about her dad and the will." I don't mention that she might also be pregnant. "And I didn't see it. Well, not quickly enough, anyway."

There's a short silence on the end of the line. "Don't give up on her," Mom says quietly.

"I'm not." I sigh deeply, drying off my hair with the towel. "It's gonna be kinda hard though. She's flying back to Virginia this morning."

"And you can't see her first?"

"I don't want her to feel like I'm pushing her. She was real adamant we were through. I think I need to give her some space."

"I think you need to let her know you're not giving up first, and then give her some space, so she knows you're still there if she needs you," Mom says. "She's not psychic, Paul. If you don't tell her you're waiting for her, she's not gonna know."

She has a point.

"Did you call for a particular reason?" I ask her. "Is everything okay with Dad?"

"Yes. Your father's fine. He's a bit tired, but I think that's just him recovering from Christmas."

"So there's no reason for this call?"

"Just call it mother's intuition. I didn't sleep very well last night. I had a feeling something was wrong."

"They used to burn witches, you know," I tease, smiling for the first time since yesterday evening.

"I know. But you're my son. I always know when you're not happy. And you're not happy. You were with Lottie. Try and work it out, Paul. She's good for you."

"I know she is." She's the best thing that's ever happened to me, or will ever happen to me. And not being with her is breaking me apart.

I get dressed in jeans and a button down shirt and wander around the apartment. I could go out, but I'm not sure where. I could do some work in my office that I've got set up here, but I doubt I could concentrate. The only thing I can think about is Lottie. She's booked on the eleven o'clock flight out of Logan, which is about twenty minutes from here. It's just before ten. I could go… I'd be cutting it fine. But… I look at my keys, which are still lying on the table where I threw them last night. I could go and see her before she leaves. Couldn't I? I know I said to my mom that I don't want Lottie to feel like I'm pressuring her, but my mom was right, if she doesn't know I'm not giving up, how will she know she can turn to me when she needs me, which according to Fin, she will.

I go through into the bedroom and put on my shoes, then grab my keys and run straight to the elevator. I said I'm not giving up. Well, I'm not.

My car's parked in the basement garage where I left it last night and I get in and start the engine, pulling out and heading for the exit. Out on the street, I hit traffic almost straight away, a long line of cars ahead of me, a mass of brake lights as far as I can see. I check the time. It's still a few minutes before ten. I can make this…

There's a break in the traffic and I floor the gas, tearing through gaps, driving like a lunatic, before I hit more hold-ups.

"Fuck it." I slam my hand on the steering wheel and screech to a stop.

Ten minutes later, I'm moving again, and within seconds, the reason for the delay becomes clear as I drive past a minor accident that's blocking one lane of the highway. Fabulous.

At least the way ahead is clear now and I take advantage, tearing up the road.

I reach the airport parking lot at ten-thirty, unsure whether I'll be too late. They've probably called her flight by now. But I guess there's a chance she's running late. Isn't there? There's always a chance.

I park up and run for the terminal, making for the departure area.

One look at the board tells me her flight's already been called, but I go over to the American Airlines desk and wait while a woman in front asks interminable questions about baggage allowances before finally moving off.

"Hi," I say to the blonde behind the desk.

"Hello," she says, with a low husky voice, looking me up and down. *Oh, please…* "How can I help?"

"I'm looking for someone who's booked on the eleven o'clock flight to Roanoke."

"That flight's already been called," she says unhelpfully.

"I know that, but can you tell me if this passenger has checked in? She's my girlfriend… well, she was my girlfriend, before I behaved like a dick…" Why the hell did I just say that? To a complete stranger.

She stares at me for a moment and her demeanor changes. She goes from sexy, interested siren, to sympathetic co-conspirator almost in the blink of an eye. "I'm not supposed to give away that information," she says.

"Please," I beg.

She glances around. "Okay. What's the name?"

"Charlotte Hudson," I say quickly, remembering at the last moment to use Lottie's proper first name.

She taps the keys on her computer a few times, then looks up at me again. "Yes," she says. "She checked in twenty minutes ago."

I feel my body sag. "Okay. Thanks anyway."

She gives me another sympathetic look. "I'm sorry," she murmurs.

I give her a slight smile, because it's the best I can manage, and wander out of the building and back toward the parking lot.

I know Lottie's flight isn't direct. She's got a layover in Charlotte for an hour, which means she won't get into Roanoke until mid afternoon. She's unaware of this, but I have my own private plane. I could fly down there and I'd probably arrive before her… but would that be too much? Would she think I was being a knight in shining armor, showing off and waving my money in her face when she feels like she's about to lose everything? It does seem like a 'grand gesture', and I'm not sure she'd appreciate that.

I get into my car and lean back in the seat. I guess there's a chance she'll turn her phone on while she's in Charlotte, waiting for her connection. Even if she doesn't, she'll be bound to check her messages when she gets home. Won't she? Of course she will…

Chapter Sixteen

Lottie

My flight landed on time, at just after three thirty, but I then had an hour and a half's bus ride from Roanoke to my apartment in Blacksburg. A cab would have been quicker. It would also have been a lot more expensive.

Luckily, the bus stop is only a hundred yards or so from the apartment block and I let myself in at just before six. It feels cold and lonely in here and I turn up the heating and then go around switching on the lights, not that it helps. I dump my bag by the couch and throw myself down on it, trying to take in how much my life has changed in the week or so since I was last here. I've met the man of my dreams, fallen in love, lost my virginity, broken up with the man of my dreams… and now I might be pregnant and facing the prospect of imminent homelessness. It's not the way I expected to spend the holidays, that's for sure.

I remember my phone died just as I got to the airport and get up again, going into my bedroom to plug it into the charger I left in there. The spare one which I took away with me is in my bag still, but I can't be bothered to unpack now.

I lie down on the bed, as the phone buzzes back to life and then beeps twice, telling me I've got messages. I imagine it's Jack, wishing me a good flight and then wondering why I haven't responded. He was worried about me last night when he dropped me back at Catrina's house… I can't bring myself to call it 'home' anymore. It isn't. I'm tempted to ignore the messages and go to sleep, but I know Jack won't let up, so I turn over and grab my phone, checking the screen.

Sure enough, the first message is from Jack.

— *Hope you're feeling a bit better today. Have a safe trip back to Virginia. Text me when you get in, just so I know you're safe. And call me anytime if you wanna talk. J xx*

I type out a quick reply to let him know I've arrived safely, and then check the second message, expecting it to also be from Jack, asking where I am. It's not; it's from Paul.

—*Lottie. I came to the airport to try and see you, but you'd already boarded your flight. I'm sorry I missed you. Really sorry. I wanted to tell you that I hope you have a safe trip back to Virginia. I also wanted to say that I know you're not sure about me, or about us, but I'm here for you if you need me. And I'm not giving up on us. I'll never give up on us, because I love you. Paul x*

The screen blurs and I drop the phone onto the comforter, turning over and curling up into a ball. He came to the airport? Why would he do that? Has he forgiven me? Does it matter? Do I even want his forgiveness? Do I want him back? I let out a sob. Of course I do. I want him back, like I want to take my next breath, and I need his forgiveness just as much, but at the same time, I can't handle the feelings of jealousy I get whenever we're together. I can't handle not knowing what I am to him, what he wants from me, whether I'm enough for him. I blink back my tears, reach over and pick up the phone, and re-read his message. He says he'll be there for me. I don't doubt he will. His words are so sincere, I can't possibly doubt them – or him. I clutch the phone to my chest and turn onto my back, staring at the ceiling, thinking about him; thinking about his smile, his eyes, his arms around me. Oddly, I'm not wondering about what he's doing, or who he's with. Does that mean I don't care anymore? Or does it mean I trust him?

I hear a key turning in the lock. Heather's home from work, and I sit up on the edge of the bed, reaching for a Kleenex from the box on my nightstand.

"Lottie?" she calls.

"In here," I reply, wiping my eyes and nose.

She appears in the doorway, leaning against it.

"Oh God… what's wrong?" she asks, coming right over and sitting beside me.

"It hasn't been the best Christmas," I tell her, although that's not strictly true. Christmas itself was magical. What happened afterwards spoiled everything. She puts her arm around me.

"Wanna talk?" she asks. She's a good friend, and I can't tell her nothing. Equally, I'm not ready to tell her about Paul. Not yet, anyway. I'd rather wait until I know whether I'm pregnant first. If I'm not, then I don't really have to tell her anything. I can just do what I suggested to Paul, and pretend it never happened – because that's gonna be real easy. And if I am pregnant, then I guess I'll have to come clean. For now though, I'd rather keep it all to myself. I'd rather conceal my shame at being so childish, so jealous and pathetic, just for a while longer. At least until I can understand why I pushed away the best thing that's ever likely to happen to me, anyway. Then I might be able to explain it to her – because at the moment, I'm struggling to figure it out for myself.

What I can tell her about though, which gives me almost as good a reason to be lying in the dark crying, is what I discovered about my father's will. I owe her that, being as she may end up being evicted too.

"Why don't I put a pizza in the oven, and you can tell me all about it?" she offers.

"Sounds good," I reply, and she gets up, going through to the kitchen. "I'm assuming this had something to do with your wicked stepmom?" she calls over her shoulder.

"You assume correctly," I reply, grabbing another Kleenex and following her.

Over pepperoni pizza, which we eat together, sitting on the living room floor, I explain what happened when I went to see Anthony. Luckily, she doesn't query how I was paying for his services. I think her shock that Catrina has the right to evict us from the apartment overrode every other thought process.

"You must feel so… I can't even think of the right word," she says, reaching over and giving me a hug.

"Neither can I. Well, I can. Right now I feel tired. Bone tired. And I'm sorry. I know this affects you too…"

"Don't," she says. "I can always work something out. This is a much bigger deal for you. I'll be fine…"

She's being very understanding.

"Thanks for listening," I say, clambering to my feet and gathering up our plates.

"Anytime," she replies.

I get to the threshold of the kitchen before I realize how rude I've been.

"I didn't ask about your Christmas," I say, leaning on the doorframe. "How did it go?" She didn't go home to see her folks, but stayed here because she wanted to spend some time with Simon, her boyfriend of about three months. Things were getting fairly hot between them before the holidays, and I know she was hoping for more.

"It went…" She blushes. "It went really well. Simon came over on Christmas Eve, like we planned." I notice the smile twitching at the corners of her lips.

"And when did he leave?" I ask.

"Yesterday?" She says it like a question, presumably because she's not sure I'm going to believe her. Then she looks up at me. "We were having such a great time together, we just lost track of the days."

I smile down at her. "Why did he go yesterday? He could've stayed longer…"

"I didn't want to presume," she says, lowering her eyes again. "This is your place, after all."

"Well, it is for now," I try to joke, and go on through to the kitchen, dumping our plates by the sink. "And I really don't mind if you want to have your boyfriend to stay," I add, once I've come back into the room.

She smiles up at me. "I'll let him know. He's gone out with a couple of the guys from the football team tonight, but maybe he can come over tomorrow?"

"Sounds fine." I've met Simon several times, when he's come into the bookstore, or called by to collect Heather to take her out somewhere. He's a nice guy. And I wonder whether that's what Heather meant when she said she'd be fine. Perhaps she's thinking that she'll move in with Simon.

"Why don't you go to bed? You need to sleep," she says.

"Yeah. I do. See you tomorrow," I reply, turning and going down the hallway and into my bedroom. I close the door, but don't bother with the light. I've got every intention of just falling into bed. I undress, leaving my clothes where they fall, then sit on the edge of the mattress. My phone's charged now, so I unplug it from the wall and check the screen. There's another message. It's timed at eight thirty-six and it's from Paul. Again.

— *__Please, Lottie. Just send me a message so I know you got home okay. I'm worried about you. Paul x__*

Paul

I've spent all afternoon and evening pacing around my apartment. I haven't eaten and I can't relax. I need to know she got home safely, that she's okay.

At just after eight-thirty, when I hadn't heard from her, I sent another message, just asking her to let me know she got home. I'm going insane here.

I guess it's around an hour later, when my phone finally buzzes and I pick it up, almost dropping it again in my impatience. It's from her.

— *__Home safely. L__*

That's it? No kisses? No 'I love you'? Nothing in recognition of the time we spent together. Just 'home safely'. Jeez, that's cold. Does she hate me that much?

I sit back and let my phone drop onto the couch beside me.

I'm not sure why I'm even surprised. She ended it with me. She told me to go. Hell, she even told me to start another list. She couldn't have made it any clearer that we're through, and just because my best friend and my mom think she needs me, doesn't mean she does.

Except I think she does.

Well, she needs someone, anyway.

And I want it to be me.

The last few days have been the worst of my life.

Sunday was probably the hardest. I knew Lottie would be back at work, so I worked too, just to try and keep busy, planning my visit to Detroit, which I've set up for two weeks' time, when the new designer says he'll have something to show me.

In the evening I decided I couldn't face sitting by myself in the apartment, so I went and sat by myself in the restaurant where I first saw Lottie. I think that was probably a mistake. Apart from the fact that the place seemed to be full of couples, laughing, holding hands across the table, staring into each other's eyes, all it did was to remind me that she's not here… and based on her text message, there's a fairly good chance she may never be here again.

Yesterday and today, I've had meetings all day, which helped to keep me occupied, and I decided to learn from my mistake of Sunday night and stayed home in the evenings. I'm not gonna say it was any easier, but at least I wasn't moping in public.

Being as it's New Year's Eve today, I decided to close the office early so everyone can get to whatever parties they're attending. Personally, I'm going home. I'm not in the mood for partying.

I get back to my apartment at around five and take a long shower, then change into jeans and a t-shirt and order in a Chinese. I can't sit and do nothing. All I'll do is think about Lottie, and wonder what she's doing. I can't keep torturing myself like that, so I put a movie on and open a bottle of wine while I wait for my take-out to be delivered.

The opening credits have barely finished when my phone rings. I pick it up, knowing it won't be Lottie. I'm realistic enough to have stopped hoping already. I'm right. It's Fin.

"Hi," I say, putting the phone on speaker and letting it rest on the arm of the couch.

"You sound great," he replies.

"Thanks."

"What the fuck is all that noise?"

"It's Jack Reacher." I turn down the volume on the TV.

"That's better," he says. "I've just finished a twelve hour shift. The last thing I need is Tom Cruise kicking the crap out of someone. It's too much like work."

"Why? Have you been kicking the crap out of someone?" I tease.

"No, you fucking idiot. But I did spend a few hours of my shift trying to save the life of a sixteen year old kid whose dad had used him as a punchbag."

"Fucking hell."

"Yeah."

"How did it go?" I ask.

"He's stable. He'll make it."

"And the dad?"

"No idea. The cops dealt with that at the kid's home. We just had to pick up the pieces."

"Do you wanna come over?" I ask. "I've just ordered some take-out, but I can call up and change the order."

"I'd love to, but if I don't sleep soon, I'm gonna die." He pauses. "I only called to see how you're doing. I meant to get in touch before now, but work's been crazy."

"I'm okay," I tell him, although I don't feel even vaguely okay. But he's got enough problems, from the sound of things.

"Yeah, I believe you. How about you run that by me again – and try the truth this time?"

"I feel like shit. How's that?"

"It's honest," he says.

"I—I drove out to the airport on Saturday," I confess.

"Why?"

"To try and see Lottie before she went home."

"Jeez. What happened?"

"I got there too late. I missed her."

"Oh, man." I can hear the sympathy in his voice. "What were you gonna say to her, if you'd seen her."

"I was gonna start off with sorry and take it from there. I know our fight was my fault. I should've spent less time worrying about Jack and paid more attention to her." I take a breath. "And I needed to let her know that I'm still here for her, whenever she needs me." *If* she needs me.

"It's a shame you didn't get to tell Lottie that."

"Well I did – or at least some of it – but I had to say it in a text message."

"Did she reply?" he asks.

"No, not until I sent a second message asking her to let me know she'd arrived home safely. Then she replied."

"And?"

"And her response was kinda monosyllabic."

He falls silent for a moment, then says, "What are you gonna do now?"

"I've got no idea."

"You're not giving up, are you?" He sounds like the idea surprises him. Giving up isn't something I want to consider, but like I said, I'm becoming more realistic.

"No, I'm not giving up." *Yet.* "But I'm not convinced there's anything to keep fighting for," I point out.

"Why? What's changed? You haven't stopped loving her, have you?"

"No, of course not."

"In which case, my question stands: what are you gonna do?" He pauses. "I mean," he continues after a few moments, "it's all well and good sitting here in Boston and sending her text messages, but that's not getting you very far, is it?"

"Yeah, I know. But what if she really doesn't want me back? What if she's better off without me?"

"You honestly think that?"

"I don't know what to fucking think, Fin."

"Then go down there and find out, man. Surely it's better to know, isn't it?"

I wonder if it's dawned on him that while I'm not ready to give up on her, or on us, maybe I'm scared of discovering that she doesn't love me, even though she said she did, and maybe I'm terrified that there really is no future for us. At least this way I can keep kidding myself.

"Give her until the weekend, if you must," he says softly, maybe guessing something of how I feel. "But then go see her… work it out with her."

"And if I can't?"

"Then at at least you'll know." God that sounds horribly final. "You okay?" Fin asks.

"No. But I was just wondering if it would be really antisocial of me to call my lawyer on New Year's Eve to get hold of Lottie's address."

"You don't need to disturb his New Year," Fin points out. "You're not going to see her until the weekend."

"I know, but I want to do something."

"Then turn Jack Reacher back on and practice your 'I'm sorry' face," he jokes.

"Oh, don't worry," I reply. "I've got that perfected."

Chapter Seventeen

Lottie

I slept through New Year's. I've got no idea why I'm so tired, but I didn't feel like celebrating anyway, so the fact that I don't seem to be able to keep my eyes open after about nine-thirty in the evening wasn't really a problem.

Today's Thursday and I'm not working, thank goodness. I stayed in bed until I heard Heather and Simon leave, then dragged myself into the shower. I didn't bother looking in the mirror; I know I'm a wreck, and I don't need visual confirmation. However, I realized I was feeling a bit stubbly 'down there', so I got a new razor from the bathroom cabinet, and that's when I found a brand new packet of sanitary pads staring back at me, just to remind me that my period's due tomorrow. That was all it took to set me off, and I wound up sitting on the bathroom floor crying my eyes out, grateful that there's no-one here to witness my humiliation.

I'm still sitting here, leaning up against the side of the bath, surrounded by balls of screwed up toilet tissue, when I hear my phone ringing. I can't even be bothered to stand, so I crawl back into my bedroom and check the screen. It's Jack, thank God.

"Hello?" I lean back against my bed and bring my bent knees up to my chest.

"Dear God, what's wrong?" he says.

"I—I can't do this," I whimper.

"Can't do what?" he asks.

"Anything. I'm pathetic. I can't even manage to get a damn razor out of the bathroom cabinet without crying."

"What made you cry?" I wonder if he's trying not to laugh. I wouldn't blame him if he did. I know I sound pitiful.

"The sanitary pads that were in there next to the razors."

"Why? What did they do?"

"They didn't do anything, you idiot. They just reminded me that my period's due tomorrow."

"I know," he says, more seriously. "But look on the bright side, you've only got a couple more days and you'll know… one way or the other."

"I'll know tomorrow," I tell him. "I'm as regular as clockwork."

"So you could take a test tomorrow?" he asks.

"Yeah, I guess. I don't think I can do this by myself though."

"Would it help if I came down there?" he offers.

"Tomorrow?"

"I can't, not tomorrow, but I can come on Saturday. I was gonna ask if I could anyway."

"Why?" I ask.

"Because I wanted to talk to you about Alex."

"What's happened?" I push my own problems to one side for a moment, remembering that he spent the last few days with Alex and his parents. "How did New Year's go?"

"Weird," he replies simply.

"In what way?"

"Alex was like a completely different person," he says and I can hear the sadness behind his words. "It was like he felt he had to pretend to be someone else for his parents, or something. He wouldn't touch me, or show me any kind of affection in front of them."

"You're back home now, aren't you?"

"Yeah. We got back this morning. Alex has just gone to the store to get some supplies."

"And?"

"And what?"

"How are things now you're back home?" I ask.

"Well, it's a bit soon to tell. We've only been back for twenty minutes."

I take a deep breath. "Have you tried speaking to him about how you feel?" I ask.

"No. Not yet. I wanted to try and get my own head around it first." He pauses. "That's why I was gonna ask if I could come see you at the weekend. I know you'll be working – at least for some of the time – but I need to get away and talk to you."

"You know you can come here. You're welcome anytime. Heather's boyfriend has pretty much moved in, but they keep themselves to themselves, and the couch is always yours."

"Thanks, Lottie," he says. "You can advise me on what to do about Alex, and I'll hold your hand while you do your pregnancy test…"

"Not literally, I hope," I interrupt.

"No, not literally."

After my shower, I went and did some grocery shopping and then fell asleep on the couch. Like I said, I don't know why I'm so tired, but it's getting ridiculous.

It's my phone ringing that wakes me and, when I check the screen, the number that comes up is one I don't recognize. I never take calls from numbers I don't know, so I let it ring out and go to voicemail. My phone beeps within a couple of minutes and I pick up the message. It's from Anthony, Paul's lawyer, asking me to return his call as soon as possible. I guess now's as good a time as any, so I press re-dial.

"Anthony Bolton," he answers.

"Hello. It's Lottie… I mean Charlotte Hudson."

"Oh. Hello Miss Hudson," he says. "Thank you for returning my call so promptly."

"Well, I assumed you'd have something important to tell me, or you wouldn't have phoned in the first place."

"You assumed correctly." His voice is serious and I sit up, paying more attention. "I've heard back from Mrs Hudson."

"You have?"

"Yes. I wrote to her on the day of our meeting, and she's finally responded today – by email," he explains.

"I see." That sounds just like Catrina. Anything to be awkward. "And what did she say?" I ask.

"She's come up with a completely implausible story about having made a mistake with your allowance. Judging from the tone of her message, I imagine she's been in contact with a lawyer, and they went through everything with her and told her she should've been paying it. To save face, she's pretending it was an error, rather than something she did intentionally."

"So what is she going to do?"

He coughs. "She's already done it. Evidently the arrears have been paid into your account already, including the January payment, which was due yesterday, and she's guaranteed that all future payments will be made on time, on the first of each month."

"Well, that was a lot easier than I expected." I flop back onto the couch in relief. I honestly thought she'd find some excuse not to make the payments, and we'd end up in a long legal battle over it.

"Unfortunately, that's not the end of it," he says and I sit forward again.

"Why?"

"Because she's done exactly what we feared she'd do." I feel my blood run cold. "I'm sorry, but she's given you notice to leave the house… and the apartment. You'll get the official notification in tomorrow's mail. I just wanted to forewarn you."

I seem to have lost the capacity to speak.

"I'm guessing that, in looking through the will, her lawyers pointed out her right to evict you from the apartment as well as the house, and she decided to go for maximum revenge," he continues.

"How long have I got?" I ask him, finding my voice.

"Two weeks," he replies. "I hope you don't mind, but given the short notice she's allowed you, I've already arranged with her to have your possessions from the house shipped to you in Virginia. I emailed her earlier and she's confirmed the housekeeper can pack them up and they'll be sent on to you by overnight delivery. You'll have everything sometime tomorrow."

"And then I've got two weeks to vacate this place?"

"Yes," he confirms.

"But I can't go back to the house?"

"You can during those two weeks," he says. "I just assumed you'd rather not… and that you'd be busy looking for somewhere else to live."

"Th—Thank you," I stutter out.

"Please don't thank me," he says quietly. "I'm just sorry our actions have resulted in this."

"You mustn't apologize. I knew the risks."

"I've repeated my request to Mrs Hudson to forward me a copy of the balance of your trust fund. As yet, she hasn't been forthcoming with that, but I'll keep pressing for it. If your stepmother has spent any of it, I'll instigate proceedings against her. I'm assuming that's what you want me to do?"

"Yes… yes, I think I do."

"Okay. I'll keep you informed."

"Thank you, Mr Bolton."

"Please, call me Anthony," he says, and we end the call.

I lie back on the couch. My worst fears have come true.

I'm homeless.

Heather gets back at just after seven, with Simon in tow.

"Can we talk?" I ask, as soon as they walk in the door.

"Sure." Heather looks at me. "Something's happened… What's wrong?"

"Should I leave?" Simon offers.

"No. Stay. This may end up concerning you too," I reply and they sit down on the couch. I take the chair and lean forward on my elbows. "There's no easy way to say this, so I'm just gonna tell you. My stepmom has taken possession of the apartment."

"The bitch," Heather says under her breath. "How can she do that to you?"

I shrug my shoulders. "She's legally entitled to…"

"That doesn't make it right," Heather replies.

"No, but I'm not gonna waste my time and energy fighting her. We need to think about where we're gonna live."

Simon puts his arm around Heather, pulling her close and she looks up at him. "We've already talked about it," she says, turning back to me. "Simon said that, if this happened, I could move in with him… But that feels like such a horrible thing to do, to abandon you."

"Well, my allowance has been reinstated, and the arrears paid in full." I checked my account earlier and the balance was just over fifteen thousand dollars, so at least Catrina's stuck to that part of the bargain. "I can probably afford to rent a small place…"

"So if I move out, that helps you?"

"Well, it means I can get a studio apartment, yeah."

"Does this apply to the house as well?" Heather asks.

"Yeah. She's sending all my things over. They'll be here tomorrow." I sit back into the chair. "Except I'm working, so…"

"I'll sign for them," she offers.

"Thanks."

"And I'll help you out with packing and moving," she says.

I give her a weak smile. "Thanks." I hadn't thought about packing, or moving. I can't think about any of it at the moment. My head's too full.

Simon offers to cook us spaghetti bolognese and, while he's making it, Heather and I go online and start looking at apartments. There's not a lot available really close to the college, and I can't afford a car, but we manage to find three small apartments that I can just about manage to pay rent on, and that I can look at next week. I'm working tomorrow, and Jack's here for the weekend, but I can start looking seriously on Monday and hopefully one of these three will fit the bill.

I've just closed my laptop when my phone rings and for the first time in ages, I actually smile. It's Mrs Hemsworth.

"Hello," I say, picking up. Heather gets up and goes through to join Simon in the kitchen, to give me some privacy.

"Hello, Lottie," she replies. "How are you?"

"I've been better," I tell her.

"I can imagine." The sound of her voice makes me want to cry, again, but I try to stay strong. "I just wanted to let you know that all your things left here about an hour ago, and the delivery company assured me that they'll be with you by four tomorrow afternoon."

"I'll be working, but my friend Heather's gonna be here to sign for them."

"Okay," she says, and then pauses. "And there's one other thing…"

"Yes?"

"I—I've handed in my resignation."

I sit forward. "You've what?"

"I can't keep working for her, Lottie. Not after this. I've spent the last few years watching that damn woman try and drag you down, but this is the final straw."

"Does Jack know?" I ask her.

"Yes. He's left too. I called him this afternoon and told him what had happened and he came right over. Mrs Hudson was her usual flirty self with him, but he stopped her in her tracks and gave her a piece of his mind. I wish you'd been here to see that." She chuckles. "He told me he's coming to see you on Saturday, so I'll let him tell you all about it."

"What are you going to do?" I ask her.

"Oh, I'll find something," she replies, dodging my question. "I'm more worried about you. Have you started looking for somewhere else to live yet?"

"Sort of. I've been on the Internet and found a few places I can go and see next week."

"Well, that's a start," she says, sounding optimistic.

"I feel so guilty." The words pour out of my mouth at the same time as the tears start to fall.

"Why? What on earth have you got to feel guilty for?" she asks.

"If I hadn't decided to try and get my money back, none of this would have happened. You'd still have a job, and Jack would still be fully employed."

"Just stop… right now," she orders, with a firmer tone than I've ever heard her use before. "I'd probably have left soon anyway. I was only hanging around for you, and as soon as you moved out and found a place of your own somewhere, I'd have resigned. Once your daddy died, you were always my only reason for staying."

The tears fall harder. "Why did he do this to me?" I wail.

"I don't think for one second that he meant to, Lottie," she says calmly. "I don't think he realized. I worked for your father for over fifteen years and I know he'd never have done anything to hurt you."

"Then why does this hurt so much?"

"Because it sucks," she replies. "But that doesn't make it your father's fault. Try not to blame him."

I grab a Kleenex, wipe my nose and square my shoulders. "I'll try," I whimper.

"That's my girl," she says.

Heather's been a star and not only waited in all day on Friday to sign for my boxes, which are now filling one end of the living room, but she's also swapped shifts with me. So, I'm working Saturday morning and taking her Tuesday shift all day, which means I'll be here for Saturday afternoon when Jack arrives and can spend Sunday morning with him, before he flies home at lunchtime. And I'll be free on Monday to go and look at the three apartments we found on the Internet.

My Friday has been uneventful, in every sense of the word. The shop was quiet, which meant the day dragged past, and gave me time to think about the fact that my period didn't arrive.

By the time I get into bed, exhausted as usual, I have to face that fact that I'm officially late.

Paul

I've flown down here in my private jet, because I had a breakfast meeting thrown at me last thing yesterday evening, for eight this morning. Ordinarily, I'd have postponed, but it was an important client, who has no family and doesn't understand the concept of weekends. But then, I guess, it wasn't all that long ago that I wouldn't have understood it either. By the time I finished with him, I knew that, if I'd flown on a commercial airline, I wouldn't have been able to get to Lottie's place until early evening and I wanted to spend some time with her to try and work things out. So, I called my pilot on the way to the airport and had him make the arrangements.

I've hired a Mercedes AMG GT for the weekend and I pull up into the parking lot outside Lottie's apartment block at just after three in the afternoon, which I figure gives us at least twenty-four hours to talk, before I have to fly back to Boston. That's assuming she'll talk to me, of course.

Since Thursday afternoon when I spoke to Anthony to get Lottie's address, I've spent every waking moment – and a fair few sleeping ones too – worrying about what he told me Catrina's done. I don't know why I'm even surprised that the bitch has taken possession of Lottie's apartment, but I am, and my immediate reaction was to fly down here straight away. I know how that would've looked to Lottie, but the thought of her worrying about the future was too much for me. It was Fin who talked me out of it in the end. And he was right. Lottie needs me, my time, my commitment, and my love, not my money. And I need to show her I'm in this for the long haul, not just the grand gestures.

I climb out of the car and grab my jacket from the passenger seat. I brought a bag, containing some clothes, but I leave that in the car. I'm not making any assumptions. None at all.

I lock the car and start walking over to the main entrance, just as the door opens and Lottie appears, followed closely by Jack. I feel the hairs on the back of my neck stand on end, but I swallow down my jealousy and keep walking. They haven't spotted me yet and are talking, their heads close together as they come down the steps.

"Hello," I call out.

Lottie looks up and pales, her mouth opening.

"Hi," Jack replies, looking a little confused. He glances at Lottie and then turns back to me again. "I don't think we've been properly introduced. My name's Jack McKenzie."

"Paul Lewis," I reply, even though I'm pretty sure he knows my name just as well as I know his.

I shake his offered hand, without taking my eyes from Lottie.

"You're here," she says, clearly bewildered by my presence.

"Yeah. I came to see you."

"Why?" she asks.

I let out a breath. I'd rather not do this in front of Jack, but what choice do I have? "Because we need to talk," I say.

"I think we've said everything that needs to be said," she replies, her voice taking on a really hard edge.

"Well, I don't. Anthony told me what happened with Catrina and your apartment…" I begin and her eyes narrow.

"Oh… so you thought you come and take over, did you? You thought you'd come and prove how pathetic I am and what a hero you are."

"Lottie," Jack hisses under his breath.

I hold up my hands to stop him. "No, it's fine." I move a little closer to her. "That's not what I thought at all," I tell her. "I've known about it since Thursday afternoon. That's two days, Lottie. If I really wanted to come riding in here like a knight in shining armor, I'd have done it before now, a lot more comprehensively – trust me."

"So… so don't want to help me?"

Jack stares at her, shaking his head. "Are you being deliberately contrary?" he says.

"No." She looks up at him. "I just don't know why he's here." She nods at me.

"I'm here because I want to talk to you," I explain and take a deep breath. "I was coming down here anyway, before Anthony told me about Catrina's latest move, because I wanted to see you. But if you need my help, then you've got it."

"If I agree to get back together with you?" she asks, narrowing her eyes again.

"No," I say, raising my voice a little. "I'll help you regardless."

"Well, I don't need your help," she says defiantly.

Jack huffs out a sigh. "I think I should let you guys talk privately," he suggests. "I'll go back inside."

He turns to leave, but she grabs his arm, pulling him back. "No... don't," she says, with a hint of desperation in her voice.

I stare down at her. She looks really tired and like she's been crying. "Would you like me to go instead?" I ask, hoping she'll say 'no'. I'll talk to her in front of Jack, if that's what she wants. I don't care, as long as she gives me a chance. She doesn't reply. Instead she looks down at the space between us and that's all the answer I need. I feel the intense aching in my heart start to spread throughout my body. This is my worst nightmare coming true, right in front of me. She really doesn't want me back. "My offer stands," I say quietly, willing her to look at me. She doesn't. "If you need my help, call me. Anytime. I'll do whatever you need me to – no strings, I promise. Lottie, I—I honestly only flew down here so we could talk. The only grand gesture I intended to make was to tell you that I love you, and that I always will; that I need you more than I ever did, and that I'll always be here for you, even if you don't want me. But I guess that's it, isn't it? You really don't want me, here – or anywhere else." I lean down and very gently kiss her cheek. "I'll see you around," I whisper, and let her go.

I go back to my rental car and get in behind the wheel. I don't look back. I can't. I can't bear to see her again. I put the car in 'drive' and floor the gas. I need to be anywhere but here.

Chapter Eighteen

Lottie

I look at his back, walking away from me and everything starts to spin. I feel myself falling...

"Whoa," Jack says, catching me in his arms. "Come here." He picks me up and carries me back into the apartment block and straight into the elevator, pressing the button for the second floor. He doesn't say a word the whole time we ride up. He just looks at the display above the doors, waiting for it to reach my floor, then when the doors open, he carries me out and to my apartment. "Where's the key?" he asks.

"In my purse," I whisper.

He sets me down gently on the floor, pushing me back against the wall, and reaches inside my purse, pulling out my keys and letting us into the apartment. He takes my hand, pulling me inside and straight over to the couch.

"Sit," he says, and I obey, falling back into the seat behind me. He disappears into the kitchen, returning moments later with a glass of water, which he hands to me. "Drink," he says.

I take the glass and have a sip of water while he sits down on the chair opposite me.

"Are you mad at me?" I ask him. He's being very abrupt.

"No. I'm confused by you, but I'm not mad at you."

"Why are you confused?" I ask, leaning back into the couch.

"Because I don't understand why you were so horrible to him," he says. I can feel myself blushing, and close my eyes. "It's not like you

You're one of the kindest people I know. And I get that you've had a whole load of shit dropped on you in the last few days, but the guy came down here to see you, to try and work things out with you. Even if you don't wanna know – which I don't believe for one second – there are nicer ways of telling him that, Lottie."

I burst into noisy tears and feel him come closer, taking the glass from me and sitting beside me, pulling me into his arms.

"Why'd you do it?" he asks. "You're so obviously still in love with him."

"Because it's over," I tell him, through my tears.

"Well, he doesn't want it to be over. And neither do you, do you? Not really."

"It doesn't matter what I want," I reply. "Once he knows I'm pregnant, I won't see him for dust. It's better this way… for both of us."

He takes a deep breath. "You don't know that," he replies patiently. "It may not have dawned on you until a few days ago that you might be pregnant, but do you honestly think it didn't occur to him? He's a lot older than you are, and a lot more experienced…"

"Thanks, I needed reminding about that," I mutter.

"Well, he is. But you're missing the point. I'm pretty sure he'd have been able to work out that forgetting to use a condom has potential consequences. That hasn't stopped him from wanting you, or from trying to be with you. I'm fairly sure he'd have worked it out straight away, but he still invited you to his family's home for Christmas, he still told you he loves you. If he really was bothered about the idea of you being pregnant, trust me, he'd have disappeared long before now. And besides, you don't even know you are pregnant yet. So you're worrying over nothing." He leans back and looks at me. "Are you feeling better?" I nod my head. "Shall we go back out and see if we can actually get to the pharmacy this time?"

"Okay." He gets up and pulls me to my feet. "I was horrible to him, wasn't I?" I whimper.

"Yeah. But he'd still take you back," he says, leading me to the front door.

"You don't know that," I reply.

"Yeah I do. I saw his face. I don't think it matters what you throw at him. He'd take you back in a heartbeat."

We get back to the apartment and read the instructions inside the packet. It says I can do the test now, but because I'm only one day late, I'll get a more accurate result if I do it first thing in the morning.

"I think accuracy is quite important at a time like this," Jack says quietly.

"But that means waiting until the morning," I point out.

"You've waited this long," he reasons.

I nod my head and take the packet through to my bedroom.

When I come back, Jack's making coffee and he brings it in, sitting beside me on the couch.

"Tell me about Alex," I say, partly because it'll take my mind off my own problems, and partly because I've been a lousy friend to him of late.

He sighs and puts his cup down on the table. "It feels kinda insignificant next to what you're going through," he says and shrugs his shoulders.

"Except you're obviously worried about it. And it's a good distraction," I say, honestly.

He smiles. "As long as you're sure…"

"I'm sure."

He nods. "It was really weird," he says. "I know I'm the more physical of the two of us, but Alex is normally quite affectionate."

"Yeah, he is." I've seen them together. Alex doesn't usually hold back.

"Except when he's with his parents, it seems." He rolls his eyes. "They insisted on separate bedrooms, which is fair enough, I suppose, but I felt like we were complete strangers. Even when I tried to kiss him at midnight on New Year's Eve, he pulled away and just gave me a quick hug."

"But he's been okay since you came home?"

"Yeah." He smiles over at me. "Everything's been fine."

"Then maybe you should give him the benefit of the doubt. It's early days for his parents. He's probably just giving them time to adjust."

"I guess…"

"You're only worrying because of what happened with your ex," I tell him. "But Alex isn't your ex. He loves you."

"Am I asking too much of him?" he asks, looking me in the eyes.

"No. I don't think you're being unreasonable at all. You just need to give him and his parents time to get used to things."

He smiles. "I was so worried he didn't want me anymore," he admits.

"Maybe you should try telling him that?" I suggest.

He nods. "Yeah, maybe I should."

"And maybe explain about your ex too, so he knows how you feel?"

He moves closer and pulls me into a hug. "What was that for?" I ask him.

"Being such a good friend." He leans back and looks at me. "Now, if we can just sort out your love life…"

"Know any good miracle workers, do you?"

He rolls his eyes and hugs me again.

Over dinner – a take-out which Jack insisted on paying for – he tells me about the scene Catrina created when he told her he wasn't gonna be coming back to work next week. A smile lights up his face.

"I wish you'd been there," he says. "She was practically begging me to stay."

"I'd have loved to see that."

"I managed not to get personal about it. I didn't want to actually insult her, because I didn't want to lower myself to her level, but I let her know I wasn't gonna come back… not if she was the last home owner with a garden in the whole of Massachusetts." He grins. "I think my words were – 'hell's gonna freeze over before I set foot on your property again'. And I remember emphasizing the 'your' in that sentence, just to give her a hint as to my reasoning."

"Did she get it?" I ask.

"No." He smirks. "She's not bright enough to get subtlety."

"So, what are you gonna do?" I ask him. "You worked for her three days a week. She must've made up a sizeable chunk of your income."

"She did. But in a way she's done me a favor."

"How?"

He turns in his seat to face me. "Because in leaving her, I've been forced to take a long hard look at what I do. I've been a casual gardener and handyman for too long, Lottie. I need to grow up and start using my degree properly."

"You have a degree?" I don't mean to sound so shocked, but I can't help it. "Sorry, that came out wrong."

He laughs. "No, that's okay. I know it's not the kind of thing you expect of someone like me, but yeah… I have a degree in landscape architecture."

"You do?" I had no idea.

"Yeah. I just never wanted to get into using it. I've always enjoyed getting my hands dirty far more than the thought of handling the business side of things…"

"And now?"

"Well, I sat down with Alex last night, and he's gonna help me get properly set up. He said he'll deal with as much of the paperwork as possible, so I can still focus on doing the thing I love best, and start incorporating more garden design into my work, rather than just doing maintenance all the time."

I smile over at him. "So, given all of that, can you explain why you were so worried about Alex's commitment to you?" I say.

"I know," he admits, shrugging his shoulders. "Can we put it down to temporary insanity?"

"No," I reply. "We'll call it fear. Fear of being really loved – for who you are."

He leans into me. "Well, that makes two of us, doesn't it?"

I wait until I hear Heather leave for work and, with a bladder fit to burst, I grab the packet from my nightstand and make a dash for the bathroom.

A few minutes later, I emerge, bringing the test and the leaflet with me, just in case we need to refer to it again.

Jack's sitting on the couch, the blankets pushed to one side. He's wearing shorts and a t-shirt, still looking sleepy and disheveled.

"How long do we have to wait?" he asks.

"Two minutes."

I put the test down on the coffee table and sit beside him. He brings his arm around me and we lean into each other.

"I can't bear to look at it," I say and bury my head in his chest, hearing his heart and my own beat in imperfect time. After what feels like forever, Jack leans forward, then lets out a long, slow sigh.

"What does it say?" I murmur into him.

"It says you're pregnant," he replies simply.

I lean back and stare at him.

"You're sure?"

"Yeah." He shows me the stick, with the word 'pregnant' in the little window. Oh God. "This can't be happening."

"Calm down," he says, putting the stick back on the table and taking my hands in his. "You don't need to panic."

"I don't? It damn well feels like I do."

"What I mean is, it's early days. You've got time to work out what you wanna do."

"Well, I can't have a baby by myself, that's for sure."

"You don't have to be by yourself."

"I know you mean well, Jack, but you and Alex have your own lives. Hell, you just told me last night that you're gonna be starting a new business. I mean—"

"I wasn't talking about me and Alex," he interrupts, looking me in the eyes. "I was talking about Paul."

I shake my head. "He won't wanna know."

"We already had this conversation, didn't we? You don't know what he wants."

"Jack, he's a multi-billionaire. He flies around the country – around the world – at a moment's notice. He's not the settling down kind."

"He seemed pretty damn keen on settling down with you when he came here yesterday."

"That's different. He didn't know I was pregnant."

"Like I told you yesterday, I think you can be fairly sure he'll have worked it out as a possibility. He wasn't going anywhere that I could see. And anyway, he's the kid's father. He has a right to know. You can't take that away from him, Lottie."

I know he's right, but therein lies my biggest problem and my biggest fear, now that I know for sure. I look up at him and shake my head slowly. "The thing is, if we were going to get back together, I'd rather he did it for me than because I'm carrying his child." There. I've said it out loud.

He smiles. "There really is no pleasing you, is there?" he says. "The guy came all the way down here to see you. He told you he still loves you and wants to be with you. He told you he'd be there for you, no matter what. He put his feelings out there – in front of me. That can't have been easy for him. What more do you want him to do, break open an artery and bleed his love all over the sidewalk, just to prove it to you?"

I stare at him and then he blurs as my eyes fill with tears, which start to fall down my cheeks. "I don't know what I want," I whisper, and he pulls me into a hug.

He holds me while I sob and, once I've calmed, he pulls back and looks down at me. "Make me a promise?" he says.

"Yes."

"Promise me you won't do anything without me."

"I promise."

He nods his head. "Shall we have a coffee?" he suggests.

"Sure. I'll get it."

"Great. I need the bathroom."

I go through to the kitchen and fill the coffee machine with water. Then I lean back on the countertop and hug my arms around myself. I can't believe that six months ago, my dad was still alive, I was studying for my degree with a fairly certain future as an architect in front of me and a loving home to to go back to whenever I needed it. Now, I'm homeless, pregnant and I've broken my own heart, not to mention alienating the only man I've ever loved, and the father of my unborn child. I'd give anything for him to be here, just to hold me and tell me everything will all be okay, because he loves me. It's not going to happen, but that doesn't stop me needing it.

Paul

Fin makes it over by the middle of Sunday afternoon. He worked until midnight on Saturday and slept in late, but came over as soon as he picked up my slightly garbled message, which I left when I got back from Virginia, feeling tired and devastated.

"I'm sorry I keep calling on you," I tell him as he exits the elevator.

"It's what friends are for," he replies, going straight into the kitchen and putting a cup under my pod machine. He selects a strong espresso and presses the button.

"Except I think you could use some sleep." I state the obvious.

"Yeah, but I can catch up later. I've got tomorrow off." He grins, bringing his coffee over to the couch and sitting alongside me. "Wanna tell me what happened?"

"I flew down to Virginia as planned," I tell him, getting straight to the point.

"And?"

"And her friend was there."

"Jack?"

"Yeah."

"Oh."

I turn to face him. "No," I say quickly. "It was fine. If anything, he seemed to be on my side."

"Your side?" he repeats. "Was there a need to take sides?"

"Yeah. Lottie assumed I'd flown down there to be the big hero and rescue her from homelessness. I told her, if that had been my plan, I'd have gone straight down there on Thursday."

"You didn't tell her I talked you out of that, did you?"

"No. I'm not that stupid."

He heaves out a sigh of relief. "Okay. So what happened?"

"She made it really clear she didn't want me there. Jack offered to leave and she told him not to. So I offered to leave instead…"

"And she told you to go?" he guesses.

"As good as. Her silence was deafening."

He shakes his head. "What did you do?" he asks.

"I told her I'd still help her if she needs me to – no strings attached – but that I don't think she loves me, or needs me… and then I got the hell outta there."

He puts his cup down on the table. "That sounds kinda final," he says.

"It felt kinda final." I lean back on the couch. "And it fucking hurts."

"And you're sure she's not with this other guy?" he asks.

I nod my head. "Yeah. Now I've met him and seen them up close together, I think they really are just friends. I don't think she wants him. But she doesn't want me either. That much was clear."

He picks up his cup again, draining it. "I need more of this," he says, getting to his feet. "You want one?"

"Okay."

He goes over to the kitchen again just as my phone rings. It's not a number I recognize and I normally ignore them, but for some reason, I decide to answer it.

"Is that Paul Lewis?" The voice on the other end is male and unfamiliar.

"Yeah. Who's this?"

"It's Jack. Jack McKenzie. Lottie's friend. We met yesterday… outside her apartment."

My blood turns to ice in an instant. "Is Lottie okay?"

"It's Lottie I want to talk to you about," he says evasively.

"Is she okay?" I ask, raising my voice and standing up at the same time.

"I'd be lying if I said 'yes'," he replies calmly. "But life's thrown a lot of crap at her lately. She's hardly gonna be at her best, is she?"

"No, I guess not."

"Look," he says, "I need to talk to you and it'd be a lot easier to do that face-to-face. Can we meet up somewhere?"

"Sure. You can come to my apartment, if you like."

There's a moment's hesitation, then he says, "Okay. I'm still at the airport. I'll get a cab into the city. Can you give me your address?"

I tell him, and he says he'll be with me in thirty minutes.

"Who was that?" Fin asks as I drop my phone back onto the couch.

"That was Jack."

Fin puts the coffee down and stares at me. "Lottie's friend Jack?"

"Yeah."

"Is she alright?" He's obviously thinking the same way as me, and I'm touched by his concern for my girlfriend, even though he's never met her. It's odd, despite my disastrous trip to Virginia, I still think of her as my girlfriend. I think I always will. "Paul?" He nudges me out of my thought process. "Is she okay?"

"I'm not sure. He was kinda non-committal about that."

He nods his head slowly. "And did I hear you arranging for him to come here?"

"Yeah. He's still at the airport. He's gonna come straight over."

"Before he even goes home?"

"Yeah." I glance up at him. "Does that seem odd to you?"

"It seems like he really wants to talk to you."

"How did he even get my number?" I wonder out loud.

"Maybe Lottie gave it to him?" he suggests.

"I highly doubt that."

"Yeah, so do I."

Jack arrives just over thirty minutes later and I buzz him in. As soon as he comes out of the elevator, he offers his hand. I take it and we shake, before I stand to one side and let him in, making the introductions. Fin goes into the kitchen to make more coffee and Jack and I sit on the couch staring at each other.

"How did you get my number?" I ask him to break the ice.

He smirks. "From Lottie's phone."

"It's passcode protected," I reply.

"Yeah, but the passcode is her birthday. Easiest thing in the world to get into."

"And you broke into her phone to get my number because…?"

"Because you need to go back and see Lottie," he says simply. "She's upset."

"*She's* upset?" I reply, feeling a little incredulous that he just said that. "How do you think I feel? She dumped me on my ass… on the street – twice. I tried to make it right, even though she was being pretty fucking perverse. You saw her. She wouldn't even look at me. I love her, but there are only so many beatings a guy can take…" I let my voice fade.

"I know she was being difficult," he says soothingly, "but she's in a really tough place right now." He looks me up and down. "Can I ask you a question?"

"Sure."

"Are you reluctant to go back there because you see me as some kind of threat?"

I stare at him for a moment, aware that Fin's just come back in with coffee and is standing to one side, watching and maybe wondering if he's gonna need to step between us. "No," I reply.

Jack nods his head thoughtfully. "It's just that Lottie told me that you thought there was something between us," he explains.

"She told me you're her friend and I believed her." He tilts his head to one side. "Eventually," I add, and he smiles.

"Just out of interest, why'd it take you so long to believe her?" he asks.

I take a deep breath. "You want the honest answer?"

"Of course."

"Because I saw you and her in the restaurant that night. I saw you kissing her fingers. That image is kinda seared into my head, so whenever I see you together, I see that."

He sits back and shakes his head. "That's all my fault," he says. "I was fooling around. I didn't mean anything by it."

I lean forward, looking back at him. "Can I ask you a question?"

"Yes," he replies.

"Do you want her?" I hesitate, then continue, "I know she says you're just a friend and, maybe to her, that's all it is, but is it more to you?"

A smile twitches at the corner of his lips and then he starts to laugh. I glance at Fin, but he shrugs his shoulders, putting the coffee down on the table in front of us, and sitting on the far end of the couch.

"It's nothing like that," Jack says eventually, leaning forward and looking at me. "We really are just friends. Lottie's very beautiful and I can understand why a lot of men would want her, but I'm not one of them." He pauses. "I should probably explain here that I'm gay, so I'm the very last person you need to feel threatened by."

I look at him for a moment. "If you're gay, why the fuck were you sucking on her fingers in that way. That was a really sexy, intimate kinda thing to do…"

He smirks. "Because you wouldn't take your eyes off of her, even though you were there with another woman. All evening you were undressing Lottie with your eyes and ignoring the woman you'd walked in the door with. I thought you were looking at her as a potential conquest and that maybe you needed to realize you can't just take women whenever you want to; that maybe you might have some competition – even if you didn't in reality."

Fin laughs out loud. "Nice touch," he says and I turn and glare at him.

"Obviously, if I'd known you and Lottie were gonna fall in love and get serious with each other, I'd never have done it," Jack explains, shrugging his shoulders.

I shake my head. "No… Thinking about the way I used to behave, I probably deserved it."

"There's no 'probably' about it," Fin remarks and I look over at him. "Are you still here?"

"Always," he replies and takes a sip of coffee, grinning at me.

I turn back to Jack. "I appreciate you coming here and telling me this, but I can't see how it helps. It doesn't explain why Lottie reacted the way she did yesterday, why she won't give me a chance to try again, why she won't even talk to me. She's made it clear she doesn't want to be with me…"

"You wanna be with her though, right?" he interrupts.

"Yeah. Of course. More than anything," I reply. "But I can't make her love me, can I?"

"You don't need to," Jack says. "She already does."

"She's got a damn funny way of showing it."

"Yeah, well like I say, she's in a really difficult place right now. It's partly to do with the apartment, and the house, and Catrina. And she's still grieving…"

"And?" I prompt. "There's something else, isn't there?"

"Yes, but I can't tell you what."

I get to my feet and look down at him. "Is she okay? Has something happened?"

"She's not sick or anything, and she's not hurt… well, other than having a broken heart. But something's happened, and you have to go back to her and work it out," he says. "She might be stubborn as hell, and unwilling to admit it, but I don't think she's ever gonna need you more than she does right now."

I don't even bother to look at Fin. I grab my phone and my keys. "Make yourselves comfortable… stay as long as you like. I'll be back… sometime."

I head toward my bedroom, picking up my overnight bag that I still haven't unpacked from yesterday, and taking my jacket from the closet in my dressing room, before returning to the elevator, and calling my pilot before the doors have even opened.

Chapter Nineteen

Lottie

I know Jack was only here for a couple of days, but the apartment already feels empty without him, even though he's only been gone for a few hours. And I feel really alone. I don't think I've ever felt so alone. Jack's the only other person who knows my secret and, for the time being, I want to keep it that way. This is my mistake and if I do decide to have a termination – which is a possibility that keeps rolling around my head – I don't want anyone else to know. So, I have to keep this to myself. Fortunately, Heather said she's going to go around to Simon's place after she finishes at work, and she'll stay the night there. Normally I don't much like being by myself, but I need some time with my own thoughts, without having to pretend to anyone, and I guess I'd better get used to it, being as I'll have to start living alone fairly soon. I haven't bothered to clear anything away since Jack left, so the blankets are still on the couch, and I've spent most of the afternoon lying there, curled up in them, watching movies and trying to pretend my life's not really falling apart.

On top of everything else, I'm now feeling sick. I doubt that's got anything to do with the pregnancy though, because it's nine in the evening, not the morning. It's probably to do with the fact that I haven't eaten anything since Jack left. I can't face cooking and the thought of having take-out again makes me want to really vomit, so I go through to the kitchen to make some toast. I can handle toast, and am just getting out the bread, when the doorbell rings.

I go into the hallway and call out, "Who's there?" It's too late in the evening to just open the door.

"It's me."

I'd know his voice anywhere. What I don't know is what he's doing here. Again.

"Why are you here?" I ask.

"To see you."

"Why?"

"Because we need to talk. Ideally I'd prefer to do that without a door between us, Lottie."

I reach out, my hand shaking, and open the door.

He's standing in front of me, wearing jeans, a t-shirt and a black leather jacket, his hair just a little disheveled, and like he needs a shave. He looks beautiful.

"Can I come in?" he asks softly, staring at me.

"Nothing's changed, Paul," I tell him, not answering his question, but blocking the doorway and keeping my voice down. "We don't belong together." *Especially not now.*

"Bullshit, Lottie. You belong with me and I belong with you. And we both know it. I've just spent a week away from you and it's been torture." He stares at me for a moment. "I'm pretty sure it's been the same for you too."

I want to tell him that he's right, but I can't.

"Can you think of anything that's happened to you in this last week that being with me wouldn't have made better?" he asks. "Because I know that every single thing in my life would've been so much better with you in it."

I can feel a huge lump forming in my throat, but I can't let this happen. I can't let him know my secret. He'd stay out of obligation, out of duty, not because he wants me…

"I'm sorry," I say, thinking on my feet.

"Why?"

"Because you've wasted your time coming down here – again."

"I have?" He looks confused.

"Yes. You… you saw me with Jack yesterday, didn't you?"

He nods his head. "Yeah. What of it?"

"Well, we've decided we want to be more than friends. He spent the night..." I leave that sentence out there for him to interpret, then add. "It doesn't matter what you say or do... I'm with Jack now."

He leans against the door frame and folds his arms across his chest. "Really?"

"Yes. Why are you looking like that?"

"Because I know you're lying."

"Seriously, Paul. You're not the only man in the world. I know we had a good time, but it obviously wasn't meant to be..."

"Stop lying to me," he barks. "I've spoken to Jack. He came to see me when he flew back to Boston..."

I don't hear any more. Everything starts to spin and then he fades to blackness.

Paul

I catch her just as she's about to hit the floor and pick her up, carrying her inside and kicking the door closed behind me. The small hallway leads into a living room, which is – frankly – a bit of a mess. There are blankets screwed up in a heap on the couch, a whole mass of stuff on the low coffee table, including Kleenex and used cups, and there's a pile of boxes stacked in the corner of the room. Still, I guess those could be Lottie's things from Catrina's house. I don't care about the state of the couch, Lottie needs to lie down, so I go over and place her carefully along its length, moving the blankets onto the floor, and kneeling down beside her, holding her hand in mine.

"Lottie?" I tap her hand. "Lottie?"

Very slowly, she opens her eyes and looks up at me, then around the room.

"How...?" she says. "How did I get in here?"

"You fainted. I carried you in."

"I fainted?"

"Yeah." I move a little closer. "Do you feel okay? Do you want anything?"

She shakes her head, using her arms to prop herself up a little. "No. I'm fine."

"Then can you tell me why you were lying to me?" I ask her. "I've spoken to Jack. He told me I should come back and see you. He also told me he's gay, so I know you're not seeing him, or sleeping with him. Why would you say that to me?"

She stares at me. "Why did he tell you to come back here?" she asks, avoiding my question.

"He told me something happened to you. He wouldn't tell me what, he just said I should come back," I explain. "Now, why did you lie to me?"

She swallows hard. "Can I have some water first?" she asks.

"Sure."

I get up and go into the kitchen, which is through a doorway off to the left and I manage to find some glasses in the third cabinet I try. There's a bottle of water in the refrigerator, so I pour some out and carry it back through, handing it to her and kneeling back down beside her.

She takes a couple of long sips and then turns and places it on the table. My eyes follow her movement and I notice all the crap that's lying on its surface. There are about half a dozen used Kleenex, two coffee cups, a folded leaflet and a white stick. My heart stops beating as my gaze settles on that final object and I immediately recognize what it is, and I lean over and pick it up, reading what it says in the small window on the side.

"You're pregnant?" I look down at her.

She nods her head and, without warning, bursts into tears.

I drop the stick back on the table and sit up on the couch, pulling Lottie into my arms, holding her close to me.

"Why didn't you tell me?" I say to her. "I was here yesterday. You could've told me then."

"I didn't know yesterday," she cries, pulling back a little, "not for sure. Jack and I were just heading out to buy the test when you arrived. I only did it this morning."

"So this is what Jack meant when he said something had happened? You found out you're pregnant?"

"Yes. But you don't have to feel obligated."

"Like fuck I don't."

She stares at me, sniffling. "I don't want that," she says through her tears.

"You don't want what?"

"I don't want you to feel like you have to come back to me. I know you can't forgive me for the things I've said and done…" Her voice fades to a whisper and she starts sniffling again.

"And how do you know that?"

"Because I saw you drive off the night we argued outside the restaurant. I know how mad you were with me. I know you can't forgive me for that."

"Really?"

"Yes. And then there's all the things I said to you yesterday," she continues. "I was so difficult, so… what was Jack's word…?"

"Contrary?" I offer.

"Yes. Contrary. It's the perfect description of me. I'm sorry I just lied to you about Jack," she whispers. "He did stay the night, but not with me. He slept on the couch. I promise."

"I know, but why'd you say it, Lottie?"

"Because I'm scared."

"What of?"

"That you'll feel obliged to come back, out of duty, out of responsibility. I don't want that."

She stops talking and reaches over, grabbing a Kleenex from the box on the table and holding it over her face.

"You finished now?" I ask her. She pulls down the Kleenex and looks at me. "Can I speak?"

She nods and I take her hand in mine, holding it on my lap.

"Firstly, you're right. I was mad with you outside the restaurant. But I was only mad because you told me to start another list. I didn't understand how you could suggest something like that. I love you, Lottie. Why the hell would I want to be with any other woman? It hurt that you could even think I'd wanna do that. I drove away because I didn't wanna argue anymore. But I didn't leave. I couldn't leave, not completely. You were obviously hurting, and I'd never leave you hurting, Lottie, you must know that." She lets out a slight sob. "I parked up," I continue, "and then I saw Jack arrive and, yeah, I'll admit, I didn't like it. At the time, I still wasn't convinced that you guys were just friends, and I drove off."

"You did more than drive off," she interrupts.

"Yeah, okay." I shrug. "But I calmed down real fast and realized I was actually happy that you had someone to comfort you."

"You were?" Her eyes widen in surprise.

"Yeah. Obviously I'd rather it had been me, but I was glad you had someone." I take a breath. "As for not forgiving you for the things you said, you were in a shitty place that evening, and I wasn't being very helpful or sympathetic. You'd just found out about your dad's will, and all I could think about was that I needed to talk to you about something else, and that you'd just taken a call from Jack and it sounded to me like you'd rather speak to him without me being there."

"Only because he wanted to talk about Alex... his partner." She pauses, then stares at me. "And what did you want to talk to me about?"

"About how I'd been with you that first night we were together. I knew I hadn't treated you right and I wanted to apologize for rushing you, for forgetting the condom and for making you leave like that. I knew whatever it was that had made you leave was down to me... and I wanted to straighten it out."

"Well, I suppose we kinda did."

"Yeah." I smile at her. "Just not in the way I wanted to." I sigh deeply. "Whatever you said to me on the sidewalk that night, I deserved it. You needed a safe place and all I gave you was doubt and criticism. If anyone needs forgiveness, it's me. And I'm sorry."

She reaches out with her free hand and touches my arm with her fingertips. "You have nothing to be sorry for," she says.

"Yeah… except not protecting you." She tilts her head to one side. "I forgot the condom, remember?" She nods her head and lets her eyes fall to her lap. "Can you look at me?" I ask her. "Please?" She raises her face to mine. "I'm sorry I forgot the condom. I'm sorry I didn't protect you that night and I'm sorry I made you feel anything but wanted with my stupid, thoughtless words. You are wanted. I want you so much I ache for you." I take her other hand and hold both of hers in mine. "I'm sorry I didn't believe you about Jack, and I'm sorry I didn't listen to you. I should've been there for you, supporting you, not arguing with you about things that don't matter." I take a breath, but not a long enough one for her to interrupt. "I want us to get back together," I tell her and she opens her mouth to speak. "Wait," I say quickly. "I'm not done yet." She closes her mouth again, but the doubt in her eyes is ever present. "I want us to get back together," I repeat, "because I know we're right for each other. And that has nothing to do with you being pregnant. When I sent you that text last week, telling you I wasn't giving up, I didn't know you were pregnant. When I came to see you yesterday to try and talk to you, I didn't know then either."

"But you must have suspected," she says, doubtfully. "I mean, even though it didn't dawn on me, surely you're… you're experienced enough to have worked out that it was a risk."

"Yeah, I had worked it out. And that was one of the things I was gonna talk to you about that night after we went to see Anthony. I wanted to let you know that, if it turned out that you were pregnant, then we'd deal with it, together. It was something I'd been wanting to say to you for a while, but you hadn't confirmed it either way, so at the time I sent that message, and at the time I spoke to you yesterday, as far as I was concerned, it was just you and me. You were the only thing I was thinking about. Well, you and me. Us. I want you, Lottie. Just you. I'll introduce you to a friend of mine called Fin, and he'll take great delight in telling you what a hopeless wreck I've been for the last week. I don't even wanna think about how much time he's spent on the phone and at my apartment, talking things through with me, helping me get through this. I don't think he actually saw me crying, but…"

"You were crying?" She's shocked.

"Of course I was. I'm lost without you." Her eyes soften and she sits upright. I let go of her hands and pull her into me, feeling her body close to mine.

"I'm lost without you too," she murmurs, and I feel my heart swell in my chest.

I lean back and capture her face in my hands, then brush my lips across hers. She moans softly and opens up, our tongues clashing and dancing as she clambers onto my lap, straddling me, and brings her arms around my neck, pulling me closer, her breasts crushed against my chest. She's breathless in moments, but so am I.

I break the kiss eventually, but keep my lips within touching distance of hers. "I know that since your dad died, you've gotten out of the habit of being loved," I whisper, "and I know this is hard for you, but let me love you. Please?"

She gazes into my eyes, but doesn't respond, and then eventually, she murmurs, "I want to, so much. I love you, Paul, I honestly do, and I'm sorry for all the things I've said, and for being so horrible to you."

"You weren't horrible."

She shakes her head, like she doesn't believe me, then says, "The thing is, I don't really see how we can make this work. We don't know each other very well, but we're evidently going to be parents. I mean… how can we…"

"Hey. Stop panicking. By my calculation, we've got nine months to get to know each other before the two of us become three, haven't we?" I say and she smiles, just lightly.

"I suppose. But…" She pauses. "I don't even know what I am to you."

"What do you mean?" I ask, stroking her hair.

"What am I to you?" she asks, with a hint of desperation in her voice. "You've never even called me your girlfriend."

"Yes I have."

"No you haven't," she replies.

"Well, I have to my friends and family. Morgan had a great time making fun of me over that. Hell, I even told the woman behind the desk at American Airlines that you were my girlfriend, and that I'd been a dick to you… That's why she took pity on me and looked up whether you'd checked in for your flight or not."

She shakes her head and smiles at me. "You weren't a dick," she says softly.

"Yeah, I was. I let you go. That makes me a prize dick." She giggles. "I always think of you as my girlfriend in my head, Lottie. Even when we've been apart, you've still been my girlfriend in here." I tap the side of my head. "And in here." I cover my heart with my hand. "And if I haven't said it out loud to you, then I apologize." I kiss her gently on the lips. "I didn't realize a label mattered to you so much, but as far as I'm concerned, you're a lot more than my girlfriend. You're the woman I love; the woman who's evidently carrying my child; the woman I want to spend the rest of my life with – even if I don't always understand you, and probably never will." I kiss her again a little more deeply, then pull back and look into her eyes. "But if you're that desperate for a label, how about 'wife'?"

Epilogue

Lottie

I feel like a beached whale. I look like a beached whale. And as it's now the end of August and boiling hot, I look like a lobster colored beached whale. It's not an attractive look, although Paul tells me all the time how beautiful I am and how much he loves me.

I can still remember my feelings of desolation at the beginning of the year, when I thought I'd lost everything. My home was being taken from me by my stepmom, I'd dumped Paul because I thought we were wrong for each other – although I would like to plead early pregnancy hormones in my own defense for my behavior toward him at the time – and I was still grieving for my dad, who I assumed had left his homes to Catrina, with no care for me whatsoever.

Being made homeless was stressful, but after Paul and I made up that evening, he made himself a coffee and fixed us both some pancakes. He didn't feel like toast, and I didn't want anything heavy. Pancakes seemed like a good compromise and Paul insisted on making them while I rested. I don't know how I managed it, but we sat up until gone midnight and talked through his proposal, being as he'd asked me to be his wife, and he agreed to give me some time to think about it. I didn't doubt his love for me, or mine for him. But I wanted to spend more time with him before making such a momentous decision. He was fine with that and, once I'd stopped crying, out of sheer relief and happiness, he carried me through to my bedroom and made love to me so gently I thought my heart would break.

The next morning, he called his assistant and told her he wasn't gonna be in the office for the rest of the day and then he came with me to look at apartments. The first one was so bad, Paul wouldn't even get out of his rental car, and we drove straight off again, but we eventually found somewhere acceptable which wasn't far from college. It was just a small one bedroom apartment, but it was big enough for me. Paul obviously offered to buy me somewhere else – much bigger and smarter – but I convinced him there was no point. I didn't intend to live in Virginia after I finished my degree, so renting for those last few months made sense. He insisted on helping me move, and paying my rent, which meant I could give up my job at the bookstore and use my allowance to live very comfortably. I was glad of that, being as the worst early pregnancy symptom I had was complete exhaustion. I slept all the time. Usually on Paul, whenever we could be together. And he did his best to ensure we were together as much as possible. He even re-arranged a trip he'd planned to Detroit, and got the man he was going to see to fly down to Virginia instead – at Paul's expense, of course – and booked the guy into an executive suite at a nearby hotel, so they could meet there each day and discuss their business. Although he was busy all day, sometimes into the evening, Paul was able to spend a few extra nights with me, which I really appreciated, being as the timing of that trip coincided with the onset of my morning sickness, and having him there, rather than in Boston, or Detroit, made all the difference.

Once the guy had gone back home and my lectures had started again, Paul came to visit every weekend, arriving on Friday afternoon and leaving again on Monday morning. That was a good thing, because it meant he was with me when Anthony got in touch to tell me that he'd received the statement of my trust fund from Catrina. He explained that there were some discrepancies and sent through copies, which made no sense to me, but Paul looked at them and hit the roof. It transpired that Catrina had spent nearly forty thousand dollars out of my inheritance, although she'd done her best to disguise it as necessary expenses for me. Being as I was only weeks away from graduation, I decided not to pursue her for the money, but to insist that Anthony become a joint trustee to prevent her from spending any more. Being nearly five months pregnant, I didn't need the hassle. And besides, I didn't want to waste any more time on her. She's in my past as far as I'm concerned. And I'm much more interested in my future. With Paul.

We've had so much fun together, discovering each other's habits and foibles. I know that he's more of an owl than a lark; that he prefers non-fiction to fiction; that he likes action movies, but will watch a rom-com if I ask him nicely; that he thinks everything can be made better by the addition of garlic… and cheese; that he's not overly keen on chocolate, but doesn't mind buying it for me; that his taste in jewelry is exquisite and that he loves me. Very much. He never pressured me to give him an answer to his proposal. He didn't even mention it. He just let us spend our time together, being relaxed and happy, and letting me know he's always there for me, and allowing me to accept that, which I think we both needed.

Then, two weeks before I graduated, Paul came down to Virginia early one Friday morning. I had no lectures that day, so he flew us both up to Maine, where he showed me round a house, just a few miles down the coast from his parents' place. I fell in love with it straight away and he said that was just as well, because he'd bought it for us. While showing me the master bedroom, he got down on one knee and asked me to marry him again. He was looking into my eyes, his own filled with hope, and holding out a tiny box, inside which was a perfect solitaire diamond ring. I burst into tears, and accepted him on the spot. I don't think he's ever held me so tight as he did at that moment and when he slid the ring onto my finger, I knew it was the right thing to do. I knew I'd found my home; my safe place.

Since then, we've been spending our weekends at the house, and now I've graduated, our weekdays are spent at his apartment in Boston. Being fairly pregnant by the time I left college, I didn't see the point in trying to get a job, so I've been helping Jack get his new garden design business off the ground. So far, it's going really well.

Mrs Hemsworth accepted Paul's offer to come work for him. She doesn't live with us in Boston, because we kinda like having the place to ourselves, but she keeps house for us up at Cape Elizabeth and, when we're not there, she goes and helps Paul's mom. They've become friends over the last few months, and I know Paul's relieved, knowing his mom has someone close by that she can turn to. It means Linda gets a break from being a carer the whole time and gets to have some fun herself. And when we're up there, Mrs Hemsworth cooks us the most incredible meals, especially her sticky ribs, which have become a firm favorite with Paul. I guess that also helps explain my resemblance to a beached whale.

Paul's also helped me come to terms with my father's will and the circumstances surrounding it. I don't blame Dad anymore. I know it was a mistake and he'd never have knowingly done anything to hurt me. I've rebuilt my mental relationship with him, and my memories of him are back to being happy ones again. Thanks to Paul.

It's the last weekend in August and, being as the baby's due in a couple of weeks, Paul's decided we're going to make this our last stay up in Maine until after he or she is born. I say 'he or she' because we decided not to find out the sex, but to wait and see. However, the house is too far away from the hospital and Paul doesn't want to take any risks. So, because it's our last weekend, and the summer's drawing to a close, we've invited everyone to stay.

That means we've got Jack and Alex – who have resolved their differences, which were mainly in Jack's head, I think – and Fin and Brad, all staying over. I've met Fin and Brad quite a few times since I graduated and moved in with Paul. I get on really well with both of them. They're good friends to Paul and we've had some fun times over the summer. Linda and Michael are also here for lunch today, and it's good to see that Michael's condition hasn't worsened at all since his diagnosis.

We're having a barbecue, which Paul's commandeered, together with Brad. Everyone else is sitting around the pool, and Mrs Hemsworth is in the middle of making one of many salads.

"You should come and sit down for a while," I tell her, coming into the kitchen to fill up the jug with iced water.

"I will, when I've finished this."

As far as we're concerned, Mrs Hemsworth might cook our meals, but she's part of the family and when we're here, she usually eats with us. Apart from anything else, she's our source of local gossip.

"You couldn't get me another couple of tomatoes out of the refrigerator, could you?" she asks.

"Sure."

I reach my hand inside and feel a trickle of water run down my leg, followed fairly quickly by a gush, which splashes onto the tiled floor.

"Oh…" I say quietly.

"What?" She looks over at me, then at the floor by my feet. "Oh my," she says, then smiles at me. "Stay where you are."

"I wasn't planning on going anywhere."

I close the refrigerator and watch as she goes out through the bi-folding doors onto the deck. She walks straight up to Paul, who turns to her, his expression altering as he hands the fork he's holding to Brad, and goes over to Fin, who's relaxing by the pool. He looks up, then stiffens and stands. They both come inside, wearing nothing but board shorts.

"Your waters just broke?" Paul says, looking at me, then at the floor.

"Yes… so it would seem."

He takes both my hands in his and looks into my eyes, a smile forming on his lips. "Your timing…" he says, shaking his head slowly.

"Move out the way," Fin urges, giving Paul a nudge. "Are you getting any contractions?" he asks.

And at that precise moment, a sharp pain grips my abdomen and I start to breathe hard and heavy, reaching out to clasp Paul's hand and staring into his concerned face.

"I'll take that as a 'yes'," Fin says and turns to Mrs Hemsworth. "Call 911," he says. "Tell them I've got a pregnant mom, thirty-eight weeks gestation, contractions underway, waters broken, doctor on the scene, paramedics required. Got that?"

She nods at his calm instructions and goes to the phone.

"What's happening?" Jack and Linda appear in the doorway at the same time and take one look at the scene, before rushing over.

"We're going upstairs," Fin says, taking charge. He looks at me. "Can you make it?"

"I'll carry her," Paul says and lifts me into his arms. "Everyone else stay down here and... find something to do."

"I could have walked," I tell him as he starts to climb the stairs, just as another contraction strikes and I grip his arm, digging my nails in.

"Yeah, of course you could," he replies, wincing.

"Shit," Fin whispers from behind us.

"Why did you say 'shit'?" Paul asks over his shoulder.

"No reason."

I can tell from the look on Paul's face that he's not convinced, but he looks down at me and smiles. "Well, this isn't quite what we planned, is it?"

I shake my head. "Has anything gone to plan yet?"

He leans down and kisses me, just as we reach the head of the stairs. "No, but who cares as long as we're together."

Paul

This was the very reason I'd decided against coming up here from now on... and look what's happened. The only saving grace we've got is that Fin's here. Thank God.

I carry Lottie into our bedroom and she grabs my arm again, sticking her nails into my flesh. Jeez, that really hurts, but I try to put a brave face on it as the pain courses through her.

"Christ, that hurts," she breathes, as she comes out the other side.

"You're doing really well," Fin says, then looks at me. "Lie her on the bed and I'll..."

"No, you can't," Lottie interrupts.

"I can't what?" Fin asks.

"You can't lie me on the bed. We only bought it a couple of months ago… it's gonna get ruined."

"Does that really matter?" I ask her. She stares at me and I huff out a sigh. "I'll take you to the guest room. Okay?"

I'm pleased now that we bought a house with seven bedrooms. Even having Fin, Brad, Jack and Alex here to stay, we've still got two guest bedrooms, having converted the room next to ours into a nursery.

I go back out into the hallway and carry Lottie along to the room on the other side of our bedroom, which isn't being used this weekend. The bed isn't made up, and is just covered with a simple white sheet.

"Is this okay?" I ask her.

She nods her head, gripping my arm again.

"Can you open the windows?" she whispers, through her pain.

"Yeah. Just let me put you down first."

I lie her on the bed, with her head on the pillows and step back, as Fin closes the door and takes my place beside her, and I go and open the large windows that overlook the ocean, letting in a gentle sea breeze and the sound of the waves crashing on the rocks below the house.

"Okay," Fin says. "We're gonna get a lot more intimate than either of us probably ever anticipated." I turn and realize he's talking to Lottie, and go back over to the bed, standing opposite him and looking down at her. She's staring at Fin, kinda scared and I sit and take her hand in mine. "Just remember, I'm a doctor and I've done this before."

"How many times?" Lottie asks.

"Enough," he replies evasively and I glance up at him. He ignores me and goes into the adjoining bathroom, where I hear him washing his hands. "Can you get undressed?" he calls out. "You can keep your t-shirt on…" His voice fades. "And Paul… fetch some towels, will you?"

"If you're giving me things to do to keep me occupied…" I say impatiently.

"I'm not. I need towels," he replies.

Lottie looks up at me.

"It'll be okay," I tell her and she nods her head. "I'll be thirty seconds."

I kiss her quickly and run out of the room and along the hallway to the closet, where I grab a handful of bath towels, and run back. Fin is still in the bathroom and Lottie has managed to get her skirt off.

"You okay?" I ask her. I know it's a dumb question, but I can't think what else to say.

"Can you help me?" she asks, and I dump the towels on the end of the bed and, while she raises her hips off the bed, I pull down her panties, and deposit them on the floor with her skirt.

"I'm scared," she says.

"Fin won't let anything happen to you," I tell her. I have every faith in him.

He comes back out, drying his hands on a fresh white towel, which he drops on the floor. Lottie pulls her legs up, then puts them down again, then pulls her t-shirt down too, despite her enormous bump, and tries to cover herself. I want to tell her that Fin will have seen it all before, but I doubt that's gonna help.

Without even really looking at her, Fin picks up two of the towels from the end of the bed and hands them to me. "Place those underneath Lottie," he says, going back and picking up a third, which he keeps hold of.

I do as he says and once she's settled again, and had yet another contraction, he places his towel over her lower abdomen, covering her.

She glances up at him and whispers, "Thank you," and he smiles at her and checks his watch again.

"Okay," he says and gives her a smile. "I'm gonna need to examine you." He comes to where I'm sitting. "Move around the other side, Paul," he says and I do as he suggests, getting onto the bed and giving him more room. He places his hands on her knees and pulls them up and apart and then settles himself in position so he can see between her legs. His facial expression alters dramatically, and I see a look of surprise cross his eyes.

At that moment, Lottie squeezes my hand, crushing the bones for all she's worth.

"I—I want to push," she cries and my eyes dart from her to Fin.

"Yeah," he says, still quite calm. "That's okay."

"It is?"

He looks from me to her. "I can see the baby's head… so yeah, it is."

Part of me wants to ask if we shouldn't wait for the paramedics, but I know that's a really dumb suggestion, so I keep quiet and let him do his job.

"Remember your breathing," he says to Lottie as the next contraction strikes. "That's it," he urges. "Good girl… Keep pushing."

Lottie screams in pain and I move closer cradling her in my arms. This has to be the worst thing ever. Having to watch her go through this, and not being able to do a damn thing about it, is torture.

Everything subsides for a moment, and Lottie breathes deeply.

"That was great," Fin says, encouragingly. "Just keep doing what you're doing."

Within moments, Lottie clutches my hand once more and a deep, throaty howl of pain comes from her mouth as she pushes with everything she's got.

"Keep going… keep going," Fin urges.

The contraction subsides and we all relax once more.

"One more," Fin says. "Just one more." He reaches behind him and grabs another towel, laying it out on the bed in preparation.

I'm vaguely aware of voices coming from the front of the house, and then footsteps on the stairs, just as the next contractions starts.

Lottie screams in pain again. "Go on, Lottie," Fin commands. "Keep pushing." She glares at him and, lifting her chin onto her chest, she gives him one last push.

"That's it!" he cries, as the door opens and two paramedics stand on the threshold, looking at us, broad smiles on their faces.

Lottie sinks back in relief, her eyes closing in sheer exhaustion, her hair matted to her damp forehead, just as we hear our baby cry for the very first time.

The next few minutes are a blur. I'm aware of the paramedics coming into the room, talking to Fin for a moment and then the baby being wrapped in a towel. Someone must have cut the cord, because the next thing I know, Fin's standing above us, cradling a tiny bundle.

"You've got a daughter," he says, his voice thick with emotion as he lays her in Lottie's arms.

"Is… is she okay?" I ask him.

"She's perfect. Just like her mom," he replies, smiling down at us. "I'll leave you guys alone for a while."

I hold my hand up to him and we shake. "Thanks, Fin," I say with feeling.

"My pleasure." He gives me a nod and returns to the end of the bed, where he talks in hushed whispers to the paramedics.

"We've got a daughter," Lottie says, staring at the bundle in her arms.

I move closer. "Yeah, we have." I push the towel to one side and reveal a tiny pink face with tufts of pale brown hair, and I fall in love all over again.

The paramedics pronounced that mom and baby were perfectly well and didn't need to be taken to hospital, so once Lottie had rested for a while and the baby was asleep in Fin's arms, I carried my future wife back to our room.

"I don't need to stay in bed," she said as I lay her down.

"Well, you're going to. Just for today."

"But I'm perfectly okay."

I sit beside her on the bed. "Having seen what you just went through, you deserve a rest and a little TLC. And that's what you're gonna get."

She smiles up at me and relents. "Okay, but just for today."

"I'll go and get the baby," I tell her. "And then you'd better get ready for some visitors. The whole family's downstairs, and they're all gonna want to come see our little girl."

"Family?"

"Well, I know only Mom and Dad are family in the strictest sense of the word, but I think of them all as family really," I explain, and she gives me a very tender kiss.

"I'd better put on something a little more presentable then," she replies.

"Want some help with that?"

She goes to get up, shaking her head, then winces. "Hmm, I think maybe I do."

Knowing the baby is perfectly safe with Fin for the time being, I spend a little while with Lottie, helping her shower and change into a nightdress, before getting back into bed. She's never worn a nightdress before and it looks kinda weird, but at least she's presentable for everyone, and we bought one that has buttons up the front so she can breastfeed, which is something she was adamant she wanted to try.

Once she's settled, I return to the guest room, where I find Fin sitting in the chair by the window, with our daughter nestled in his arms.

"You look kinda comfortable like that," I tell him from the doorway.

He looks around and gets to his feet with ease, walking over to me. "I was just giving her some advice," he says, smiling gently.

"You were?"

"Yeah. I was just warning her off of guys like us."

I laugh. "Damn straight," I reply. "She's not going anywhere near guys like me." Well, like I used to be, anyway.

"And me," he says, looking up at me.

"You're not so bad," I tell him.

"You wanna try telling Rachel that?" Rachel is a woman he's been seeing for a couple of weeks. As far as Fin is concerned, it's a fairly casual thing, but judging from the number of times she's called and texted him over this weekend, I think she sees it as something a lot more serious and I know it's bugging him.

"No, but maybe you need to," I reply. "I think you need to have a long talk with her."

He shrugs. "Yeah, I do. But not right now. I've kinda got my hands full at the moment." He gazes down at my daughter again. "You know, it's not something I've ever thought of trying before," he admits, "but after today, I've gotta tell you, I'm kinda jealous of you guys."

I'm surprised. "Which part?" I ask him. "Being settled, or having this little one?"

He hesitates for a moment, then whispers, "Both."

"Well, you'll find the right woman one day, and until then, you'll definitely be the baby's favorite uncle," I say as he reluctantly hands her over to me.

"I should damn well hope so." He smiles at me. "How's Lottie?"

"Sore."

He smirks. "That'll pass."

"Now we're on our own, can you tell me why you said 'shit' like that when we were coming up here earlier?"

"Because Lottie's contractions were so close together. Ideally I didn't want to have to deliver your baby all by myself."

"Why not?"

"Because I've only done it twice before…"

"Excuse me?"

"Just because I'm an ER doctor doesn't mean I get to deliver babies all the time. Generally, they go to the maternity department. If they do end up with us, it's usually because there's something else that's wrong. We usually deal with the 'something else' and call down one of the maternity docs to deal with the delivery. So… I've done it twice in my whole career. Today makes it three times."

"Fucking hell," I whisper.

"Yeah." We stand for a moment and stare at each other. "Don't sweat it, Paul. It's something where Mother Nature kinda takes over," he adds eventually. "Unless there's a problem… which there wasn't."

"Well, next time, I'm gonna make sure we're nearer the hospital. For everyone's peace of mind – including yours."

"Next time?" he smirks. "Have you spoken to Lottie about that?"

"No, not yet."

"I suggest you leave it for a while before you do."

I nod my head, grinning. "Yeah, I think I might. And now, I'd better take my daughter in to her mom before she comes to find me." I turn to leave and he follows. "I guess everyone's gonna want to come up and see us," I say as we reach the doorway.

"You bet they are."

We pass through and he closes the door behind us. "Can you go down and say it's fine for them to come up, but can they just give us ten minutes first?"

He nods his head, and is about to move away when I grab his arm. "I owe you," I tell him simply.

"No you don't," he replies. "I think I told you once that friends don't owe each other anything, remember?"

"This is different. This was about Lottie, and our baby, which means I can't even begin to repay you, but if there's ever anything you need – and I mean anything – then you just have to say the word. Okay?"

He nods his head, pats me on the arm and goes downstairs.

Back in our room, I lay the baby in Lottie's arms and then lie down on the bed beside her.

"You look beautiful," I tell her honestly.

"I look a mess," she replies.

I shake my head. "You've never looked more beautiful to me."

She smiles and we lean into each other for a brief kiss.

"Everyone's gonna be coming up here in a minute," I continue, "but I wanted to talk to you alone first."

"You did?"

"Yeah. We never did set a date for the wedding, did we?"

She swallows and looks at me. "No."

"I knew you didn't want to get married while you were pregnant, but I really don't want to wait much longer. So… how does Christmas sound?"

"Christmas?"

"Yeah."

She grins. "It sounds perfect." She pauses. "And while we're on our own… Can we talk about the baby's name?"

"Sure." I lean in closer. "I thought we could name her after your mother, if that's okay with you?"

Tears form in her eyes. "I—I was going to ask if we could do that too. I didn't want to presume, but…"

"Your mom was a very special woman," I add, wiping away her first tear with my thumb.

"I didn't know you'd met her?" she queries.

"I didn't. But your dad loved her. He talked about her all the time. And if she was anything like you, then she must've been special."

"So, Olivia it is then," Lottie says after a long pause, looking down at our baby daughter.

"Yeah." Right on cue, Olivia lets out a little whimper and screws up her face before settling down again. "I guess this means you've got another label," I tell Lottie as she kisses Olivia's soft head. She turns to me inquiringly. "You're my fiancée, my soon to be wife, and now you're a mom."

"And we're a family," she replies, smiling.

"We'll always be a family," I say, just as the door opens and the rest of our family comes in to join us.

The End

Keep reading for an excerpt from Suzie Peters' forthcoming book
Believe In Me
Part Two in the Believe in Fairy Tales Series.
Available to purchase from February 22nd 2019

Believe In Me

Believe in Fairy Tales: Book Two

by

Suzie Peters

Chapter One

Lily

I open my eyes and stretch my arms above my head, then pull back, the pain jolting me fully awake and making me suck in a sharp breath. It's a struggle to ignore the nagging spasms that continually rock my body, but I make the effort and raise my head, glancing across to the window, and noticing my cardigan still lying over the back of the gray leather chair. *Of course.* I came up here to fetch it after lunch, but I seem to have fallen asleep. How long for, I have no idea.

I turn over and look at the clock, then sit up, wincing in pain again. How can it be four o'clock already? That means I've been asleep for over two hours. I was going to go shopping, although how I thought I'd do that, considering how awful I feel, I've got no idea. I guess it was just a need to escape. A need to get away from this house, from the watchful eye of the housekeeper, Mrs Gibson, whose dark presence reminds me far too much of Mrs Danvers, a character from my favorite book *Rebecca*, by Daphne du Maurier. I know she's nowhere near as sinister as her fictional counterpart, but it wouldn't hurt her to crack a smile once in a while. It was a need to be out in the cool autumn air, among other people, to think, to be myself, to wonder what went wrong, and why Kevin doesn't love me anymore, or whether he maybe never did.

I go to the bathroom, returning a few minutes later, still drying my hands, and sitting down on the edge of the bed, just to rest my legs. They're so painful, I'm not sure where to put them, and my feet still feel like they're on fire, like hundreds of tiny red-hot pokers are jabbing into me continuously, but in going to the bathroom, I've noticed that I seem to have developed a new symptom now as well, and I dump the towel on the bed and look down at my hands. They're a normal color, and they're not swollen, but they're completely numb. I raise my right hand, holding it up to light streaming in through the window and touching it with my left, even though I can barely feel the contact, and my bottom lip starts to tremble as tears threaten to fall. I'm scared. My phone is lying on the nightstand and I reach for it, but then pull back. I could call Doctor Fletcher, but what would be the point? I've been to see him four times in the last two weeks, and every time he tells me I've just got a virus, and that I should get plenty of rest and keep taking the tonic I've been using ever since I first started to feel so run down. Can I face the humiliation again? Can I handle the look that he gives me? The one that says he thinks I'm making it all up, that I'm attention seeking? I shake my head and lie down again. Maybe some more rest will help... Maybe this is just a form of shock, a reaction to Kevin having come home so unexpectedly last night, and the discoveries I made while he was in the shower. Not that they were discoveries really, being as I've already known about him for so long. I've just been trying to pretend it's not true.

My mind drifts back to the feeling of panic I experienced when I heard his key in the lock yesterday evening. I don't know why I panicked. He's never hit me, or harmed me in any way, but I suppose I've gotten used to being by myself. It was a Saturday night, and I wasn't expecting him to come home, not when he hasn't been here for the last three weeks...

"Hello?" He called his greeting like a question, as though he thought I might not be home.

"Kevin?" I'm not sure why I doubted who it might be. Other than myself and Mrs Gibson, no-one else has a key to the house.

"Who else would it be?" I could hear the shortness of his temper already and found my hands were sweating. I remember wiping them on my jeans and sitting up on the couch to greet him, despite the pains that were wracking through my body.

He appeared in the doorway, wearing a suit, with the tie undone, looking as handsome as ever, and younger than his thirty-five years, his dark hair swept back and his brown eyes boring into mine.

"You look like a wreck." There was more than a hint of disdain in his voice.

"I'm not well."

"Really? Still?" The disdain turned into disbelief.

He walked over to the drinks cabinet and poured himself a whiskey. Neat. No ice.

"Yes."

He nodded his head, stared at me for a moment, and then announced he was going for a shower. Within moments, he was back again.

"You moved into the guest room?" His voice was like thunder and I raised my hands to my head, just to steady it.

"I thought it might be easier... what with me not being well." I didn't make eye contact with him, because I wasn't telling him the truth. Well, not entirely anyway. I did think it might be easier if we weren't sharing the same room, but that wasn't because I'm sick. It was because the last time he was home, which was three weeks ago, I'd overheard him having a conversation on his cell phone. He was in his home office and I'd gone to bed early, because I was tired – I wasn't sick back then, just tired. However, I needed a drink and came downstairs, and that's when I heard him, telling someone – presumably his lover – how much he was going to miss her over the weekend, that he was bored rigid already, having to be here with me, that he couldn't wait for Monday when he could be inside her again and that he was hard just thinking about it. I'd stood outside the door, mesmerized, and listened to him describing the things he'd done with her just that afternoon, telling her how sweet she tasted, and how how much he enjoyed coming in her mouth. Then I'd heard his groaning climax as the tears rolled down my cheeks, and I realized my fantasies of a supposedly perfect marriage were just that... fantasies. My long-held suspicions were accurate. My husband was having an affair. That was bad enough – obviously – but I think what made it worse was the knowledge that, ever since he'd know me, he'd denied me the intimacy and pleasure of oral sex, but had seemingly enjoyed it with someone else. It was something I'd always wanted to try, and it still is, and yet he made me feel like such a slut whenever I suggested it. I can still recall the look of revulsion on his face, even now. But I guess it was only me who repulsed him.

He went back to the city on the Sunday evening and I moved out of the marital bed…

"Easier for whom?" He took a step into the room and for the first time in our marriage, I felt really scared of him.

"Both of us?"

He stood still, looking at me silently for a while and then just turned and left. I wondered if he realized I know about 'her', and whether he cared.

I didn't see him again last night, mainly because I went to bed before dinner, but this morning, I was hungry and I decided to go downstairs to find something to eat. On my way, I passed our bedroom – well, the room that used to be our bedroom. The door was ajar and I could hear Kevin in the shower, singing slightly out of tune, just like he always has done. I could also see his phone, lying on the bed, as though he'd just been using it.

Call it curiosity. Call it stupidity. I knew no good could possibly come of it, but like a bomb on self-destruct mode, I pushed the door open and crept into our room – well, his room. I wasn't sure whether he would have changed the passcode to his phone from the days when I was his trusted PR assistant, used to sending his messages because he was too lazy, but I tried it anyway, and it worked. With half an eye on his bathroom, I went straight to his message app, where I discovered a series of texts from someone who he'd named as 'C'. They were very explicit, very detailed, describing all the things they wanted to do to each other, or had recently done and were re-living. I was immediately transported back to that evening a few weeks ago, when I'd stood outside his door and listened to him on the phone. This must be 'her'…
I was surprised, not by the language, but by how romantic they were at times. I had to go back to the early days of my relationship with Kevin to recall the last time he'd said anything like that to me. And yet he

seemed to have been communicating with this woman for months and months. Maybe even years... I scrolled back further and found more messages, some going back to before he and I even met. A lot of them were the same, full of raunchy commentary on their sex lives, but then there were some which contained details of money changing hands between the two of them. She couldn't be a prostitute, surely? I shook my head, despite the pain. Of course not. The amounts were far too much, and she was paying him, not the other way around. The messages also mentioned Kevin attending business meetings with the woman, which confused me. I was about to put the phone down, fearful of being caught out, when I noticed a single message dated three weeks ago, from the last time Kevin was here, to someone called just 'M'. With a trembling finger, I clicked on it and gasped at the graphic content. It made the others seem tame by comparison and, although I'm no prude, I wanted to be sick.

I put the phone down where I'd found it and fled his room, returning to my own, my hunger forgotten. He left the house about a half hour later and I showered and dressed, before going downstairs. Mrs Gibson was hovering in the kitchen and told me I looked like I could do with some of my tonic.

"It'll pick you up." She gave me her best attempt at a smile, which was more like a grimace.

"I'm not sure it's working." I think I felt better before I started taking it, if I'm being honest.

"Well, you know what the doctor told you." Making it clear she wasn't going to take anymore arguments from me, she tipped a spoonful of tonic into a glass and added some orange juice, passing it across the breakfast bar.

"Where's my husband gone?" I sipped the drink, grateful that at least it didn't seem to taste of anything and that whenever she mixes this up for me, I can just enjoy the fresh-tasting juice and hope it's doing some good at least.

"He went to play golf."

"He's coming back later?"

"As far as I know, yes." Her voice was flat, monotone, disinterested. But then it always is.

He didn't come back by lunch, so I had an omelette and salad, made by Mrs Gibson, and then decided to come up and fetch my cardigan, before going out… and that's when I fell asleep.

I turn over, wiping away the tear that's rolling down my cheek. Where did it all go so wrong? Maybe it's my fault. Maybe I shouldn't have married him in the first place. I take a deep breath, trying to steady myself. Of course I shouldn't have. Let's face it, would you marry a man you caught with a semi-naked woman in his office just three days after he'd taken your virginity? Of course you wouldn't. So why did I? Was it because he held me in his arms and told me it was a mistake, that it would never happen again, and that he couldn't live without me? Was it because he sat me down on his couch and knelt before me, with tears in his eyes and convinced me I was the only woman he'd ever loved – and would ever love? Was it because he spent the next couple of weeks doing everything in his power to regain my trust, and then took over a whole restaurant for the evening, and proposed to me in the most romantic way imaginable? Or was it because, at twenty-five, I had nothing else? I had no family, no-one else to turn to. I felt like being with him was the best I could do… because it was easier to bury my head in the sand and hope for the best, than to face the truth? Whatever it was, I married him. That was over a year ago now and it was the worst decision I've ever made – apart from getting involved with him in the first place.

Those first few months of our marriage were a whirlwind of rallies and meetings, dinners and parties, and occasional sex, when he could fit me into his schedule. My head was spinning most of the time as my role changed from PR assistant to future Senator's wife, married to a man I'd known for less than half a year, and I didn't have time to notice anything out of the ordinary. Then he was elected in the mid-terms. In reality, once the celebrations had stopped, what that meant was that Kevin and I spent even more time apart, because he decided to 'surprise' me, by buying this house in the country. To be honest, I liked the idea. I'd never warmed to his Boston apartment; it was very much a bachelor pad, and I hated the reminders of his previous life. This way, I reasoned, we could build a life together, away from all the hubbub of the state capital, and its politics. Of course, what he didn't tell me straight away was that he intended to spend most of his time in the city, leaving me by myself out here in the middle of nowhere, because I don't think he could have bought a more isolated, or isolating house. It's right on the fringes of the state, and at least ten miles from the nearest town. There are another couple of homes nearby, but they're not visible from ours, so there's a definite feeling of loneliness here. Being as he'd made it clear he no longer wanted me to work for him, right from the moment we'd married, I questioned the fact that we'd be spending so much time apart, but he told me he liked the idea of me keeping house; he valued the traditions of a stay-at-home wife… and then he promptly employed Mrs Gibson, and made my role redundant. So, all I had left to do, was to look the part, to make occasional appearances and hold his hand in public, whenever necessary. It wasn't the most fulfilling job in the world, but in a way, I'd known what I was signing up for. I couldn't complain. Not that he was home enough to listen anyway.

The first real clue that things weren't right came in the spring, so about six months into our marriage, when I noticed that he started ignoring his cell phone. He'd check who was calling and then decline the call, usually giving me a loving smile, or a squeeze of my hand at the same time. He did that a lot. I didn't worry about it, assuming it was a reporter, or an aide he didn't particularly want to speak to while he was with me. Then, after another month or two, he started taking the calls, but leaving the room and going into his office, or out onto the deck. Again, I didn't think too much of it. A lot of the things he had to discuss were confidential and I knew it wasn't always possible for him to speak in front of me. He told me he loved me, and we were still having as much sex as we could, considering he was in the city most of the time, and I was kicking my heels out here in rural Massachusetts.

I recall a conversation I had with his brother, Eric at around that time, at a family barbecue. Eric lives in a luxurious house about a half hour drive from us, and still runs the family firm, making optical lenses, where Kevin also worked as the CFO until he decided to run for political office. Even though it was a Sunday, Kevin had taken a call and disappeared into his brother's house, leaving the rest of us sitting outside. Eric's wife, Isabelle, had made a joke that Kevin looked guilty and maybe he was having an affair, and Eric had turned around from the barbecue and told her that there was no way Kevin would do that. He'd then switched his glance to me and I'd thought he was about to pay me a compliment, when he'd smiled just lightly and said that there was no way Kevin would risk his career by cheating. I felt so deflated by that, I didn't even notice at the time how quiet Kevin was all afternoon, or how impatient he was to get back to the city that night – to the point where he didn't even kiss me goodbye... that realization came later.

I start at the sound of the front door slamming shut. Kevin's home. His footsteps ring out on the wooden stairs and I feel my hands sweating again. Why am I reacting like that to him?

The door to my bedroom is closed but he doesn't knock. Instead he just walks right on in.

"What are you doing in here?" he says harshly.

"Resting," I reply, not bothering to turn over.

"Tell me something I don't know," he says.

I take a breath. "Are you going back to the city?" I ask.

"No, not tonight. I've got to see Eric tomorrow at the office." Although Kevin doesn't work for the family business anymore, he still retains a shareholding and has to attend monthly meetings. I'm not sure it's been a month since their last gathering, but I don't count the days.

"So you'll go back tomorrow?"

"Yes. I'll go back right after the meeting," he replies and from the nearness of his voice, I can tell he's come further into the room. "Why? Are you trying to get rid of me?"

"Of course not," I lie, making an effort to sound as carefree as possible.

"It's a lunchtime meeting," he says, as though I'm interested. "I'll work from here in the morning..." His voice fades and I feel the weight of him sitting down on the bed. "Why did you really move in here?" he asks.

I turn to face him, wincing at the pain. "I explained. I thought it would be easier." He nods his head, clearly feeling more amenable than he was last night. "Why do you ask?" I add. He shrugs his shoulders but doesn't reply and I struggle to sit up. "Can I ask you something?" He stares at me, but still doesn't respond. "Are you having an affair?" I know he is, but I want to see how he'll react.

He shifts on the bed and looks out the window. "What on earth would make you think that?" He turns and looks at me again. "Is that why you've moved in here? Because if it is…"

"No." I shake my head, laying back down again. "I genuinely thought it would be better if I didn't disturb you when you're here." *Not that you're here very often.*

He gets up. "Well, I'm sure you know what's best," he says and I notice he didn't answer my question. I didn't need him to, but I think it's interesting that he didn't even bother to lie.

As he closes the door behind him, I wipe away the tear that's fallen onto my cheek and wonder why it hurts that I'm not even worth lying to anymore.

Fin

"Do you think next time we come up here, you could make it slightly less exciting?" I comment to Paul. He's standing in the lobby of his huge beachside home in Cape Elizabeth, Maine and our friend Brad and I are just saying goodbye to him and his fiancée, Lottie, after a very eventful weekend.

"I can guarantee I won't ask you to deliver another baby," he replies, smiling down at the newborn cradled in his arms. I never thought I'd see the day when my best friend would be a father, but I guess love does that – well, love and forgetting to use a condom, anyway.

"Why don't I feel reassured by that?" I go over to him and give him a minute to shift baby Olivia to his other arm so we can shake.

"Thanks again," he says, with disarming sincerity, keeping hold of my hand. "For everything."

"I'm not gonna say 'anytime', because I nearly had a coronary," I reply, smiling at him. "And being as I'm the only doctor here, that might have given you a problem. But you know where I am… okay?"

He nods and I turn to Lottie. She's undeniably beautiful, although she still looks kinda tired, and at the moment, I think she's also a little embarrassed. I guess that could be because I delivered her daughter yesterday afternoon and we got more intimate that I ever thought we would, considering she's engaged to the man who's been my best friend since high school.

"Take care of yourself," I say to her, breaking the ice as best I can.

She nods her head and then, without saying a word, she puts her arms around me, which takes my breath away for a moment. "Thank you, Fin," she whispers.

I hold her gently and glance across at Paul, who smiles, then wanders over.

"You can put her down now," he says, letting me know his generosity only goes so far.

I turn and grin at him, but Lottie speaks first. "I was just saying thank you," she says. "We owe him a lot." She smiles back at me as he pulls her into him and she nestles against his chest.

"I know. We owe him everything," he says, kissing the top of her head. "But that doesn't mean I'm gonna let him take liberties with you."

"I wasn't…" I point out. "But at least let me have a last hold of your daughter. I'm probably not gonna see her for a few days, and I know how much babies change."

I've enjoyed every minute of holding this precious bundle and, as he hands her over, I look down into her beautiful face and plant a gentle kiss on her forehead. "Don't let your daddy spoil you too much," I whisper. "Just because he's a billionaire…"

"He's not gonna spoil her at all," Lottie says smartly and we all turn to look at her.

"I'm not?" Paul scratches his head, as though confused.

"No, you're not," she replies, quite seriously. "I don't want her to grow up with no idea of the value of a dollar."

Paul laughs. "Well, that's not gonna happen," he says. "She's my daughter, remember?"

Lottie comes over and takes Olivia from me, holding her close and looking down at her. "Yeah, and she's mine too," she says, going back to Paul. "And that means she's gonna understand what money can do – and what it can't…" For someone who grew up with a millionaire for a father, Lottie's got her feet very firmly planted on the ground. That said, her father was a great philanthropist, and I don't think the apple has fallen too far from the tree in her case.

"Yes, ma'am," Paul replies, putting his arms around Lottie and pulling her into him, her back to his front, and then placing a protective hand on Olivia as well. They look like the perfect family and I hate to admit it, but I'm feeling more than a little jealous.

Brad steps forward. He's been quiet this weekend – but then there's been a lot going on.

"When are you coming back to the city?" he asks.

"Probably Tuesday or Wednesday," Paul replies. "I can work here for a few days, and Lottie wants to take some time to recover."

"But we need to get back to normality," Lottie adds. "Otherwise it's gonna feel like we're on one long vacation… and we're not. Even if we'd like to be." She looks up at Paul and he bends and kisses her gently.

"Maybe we can get together one evening?" Brad suggests. "If you think you're gonna be up to it?"

"Sure," Paul replies. "Why don't you guys come over to the apartment?"

"Sounds great," Brad says. "We can get take out, and drink beer, and Fin and I can laugh about how little sleep you guys are getting."

"Nice," Paul says. "Thanks for that. I was hoping you'd say you'd watch Olivia and let us crash for an hour or two."

"No chance." Brad grins.

Getting together at least once a week is something the three of us have done for years. In the past, we used to compare notes on work, life and relationships, or at least the women we'd slept with recently. We strictly avoided politics and religion – not that I think any of us has particularly strong views on either subject. When Paul got together with Lottie though, we just kinda started involving her too. It wasn't a conscious decision. It just happened. Obviously, we no longer talked about our female companions – at least not in the same way, anyway. But it has proved useful occasionally for Brad and me to get Lottie's input. I'd been planning on talking to her this weekend about the woman I've been seeing for a couple of weeks – Rachel – but other events got in the way… like Olivia being born two weeks early.

"Call me," Paul says to me. "We'll set something up."

I nod my head and, after we've all shaken hands, given Lottie another hug and kissed the baby one more time, Brad and I climb into his Jeep. We decided he'd drive up here and I'm now relieved we did that, because I'm tired and am glad to be handing over the responsibility for getting us home to someone else.

"That was a slightly different weekend to the one we expected," he says, once we've been driving for a few minutes.

"You can say that again." I'd been looking forward to this weekend for ages. We've been up here for several weekends with Paul and Lottie since Paul bought their place back in the spring, but this time, I really needed the escape from Rachel – not that she let me. She's been phoning and texting me the whole time, to the extent that I turned my phone off yesterday lunchtime, because I couldn't handle it any longer.

"Paul seems to have taken to fatherhood like a duck to water," Brad says, interrupting my train of thought. I'm not ungrateful. The last thing I wanna do is spoil the last few hours of the weekend thinking about Rachel.

"Yeah, doesn't he?" I turn slightly to look at him, and although he's concentrating on the road, like any good cop should do, I can tell he's deep in thought.

"Who'd have thought, a year ago," he continues, "that Paul Lewis would be settled down, engaged, with a baby daughter and planning his wedding?"

"Not me, that's for sure."

Paul was a renowned bachelor, with a 'little black book' to prove it. Well, it wasn't really a little black book. It was an encrypted file of women who would happily tend to his every whim and pleasure. At least that's how it's always seemed to Brad and I, anyway. They'd hook up with him for an evening – because he never spent the night with any of them – and not seem overly bothered that he failed to contact them again for weeks or months at a time. Lucky asshole… He's never had to contend with the likes of Rachel and her never-ending demands. I know he enjoyed his way of life too. At least he thought he did, until he met Lottie and she just blew him away. Not that I'm overly surprised. When he first introduced us to her properly, after they'd found out she was pregnant and had overcome a few early teething problems, Brad lost the power of speech for a good five minutes. I had the advantage over him, being as I'd seen her before, from afar, even if I hadn't actually met her. Even so, I wasn't prepared for how beautiful she is close to, and it took me a moment or two to recover my senses sufficiently to be able to string a sentence together. Paul, naturally, found all of that highly amusing and didn't let us live it down for weeks.

"I'm not sure I'm cut out for that," Brad says, a little dreamily, almost like he's forgotten I'm in the car and is thinking out loud.

"Really?"

He glances across at me. "No," he says. I wonder if there's a hint of sadness in his voice, but he dispels that thought by grinning broadly. "Although you looked very much at home holding the baby."

"That's just because I'm a doctor," I remark and he nods his head slowly, like he doesn't believe a word I'm saying.

"Yeah, right," he says softly. "Doesn't the thought of monogamy scare you?" It's a serious question, which I guess means it requires a serious answer. The problem is, I don't have one. I know I mentioned to Paul yesterday that I felt a little jealous of what he's got with Lottie, but I haven't really had time to think that through.

"I don't know," I reply, gazing out the front window. "I guess if you find the right person…"

"But how do you know they're the right person?" he asks.

"I guess you just do." I look over at him again. "Maybe you should be asking Paul this, not me. Let's face it, I'm thirty-four years old and I've spent my entire adult life chasing women."

"And you've never once considered settling down with one of them?"

"Hell, no."

He chuckles. "Me neither," he says, shuddering. Brad's been known to date women for a whole month before now, which compared to Paul and myself, qualifies as a long-term commitment.

"Not one?" I ask.

He shakes his head. "No. I can't imagine only ever making love to just one woman, or waking up beside her every single day for the rest of my life." He glances at me again. "How does that even work?"

"I've got no idea, man."

But the thing is, after seeing Paul and Lottie together and observing their love for each other and their baby, I'm kinda interested in finding out. If only I could work out how.

Brad drops me at my apartment building and I grab my bag from the back seat.

"Call me tomorrow," he says. "We'll set something up for during the week and you can let Paul know."

"Sure." I need to get into work and see how my shifts are fixed for the week before I can decide when to meet up, and while Brad's shifts are a little more settled than mine, I know he'll need to get his feet under the desk again prior to making any personal arrangements. Unlike Paul, our time isn't quite so much our own. Not that either of us would change what we do – not for anyone.

I go up in the elevator to the fifth floor, and let myself into my apartment, dumping my bag by the door and flopping down onto my black leather couch. It's weird. I'm exhausted, but a little high at the same time. I've only delivered three babies in my whole career – Olivia being the third – and while I was terrified to start with, it went really smoothly, which has left me feeling kinda pleased with myself. I don't know why though, being as Lottie did all the hard work. Call it professional pride that I didn't fuck up.

I pull my phone from my back pocket and turn it on again. It's been a huge relief having it switched off for the last twenty-four hours or more, but now I'm back home, I should probably put myself back in touch with the rest of the human race. Apart from anything else, if there's an emergency at work, they might need to contact me.

As it sparks into life, it beeps over and over again, multiple times.

"Fucking hell," I mutter, under my breath, because I know these are messages coming in from Rachel. The only thing I can say about her is that she's persistent.

I gave up taking her calls at around one pm yesterday and turned my phone off. There are three more voicemails and twelve text messages, and to be honest, I can't be bothered to even check them. I need to stop this. Now.

I go to my contacts list and dial her number, waiting for it to connect.

"At last," she says, huffing out an impatient sigh. "Where the hell have you been?"

"Away," I reply abruptly.

"Away where?"

"In Maine, with some friends of mine."

"And when were you gonna tell me about this?" she demands.

"I don't have to tell you my every move, Rachel. We're not joined at the hip."

"I'm still entitled to know where you are," she says. *Entitled?* Who the hell does she think she is?

"You're not entitled to know anything," I reply harshly.

"So, what were you doing with your friends... all weekend?" she asks, ignoring my comment.

"If you must know, I was delivering a baby for one of them," I respond and wait for the fireworks. I don't have to wait long.

"You were what?" I don't bother to repeat myself. I'm pretty sure from her reaction that she heard me. "Whose baby was it?"

"Not mine, if that's what you're implying," I remark. "The labor started two weeks early and I had to step in."

"Why? Couldn't this woman get herself to a hospital in time?"

"No, Rachel. She couldn't."

There's a pause. "And you know her?"

"She's the fiancée of a friend of mine, yes."

"So you'll be seeing her again?" She seems surprised.

"Of course I will. I'm gonna be seeing her next week sometime. Well, I'll be seeing all of them, actually."

"Oh, will you now?" she says, like she's planning on changing my mind.

"Yeah, I will."

"But how can you?" she asks. "I mean… I mean, you know what she looks like naked. How are you going to be able to look each other in the face?"

"Oh, grow up, Rachel. I'm a doctor. I see naked women all the time."

"And I'm supposed to like that, am I?"

"Frankly, I don't give a damn whether you like it or not." I'm really losing my patience now. "The fact is that when I'm working, I'm not interested in what my patient looks like, other than to assess their injuries or illness. I'm not looking at them from any perspective other than what they need me to do for them, and in Lottie's case, she needed me to safely deliver her daughter. Period."

"Even so," she says, obviously wanting to continue the argument, despite everything I've said, "it can't have taken the whole weekend to deliver the baby."

"It didn't," I reply. "But what's your point?"

"My point," she says, "is that I've been calling you and you haven't returned one message. Not one."

"No."

"Why not?"

I guess it's time to be brutally honest. "Because I didn't want to."

"But you were okay with fucking me, weren't you?" she shouts, losing it in fairly spectacular style. "And no doubt you'll expect me to drop everything, including my panties, and come over there whenever you click your fingers. Well, let me tell you—"

"No," I interrupt before she can go on.

"No what?"

"No, I don't expect you to drop everything. I never did. Whatever you think, Rachel, I've never expected that of you, or any woman. I'm not that kind of guy." I'm really not. I may fool around, but it's never just on my terms, not in the way she's making it seem, anyway.

"Oh, really?" There's a really unattractive hint of sarcasm to her voice.

"Yeah. Really."

"So you'd turn me down if I came over there now, would you?"

"Yeah, I would." There's a stoney silence on the end of the line. "I think it's best if we call it quits, Rachel, before one of us says something we both regret."

"I don't think I could regret anything I said to you," she replies. "You're a two-timing, cheating, using asshole, and I…"

"I've never cheated," I say, speaking over her and raising my voice. "But being as that's what you think of me, let's just forget the whole thing."

Even as I'm hanging up the call, I can still hear her screaming abuse at me. But as I put my cell down on the couch beside me, the feeling of relief that she's in the past and I never have to see her again, is almost overwhelming.

… to be continued

Printed in Great Britain
by Amazon